To Susan,
With best wishes,
Diana Branisteanu
June 2021

Life Under the Dark Sky

A Novel based on a True Story

Diana Branisteanu

Life Under the Dark Sky

ISBN 9781460964316

For my loving family, especially for Hedwig, my mother-in-law.

Chapter 1

The sun was rising from behind the mountain, sending rays of warm light over the little town which sat around and along the river valley. Traisen was bigger than a mountain village, yet not quite a town. It was an ancient place not far away from Vienna, where people found plenty of resources for farming on the high green hills, which were heaven for cattle and sheep. Over decades the trade of home-made goods and farmers' products had made Traisen a self-sufficient community. The factory at the edge of the town was relatively new, and employed a large number of the town's younger generation, who were eager to learn and earn money. The land was blessed with natural resources, bright summers, and white winters, and everybody was minding their own business, living in harmony and good faith.

This was the town in which Heidi grew up and went to school. Her family was not rich, but not poor either. Her father was well-known in the community and well respected. He was a shoe master, and while repairing the shoes of almost everybody in town was kept well informed of everything that was happening at any given time. Heidi was his second daughter, and the one that, over the years, began to take after him more and more. He loved all four of his children dearly. He often thought how different they were, and about how each one had something special that made his life worthwhile.

Teresa, the oldest, was born in 1920, and had been blessed with the gift of cooking. She could turn any meal into a treat. She was now a young lady, and had already learnt a lot from her employment as chef assistant, and at times even chef herself, in the lavish castles of the wealthy inhabitants. While doing this, she had also learned to be organized, and picked up a little bit of book-keeping too. She worked for two years at Rosenburg Castle for Grof Hoiu, a very well established man, whose family had inherited old money and properties.

Johan, his only son, born in 1927, was a happy boy who was often spoiled by his older sisters and his mom. There was no doubt that, as long as the world did not plummet into the turmoil of war, he would grow up to be a fine man. Sometimes his father wondered what the future would bring to all of them. He was a veteran of the First World War himself, and knew only too well what it is like to be a young man living through those uncertain times when all hell breaks loose.

Louisa, the youngest, was still in elementary school, and had no worries. The nest of her family and a couple of friends of the same age were enough to make her happy.

And there was Heidi, born on October 11th, 1924, who was now seventeen. Heidi was a free spirit, always ready to discover something new, always willing to see more than Traisen had to offer, to travel, to meet people, and determined to pursue her way in following her dreams. But what dreams can a seventeen year old have when her country was about to be torn apart, caught in the middle of a world war? She knew that life is precious, is meant to be lived one day at a time, and is meant to be made the most of. She had the personality of a leader: she was a quick decision maker, insightful thinker, and possessed a great deal of courage and honesty. Even at that young age she had life experience that prepared her for always being on her feet.

She had just come back from Vienna. Ah, Vienna! The city that mesmerized her! Capital of an empire for more than a century, capital of waltz and music! Living in Vienna for almost a year was a dream come true for Heidi. She could not believe her luck when she had found work there the previous summer. Through one of her mother's acquaintances, she had discovered that a respected family, Mrs. and Mr. Wolfang, needed a nanny for their two year old daughter, Klara. Knowing that Heidi was a brave girl who could be trusted, who was yet sweet and amenable with young children, she received a good recommendation for the job, and then off she went to the city of glamorous parties, glorious history, and majestic music.

On a morning like this Heidi could not help thinking back on her time spent in Vienna. Thus far it had been the best time of her life. She still regretted that she could not stay for longer. Having to return home proved to her that one cannot hang on to good times forever, and that only change is constant. Even so, she would treasure that chapter of her life as long as she lived. Happy memories were meant to help her along the way, and give her strength during tough times.

Four years before, in early 1938, Hitler had consolidated his power in Germany and was ready to begin his planned expansion. He had personal ties with Austria, having been born there, and tried to gain popular approval for the unification of Austria with Germany through diplomatic channels. First, he reinstated full party freedom, released imprisoned members of the Nazi party and let them participate in government. The political scene changed drastically for Austria, and in a short time the German troops crossed the Austrian border. Nazi flags and Nazi supporters greeted Hitler on his journey to Vienna. It all looked like an enthusiastic welcome, and he arrived in the capital city on April 2nd, 1938. By then Austria had become the province of Ostmark and part of Germany and the Third Reich. The Anschluss was ratified by a plebiscite that won the support of an overwhelming majority. People were scared and confused, and the vote was not anonymous. The Austrian nation was losing control over its own legitimate identity. Hitler, through his SS officers, arrested prominent representatives of the First Republic Party, Social Democrats, the Communist Party, and other potential political dissenters, as well as Jews. They were either imprisoned or sent to concentration camps. The Austrian population was reduced to obeisance on the threat of similar treatment. Even in a small town like Traisen the German political pressure was present, and nobody could be trusted anymore. People were talking out of fear, and the Nazis had already infiltrated every part of the country with spies.

Heidi's father, Frantz Souisa, advised his family to keep a low profile and not make any kind of comments in public or express any opinion regarding the day-to-day deterioration of life or political concerns. He knew that this was the only way to survive and keep his family safe. He was thinking of his kids, and, from what he heard, it sounded as though Germany was planning to expand into Czechoslovakia and Poland. Nobody could stop the war, or the power of the Third Reich.

Chapter 2

In the summer of 1938 Heidi finished school and wanted to begin learning a profession. The apprenticeship program she was interested in was not available at that time. She wanted to become a hairdresser. She herself had beautiful shoulder-length locks, the color of copper. At that moment, though, there were no places available for training in that field. She put her name on a waiting list, but, with war and its attendant chaos looming, the chances of her being enrolled were slim.

Her older sister, Teresa, was attending a specialized program in cooking and restaurants. Her placement at Grof Hoiu's castle was giving her experience and knowledge.

There were not many places to get a job. Young men were being sent to the army, and the only work to be found for girls was as a house-helper for the soldiers' wives. That wasn't what Heidi wanted, and certainly not in Traisen. She wanted to go to a big city to see new places, meet new people, and discover the world. It was two years later that she received the offer to go to Vienna and take care of little Klara and help her mother, Elisabeth Wolfang, around the house. Elisabeth was a young mother only eight years older than Heidi, and she and her husband had been married for three years. They had a nice spacious apartment close to St. Stephan's Cathedral in the centre of Vienna. Despite the German occupation, the city still looked glamorous to Heidi.

Elisabeth was happy to meet Heidi. She needed help in the house and with little Klara. Her husband Karol, who was an officer, had been called up. He had not been sent to the front yet, but was teaching a regiment of infantry at a cazarm outside the city. He stayed there during the week and only came home on weekends. Elisabeth had a maid who came to the home three times a week. Heidi was employed to be Klara's nanny and her mother's companion. The uncertain times, due to the political climate and threat of war, made Elisabeth nervous, and she feared for the safety of her family, and, even more, for their future. Having Heidi around helped relieve some of her anxiety.

Heidi was full of life, happy to move to the big city, willing to help and fascinated by her new life, so different from the one she had had in her small town. Little Klara was an adorable toddler with curly blond hair and big blue eyes. The first time she saw her, Heidi thought that if she were ever to have a child she would like him or her to look like Klara. The girl was happy, cute and friendly. Within a week Heidi and Klara had already developed a special bond, playing, taking short walks, and having breakfast, lunch and dinner together, all the while having fun. Elisabeth was pleased to see how helpful, resourceful and loving Heidi was with her child. Elisabeth trusted her, and Klara loved her. Soon Heidi became part of their family, and seemed almost like the younger sister Elisabeth had never had. Along with taking care of Klara, Heidi grew closer to her mom.

The maid, Sylvia, was in her twenties, a decent young woman who was dedicated to her work, diligent and friendly. Heidi liked her from the beginning. Their employer was a good woman and Heidi and Sylvia appreciated their good luck.

The Wolfang residence was a nest of harmony in which one could easily forget about the chaos that existed outside its walls. Even though people in Vienna tried to remain calm, and stores, banks, schools, and cultural establishments stayed open, the fear of the war was present everywhere. Most of the men suitable for service were already enrolled in the army, and those left at home were older or too young. Rich, ordinary, and poor men were all equally affected by the war. It seemed as if society had brought down its class barriers and become one mass of people trying to survive and stay sane. For the moment, Vienna was calm, the Danube was blue, and the bells of St. Stephan's Cathedral rang out every hour, measuring time. The golden leaves trembled in the wind and fell on the sidewalks, making a nice warm rug underneath people's feet. Elisabeth gazed out the window, thinking of her husband. Sooner or later he would be sent to the front, and who knew what the future would bring for them. She heard the laughter of her daughter coming from the other room where she played with Heidi, and instantly felt stronger, knowing that, no matter what, she'd have her little girl to keep her going. There was also her cousin Thomas who visited her regularly, and since he was a student at The Medical Institute of Vienna, he would not have to go to the army. If worst came to worst, she and Klara would not be alone.

Thomas was an easy-going young man. At twenty two, he had good life experience, a few good friends among his school mates, and a powerful determination to become a doctor. His family lived in St. Polten. Elisabeth was like a sister to him, and the only family he had in Vienna. He lived in the student residence, but very much enjoyed visiting his cousin. On occasions he took Elisabeth out for lunch or dinner to cheer her up and help her forget her worries. Since Heidi had come to look after his adorable niece Klara, the place had become livelier and he really looked forward to paying them visits. Thomas had a good sense of humor, and knew a lot of gossip from the university. He always tried to share a funny story, or make some entertaining plans when he was coming over. He knew what was going on in his country and around Austria. The war was already part of life, but he did not talk about it much and minded his own business. In such times, everybody tried to cope with the situation in their own way. Thomas chose to take care of his family and focus on his studies rather than fill his life with worries about the world coming to an end. He was, by nature, an optimistic and strong person. The three young ladies, even Klara, always looked for-wards to his visits. Occasionally he brought candy or cookies from the corner coffee shop. With Thomas around, Heidi got a taste of social life in the big city. On Thursday nights short silent movies played at the nearby Cinema, and the entrance fee was very cheap. While Elisabeth had seen most of the shows the year before with her husband, she encour-aged Thomas to take Heidi out and enjoy the movies. Heidi loved it, and laughed with all her heart watching Charlie Chaplin's meaningful play. At other times there would be soirees taking place that Thomas knew about, usually at one of the remaining open restaurants, where student live bands put together singing concerts for the benefit of the Red Cross organization. He always attended these in the company of his cousin or Heidi, and it was then that Heidi learned the tango and even the waltz. Thomas was a good dancer and great company. For a few shillings' donation, and the cost of a slice of apple pie with a glass of water, they could spend more than three hours enjoying the music and swirling on the dance floor. Walking home afterwards on dark streets was a powerful reminder of the ugly reality, but, for Heidi, the excitement of such evenings overcame the fear of the war, and by the time she got home and went to bed felt as if the world, at least, was good. Usually, the next morning over a thin breakfast she would give Elisabeth a detailed update about the previous evening, with much enthusiasm. Sometimes there were even funny stories to tell, and they would have a good laugh. Those moments, however, were soon replaced by the anguish that Elisabeth felt listening to radio news from the front, while Heidi went about her day with Karla. One day passed after another, and without so much as a notice the season changed from colorful autumn to gray and white winter.

After losing battles against England and having been weakened on the Western front, Germany shifted its military focus toward the East. The invasion of the southern Soviet Union got off to a good start, and German armies surrounded more than half a million Red Army troops east of Smolensk. The German armies began the drive toward Moscow, and certain German politicians made glowing predictions of the end of the war. But soon thereafter, while the temperatures fell on the Moscow front and heavy snow followed, the German tanks were immobilized. In the southern Soviet Union, the Germans were more successful, and gained territory in Crimea and Ukraine. By late 1941, major cities in Germany began to suffer nightly bombings, while at the same time the Allies also registered heavy losses.

In mid-December, while civilians in Vienna were trying to think about the coming Christmas, Hitler and Mussolini declared war on the United States, which reciprocated in turn and declared war on Germany and Italy. Soon after, Hungary declared war on the United States and the United Kingdom. Romania and Bulgaria followed Germany and entered the war against the United States and England. The battles were fought on ground, sea, and air. Austrian soldiers were part of the German Army. There were daily reports of lives lost or soldiers missing in action. Elisabeth's husband was due to leave Vienna soon after Christmas for service on the front. Germany needed more and more troops on every active region of the map. The normality of life had been shattered by the war, and the joy of Christmas was a dim memory for most Austrians.

A decorated branch of a pine tree on a coffee table in Elisabeth's living room was the only sign of the holidays. Klara was happy to see the colorful so-called Christmas tree, and, on Christmas morning, to discover a knitted doll underneath it. Heidi and Elisabeth had made the doll in secret over the course of a few late nights. The child was happy, and everybody tried to see the holidays though Klara's joyful eyes. They celebrated Christmas around the dining table with some traditional meals that weren't easy to prepare, given the lack of food supply in the grocery stores. But at least they were all together for the day, Elisabeth, Karol, Klara, Heidi, Thomas and Sylvia. The carols sung in St. Stephan's Cathedral gave the end of the year a festive atmosphere. People gathered at church to pray and listen to religious music, passing the time and hoping that God would stop the insanity of the world.

The New Year of 1942 came without glory, putting an end to the brief holidays that some privileged officers from the army had spent with their families. Elisabeth's husband had to leave Vienna on January 2nd and join his detachment to leave for eastern Germany. Elisabeth was devastated, not knowing if she would ever see Karol again. She sobbed all day long for days at a time, hardly able to even keep up a brave face for Klara's sake. Heidi spent lots of time with the toddler in order to afford Elisabeth some privacy. Sylvia, whose brother had had to go to the front at the same time as Karol, was a mess herself, and together with Elisabeth intently followed the radio news about the front. The house became a war news center, touched by the war in many ways, and nothing seemed to be the same. Even the little girl was affected by the adult's anguish: she began to cry in her sleep, and woke Heidi up more than once every night.

Thomas's visits lost their sparkle. Where before they had made plans to go out and live life, at the beginning of the year all they could talk about was the news from the front and Hitler's plans for an offensive. The young man always knew something more than was allowed to be said on the radio and the three women now waited for his visits for completely different reasons than they had before. Thomas was torn between the ugly truth he had to deliver from his campus sources and the protective care that he felt toward his cousin and his little niece. He also assumed the role of male figure in Elisabeth's family after Karol had to leave. He wanted to help and be there for the Wolfang household. One day after another went by and finally, at the end of January, Elisabeth received a letter from her husband and began to relax a little. She was happy that Karol was safe and sound, and full of gratitude to the dear Lord for having mercy on him. That evening Thomas took Elisabeth to a nearby theatre to see a play and forget her worries.

As the old saying goes, human nature adapts to any conditions after a while. Elisabeth started to accept her life lived on a knife blade, torn between fear and hope. Heidi, who knew that her family and loved ones were safe in Traisen, and not having anybody close to her heart enrolled in the German army, was in a better position to lift Elisabeth's spirits than Sylvia was. At seventeen, Heidi was wiser than other girls her age. She knew from her dear father, who was a veteran of WWI, that there were many hidden aspects to the conflict that Hitler had started three years before. While most Austrians, at the beginning, had seen Hitler as a liberator who would give Austria prosperity, the Souisa family had the feeling that nothing good could possibly result. But life is lived one day at the time, and, thus far, Heidi's family had remained much better off than many Austrian families, the Wolfangs included. Heidi's optimism gave Elisabeth strength, and Thomas was grateful for that. For this reason, in return for her helping his cousin cope with this difficult time, Thomas really wanted to make Heidi happy.

By February, winter was in full cry, covering Vienna with a thick blanket of snow. In times of peace it would have been welcomed, but given the poverty that the war had brought for the last three years, the population was hit hard by the cold and snow storms. Heating homes was a huge challenge as the supply of fire logs and gasoline were not enough for a long heavy winter. Also, warm clothing had been worn out, and no new ones were available. The factories were sending produce to the army first, with only the remnants left over for the civilian population. The fear of catching diseases kept people indoors for the most part. Heidi liked the snow. It reminded her of her childhood, the winter sports that she enjoyed in Traisen, skiing on the mountain's slopes or skating on the frozen Traisen River. She liked to take Klara to the neighborhood park and make snowmen, or pull her on the slide around the plaza. Thomas joined them on occasions. At other times, he borrowed skates from his school mates, and took Heidi or Elisabeth to an improvised ice rink for a few hours of fun on ice. Both young women were good skaters, and the physical exercise did them good. Once again, Heidi enjoyed life, despite the war and the dangerous times. With her optimistic nature, she was able to bring the smiles back to Klara, Elisabeth, and Silvia's faces.

The crisp cold wind caused roses to bloom on the young women's cheeks, while sliding across the ice gave them a feeling of freedom. The news from the Eastern Europe front was that the Axis powers, the German Army and its allies, were doing better now that spring approached. Days followed on one another, and Vienna was about to change to another season. The snow gave up, the black earth was revealed again in the park, and the streets were washed by the melting snow and ice.

At the end of March, disturbing news was heard. Hitler began another cruel war against the Jews. Those living in Berlin had to clearly identify their houses and obey The Third Reich. From then on, concentration camps were ready to receive their tenants on Death Row. But this detail was kept secret at that time, and few people could even begin to imagine the genocide that was shortly to follow.

As always, the future was unknown and the present liable to change in a split second. Europe, North Africa and Asia became a battle field, and nobody could tell for how long or at what price. It seemed like Hitler's desire for power had no limits, and was constrained not only to land but included also the extermination of selected population and societies. There was no precedent for the madness of this kind of self-proclaimed leader. All the bad news filled the Wolfang residence with fear and sadness, and the lack of nutritious food and vitamins weakened the resistance to infections, flu and colds.

At the beginning of April, Heidi began to suffer from a toothache, which cut into her vivacious attitude. The few medicines that Elisabeth had in the house did little to help. Day by day Heidi was losing the battle with an infection of her front teeth. This was the last thing that she needed, and plain bad luck. In a week, in addition to the pain, her face started to swell and complications occurred. A short, painful visit to a dentist advised her to seek treatment in her home town and take time to heal and recover. If she did not do so, she was likely to lose her front teeth and contract septicemia, which would lead to worse consequences. Elisabeth understood that Heidi had to go home and take care of herself. She felt sorry about losing Heidi, and did not know how she and Klara would cope with this unexpected situation. Sylvia could take over Heidi's duties in the house and with the child, but she could not replace the ray of optimism that Heidi's personality always brought to Elisabeth's home. She was irreplaceable, and everybody knew that her departure was not a good sign. Heidi was also sad to leave Vienna and the friends she had made behind. There was the desire to, and possibility of, return after she recovered, but given the uncertainty of everything during the war, that hope was very slim. Klara, Elisabeth, and Sylvia said a tearful good bye, and Thomas took her to the rail station. Together, they took the train to St. Polten. The young man wanted to make sure that she got home safely, and used this opportunity to pay his parents a visit. For the first time in a year he felt like seeing his family and getting close to his parents. It was almost as if an urge to hold and protect them were animating him. For the first time, he felt the fear of facing the future, and going home was meant to give him strength. Once arrived in St. Polten, he put Heidi on an old bus to Traisen, but not before hugging her and wishing her well.

Heidi knew that she might not see him and his cousin again, which made her very sad. In the time she spent in Vienna she had learnt a lot and grown up faster than she would have had she stayed home. Most importantly, she discovered her strength and the positive influence she had on people, the fact that she could touch other people lives and be empowered by helping others. Thinking this, the toothache seemed to fade a bit. In the wake of the many losses that families started to suffer due to the war, she was happy to see her family again. Waving good-bye to Thomas through the bus window, she was going home to her loved ones.

Chapter 3

Heidi's mother, Josephina Souisa, was hanging washing on the line in the backyard. The sun would dry them in no time. So far, the summer had been sunny and her small vegetable garden had suffered. Weeds were growing faster than the crop, and Josephina would have to attend to it next. Perhaps she would have to water in the evening. That was a hard task, since the water had to be carried in a bucket from the river. The house they lived in was built on a hill's slope. From the front view, it had three stories, but the backyard was at the same level as the third floor. The Souisa family lived on the third floor, with the entrance from the backyard directly into the two bedroom apartment. The twenty three steps that led along the side of the house to their main door became quite tiring for Heidi's parents.

Before the war, Frantz Souisa had begun working from home in his improvised little repair shop in a storage room. He still spent a lot of time in his working room, but he now had fewer and fewer clients. People had no money to pay for his services, and most of his fees were paid in the form of bread or oil tickets, or by rendering services in return. It was a time of war and people did not need money. They needed food and shelter to survive.

The home was cozy. The furniture was old but solid, and had a nice turn of the century touch. The armoire in the great room held a few interesting things that marked the history of the family: faded photos, old coins, and a few pieces of jewelry that the Souisa girls treasured.

Heidi and Johan were now old enough to help their parents, who were grateful for that. Now that Heidi was back home and almost recovered from her tooth infection, she was eager to take on the tasks that were too hard for her parents.

Heidi was looking out the window along the street. Across the street was the railway, and across the railway the Traisen River flowed down from the mountains. It was already August. Since she had come back from Vienna in April, she had focused of her health and tried to recover. It was a slow process, as a result of which she lost weight and felt weaker, but that did not stop her from taking on some temporary jobs and earning goods and food as pay. She found out that every time she stayed home for more than two weeks, the officials from City Hall found out about it and sent her messages to come in for a report. Spies were everywhere, and informants from within the community worked for the SS and German Army, who controlled everything, including the lives of civilians. A couple of times she had to go to Town Hall and explain what she had been doing and who she worked for. The fact that she was only seventeen did not stop the authorities from questioning her.

The German Army started to look into enrolling unmarried or childless women for the performance of tasks behind the front in order to release men from those duties, so that they could be sent into battle. The losses of the Axis armies had to be replaced by new soldiers.

'Oh, my! Is that Teresa?' Heidi could not believe what she was seeing. Teresa was coming down the street toward the house. She had no idea that her sister was coming home. Teresa had been working at Grof Hoiu's castle for two years now. Every time she came home for a visit she announced her arrival ahead of time and was expected, but today she had not sent any message, and yet here she was, almost arriving at the building. This made Heidi wonder if everything was alright with her sister. She turned to the door and headed out to meet Teresa, shouting the unexpected news to her mom in the backyard.

'Good Lord, Teresa, what a surprise! Let me hug you sis. Mom and dad will be in shock seeing you here all of a sudden!' Heidi said, jumping the stairs two at a time to meet her sister.

'Heidi, I'm so happy to see you! But not so happy to be home. I'll explain later. Where are the others?'

'Mom and dad are at home. Johan is helping the farmer up on the hill to make hay for the winter. Louisa must be downstairs at the neighbor's place playing with their daughter. Let's get inside, and I'm all ears.'

'Teresa!' her mother exclaimed 'What on Earth are you doing at home? Are you all right? What happened? Frantz, Frantz, your daughter

14

came home, can you believe it?' Josephina Souisa hugged her older child, her heart pounding in her chest.

Frantz came out of his shop to greet his daughter. He was happy to see Teresa, and at the thought that, once more, the whole family was together. Many families were facing the hardship of seeing their older children leaving home, having to join the army. Traisen had begun to lose its younger generation, not knowing how many of the departed would have the chance to return. In many houses parents were sad and lonely, and, knowing this, Frantz felt lucky that once again they were all under the same roof.

'It is good to see you. I feel better already,' Theresa said.

'What do you mean you feel better? Are you sick?' Heidi asked.

'Let's sit, shall we? Give the girl some space and something to eat, Josie. Heidi, please go and ask Louisa to come home. She has to welcome Theresa,' Frantz said, and Heidi disappeared through the door in a hurry, eager not to miss any of the details of her sister's unexpected return home.

Over a frugal snack consisting of a cup of yogurt and a piece of bread, her family gathered around the kitchen table, Teresa begun to talk about the events that had brought her home.

Her employment at the castle was good and she learnt a lot. She was doing what she liked most, and she became a chef assistant. Her skills were recognized by the Hoiu family. She was diligent, and dedicated to her profession. Work was tiring, but rewarding. Furthermore, in the last six months she fell in love. Hans Ellis, the young man in charge of Grof Hoiu's stables, had had an eye for her from the first day of his job. When he came into the marble floored kitchen to get a glass of water and saw Teresa, he spilled the water all over himself. Teresa smiled, trying hard not to laugh at him, and gave him a napkin. He was a tough man, and being sloppy was out of his character. It must have been love at first sight, and it was mutual. Teresa and Hans became an item, and spent all their free time together. Hans was twenty two, one year older than she was. He had not been called to army duty yet as, having an ill mother, three younger siblings, and no father at home, he was the only bread winner in the family. He was from Krems, on the other side of the Danube. From February to June Teresa had a good time, wrapped up in her romance and content with her work. She was not overly worried about the war, since she knew that her family was safe, and nobody close to her was in immediate danger.

Then she felt the pain in her legs, followed by the swelling. At first she did not pay much attention and tried to ignore the signals which her body was sending. Two weeks later the pain intensified, and Grof Hoiu's doctor sent her to the hospital in St. Polten. They investigated her condition and diagnosed her with chronic venous insufficiency. The recommendation was to go to a sanatorium to recover, and not to stand for more than a few minutes at a time. The truth was that standing for ten hours a day on the cold marble floor in the kitchen had brought upon the illness in the first place. She was told to get another job that would not require as much standing on her feet. The three weeks spent in the sanatorium did her good physically, but tore into her soul. Quitting Hoiu Castle meant quitting a career that she loved, and also leaving Hans, the man she loved. The Hoiu family was sad that Teresa had to be let go: they were found of her and wished her the best, but, for her own well-being, she had to go. Hans, on the other hand, could not accept seeing her leave so easily. He was concerned about her health, and wanted her to get well, but her having to go home made him very sad. It looked like he was going to lose her, and all his dreams for a future together with her broke into a million pieces. Teresa was as upset about the situation as he was. Finally, a week before she had to leave, Hans proposed to her. It was a beautiful moment, in which they promised one another undying love and decided that when the war ended they would find each other and get married. All they could do for now was to have faith that they, and their love, would survive. It was more like an agreement than an engagement, but that was all they could do to soften the separation. Of course, Teresa was concerned about the fact that he might have go to the army after all if Hitler needed more troops. She hoped that one day he would come and find her in Traisen, and that they would then be together until death. The day she left the castle was bitter-sweet for both of them.

Now here she was, at home with her family, and she could not even be happy about it. Her heart was where Hans Ellis was, and was hurting.

Teresa told everyone about her illness, but left out her love story with Hans. Her mother had tears in her eyes, her father tried to encourage her, Louisa did not understand much, and Heidi thought that it was ill-fate that both of them had gotten sick and had to come home when they would have rather had stayed and kept their jobs.

Later in the evening Johan came home and was surprised to see his older sister. He was happy about it, but he was too tired to notice that everybody was sad.

When they went to bed and the lights went off, Heidi, whose intuition made her think that Teresa had kept something secret, asked her sister if there was more to the story that she had already told her parents. It was then that her sister started to cry quietly and tell her all about Hans. Heidi embraced her sister, held her tightly until the tears dried on her face, and both fell asleep wishing for better dreams.

The next few weeks flew by. On the Eastern front, the German Army approached Stalingrad and the fighting intensified. The news became more and more frightening. What they gained in distance, they lost in numbers. The casualties were never revealed, but, from the letters that sporadically came from the eastern front, people knew that a lot of soldiers had perished or been taken hostage. In Western Europe the Allied Army won and lost by turns, and it looked like victory was still far from their grasp. The war spread to North Africa, too: the British Army was involved in some battles in Morocco, while the battle of Malta claimed a lot of lives.

Heidi and Teresa found out that they had to report to the Unemployment Office on September 1st. The sisters smelled trouble and could not decide whether to be afraid or angry about the appointment.

'Teresa, what do you think is going to happen when we go there?' Heidi asked her sister. 'It is strange that we both have to go at the same time. I have been able to avoid all these appointments for the last two months. I think that some spy must have turned us in once you showed up at home. People are so submissive to the German occupation these days. It makes me sick just thinking of it.'

'I can tell you that we should be prepared for the worst when we go to that office. I heard that near St. Polten they started to enroll young women into the army. It sounds like Hitler also has a plan to take boys as young as fourteen or fifteen and train them for the army,' Teresa said while she combed her hair.

'Good Lord sis, don't tell me that Johan is in possible danger too! Mom and dad would be devastated if he has to go to the army. Besides, they need him here for help,' Heidi added with horror.

'It's quite possible, unfortunately. But let's not become paranoid just yet. Tomorrow we will go there and keep our cool and see what happens. I am as scared as you are, but we cannot change our destiny.

Ever since I left Grof Hoiu's castle I feel like my life has no meaning anymore. I had to give up on all that mattered to me, and this stupid war is going to kill us.' Tears filled Teresa's eyes, and she turned away and left the room. Heidi knew that her sister was very depressed, and was suffering because she missed Hans so much. She saw that Teresa slept with Hans's picture under the pillow. Sometimes, at night, she heard her crying silently. Love must be full of trouble, Heidi thought, judging by the look of Teresa. Her sister was twenty one years old, and this was her first love. When Teresa showed her Hans's picture, Heidi admitted that he was handsome, and that he had a very profound look on his face. But that was all she noticed, and her heart did not skip a beat, nor was she jealous of her sister. If love makes you feel so miserable, she was not in a hurry to find it. If anything, she felt sorry for Teresa and her unhappiness.

'Tomorrow, when you go to Town Hall, be careful what you say, and you better not express any opinion about the war. Try not to argue with people over there,' Frantz Souisa advised Heidi. 'Your sister is so angry about everything and I'm afraid her big mouth will get her in trouble. I tried to explain this to her, but all she does is turn around and run out of the room in a storm to avoid any conversation. I really do not think that her illness could have made her so sour. Whatever it is, tell her that there is no point in making the matter worse than it already is, and she should control herself and behave. Heidi, I trust you. You always have been more like myself, and I know that your judgment is solid, so please take care of your sister, even though it should be the other way around.'

'Yes Dad, I will. Please don't worry too much about tomorrow. It must be a visit like I had in the past. Nothing out of the ordinary. Do you want something from the garden, or I should go and pick up some apples from the apple tree and bring to you?' Heidi offered, trying to sound casual, to assure her father that everything was going to be all right. At that moment her mother came in, dragging Louisa by her hand and arguing with her about not helping around the house and spending all her time at the neighbors'. That ended the conversation between Heidi and her father, and Louisa's high pitch voice protesting against her mother's argument, filled the house. Frantz turned and went to his working room, feeling outnumbered by the women in his family. It seemed certain that the oldest and the youngest daughters were going through a crisis. God help them all.

The next morning it was raining. The sky was gray; a crisp wind was blowing through the valley. It looked like autumn would be coming sooner than expected. Heidi and Teresa were getting ready for the appointment. The breakfast that Josephine put on the table for all of them did not appeal much to the older girls. Johan and Louisa, having a good appetite, devoured the leftovers. There was tension in the air, but nobody dared to say anything about it. The weather did not help the mood, but rather mirrored it.

Heidi was wearing a dark blue dress that had seen better days, and was thinking about putting her rain coat on. A pair of brown shoes completed her modest outfit. Teresa had on a black skirt paired with a white knitted blouse, and looked very stylish. She had gotten some good quality clothes from Mrs. Hoiu when she left the castle. The lady had liked her and admired her skills, and wanted to give her a gift expressing her gratitude when she had to leave. Teresa's shoes were worn out, but her father polished them the night before and she looked pretty from head to toe. Teresa's appearance was a complete contrast with the way she felt inside. Heidi, on the other hand, was in an optimistic mood, not letting the nervousness take over her.

When they left the house, rushing under the rain, Frantz watched from the window and said a silent prayer. Who knows what will come their way? He thought.

The Unemployment Office at the Town Hall had a waiting room painted in a dark shade of gray, and five old chairs, each a different style. The floor was wet from the imprints of the shoes of people coming in from the rain. There were only a couple of middle age women waiting to get in. The Souisa sisters entered the building, shaking the water off their raincoats. After greeting the two women, they sat down on two of the remaining three squeaky chairs. It was a bit early. Good. They had time to catch their breaths, thought Heidi. But then, all of a sudden, the office door opened and their names were called out. Taken by surprise, both girls jumped up from their chairs, looked at each other and then slowly walked toward the open door.

Inside the office where before there had been only two civil servants, they were now joined by an additional army officer. Not a good sign, Heidi thought.

'Good Morning,' Heidi said, entering followed by Teresa.

'Are you Teresa and Heidi Souisa?' one of the workers asked without greeting them.

Not knowing which of them should answer first, both started to speak at the same time, and suddenly stopped to give one another the turn to respond.

'Since when have you been out of work? Do you know that our society cannot support lazy people hanging around doing nothing? What is the reason you are out of work?' the other man asked in an authoritarian voice.

Heidi looked at him asking herself who was supposed to answer first, and which question. Teresa was panting, shocked by the implicit accusations of laziness and irresponsibility. She looked at the German officer and saw that he was taking notes.

The silence started to feel uncomfortable, and the tension in the room could be cut with a knife.

Finally, Heidi regained her composure and spoke for both.

'I am Heidi Souisa and this is my older sister Teresa Souisa.' Saying their last name, her father's image came into her mind and gave her strength. The sense of belonging felt good.

'Both of us are currently out of work due to illness. Both of us were employed before and worked for well respected households, I in Vienna and my sister near Krems, at Rosenburg Castle. I had a bad tooth abscess that took a long time to heal, and my sister was treated for chronic venous insufficiency in a sanatorium in St. Polten. She was advised not to work in any job that requires standing for long periods of time. Her legs were badly swollen at that time. She came home a few weeks ago. In the mean time we have been helping around the house and assisting one of the farmers up on the hill. Neither of us is lazy. We are good citizens.' Heidi went on with pride.

Teresa looked at Heidi, realizing that her sister was talking for both of them while she was not able to say a word, shaken by the rudeness of the man. She felt like screaming and running out of the office, but her feet would not move.

The officer then looked at them for the first time since they had walked in the office and asked the sisters their ages. 'I'm seventeen, and . . .' Heidi started to answer.

'I'm twenty one.' Teresa continued, speaking for the first time in the meeting.

The officer took some notes again, and exchanged a glance with the other two men. Then, one of the civil workers said:

'You will receive a letter from our office within a few days with our decision regarding your eligibly to unemployment benefits. You may both go now.' Then he looked down at his papers, and waited for the girls to exit the room.

Heidi was surprised by this conclusion, and for a moment did not know if she should say thank you, good-bye or just leave the room without a word.

She heard Teresa saying 'We will be waiting for your letter. Good-bye now.' and turned toward her, took her by hand and headed to the door. Heidi followed without a word, nodding to her sister.

Back in the waiting room, when the door closed behind them, they paused for a moment and looked at each in silence. What was that all about? The meeting was brief, confusing and intimidating. It was not good news at all.

On the way home neither of them spoke, and neither noticed that it had stopped raining. They were both deeply immersed in their own thoughts.

Once they arrived home the anger erupted like fireworks. How dared they call them lazy, and treat them with such disrespect? And the German officer, what was he writing down? Heidi's intuition told her that the letter they had mentioned would bring bad news, and by that she did not mean only that the unemployment benefit would be cut off. It may be more than that to it.

Frantz and his wife listened to the girls' complaints without saying a word, trying to make sense of the heated conversation between them. Something had certainly gone wrong, and the consequences would follow. Their father slowly left the room, keeping his opinions to himself. Their mother busied herself with fixing lunch, while Louisa slammed the door on her way to the neighbors' place. Johan, who stayed home on that rainy day, wanted to find out more, asking questions over the high-pitched voices of his sisters.

'What do you think their decision will be? Did they tell you how soon the letter will come?' the boy asked with interest.

'Can't you understand that we were not told more than you and I already know? I wish I knew the answers, but I don't. All I know is that they tried to intimidate us and look down on us.' Heidi said, knowing that waiting for that damn letter would drive everybody in the family over the edge.

'Now, I'm going to change my dress, and help dad clean his shop. I'm not going to waste any more time talking about something I have no control over. Teresa, you should help mom in the kitchen and try to relax. Look, the sun is peeking through the clouds. Maybe in the afternoon we can go up to the farmer and help him feed the chickens. That way we can bring home some fresh eggs and a bottle of milk. What do you think, Johan?'

The boy nodded, and then added, mostly to himself:

'Hopefully the weather will allow us to climb the hill. You know the road to the farm must be muddy after the rain, and you can hardly walk without slipping down the slope. We need our rubber boots.'

For the next three days Heidi and Teresa busied themselves with any task around the house in order to distract themselves from the awful uncertainty of waiting. On September 5th, the mailman knocked on the door to deliver two letters. Both bore the stamp of the Third Reich. One had Teresa's name on it, and the other Heidi's. Frantz took them, thanked the postman and looked at the envelopes for a long time, before turning to find his daughters staring at him.

'Here you go, you have mail!' Frantz said, giving each of them a letter and then pulling up a chair and sitting down.

Teresa took a deep breath and opened the envelope. Unfolding the paper, she looked at her father and started to read loudly.

"To: Teresa Souisa,

This is to inform you that on October 1st, 1942 at 10am you shall report to the General Department of the Third Reich in Vienna to enroll into the glorious German Army. At that time you will be informed about your duty and the detachment you are to join. Until that date you must notify us of any changes that may occur in your health and location.

This is an order from the Third Reich, and disobedience will be prosecuted.

Colonel Rudolf Weise."

When she finished reading, she looked around the room. Her mother had tears in her eyes and her hand pressed to her chest. Her father was looking down at the floor, and Heidi was staring at her in disbelief. None of them spoke for a while. It was as if the room was a scene cut out of a silent movie with a broken sound track.

'Now, Heidi, it's your turn to read your letter,' Frantz said at last.

Heidi started to tear off the envelope, took out the letter and unfolded it. She quickly scanned the content and said:

'It says exactly the same thing, only it's addressed to me.'

'October 1st is only three weeks and three days away. Dear Lord, this is terrible news!' Josephina managed to say in horror, tears streaming down her face.

Frantz Souisa pushed the chair and got up. This was much worse than he had anticipated. He had a feeling there was a good chance that Teresa would be sent to the army, but, good Lord, now they called Heidi too? She was only seventeen years old. What was Hitler doing, taking children out of their family's nest and throwing them into war? This was outrageous. The whole thing saddened Frantz to no end. The First World War had been bad enough but this one was complete insanity. He was getting old and his health was not too good, and he needed help around the house, now when two of his children were due to enroll in the Army. He had to do something about it, but what?

The next few days went by quickly. The neighbors found out about the Souisa girls' call up, and so did the farmer on the hill. Everybody who knew them was concerned about their safety and their future. People come together during challenging times, and many tried to give the girls advice or to comfort the parents.

One morning, Frantz Souisa asked Heidi to give him the letter she had received, an envelope and a blank sheet of paper. When she had done so, he sat down at the kitchen table and started to write. Heidi looked at her father, and without a word sat down at the table too.

'I'm writing back to the S.S. Office in St. Polten. If you have to join the army, the least I can ask them is to keep you with your sister. Teresa is older, and can look after you with her good judgment, and you can look after her too. Together you have a better chance of handling whatever comes your way. If they will do me this small favor, it will serve as some relief in this awful situation that we have to accept,' Frantz said to Heidi, and then continued to write. When he had finished he sent Heidi to the post office to mail it.

Heidi took the letter and, on the way out, almost collided with Teresa, who had spent the whole morning in the bedroom. Heidi was surprised to see her ready to go out instead of helping their mother around the house. The two sisters headed down the stairs toward the street. Once outside the iron gate, Heidi said:

'Where are you going? You almost locked yourself in the bedroom all morning. We will be gone in no time and mom and dad are so upset, and it seems like you are living on another planet. They are so concerned about our departure. You should be more sensitive and try to be there for our parents, and Johan, and Louisa.'

Teresa looked at Heidi, and tears flickered in her eyes.

'I know I should concentrate more on our family, but I wish you could understand how hard it is to have to go into the army for me. I spent the morning writing a letter to Hans so that he will know what is happening with me, and find a way to keep in touch. I'm going to the post office now to mail it.'

'Teresa, I wish I understood you better, but it looks to me that all you think about is Hans instead of focusing on our future and the uncertain times that lie ahead for us. I'm going to the post office too, but the letter I have to mail is written by dad, and addressed to the SS Office.'

'What? Are you serious?' Teresa asked in disbelief.

'Yes, sis. He is asking them to keep you and me together wherever they will send us. He is very concerned about our well-being and all the dangers that await us. He wants to make sure that we will be able to look after one another and that at the end of this stupid war we both come home safe and sound. Please make an effort and be gentle with our parents. Help support the family in the short time that we have left before October 1st.'

Ashamed, Teresa put an arm around Heidi's narrow shoulders and squeezed her gently. She would mail the letter to Hans, but she was determined from then on to treasure her family and their time together. She would take care of her sister and assume the protective role of an oldest sibling. Her family deserved it, and she was part of her family. Yes, she would prove her loving and caring attitude, because she loved her family very much. Yes, Hans would have to take second place in her heart, where he belongs.

On the way home from the post office, Teresa was preoccupied by what had to be done before their departure, full of constructive ideas about how to handle their enrolment and what would be the best approach for military life.

Heidi was glad to notice that, for the first time since coming home from Rosenburg Castle, her sister was behaving normally and responsibly. She finally had her sister back. It was a bitter-sweet revelation, but if they stuck together, and the Good Lord helped them, maybe there was a chance for all of them to make it through.

Chapter 4

The train started to move from Traisen station. The locomotive was panting heavily, and the wheels' motion developed an increasing rhythm as the old yellow building was left behind. In front of it on the platform Frantz, his wife, his son, and his youngest daughter waved good bye to Heidi and Teresa, who stuck their head out of the car's window for as long as they could see their family being left behind at the station. They were first going to St. Polten, and from there to Vienna to enroll in the army. The order was to be there at 10 am, and they thus had to take the early morning train. Neither of them could sleep the night before. They went to bed late, wanting to spend as much time with their loved ones as they could. In the morning it was a rush to get to the station, and to try not to forget anything important to take along. Now that they were on their way, and had survived the dreadful moment of saying their good-byes, Heidi looked around and saw that there were only few travelers in their car: an old couple that looked rather wealthy, judging by the amount of jewelry the woman was wearing, a man hiding behind the newspaper he was reading, and a young woman trying to get some sleep.

Heidi and Teresa looked out the window, each of them holding a bag with their belongings. Mostly they had packed underwear, warm socks, and a couple of sweaters. Their papers and IDs were in their coat pockets. The train ran through the mountains in which the scenery was full of autumn colors. It was a gorgeous day.

The trip took about an hour. Once arrived in St. Polten the girls asked for direction to the train to Vienna, and were surprised to learn that it was right across the station's platform. They also noticed that the young woman they had seen on the train was coming toward them, a bit disoriented.

'Excuse me, may I ask you were Vienna is?' she said shyly.

'Do you mean the train to Vienna?' Heidi said with a smile.

'Yes, I'm sorry, I am a bit confused. You are right, Third Reich train to Vienna,' the lost girl added.

Teresa tried not to laugh at the twisted choice of words the girl was using. Heidi started to feel sorry for the poor stranger, who looked as scared as a chicken wandering outside the nest.

'We are going to Vienna too. If you like, come with us, we can look for it together,' Heidi added.

'Really? Sure, I'm coming with you then. My name is Gloria,' she said with relief.

'I'm Heidi and this is my older sister Teresa. We are from Traisen. Where are you from?'

'I'm from Lilienfeld. I have an order to enroll in the army,' Gloria went on, happy that she had found some company.

'So do we. Our appointment is for 10 o'clock. We should get on this train here; it may leave any minute now,' Teresa said in a business-like tone.

The three girls headed toward the train, hopping in the closest car. Soon the train was in motion. The trees on each side of the railway were yellow, giving a warm light under the morning sun. The two-hour trip passed by quickly as the girls were tired and slept almost the entire time after the conductor had seen their tickets.

Once they had arrived in Vienna, Gloria was amazed by the large building of the station. She could not take her eyes off the high ceilings and the grandeur of the columns.

Heidi took a deep breath, overwhelmed by all the memories of her life in the Austrian capital. She thought of little Klara, her mom Elisabeth Wolfang, and Thomas, and Sylvia, wondering what their lives were like now.

Teresa was the only one not day-dreaming. She asked for directions, and found out that the General Department of The Third Reich was within walking distance of the Central Station. Making sure that the other two girls followed her, she rushed out of the station.

On the sidewalk people were going about their business in an alert, brisk manner. The girls saw that there were quite a few people in military uniforms. On the street, they noticed that most of the cars belonged to the German Army. In front of the General Department of the Third Reich, a military bus was parked.

Heidi, Teresa, and Gloria stopped to look at the red brick building before entering it. Inside were a lot of people, and a number of soldiers directed everybody to the right booth. One of the soldiers asked them about their papers. After they had shown their letters, all three were sent to the booth marked 'Enrollment'. With some trepidation, Teresa walked toward it, Heidi and Gloria in tow.

'Heil Hitler! Give me your papers and Identification,' the women inside the booth said directly.

'Good Morning. Here you have my papers and my sister's,' Teresa said as she handed over the documents.

The woman looked at the Identification and at the girls, put a stamp on each letter that the girls had received, and with a commanding voice said:

'Go straight, and turn into the first corridor on the right. The last door on the left is the storage room where you get uniforms. After that you have to go to Room 201 on the second floor for a meeting. Make sure you don't waste too much time, the meeting starts at 11 sharp. Next!'

'Thank you,' the sisters said and went on their way, allowing Gloria to get to the booth's window. Before they reached the corridor on the right, Gloria was catching up with them.

'I was told to go to the storage, and after that to a meeting, I forgot which room.'

'Probably the same room, Room 201 as we have to go to. Let's get the uniforms now,' Heidi said as she took Gloria's hand, leading her onto the long corridor.

The storage room was huge. Shelves from floor to ceiling were stuffed with clothes, each shelf marked with the sizes of the garments it bore. A woman dressed in uniform welcomed them, and told them to pick only a winter coat, a bonnet and a pair of shoes from the supply. Heidi was surprised to see that everything was new and neatly folded. This gave her a boost. It was long time since she had got to choose new clothes. The girls did not wait for another invitation, and right away started to look for their sizes and picked out gray coats. They spent more time in the shoe section, and then put on the bonnets and tried on the coats. Half an hour later all three had a pack with a uniform, had signed a receiving document, and rushed toward the meeting room.

Room 201 had a long table covered in the Third Reich flag, in front of which stood about ten rows of wooden chairs. Half of them were occupied by other young women holding folded uniforms. There was a murmur of whispers, with nobody daring to speak loudly. Eyeing three available chairs in the second row, Teresa showed the way, and all three sat down, joggling the uniform packs and the bags they had brought from home.

After a short while three officers came through the door. All essayed a Third Reich greeting, raising their right hand. The sound of the chairs being pushed back against the hard wooden floor filled the room as the audience rose. Then, with another thud, everybody sat down.

'We will take attendance. Please rise when you hear your name called out.' The officer called all the names, and made a mark after each of those who responded. Surprisingly, there were no absentees. The second officer then started to talk.

'I am pleased to see that everybody came on time, and followed the instructions. All of you will join the Telecommunication Detachment and will help the glorious German Army to win the war. This afternoon you will be taken to the old airport site, on the Eastern side of Vienna, to begin instruction and training. Upon completion of the program, each of you will be sent to telecommunication stations at various locations in the German occupied territories.'

The third man took notes, and, when the other finished his speech, said:

'There is a bus at the front entrance that will take you all to the training school site. On the way out, you'll be given a suitcase to carry your uniform. Write your name on the suitcase's tag and board the bus. At the destination, keep the order for accommodation in the school's dormitory. After that, you'll have to attend the assembly before dinner. Good luck to everyone.'

Immediately, all three officers got up and left the room. The girls gathered their belongings, and flooded toward the door all at once, pushing each other. Seeing this, Heidi stopped Teresa.

'Hold on! We don't need to rush. Tell me what do you think of all this so far? The officers looked decent to me. Telecommunication can't be that bad! Interesting, huh?'

'We'll see. Don't set your hopes too high,' Teresa answered wisely.

Gloria listened quietly, and waited for the sisters to exit the room. In the next half an hour all the young women had their uniforms packed in suitcases and they lined up to board the bus.

On the way to the decommissioned airport, Heidi realized that they had not eaten anything since breakfast at home, and she was hungry. Their mother had slipped a slice of bread and an apple into each girl's bag before they left home, and Heidi searched hers and took out the food. Seeing it, Teresa did the same thing. Heidi looked at Gloria. The next moment the girl took a piece of pie wrapped in paper out of her pocket and started to eat. Heidi smiled to herself. This Gloria from Lilienfeld was determined to follow them, no matter what. It was funny and sweet, the natural way she stuck with them. The war had brought them together and, soon enough would probably tear them apart. For now, though, Gloria was happy that she had found somebody helpful and trustworthy, from the same area, whom she could call a friend. The wide world was full of enemies, anyway.

Vienna was full of autumn colors. Heidi looked out the bus window at the majestic buildings and tall churches they passed on the way. This time last year she was happily discovering the day and night life of the city. Fascinated by the city she never visited before, Gloria had completely forgotten to eat the pie. She was like a little child on Christmas morning. Teresa looked out the window too, but she could not see much. Her thoughts were elsewhere. Hans and she had always wanted to visit Vienna together, but their dream had not yet come true. How ironic the game of fate which had brought her here, alone, for a completely different reason!

After a forty minute drive, the bus arrived in Vienna's outskirts and the urban scenery changed to a hilly landscape covered in dry grass. Ahead, one could see the control tower of the old airport and around it there were three long, low-rise wooden buildings. The premises were encircled by a low chain fence painted green. The large gate was open. A high steel structure which resembled a hydro pole was scrapping the sky in the middle of the yard. On top of it was installed the alarm system, dominating the horizon like an eagle.

The bus pulled through the iron gate and came to a full stop in front of a building labeled "Main Building". The doors were opened and the driver told everybody to get off: they had reached their destination. The young women gathered their suitcases and formed a group in front of the main entrance beside the empty bus. Everybody looked around with disappointment. The place was like a deserted fort in the middle of nowhere. The afternoon sun lost its warmth, and a strong wind was blowing with a horrifying noise. An officer came out of the building and asked for the girls' attention.

'Listen to me, everybody! I am Colonel Rudolf Weise, and I am in charge of the Instruction Program for your training. At first, you will be accommodated in Building 2, where the dormitory is. There are enough beds there. Choose one and settle in. There is a bathroom in the building. Building 3 is for school personnel and you are not supposed to wander over there. The Main Building is where the lessons take place, and in one of the rooms your meals will be served. The training schedule will be given to you this evening at dinner, 7pm sharp. Instruction starts tomorrow morning. That's it for now. Heil Hitler!'

The colonel turned on his heels and disappeared inside the ugly building. The girls looked toward Building 2, and slowly moved in that direction.

'Can I get a bed close to you two?' Gloria asked Heidi. 'This place is so far from the city and so cold. I'm a bit scared.'

'Let's go inside and have a look at the dormitory, before all the good spots are taken,' said Teresa pushing Heidi ahead.

The dorm was a huge hall with beds on both sides, and at one end was a table with a bench and a coal stove. Once inside, everybody rushed for beds close to the stove and further away from the outside door. The Souisa sisters managed to find two spots somewhere in the middle of the room. Gloria secured a bed across the aisle from Heidi's. The bed sheets looked clean, but they were worn out by the chlorine. The pillows were hard and the blankets rough. Nothing for comfort, all for the basics! The bathroom had two sinks, one shower and two toilet stalls. It was at the opposite end, next to the outside door. A few small windows that let in a dim haze of light completed the dormitory's appearance.

'I hope the main building looks better, because this one is downright ugly,' said Heidi, more to herself than to anybody else.

'It is how it is. We only sleep here. We'll be spending most of our time in training, anyway,' Teresa replied before adding 'I'm going to lie down for few minutes. I'm tired.'

Over the next few days the girls got into a forced routine and began their learning of telecommunication and camp phone sets.

On October 11th 1942, ten days into the program, Heidi turned eighteen. It was the worst birthday of her life, and, ironically, the most important: she had just become a legal adult. Teresa and Gloria congratulated her when they woke up, and expressed their regrets about not having any presents or cake for celebration. Hugs and good wishes were all that Heidi received on that day. It was enough: she was healthy, had family and friends, and the weather was gorgeous. The sky was clear, the sun was shining, and even the powerful winds that made the nights so chilly had stopped for a while. It was like someone specifically configured the perfect day for her and her only. It was a pity that most of it was spent inside the classroom.

Heidi found the courses interesting and easy to learn, but she did not like the food and the coarse condition of the dorm. As a result, she was always hungry, tired, and cold.

In November the cold weather arrived. The coal stove could hardly keep the big room warm, and there was not enough coal to burn through the whole night. In the morning everybody in the dorm would be shivering. Heidi slept fully dressed, and the coat she had been given was always thrown above the bed blanket during the night. Teresa and Gloria adopted similar habits. The other girls complained about the freezing nights to Col. Weise, but nothing had been done to improve the situation.

The material was interesting, and the days passed faster than the nights. The girls learnt about point to point telephony, how to lay phone cable on the field and establish communication connections, and how to use the telex machine in code Bode and conduct radio communication in Morse code. Heidi, with her eager mind, was a quick learner. Sometimes, in the evenings, she helped Gloria with what they were taught during the day. Gloria made a habit of working with Heidi on all the field activities they practiced. Teresa was amused to see how clingy Gloria was to her sister.

Six weeks into the program, in mid-November, they were assigned an air attack drill. The girls were divided in groups of three or four and each group was given specific tasks to accomplish during the exercise.

The evening before the drill, everybody was reviewing what they were supposed to do the next day.

Heidi, Gloria and Teresa were responsible for sky observation and for transmitting information by camp telephone to the groups inside the telecommunication station held in the main building. Inside were three groups of three students each, who were in charge of transmitting the data by phone, telex and air waves to the so called "reception cells" which had to warn everybody to be prepared for an air strike.

'Heidi, why did we get the most risky task?' Teresa asked, reviewing the schedule. 'We are the only group that has to be outside, and you have to climb on that antenna tower all the way to the top. Aren't you scared?' Teresa continued to look worried.

'That's all right, sis, I always liked to climb trees, remember? And trees are more dangerous than this steel tower, because you never know when a dry branch is going to break under you. The steel is solid and has a ladder all the way to the top. On top I have a little platform I can stand on, and heights have never scared me,' Heidi responded with enthusiasm.

'You are really brave, Heidi. I would not go up there if my life depended on it,' Gloria enthused in praise of her friend.

'Well, instead of worrying about me being at the top of the antenna, we better make sure that we know how to connect the phone sets and lay the wires from the base of the tower, where you Gloria, are going to be, to the door of the building where Teresa will be. Remember, we have to communicate using the phone set, and not yell at one another. Did you two check the cables for length and quality?' asked Heidi. She wanted her group to succeed.

'That is all done. The phone sets are also fully charged. Gloria, are you fine with being at the base of the tower?' asked Teresa, concerned that the girl might get too nervous and forget what to do, just as she usually forgot how to talk when she was under pressure.

'Yes. I'll be fine. Whatever Heidi tells me, I'll pass it on to you, right?' Gloria confirmed.

'Then we should get a good night sleep to be well rested for tomorrow. Good night!' and with that Teresa got all bundled up in bed, followed by Heidi and Gloria.

Soon the entire room went quiet and only the flicker of the fire in the stove cast a playful light on the ceiling. By the time everybody was asleep, even that yellow-red ray had grown tired, and once the coals burned out the darkness reigned over everything. And with this, the cold November night was painfully felt inside the building.

The next morning the sky was overcast, as if painted in shades of granite and grey. The wind was blowing from the mountains, bringing with it damp cold air. The students had their usual breakfast, after which they prepared for the drill. Everybody was nervous, knowing that the scenario for which this drill was an exercise, could very well happen in reality if an air bombing raid was launched over Vienna.

At 10am the girls were ready, the wires were laid down and the telecommunication machines were ready to be operated.

Heidi started to climb the ladder to the top of the antenna, with instructions in the pocket of her coat. She paused when she was half way up: the wind was strong, and she had to exert more effort to secure her grip on the ladder. She then continued her way up to the top. On the small platform, she made sure that the wind would not blow her away, and waved to Gloria to let her know that she was all right. The phone set was tied around her waist, the cable connected to the set that Gloria was holding at the bottom of the pole. Gloria almost got vertigo just looking at Heidi. She quickly made the sign of the cross in an effort to calm herself down, and then looked toward the main building where Teresa was in position, the phone in her hands.

From where Teresa stood, Heidi looked as small as a bird. She was worried for her sister, and could not wait for this exercise to be over. Col. Weise started to speak on the megaphone, announcing the beginning of the drill. Shortly after his speech the air alarm started, the sound unbearable, loud and terrifying, giving everyone goose bumps.

Heidi's heart almost jumped out of her chest when the siren began to sound directly next to her. Out of instinct she lowered herself onto the tiny platform, grabbed the phone and started to shout the imaginary directions of a possible attack, sending the information to Gloria who then passed it on Teresa and ultimately to the groups inside the building. The accuracy of the transmission was important, and they were to be judged on its basis.

Gloria was terrified by the siren's noise and the rapidity with which she had to receive and transmit the information, but she pulled herself together and performed well under pressure. Teresa was surprised to notice that Gloria's message was said correctly, for a change. She was quick in retransmitting it inside, all the while with her eyes glued to her sister's post.

The drill lasted 20 minutes. For Heidi it seemed like an eternity. The wind tore at her with its savage forces and shocking noises. The siren beside her was agonizing: she spoke into the phone's receiver not hearing her voice at all.

When the drill was over, Heidi was deaf, or so she thought. The world was still and silent around her. All she could feel was the wind's force, but the noise was gone. She closed her eyes, and it felt as if she was flying. The slight movement of the antenna due to the wind was like the tremor of an earthquake. Heidi did not move, curled like a ball on the top platform.

On the ground, Teresa called her sister, but received neither sign nor sound as a reply.

'Heidi, Heidi!' Gloria yelled from the bottom of her lungs. No answer, no movement from up there.

'Oh my God! No! She is dead! Teresa, Heidi is dead!' Gloria started to cry, her entire body shaking with sobs.

'Stay right here and watch her. I'll run to the building to get help,' Teresa told Gloria, and headed toward the building. Gloria followed her.

Teresa stopped, grabbed Gloria from the shoulders and pushed her back.

'I told you to stay where you are, and watch my sister while I bring help. Do you understand me?'

'She is dead, she is dead, what can we do?' Gloria wailed.

'Listen to me: watch her and talk to her. She is not dead. I'll go get help!' Teresa's look was as sharp as a blade, and stopped Gloria in her tracks. The girl did what she was told, tears streaming down her face.

From the building the other students came out, followed by the off duty guards and Col. Weise. Everybody looked up at Heidi. Nobody saw any movement up at the top of the antenna. Teresa pleaded for help, rushing everybody toward the bottom of the tall pole.

Up above, Heidi slowly opened her eyes and looked down without moving. She still could not hear, but she could see the crowd gathered below her. Her mind began to process information, trying to understand what was going on. Everybody was making signs towards her with their hands. She could see Teresa's shocked expression, Gloria's crying face, and Col. Weise's worried gaze among the others. She realized that they were trying to tell her something, but she could not hear a thing. Keeping her head in the same position she rotated her eyes, and saw the horizon and the grey sky. Then she moved, and found her balance. Seeing this, the crowd began to cheer and clap their hands. Teresa started to cry, thanking God that Heidi was all right. Gloria let out a scream of joy and hugged Teresa, jumping up and down.

Col. Weise put the megaphone to his mouth and asked Heidi to carefully descend from the tower.

Suddenly, like a cork from a bottle of champagne, Heidi's ears popped and she began to regain her hearing. The noise of the wind, the voices from bellow, and the officer's orders hit Heidi all at once. She regained her composure and looked down the ladder, but at that moment fear took over her. Her feet were glued to the platform and her hands held tightly onto the thin rail. This was nothing like getting down from a tree, by moving from one branch to another; this was a straight vertical ladder, fifty meters long.

'Heidi, come down, the drill is over,' said Teresa as loudly as she could.

'I'm not coming down. I cannot do it!' Heidi managed to articulate.

'Yes, you can! Just hold tight onto the rail and do not look down,' responded Teresa.

'Heidi Souisa, you must descend the tower now!' Heidi heard Col. Weise command.

Terrified, she said, 'I can't, I'm too afraid, sir!'

Col. Weise understood and quickly formulated another plan. He ordered a soldier from among the off-duty guards to climb up and give Heidi help, while also instructing the crowd to move back from the antenna in order to give the soldier some space to begin the rescue mission. Everybody complied, and in no time the soldier was beside Heidi. He took some time to talk to her, while all the people on the ground quietly waited, their eyes fixed on Heidi.

Five minutes later the descent begun. The soldier was coming down first, followed by Heidi, one step at a time. Another ten minutes later, with about twenty happy faces staring at her, Heidi put both feet on the ground. Cheers and hugs welcomed her. When the enthusiasm had calmed down a bit, Col. Weise asked everybody to go inside the classroom and analyze the results of the drill exercise. The task had without doubt been accomplished well, and Heidi was seen as a hero. After all, who would have wanted to be up there, watching for the arrival of the enemy's planes? That was by far the most difficult task, drill or not.

Col. Weise was satisfied with the way the instruction was going. The students were agile and fast learners. Despite the poor accommodation and the thin meals, all the girls had a good attitude to their studies. They would have become fine members of the Third Reich Army by the time the program had concluded. As a reward, he would propose to the Army's Major Stat that everybody be given a well-deserved vacation over the winter holidays.

Once December had come, winter rolled in with bitterly cold weather and freezing nights in the dormitory. Some of the girls got cold. Some took turns to watch the fire, and keep it burning, but the daily coal supply was not sufficient to last throughout the night. Something had to be done. The coal was stored in Building 3. Every morning two soldiers carried the coal ration to the stove in Building 2. The storage room had an outside door.

One evening Gloria told Heidi, 'Guess what? I heard the other girls talking about making a plan to get more coal from the storage room during the night.'

'No you didn't!' Heidi stopped Gloria's speech. 'We can try to ask for more coal. We may get a larger supply.'

Gloria pulled Heidi towards her and spoke into her ear.

'I'm telling you that tonight two girls will go and bring the coal , while two others will watch for the guards. They want to put together a plan so that we all do this job on rotation every night.'

Heidi paused, and processed the information. They were proposing that they steal coal. What if they got caught? She was not sure that was such a good idea. It would probably be better to talk to Col. Weise about giving them more coal. But what if he did not approve? And then, on the other hand, Heidi considered the fact that one cannot over-rule the decision of the majority without being called a traitor.

That night, Gloria's prediction was proved right. Four girls worked together to steal coal from the storage room, and the fire burned in the stove without interruption. It was pleasant inside the room and the rest of the girls slept better than they had in months.

The next night, they decided not to repeat the procedure in order not arouse suspicion, but rather to apply the plan every second night. Teresa told Heidi to avoid getting involved in the scheme for as long as possible.

In the second week of December, at the great assembly, Col. Weise told everybody where they were to be sent after the completion of their instruction. Each girl received the decision in writing. Most were to go to different cities in the German occupied territory.

Looking at her papers, Teresa asked Heidi about her location.

'Pilsen, in Czechoslovakia. You?' Heidi answered.

Teresa sighed with relief.

'Me too.' The sisters were overjoyed that they were to be sent to the same place. Their father's letter had not fallen on deaf ears after all. They were grateful for that, and their parents would be too.

At the end of the meeting, Col. Weise gave them another piece of good news. For the hard work and diligence that everybody had shown during the time spent at the school, they were going to be rewarded with two weeks vacation over Christmas and New Year. They were free to go home from December 17th to January 2nd. On January 3rd 1943 they were to report to the communication centers as per the papers they received. Upon hearing this news, a loud cheer erupted in the classroom. Vacation was only few days away. Everybody was happy.

For the remaining nights, nobody tried to steal coal anymore. They figured that putting their good luck in jeopardy was not worth it. After all, they were to go home soon. Furthermore, the weather became milder, and, with a light snow having fallen on the ground, their foot prints leading from the dorm to the storage room would have given them away in the morning.

On December 17th 1942, everybody left the old airport premises on the same bus that had brought them there almost three months ago. This time the bus was filled with happy sounds, as all chattered about home and loved ones. Teresa, Heidi and Gloria could not wait to get to the train station and take the train back home.

Chapter 5

The end of 1942 was not a very good time for the German Army. In Western Europe the French Resistance gained momentum, and helped the Allies to weaken the Axis troops. The Germans suffered heavy losses in North Africa. The Allies' Operation Torch in Algeria and Morocco was a success due to the French Resistance's help. In Eastern Europe, the Battle of Stalingrad was a desperate struggle for the German 6th Army. Operation Uranus, launched by the Soviet Union, encircled the Germans near Stalingrad and forced their surrender. Hitler hated these outcomes, and instructed his Generals not to surrender at whatever the costs. It was a mad order, with grave consequences for the German troops. As the year came to its end, the Allies' positions looked brighter than the German's on all fronts.

In Traisen, the Souisa family had its own reason to celebrate: Christmas found every member of the family at home. For the first time since the war had begun, there were no empty seats around the kitchen table. Teresa and her mom worked hard to prepare the food for Christmas Eve dinner and Christmas Day supper. They were having roast rabbit with corn and cranberry sauce. Frantz Souisa had received a bottle of wine from one of his customers who needed his boots repaired, and Heidi baked an apple pie to be served as desert. Johan worked hard to cut logs for the stove, and Louisa decorated a big branch of pine tree, which served as a Christmas tree in the family room.

The day before Christmas it started to snow again, a fresh white blanket covering the roofs of the houses, the street, and the frozen Traisen River. The trees looked like white arms elevated to the sky, welcoming the Holy baby Jesus. At church, hymns of joy were sung by children, and, once the night grew dark, candles lit up every window.

Heidi was filled with joy to look around her and see her loved ones content and healthy. Her joy spread throughout the room and the conversation was animated by the tasty meal and the beautiful sight of the Christmas tree. Johan and Louisa were waiting in anticipation for the Christmas presents to be found under the tree in the morning. Teresa was happy to receive news from Hans, letting her know that he was well and still working at the castle. The parents enjoyed their children's company, living in the moment. Christmas morning came with appreciation for the little gifts that they exchanged. Following this, they all went to church together to attend Christmas Mass, and share the spirit with other people.

As one day followed after another the year came to an end, and so did Heidi and Teresa's vacation. New Year's Day was spent in preparation for the departure to Pilsen. Again, Heidi and Teresa had to pack up a few clothes, some food for the trip, and say their good-byes, promising that they would keep in touch with their parents and take care of themselves.

Winter was in full swing in Pilsen. The old city was covered with a blanket of fresh snow which sparkled in the afternoon sun. The historical city center with the large square plaza was dominated by the slim tower of the gothic St. Bartholomew's Cathedral. The edifice was grandiose and beautiful, inside and out. The streets had an urban charm that reminded them of the past, but also a technological asset in the trolleybus wire net and its electrical vehicles. The trolleybus operation had begun in Pilsen in 1941. It was a new form of transportation between the city center and the industrial areas, where most of Pilsen's population worked. The city was proud of the heavy machinery factory, Skoda, which manufactured trucks, cars, train cars, trolleybuses, buses, and, more recently, parts for military machines. The plant was well known in Europe and a great asset for the Nazi Army. Most of production was now directed toward supporting the war effort. Pilsen was also valuable for Germans due to its well known brewery. In times of peace, this Bohemian city had had many reasons to be proud, among which were its old heritage, the picturesque surroundings, the self-sufficient economy, the great beer, the advanced technology, and its people, who made all these things possible.

The first impression of the city for the Souisa sisters was a positive one. They were surprised by how much it resembled St. Polten and, if not for the foreign language they heard on the street, they would have thought they were still in Austria. The language barrier, though, was not a major obstacle, since lots of the locals understood German, and were able to communicate with the Nazi occupants. That was a good thing, as Germans had taken over the leadership of most institutions and factories. They also controlled the schools and the public sector.

Heidi and Teresa could see that the German occupation here was more severe and visible than in Austria. The reason for this was that Czechoslovakia had not been as eager as their homeland to welcome Hitler when he expanded the German territory in 1938. The tension between the local population and Germans had never eased. On the other hand, Pilsen was a strategic point of interest for the Nazis. The Skoda factory was working for them, and it was an important base for military research. It was also used as an Air Force Base. Maybe that was why one could sense hostility in the air. But that was politics, and the Souisa girls knew better than to get involved in it, as their father had always taught them.

The Third Reich's Communication Center, where Heidi and her sister had to go, was a three-storey solid old building in the heart of the city. The thick brick walls alluded to decent living conditions and safety. The ground floor housed the administration, the dining hall and the kitchen. The second floor had several bedrooms for the young women enrolled in the German Army, whose duties were telecommunication between communication centers placed all over Europe, from Berlin to Gdansk in Poland, Bucharest in Romania, Rome in Italy and Marseille in France. The Communication Room was strategically placed in the basement of the building. On the third floor in the south wing was the quarter which housed the instruction personnel, and in the north wing there were a couple of classrooms used for training.

Heidi quickly assessed the bedroom they had to share with two other girls, and found it rather nice and livable. There were four beds, one in each corner of the room, and a small table with four chairs in the middle. By the door there was an old-fashioned wardrobe with a dozen hangers on one side and four shelves on the other. Its two large doors were decorated with wooden panels carved in the rococo style.

'This looks nice and homey, don't you think? And best of all it's warm and cozy in here!' Heidi said to Teresa with a cheerful tone.

'I agree. It's not bad at all. What a difference from the icy Building 2 in Vienna! Let's pick our beds and get comfortable. The other two girls will be here anytime now.' Teresa responded in a tired voice. The cold outside had really gotten to her, and now, in the warmth of the room she became a bit sleepy.

'We should avoid the beds by the windows. They are more exposed to draft and other hazards. Dad always said to watch out for dangers, and take minimal risks. This city is not in our country, and we may not be too welcome here after all. We have to stay alert at all times,' Heidi said, more to herself than to her sister.

Both of them started to unpack their small suitcases, placing their clothes in half of the wardrobe. They were pleased that the room and the beddings were clean. From the hallway they heard voices and steps approaching. There was a knock on the door, and Heidi opened it to find herself facing a lovely young woman with big, warm blue eyes and curly blond hair. Seeing Heidi, she unveiled a sweet smile and started to talk in a familiar German dialect.

'Good Afternoon! I'm Mathilda Schos, but everybody calls me Ticla. I'm supposed to be your room mate. This is Karina, a girl I met downstairs who also was sent to this room.' She looked over Heidi's shoulder and saw Teresa sitting at the table in the middle of the room.

'I see that, with the two of you, our room is already complete. I can't wait for us to get to know each other,' Ticla added, still smiling. She stepped into the room, followed by Karina, who seemed to be more on the shy side.

Teresa got up from the table and came to Heidi's side, her eyes on the two newcomers.

'Hi Ticla! Hi Karina! Nice to meet you. I'm Heidi Souisa and this is my older sister Teresa.'

'You two are sisters? That is so nice. You are so lucky to be together! Where are you from?'

'We are from Austria, from a town sixty kilometers away from Vienna called Traisen. Where are you from?' asked Teresa.

With a sparkle in her eyes, visibly pleased, Ticla replied, 'I'm from Austria too, a place halfway between Linz and Salzburg. What a coincidence! Karina, what about you? I've not had a chance to ask you yet.'

Karina sat on one of the beds by the window, and with a sigh said, 'I'm Karina Schwartz from Leipzig, Germany. Apparently I'm an outsider, since all three of you are Austrian.'

Heidi noticed a trace of regret in Karina's voice, and maybe disappointment too. She also realized that the girl's German was perfect and dialect free. It usually takes some time to adjust to a new environment and new company, but Heidi was confident that the four of them would get along just fine.

'Karina, it's nice to meet you. I think we're the outsiders rather than you, since you are German born. Don't worry: we're all in the same boat. All we have to do is attend to our job and keep safe. We will be great room mates, won't we?' said Heidi, and gave the girls an encouraging smile.

The rest of the afternoon and evening passed quickly while the four young women tried to settle in and make each other acquaintance. Heidi and Teresa were seen as a team, Ticla as a comfortable fit into the group, but Karina was more reserved and kept the others at an arm's length. Teresa thought that this was understandable, given the fact that Karina had to carry the burden of her nation being the main aggressor in the war. Also, the heavy losses of the German Army on most of the fronts could have done nothing to relieve the spirit of its citizens. In her opinion, though, Teresa knew that none of them were on safe ground in Pilsen, and, because of that, it was better to be united than to fight amongst one another.

The next morning was comprised of an assembly in the big dining room, followed by the allocation of uniforms. In addition to the gray coat that they received in Vienna, everybody was given a matching skirt, two light gray shirts, a dark gray wool vest, and a long jacket with shiny yellow buttons and tresses on the shoulders. A swastika was embroidered on the left sleeve of the jacket. The girls spent quite a long time trying on the garments. By lunch time they had gone through all the formalities, they had filled in the paperwork, and in the afternoon they were given an overview of the Communication Center in the basement of the building. Their schedule was to continue working around the clock. Their shifts were posted on a big black board. The girls would work nine hours a day, with a few breaks for meals. While off duty, they were allowed to go outside and into town if they wanted to, but they had a curfew of 10:30 pm. For the late and night shifts, which were assigned by rotation, resting time was modified accordingly. At least six persons were on duty at any given time, with more people working during the daytime, or during an emergency.

Back in their room that night, Heidi reviewed her schedule for the following week and realized that she and Teresa were to work together.

'Tomorrow at 8 o'clock we start working. I hope they will train us for a day or two.'

'I heard that this center is new, and we are the first transmission detachment to work here. Where did you attend the instruction program?' Ticla asked.

Teresa was the first to answer.

'We were in school in Vienna. Upon completion of the program each girl was sent to a different place. We were lucky to come here together. What about you?'

'I attended the Radio Transmission Unit in Salzburg. We learnt all the transmission codes. I hope I'll be able to handle the job here,' Ticla said, and then turned toward Karina with a questioning look.

'I'm not sure I like to talk about myself and what I've been taught to do. I barely know you,' Karina said, trying to avoid the discussion.

'You are right. We don't know you either, but we don't have any preconceptions about you, and we're trying to become your friends. It would be nice if you appreciated it and lost some of the air of superiority that you've displayed ever since you entered that door. Don't you think, since we have to share the same space, it would be better to get along with each other rather than make everybody miserable without any reason? Yes, we are Austrians and you are German. But the war brought us together on the same side of the barricade. These are dangerous times, when we have to be united and help each other in order to survive. Is it too much for you to understand that we are not supposed to be enemies?' When she stopped talking, Heidi saw admiration in her sister's and Ticla's eyes. Karina sat on the edge of her bed, not knowing what to say. She knew that the other three were waiting for her to react. She thought about what Heidi had just said, and knew she was right, but it was hard to admit it in front of these strangers. Germans were not the most beloved of people those days, and enemies were everywhere. The truth was that she was scared of all potential dangers that lay in wait.

'I was trained in radio communications for three months in Berlin. All my classmates were sent to Amsterdam in Holland. I was the only one to come to the East. I keep asking myself why I got exiled to Pilsen? I was a good student. Why couldn't I go to Amsterdam as well?' Karina said, speaking more to herself than the others.

'Maybe you've been sent here because the mission here is more important than in Holland. Pilsen has Skoda, the big factory. It's important for the Nazi Army to secure it and keep production going. Also, the city is a strategic link between the Eastern and Western fronts. I'm sure your knowledge is very much in demand at this Communication Center,' Heidi said, moving over to sit by Karina's side.

Looking at her roommates, the German girl started to relax and almost smiled.

'Maybe you're right. I should stop feeling miserable about things I can't change and accept the fact that I'm here and have nice company with you girls. I'm sorry for being unfriendly,' she said in a quiet voice.

Ticla came to sit on the other side of Karina.

'That's all right. We should be friends from now on, and not waste our energy fighting with each other. Let's call it a night and go to sleep. Tomorrow is our first day on the job – we should be well rested.'

With that, each girl got ready to go to bed, hoping for nice dreams. Each of them was relieved that the tension in the room was diffused, and that they had hopefully gotten over a hurdle. Next morning, they were woken by the wake-up signal. They had fifteen minutes to get dressed in their new uniforms and be ready for breakfast, which consisted of a slice of bread with apricot jam and weak tea. The food seemed much worse than it had been in the training camp in Vienna.

The work day was interesting, and time passed faster because of it. The girls in Heidi's shift were all resourceful and hard workers. The Supervising Officer, Col. Helmut Schloss, was pleased with the way things were going in the Communication Center.

In just a few weeks everybody was performing well, and the daily routine became easy to follow. The information that they handled was sensitive and classified. Col. Schloss made it clear from the beginning that no personal comments were allowed to be made about it, with the focus being on the accuracy of the reception and transmission rather than any analysis of its content. Everybody learnt this discipline, and did not display any emotion over the messages' content.

Heidi could not stop thinking that, at this rate, they would soon become robots of the German War Machine. By the end of January, the Germans had lost the Battle of Stalingrad. The Soviet Red Army forced the Germans to surrender, and blocked their attempt to move the front toward Leningrad. Many members of the German Army were taken hostage. Trying to compensate for the numbers lost, Hitler instituted a new law: men between 16 and 35 and women between 17 and 45 were now liable for conscription.

Heidi took her sister aside when they got a break.

'Good grief, Teresa! If they apply this new law in the occupied territories it will affect Johan, won't it?' 'Johan turns 16 this year! You are right. He may be asked to go to the army. If that happens, he'll be in big danger, and mom and dad will be devastated. What can we do?' asked Teresa, bracing herself for the worst.

'We can't do anything about it, only get used to the idea that we may not see our brother for a long, long time. It looks like the war is now becoming more aggressive near home. The Allies are pressing the Germans everywhere in the world, even here in Europe,' Heidi continued.

Teresa saw the soldier in charge of policing their breaks make a sign for them to go back to their stations, and bade Heidi to stop talking and return to the basement. She also noticed that everybody inside was focused and alert. Heidi immediately realized that something serious was going on. Once at her telex machine, she started to read the messages coming in. They were frightening.

The American offensive, in an unprecedented bold move, was about to bomb Munich, Vienna and Berlin. The news was unfolding before her eyes. She looked toward Teresa while a feeling of fear ran up her spine. Teresa was as white as the wall, digesting the information herself, and trying to pass it on through the telecom channels. It was February 9th, 1943 and Vienna, their beautiful city, was about to be destroyed. She thought about her friends in Vienna, and how close to Traisen the war had come. In a matter of minutes, more girls were brought into the Transmission Room to help. Ticla, who had been off duty, came to Heidi's side, looking alert and concerned.

'What on Earth is happening? Air strike alarm? Where?' Ticla asked at once.

'Vienna, Munich and Berlin are under attack. We have to alert them quickly,' Heidi whispered, while her fingers typed the warning message on the telex. Ticla sat at the receiving machine waiting for replies from the affected zones. They worked in teams to speed up the process. Both girls were diligent and agile. Their goal was to give people plenty of notice to seek shelter and keep safe and thereby save as many lives as they could. This was the first time their work was making a difference in a life and death situation. Even more significantly, it was a matter of saving their own people, Vienna's civilians. That thought gave Heidi firm purpose in what she was doing, and for the first time she realized that information is power and can itself be a weapon. Afternoon changed into evening and then into night with nobody leaving the basement. Everybody was working hard to trace the developments of the air raid. After midnight, half of the workers were dismissed from duty so that they could go and get some rest for next morning's shift. Among them were Heidi and Teresa, who went to their room feeling numb. They did not know the outcome of the strike yet, but the last message received before they had left was that it was all over.

Back in the bedroom, Karina was sobbing quietly with the lights off. Heidi turned on the lamp that sat on the night table beside her bed.

'Are you all right, Karina? Why are you crying?' asked Teresa while letting herself sink in the bed's mattress.

'Why am I crying? They bombed Berlin. My people were killed by those American bastards. I hope they burn in hell for dropping bombs on German soil. That is what I'm crying about. Can't you figure it out yourself?' said Karina, the hatred in her voice was obvious.

Heidi was sad, and tired, and the last thing she wanted was a quarrel with Karina, but she did not like the tone in which the German girl had spoken to her sister.

'Karina, watch your words, and do not talk to us like that. Vienna was bombarded too, and Austrian people died tonight for no reason other than the fact that they lived in German occupied territory. We could be the next, here in Czechoslovakia, just because we happen to be ruled by the Nazis, your people, but nobody blames anybody here. This is not our war, this is World War II, and you and I are too small to pass judgments on what happens and why. So please give us a break and try to behave. We respect your feelings, and so should you. Now let's get some sleep, because tomorrow will be another tough day. Good night.'

'Good night!' Teresa said, coming to give Heidi a hug. It felt good to comfort each other. All of a sudden they felt another hug around their shoulders. Karina's arms were light, but warm.

'Good night!' she added in a soft voice.

Over the next few days they learnt about the aftermath of the attacks, and were horrified by how much had been destroyed in a matter of hours. Heidi wrote a letter home, mostly to inquire how her parents were doing now that the enemy airplanes were flying over Traisen. She also mentioned that the situation in Pilsen was rather calm, and that she and Teresa were doing well.

Ten days later, when the reply from home came, the Souisa sisters almost fought each other to open the letter. They were so anxious to read it that they almost tore it apart in the process. When they saw their father's handwriting, emotion brought tears to their eyes. Then Teresa started to read, slowly, taking in every word. It was as if the piece of paper had magical powers with which it warmed their hearts, by building a bridge of love between Pilsen and Traisen, between their home and their duty.

"My dear daughters,

Your mother and I were happy to receive news from you, and mostly we were happy that you two are safe and well. It looks like the war is getting closer and closer. Vienna was hit hard by the bombs. The Allied army has moved into Central Europe after having won the battles in North Africa and the Mediterranean regions. The Americans are very aggressive, and determined to defeat Hitler. From now on, I have a feeling that we will see more attacks and air strikes. These are affecting civilians' lives, destroying cities, and ultimately killing innocent people. There is nothing we can do about it, except to hide in shelters and pray. We heard about the new mobilization law in Germany and we fear that it may apply in Austria as well in the near future. Johan will be 16 soon. I have already started to give him advice and prepare him for the war in the event of his enrollment. He is too young to realize all the implications of this war. He thinks that going to army is a sign of becoming a man and being important. He looks up to you two with pride, and so do your mother and I, but I'd rather keep him home than send him away. We will see what the future will bring. Louisa is going to school and growing up fast. We wish she would help more around the house, but it is hard to deal with her erratic moods sometimes. Your mother and I are fine. The cold winter keeps us mostly inside the house.

There is no day that passes without us thinking of you and praying for your safety. Please do not take unnecessary risks, and take care of one another. Your mother sends you her love. God bless you!

Love,

Dad

PS. Try to write us more often. We are always worried about you two."

When they finished reading, tears were streaming down both sisters' cheeks. Their father's letter had touched their souls. The feeling was overwhelming.

'I'll make a habit of writing home every second week. We have to keep in touch more often. I'm sure our letters give joy and relief to our parents,' said Heidi. Teresa seemed to agree, but was a bit distracted. She was thinking of Hans Ellis and the fact that she had not received a reply to the letter she had sent more than two weeks before. How happy she would be if a sign from her lover came! But so far, no such luck.

'I'm wondering what has happened to Hans. He should have replied to me by now. Dad's letter arrived in less than a week,' she said in a sad voice.

Ticla and Karina also received letters from their loved ones. After the bombardment in Berlin, Munich and Vienna, everybody was seeking assurance that their families were fine. The war was happening too close to home. It was frightening.

'Tonight we are all off duty. We should go out and have a hot chocolate or some tea at the Corner Café. We received our pay not long ago and we should treat ourselves. What do you girls say?' Ticla said, taking the initiative to have some fun for a change. The atmosphere in the room was becoming more melancholic, and she needed a change. Her outgoing personality matched Heidi's. Teresa, on the other hand was too serious and absorbed in her romance, or rather lack thereof. Karina had mellowed a lot since the last discussion with Heidi, and, although she had some reservations about going out into the city, she agreed that they all needed to have some fun and see real people, not only the soldiers and the officers in the building.

The Corner Café was within walking distance of the Communication Center. The four girls entered and shook the snow from their boots by the door. The light was dim, and the aroma of the coffee was mixed with the tobacco smoke in the air. Most of the customers, male and female, were in uniforms. Heidi recognized a few girls from their detachment at a table with two German officers. There were soldiers sweet talking some young Czech women, who looked very pleased and laughed frequently. Music was coming from a Czech radio station, alternating Czech and German songs. Ticla spotted an empty table in the middle of the large room and the others followed her to it. Once seated, they started to relax, embraced by the bohemian environment.

'Wow. It is interesting in here. A diversity of people and relaxing atmosphere, don't you think?' Ticla said, looking for a waiter to order a hot drink.

'I have to admit that it is much nicer than our dining room. I like the music too, and the soft light. All I need now is a cup of hot chocolate and a biscuit,' Heidi added.

'If you ignore the dirty looks that the Czech girls are sending our way, we can actually have a good time. Unfortunately, I can't relax knowing that the majority of people here hate us,' Karina pointed out right away.

The truth was that the four of them were quite an apparition on that night. They had never been seen in the Café before. They were all pretty, and looked smart in uniform. The regular customers noticed them with admiration, and watched them closely. And how could they not notice the four young girls in uniforms? One, Ticla, was blond with bright blue eyes, one, Heidi, had curly copper hair and deep blue eyes, one, Teresa, had darker hair and velvety brown eyes, and the last one, Karina, had her blond hair pinned neatly in a chignon in the back, revealing a pretty face and green eyes.

'You girls are new here, aren't you?' the waitress asked out of curiosity when she came to take their order.

'I suppose we are. It's the first time we've come here, and we have to admit it's a nice place. We will definitely come more often from now on.' Teresa answered.

The night became enjoyable and everybody loosened up. By the time they got back to their room they felt recharged and relaxed. They also felt closer to each other, and as if there was already a bond between them. Before she fell asleep, Heidi counted her blessing: her family was fine, she and Teresa were healthy, they had two new friends in Ticla and Karina, and beyond the curtain of war there was a social life that they could enjoy from time to time, like the evening they had just had.

The month of March brought longer days and milder weather. By then, the four friends had learnt how to balance work, personal life, and military discipline. They made a habit, on the evenings when none of them were working, of going to the Corner Café and having fun by listening to the music and nursing a mug of tea.

March 21st began just like any other day, if not better. Teresa had received a letter from Hans the day before, and she was finally happy. He had written to her from Rosenburg Castle telling her that he would soon have to join the army, as his mobilization order had arrived and he was due on April 1st. The best part of the letter was the part where he had said that he loved her, and asked her to take care of herself until they'll meet again. Heidi was happy for her sister and her improved mood. They were both going in for the evening shift, and spent the day cleaning the room and doing other domestic chores.

By 6pm, Heidi was at her transmission station in the basement of the building. She and Teresa were pleased with how the day had passed by.

At half past seven a message came on the wires warning about a possible air attack on the Western part of Czechoslovakia. Following the communication procedure, Heidi reported it to Col. Schloss immediately. From that moment, the big wheel of the German defense program was set in motion, and all the girls in the building were asked to come back to the transmission center and assist with the alarm notice that was broadcast to the city of Pilsen and some other little towns in its vicinity, including Skoda plant. In the next couple of hours more messages came, warning that the Allied bombing planes may in fact only be flying over Pilsen on their way to the actual target of Budapest. Col. Helmut Schloss did not want to take any risks, and issued the code red alarm, which indicated that an air strike was expected. The girls became aware of the danger and worked diligently to pass on the messages and the orders received. Night fell over the city quickly, and the lights on the street and in the buildings went on as if nothing was going to happen.

The Communication Room received the frightening information at 9:15pm: the target of the bombing raid was Pilsen. For a moment the room went quiet, while everyone processed the news. The next minute, Col. Schloss gave the order to set off the alarms in the building and to shut off all the lights. The on duty soldiers complied immediately, and all personnel descended to the basement shelter.

'Did you telex the warning to the City Hall, and Skoda? Why are they not ringing the RAF Alarm to notify the population?' Col. Schloss thundered across the center.

'We don't know, sir why they are not applying the anti-aerial procedure. We have warned them five times already, and they confirmed the reception,' Karina replied promptly.

One soldier returning to the shelter after his round upstairs announced that the city had not blacked out and that no sirens were to be heard.

Col. Schloss was fuming. He grabbed a phone connected to the city network and made a frantic call. He was arguing with whoever was on the other end of the line, trying to have his message understood. Eventually, he hung up the phone in frustration, and immediately made another call. It sounded as though he was talking to the German Major State, reporting the situation. It was already five past ten at night.

Heidi, Teresa, and Ticla moved to a corner of the room, as did the other girls. They were advised by the soldiers to clear the area in the middle where the structure was more likely to collapse in the event of the building being hit by a bomb. Karina came to join her friends. They all sat down on the floor. Some blankets were spread around for everybody to sit on. All the girls were quiet, listening for noises coming from outside. They could not see anything outside, since there were no windows in the basement. The emergency lamp in the Communication Center was on, spreading a dim light through the room.

'I'm going to start to pray. Maybe it will help and we will be spared,' Ticla whispered in Heidi's ear.

'Come closer and just listen. Do you hear aircrafts?' Heidi answered, squeezing Teresa's hand.

The tension in the room rose in the next minutes, when the roars of airplanes were heard vibrating in the thick concrete foundation. Some screamed out of fear, some covered their faces, and Heidi and Teresa instinctively hugged each other. The big clock on the wall showed 10:30pm. Then, for five minutes or so, a period of silence followed. Just when the Heidi's heart beat became normal again, the noise came unexpectedly, like wind through a giant pipe. By the time it had intensified and everybody was paying attention to the noise, the voice of Col. Schloss shouting "Achtung Bomben!" was followed by a loud explosion. Instantly the shelter began to shake and the emergency lamp went out. The darkness amplified the horror, and Heidi felt Teresa's body trembling while clinging to her own. Heidi extended her arm and tried to touch her surroundings, checking for debris. She thought that everything had collapsed around them. What puzzled her was that the air was breathable and still clean, not dusty or smelly. She reached out and felt Ticla's arm. It was warm and it moved.

'Were we hit by the bomb? Who's this?' Heidi asked in a low voice, drained by terror.

'It's me, Ticla. Karina is here too. We are fine, only terrified.'

A few moments later, more girls started to move, and sobs were heard throughout the dark room.

'The bomb fell close to us, but did not hit. Everybody stay calm! The soldiers will get some flashlights soon. This is not over yet. Keep order!' Col. Schloss commanded.

Soon, the dancing lights of the flashlights were scanning the entire room. Heidi saw that everybody was alright and the walls were still standing. Teresa had a strange look on her face, and did not release grip on her sister. Heidi started to talk to her quietly in an effort to ease the anxiety for both of them. Ticla helped her with encouraging words and reassuring gestures, and all of a sudden Heidi felt stronger. It was as if her survival skills had suddenly kicked in and helped her to deal with her fear. The fact that the building was strong enough to resist the quake of the bomb helped her cope with the situation. But then the frightening noise came again, and another rattle shook the building. Screams were heard again in the room, but the flashlights stayed on this time. Another bomb hit the ground not far away from them, and then more explosions followed with less intensity, meaning that it was happening further away. Teresa almost fainted in Heidi's arms. Seeing this, Heidi focused on her sister's physical and emotional state.

'Teresa, don't be afraid. It sounds like the planes are going away. We are safe here, just hang on, alright? Ticla and Karina, give me a hand here to help my sister.'

'Teresa, here, lean on my back,' Karina offered as she steadied herself. Ticla took Teresa's hands and gave her a gentle massage on her wrists to calm Teresa down. Teresa, in their opinion, was having an anxiety attack, and needed to relax. With their focus having shifted from the bombing to their friend's state, the three girls felt useful and able to detach their attention from the atrocities outside.

The sound of the bombs faded away for a while, giving everybody hope that the strike was over. Some girls began to get up and stretch.

'Nobody leaves! Everybody stays seated as before. This is not over yet. The planes dropped the bombs and went away for a short while, but they will return, and on the way back, if they still have bombs on board, they will strike again just to get rid of them. They are not allowed to land loaded. We have to wait until the planes have flown back over the city. Understood?' the officer commanded.

The girls returned to their places, terrified. Teresa looked like she was having trouble breathing. Heidi urged her to lie down, not knowing what was wrong with her sister. She was now more scared about Teresa's condition than the bombing outside, and she began silently to pray for her sister. She lost track of time. That night was worse than a nightmare. She could have used some crying to ease the tension, but she had to look strong for her sister's sake. Thank God that Ticla and Karina were helping her cope with the awful situation. While she was thinking and praying, the planes returned and the sound of falling bombs delivered another shock to everybody's hearts. Three more bombs were dropped in their vicinity, accompanied by the ground shaking and the loud noise. Heidi threw herself over Teresa's body to shelter her from the horrific shock wave.

When the noise faded away and the movement inside the shelter was obvious, the emergency lamp, fixed by the soldiers, came back on. The fear was written all over the girls' faces. Slowly they got up, looking to Col. Schloss for assurance that this time the strike was over and it was safe to get out. A telex machine went off, receiving a message. The officer, having read it, turned around, and said 'Confirmation that the air attack is over!'

Instantly, a unanimous cheer erupted in the room. The girls could not stop themselves from releasing the pressure in loud exclamations. It was as if the officer had announced that the whole war was over. As inappropriate as it sounded, one could not expect much self-control from these young women who had just survived their first bombardment.

'Quiet!' the colonel shouted. 'There is nothing to cheer about. People were killed out there, and buildings destroyed. We have to assess the severity of the attack and report to headquarters. Behave yourselves! The people who were supposed to be on night shift stay in the center to supervise radio reception, while all others will slowly go upstairs and look around in an organized manner. Understood?'

'Yes sir!' the girls all responded at once.

Heidi, Ticla, and Karina helped Teresa get up. With some support she steadied herself and looked around. She was grateful that everybody was fine and the danger had passed. Slowly, the pain in her chest started to ease and her breathing became more regular.

'Let's go upstairs. None of us is on duty right now,' said Ticla and led the way for the other three.

The lights were turned on, but the ground floor was very cold. The soldiers announced that a couple of windows had been broken. They hurried to inspect the other floors for damages. The girls moved quickly toward the safe windows to look outside. Most of the street lights were damaged or broken, but a few were still standing and lit. The sight of the neighborhood was terrifying. The building across the street had been destroyed, and others down the road were either only half standing or reduced to debris. Even though the bomb fell further away, some old structures had taken a heavy blow from the shock waves. When Heidi arrived outside, her eyes filled instantly with tears. She had never seen such destruction in her whole life. Teresa looked over her shoulder and cried out loud. It was a miracle that their building had escaped the disaster. But that was not all. From the piles of concrete one could see signs of life stirring. Wounded people cried for help and for rescue. The soldiers noticed and ran outside to see how they could help. The girls, seeing this, rushed toward the main door to follow the soldiers. Heidi told Teresa to wait where she was, and asked Ticla and Karina to join her on the street.

'Oh my God! What a disaster! People are coming out of that damaged building. Do you see, Ticla?' said Heidi.

'They were injured by the debris! Some are badly wounded. Let's get closer and try to help them!' Ticla answered. All three ran toward the half-collapsed building down the street. They could hear cries for help and moans of pain. When they were close enough they saw dead bodies mingled between pieces of broken furniture and other household items. They stopped, terrified by what they saw. The smell of burnt wood and the stench of death were unbearable. The screams of ambulance sirens were heard throughout the destroyed city. Some were coming towards their street, along with some German trucks. The girls and the soldiers from the Communication Center started to help identify the injured people and signal for professional help. Not far away, some other German soldiers were putting out a fire. The night was cold but none of the volunteers noticed. They worked hard to help as many of the wounded as they could.

Karina was walking a woman to the ambulance when she saw Teresa holding onto a tree on the nearby sidewalk. She looked as if she could not breathe and was on the verge of collapsing.

'Heidi, Ticla, over here! Teresa needs help quickly!' Karina yelled at the top of her lungs.

Hearing her, Heidi ran toward her sister, anger and pity mixed in her soul. Why had her sister come outside? She told her to stay in the building. What was wrong with her? If she collapsed now while everybody was busy with the bombardment victims, who would take care of her? She was not even strong enough to bear seeing these atrocities, let alone to help anyone!

'Teresa, what on Earth are you doing here? Go inside right now! Let me help you,' Heidi said, grabbing her sister by the shoulders.

'I was afraid that you may be in danger. I can't sit inside and wait while you are here in the middle of this disaster. Good Lord, this is terrible! Dead people everywhere, and the wounded are suffering so much. What has this world come to? Heidi, come inside with me, please!' Teresa said between sobs.

'I'll walk you back to our room where you can look out the window and see me down here. Please understand that you are worsening your condition by being here. You are in no shape to help, and if you do not calm down, soon enough you'll have to be taken care of as much as these poor injured people.'

'But I want to be with you. I promised dad that I would take care of you!' Teresa insisted.

'I'll tell you what, you stay in our room, and listen to me. I'll come back here for a short while until more Red Cross people arrive on site, and then Ticla, Karina and I will return to our room. We were lucky this time, but the majority of the Pilsen population was not. I have to help them as much as I can. I promise that I will take care of myself. Nothing will happen to me tonight.' Heidi did not know how else to convince Teresa that everything would be all right.

Finally, feeling weaker and weaker, Teresa agreed to go to their room and wait there while the other three finished doing what they could to save lives. The rest of the night passed in a frenetic effort to help the survivors.

At dawn Heidi and her friends came inside. Their uniforms were dirty and stained with blood, and their faces almost black from the smoke. They were worn out by the work and shaken by the tragedy they had seen. After washing themselves as best they could, they collapsed onto their beds for a couple of hours of well-deserved sleep. Teresa was happy to see them back. She also fell into a deep sleep right away.

On March 22nd, the day after the attack, the facts of the matter were revealed. The night before had been the worst bombardment in the history of the war, up to that point. The City of Pilsen did not take the warnings seriously, and therefore did not set off the air strike alarm or carry out the required black-out. Seeing the disaster and the aftermath, they could not believe how foolish they had been, and at what price. City Hall had received contradicting messages about the air raid the previous evening. Some claimed that the planes did not belong to the Allies, but were rather German planes on the way to bomb Ukraine. The message from The Third Reich Communication Center, sent by Col. Helmut Schloss and his communication personnel was hence disregarded as being a false alarm. In the end, however, it became clear who was right and who was wrong when the bombs fell like rain over the exposed and unprepared target: the city lit up like a Christmas tree in Central Park. Now the "smart" leaders at the City Hall were sorry about the mistake they made, but it was too late. The Skoda plant, outside the city, had obeyed the warning, and escaped the bombardment. Many local workers at the plant returned home the next day only to find their families and homes had vanished in the smoke. It was a tragedy of great proportion.

Over the following days further information emerged: it had been an act of sabotage, orchestrated by the Czech Resistance. In the process, more civilians than Germans were killed, but, since any act of the war came at a price, this one was no exception.

Chapter 6

'How are you feeling, Teresa? Do you want me to bring you a tea or anything else from the kitchen?' Heidi asked. She was on a short break from work, and had come to check on her sister. Ever since Pilsen had been bombed two weeks ago, Teresa had not felt well. The nurse at the infirmary on the third floor asked a doctor from the Red Cross to come and see her. The doctor had come two days before and examined Teresa. He found that she had a weak heart beat and a constant state of anxiety. Following the diagnosis, his recommendation was for her to rest and be released from army duty. Immediately after that, Teresa was dismissed from working in the center. Now she was waiting for her paper work to go through and to recover sufficiently in order to be able to travel home.

'Thanks for asking Heidi, but I don't need anything right now. Come and sit here by my side. I want to talk to you about my leaving,' Teresa said in a concerned tone. 'Who will look after you when I'm gone? I hate myself for having to leave you here in constant danger, while I'll be home sheltered from the war.'

'Teresa, you have to go home, and should make the most out of that. You have to take care of yourself and recover. In the meantime you'll have your hands full helping our parents, Louisa and Johan, and keeping them safe. I have a feeling that soon the war will be felt there too. You have the survival skills to help them cope with whatever will come their way. As a matter of fact, I'll be relieved knowing you are all together in Traisen,' said Heidi. After a short pause, she continued, 'Please don't worry about me. Ticla and Karina are good friends, and I won't be alone. Now I have to go back to work. Just relax and I'll see you in a couple of hours.' Heidi gave her sister a hug and ran out the door returning to her duty.

Teresa got out of bed and looked out the window. The street still reminded her of that awful night. The sight was quite depressing. She was delighted that she was to leave this city and go home. Apart from her medical condition, it was a great blessing. Her active war days were over, and that was a good thing. But Heidi, who was so young, would have to stay behind, and God only knew what could happen next. Yes, the emotion she felt at the prospect of going home was a bitter-sweet feeling for Teresa, and so it was for Heidi.

Ticla came in from her shift and interrupted Teresa's thoughts.

'Hi Teresa, are you feeling better? How was your day? Mine was exhausting. Col. Schloss made us transmit every message twice. He thinks that we should cover all the bases, just in case another attack occurs and City Hall disobeys it again.'

'Do you think they will come again anytime soon?' Teresa asked, feeling suddenly afraid.

'There are no indications that the Allies will come back to Pilsen, but the will certainly strike somewhere else. The war is far from over,' Ticla conceded.

'I'll be going home soon, Ticla. You and Heidi are getting along very well. Please take care of one another after I leave. It makes me feel terrible to leave her alone here. Will you be a good friend to her?'

Ticla looked into Teresa eyes and spoke slowly. 'Teresa, I do not often make promises, and under such circumstances as war puts us in, I avoid doing so even more, but ever since I've met Heidi I've known that we will become good friends. You are her sister, but Heidi feels like a sister to me too. Don't worry. We will weather whatever comes our way together. We will take care of each other.'

Hearing that, Teresa felt tears misting her eyes. She hugged Ticla , and thanked her for being there for her sister.

The rest of April went by quickly. Initially, Heidi thought that she would be allowed to travel home with Teresa and then return, but had no such luck. Teresa left accompanied by a nurse. Her departure was tearful, but Heidi knew that her sister was better off away from the war. As far as Heidi was concerned, Teresa would take care of her loved ones at home, while taking care of her own health problems. Ticla and Karina were close enough to her, to consider them good friends and trust them. Heidi thought that she would be just fine after Teresa's leaving.

May 1st, 1943 found Heidi alone in the German Army. None of her relatives were enrolled at that time. Teresa arrived home safely and shortly after, Heidi received a letter from her father, full of advice on how to take care of herself, particularly since she was now on her own. She replied quickly, telling him that she was doing fine, and mentioning the good friends she had already made in Pilsen.

The Nazis had experienced setbacks on all fronts, in Europe and North Africa. 1943 was a turning point in the war. The Allies became more aggressive, gaining momentum in and around the Mediterranean Sea. The air raids intensified. More and more civilian casualties were recorded on German soil. The Communication Center in Pilsen became very busy, keeping up with the developments of the war.

Heidi and her roommates had to cover more shifts than at the beginning of the year, having less time to rest. The communication codes were changed every three days to ensure security, and all these changes required a training period, taking a toll on everybody.

'Good Lord, I'm so stressed out and tired,' Ticla told Heidi late one   night before going to bed.

'So am I. At this pace we will ruin our health soon. And on top of it, meals are getting thinner and thinner. Don't you think? We are overworked, underpaid, and poorly fed,' Heidi complained.

It was almost eleven o'clock at night. The girls were too tired to fall asleep. Karina entered the room quietly, thinking that the other two were fast asleep. The soft light coming through the window from the street was enough for her to find her way toward her bed. She was exhausted.

'Karina, how are you?' Heidi asked her friend.

'My goodness Heidi, I almost jumped out of my skin. Aren't you sleeping?' whispered Karina.

'Neither of us can sleep, Karina. We are too tired and hungry too,' Heidi continued.

'Tell me about it. Since Teresa left, work has become hectic. Soon all of us will get sick. The codes are changing so often that I can hardly keep up with them. My head is spinning after every shift,' Karina admitted.

'Maybe if we start making mistakes, Col. Schloss will declare us unable to meet the job requirements, and will let us go home,' said Ticla. She thought that she had just had the most brilliant idea. It seemed like a great solution to put an end to military life.

'What are you saying, Ticla?' Karina asked, getting ready for bed.

'I'm telling you that we should try not to be as efficient and perform all the duties as diligently as we do. All this effort we put in is affecting our health. Look at us: we are not able to fall asleep anymore, we are constantly hungry because of all the energy we burn in the Communication Center and, with these long shifts, we have no time to recharge our batteries. The next time the codes change I will play stupid,' Ticla announced.

Heidi thought about Ticla's idea. Was it a good idea? As long as nobody got hurt due to some minor mistakes, the plan that Ticla proposed might work. Col. Schloss might get irritated and discharge them. It was worth a try.

'I think we could try and slow down our work a bit, like getting behind with the transmission, and intentionally showing that we can't assimilate all the material that we are taught. Then we should wait and see what happens,' said Heidi.

Karina became a bit suspicious, but admitted that as long as this staged play didn't get out of control and hurt someone, they had a chance of succeeding with the plan.

After this discussion, the three friends fell asleep, dreaming of a life lived in peace.

Over the next few days each of them put the plan into action. Karina delayed transmission of the received messages, Ticla intentionally forgot to report a few messages and blamed it on her poor concentration, and Heidi stopped and asked the supervisor about which codes to use for transmission every five minutes. This went on for a while. Before long, all these "tricks" were noticed by Col. Schloss, who showed his displeasure and urged everybody to pay attention and work diligently. This detachment was one of the best he had ever managed, but all of a sudden the performance of some of the girls had declined dramatically.

In the middle of May the Allies intensified the air strikes again, targeting electric power plants. Two important dams were bombed in Germany, the Mhone and Eder. As a result, the war industries in Rhur, Germany lost electric power. Reports of the attack were flooding the Communication Center in Pilsen. These were important matters that required a lot of attention and were marked as sensitive information. Col. Schloss could not afford to be slowed down by the poor performance of his staff. The Nazis were being hit from every direction and the defense plans were crucial in keeping the German war machine afloat. Yes, work became more and more demanding, but that did not justify the small mistakes that the girls made every now and then, and the fact that they lost their focus.

By the end of May, Col. Schloss called for a general meeting in the dining hall to analyze the group's performance and to assess training needs. He had to do something to stop the downhill slide, and the diminished interest in the job that some of the women had displayed lately.

The entire personnel were seated at the tables, not knowing what to expect from the meeting. It was rather unusual, and speculations crossed everybody's mind. Was there a big announcement to be made, or was something bad about to happen, or, like Heidi, Ticla and Karina started to suspect, were some of them going to be released from duty?

The smell coming from the kitchen where lunch was being prepared at the same time could not distract the train of thought and silent questions in everybody's mind. Heidi was curious to find out what the meeting was all about. She looked out the window and saw that it was a gorgeous day outside. Summer was almost there. Five months of terror and hard work had passed since she arrived in the Bohemian city, and she was missing her family in Traisen very badly. Maybe soon everything would be over, and she would be free to go home. This hopeful thought made her smile. The mountains back home would already be covered in high green grass, and the Traisen River must have been full of trout. Her father would be so happy to welcome her home. She would be there to help her parents survive the war.

'Heil Hitler!' Heidi heard the thundering voice of Col. Schloss, which startled her, interrupting her day-dream.

The audience greeted their superior with a loud voice and large gesture. Once everybody was seated again, the officer stared to speak with authority:

'The glorious German Army fights hard to win the war, despite the pressure the Allies push against it. Our wonderful leader Adolf Hitler has the determination to defeat the enemy. Under his leadership Germany and the German people will prevail and win a better, prosperous life. Everybody who has the privilege to be part of the Nazi Army, including everyone in this room, has to give one hundred and ten percent effort to their job in order to honor the duty with which they have been entrusted.' At that point he paused to gauge the response of the audience. His gaze brushed the faces listening to him.

Heidi sensed that his displeasure was about to follow. The speech had begun in an oratory manner, far from dealing with the reality. They all knew that the "glorious German Army" was not doing all that well. The news coming hourly through the communication channels told stories of lost battles, and civilian losses when the German cities came under bombing air strikes. However, Col. Schloss was about to continue with the demagogy, on and on and on.

'Our Army has brave soldiers and wise leaders! Our Army is bound to win the war! Our Army uses the best war technology, and the most competent auxiliary personnel!' Pause again.

The girls did not know what to expect next. He certainly had their full attention.

'Everybody who fights this war as part of the wonderful Nazi Army should be proud and confident that victory belongs to us. He or she has to give their very best service and strive for excellence. Everybody in this room is a wheel of this great war machine that will punish the enemy. The importance of our work is crucial for the whole machinery to function properly. Do you understand this?'

Now things cleared up a bit in Heidi's head. The superior officer was making a plea for something. But what, exactly?

'It is a shame that for the last month our performance has decreased substantially, and is showing no signs of improvement. I do not want to consider it an act of sabotage, because then it will be handled by the Martial Court, but I'm not pleased at all with your hostile attitude toward learning and doing a good job. This is a very serious matter and I warn you that, if it continues, you and only you will be responsible for the consequences.'

At this point in the speech everybody was frowning in their chairs, and a wave of fear ran throughout the room. The threat came cold and sharp and hit Heidi and her friends hard to their cores. Would they be imprisoned and tortured for what they had done? Was it the end for them? Everything was possible during times of war, and now they were about to find out their fate.

Ticla cast Heidi a frightened look, and Karina slid down on her chair, trying to make herself invisible. Heidi thought about her dreams before the meeting and her hopes that she would be set free, and now everything not only shattered but the future was looking rather awful, similar to the death penalty. Before she even had time to imagine the worst case scenario, Col. Schloss continued in an angry tone.

'So listen up everyone! Those of you who are not able to keep up with the fast pace of this important job will be redeployed to another kind of work which will not require your brain, but will be comprised mostly of hard physical labor in a much less friendly environment. I assure you that failing in your job here will not result in your dismissal from the army. If any of you had the unfortunate idea to think this, I can only warn you that it will not be case. You will only feel sorry for your stupidity. You should consider yourselves lucky that, at this point, this is only a warning and you still have the opportunity to smarten up and improve your work to a level that will allow you to keep this job, and not be transferred elsewhere for incompetence. Do I make myself clear?'

The room went quiet; one could have heard a pin drop. The officer scanned all the faces that stared at him, one by one, with piercing eyes, as if trying to read everyone's thoughts. Most of the staff were looking down, avoiding confrontation. Heidi held the officer's penetrating gaze, and then blinked twice in a sign of approval sign. He liked it. This was what he had been looking for: acknowledgment.

'I take that as a "yes". Now, everybody back to your duties, and do not forget everything I've just told you. Meeting dismissed. Heil Hitler!'

The choir of voices in the room responded: 'Heil Hitler!'

It was already lunch time and Heidi was due to begin her shift at 2pm. Ticla and Karina were free until 4pm. The three of them gathered around a table. Lunch was to be served in half an hour.

'Holy Mother of God, sisters, what a meeting, huh? I thought I was about to faint at one point,' Ticla said to the other two.

'Tell me about it. I wished I was invisible, and deaf. He scared me like hell,' Karina continued.

Heidi was thinking back to that evening when they made a pact to play stupid in order to be able to go home. The whole plan came out of desperation and exhaustion, combined with terror and fear. Alright, so they failed, but who could blame them for trying? This was a war too large for their shoulders, and sometimes things got awkward.

'Listen to me: we have to get over it right now. Enough with the guilt and fear! We could have ended up in jail, or been tortured, for what we did or did not do, but it turned out that we are still safe and unscarred. We've learnt our lesson. The Army is too big and powerful to meddle with, so let's pull ourselves together and have lunch. There is nothing we have to worry about anymore. Let's focus on surviving rather than on feeling lousy,' and with that Heidi got up to wait in line for her meal.

Ticla gave Karina a sign under the table urging her to go after Heidi to get their lunch.

The food smelled good, which was quite unusual. For the last month they had been served a thin soup with traces of carrots and potatoes, and macaroni with gravy. Today it was chicken soup and chicken roast with mashed potatoes. It looked like Col. Schloss had ordered the meal to motivate the girls after his speech.

'This food looks delicious! I wish we received stuff like this every day.' Ticla could not believe the feast lying in front of her.

'After this meal, I think our performance will improve!' Heidi said with a wink.

'I definitely think you're right!' Karina agreed with an ironic smile.

After lunch, when each of them returned to the Communication Center in the basement, work flowed smoothly and precisely.

June 1943 found Europe under siege. The Allies were on the brink of defeating the Nazis. The attacks were quick and precise. The air strikes intensified, and Germany was the most common target.

In July 1943 the rocket scientist Wernher von Braun presented the V-2 rocket to Hitler, who had made this project a top priority. The Vergeltungswaffe 2 (V-2) was a retaliation weapon, the first long-range ballistic missile, and the first human artifact to achieve suborbital space-flight. Heidi learned from the messages that she transmitted back and forth on her job that this rocket could reach targets as far away as London. She realized, not without fear, that the war was about to shift from the conventional technology to a new level, one that was reaching into new means of mass destruction. Even though the bombs were falling further away from where she lived, and no immediate attack threatened Pilsen, what was happening across the world, and particularly across Europe, scared everybody in the center.

In mid-July bombs fell over Rome in Italy. A second attack short-ly after, in Sicily, brought a coupe d'état against Mussolini. Without any warning, the next day a major raid hit Kiel, marking another major attack on a German city.

The Communication Center found out about all these events in a state of panic. Every day there was an emergency, and every day brought increased anxiety to the Centre's crew. The girls were engulfed in fear and worked under high pressure.

For the last month, Heidi had started to feel pain all along her right leg from her hip to the toes. She tried to ignore it, and eventually it went away for a while, only to come back later in full force. On the evening of July 24th she went to bed early, thinking that some rest would solve the problem.

When Ticla came back from her shift, she had high expectations for the evening. It had been months of nothing but work, work, and work. Their physical exhaustion was exacerbated by their insecurity and fear. She and her friends had hit bottom. They had to recharge their batteries and do something good for themselves. With these thought in her mind, Ticla entered the room and was surprised to see that the lights were off. She could have sworn that Heidi had headed back to their bedroom only minutes before her.

'Ahrg , ouch,' she heard in the dark.

Ticla stopped on her feet and turned on the light. She saw Heidi curled on her bed with tears in her eyes.

'Good Lord, Heidi! What happened to you? Why are you crying? Are you hurt? Talk to me!'

'My hip hurts me badly. I can't stay still, I feel like the entire right-hand side of my body is in flames. It is hard to explain, Ticla.'

'When did it start? Just now?' Ticla sat on the edge of Heidi's bed ready to hug her friend.

'No. I've had it for a while, but it has never been so intense. I thought that it would go away if I got more rest, but my schedule was so busy I could not relax much, and for many nights I've not been able to sleep because of the pain. Now I'm at the end of the rope. It hurts all the time, and I almost get nauseous from the pain,' Heidi confessed.

'Stay right here, I'm going to get help. I'll run upstairs to alert the nurse,' and with that Ticla was out the door before Heidi could stop her.

In the doorway she collided with Karina who was coming in and could not wait to see her roommates. The most recent news of the evening was that Hamburg had become the Allies' latest target, and the heaviest assault on German soil to date was predicted. Col. Schloss decided not to ask for the entire staff in the Center that evening because of the many hours that the girls had already put in and his fears that fatigue would only jeopardize their performance. Instead, he thought that it was better to have a more focused team in the morning. Nevertheless, Karina knew that Germans all over the map were being hit hard, and it was difficult to keep the pace with all the developments of the war. She was sad and scared when Ticla almost knocked her off her feet.

'Ticla, watch out! Why are you running like that? It there a fire inside the room? Slow down!'

'Sorry! You go ahead and watch Heidi. You'll understand what is going on. I have to go!' Ticla started to rush toward the stairwell, and then went up taking two stairs at a time.

Karina looked after Ticla, and then she turned and walked into the room. She saw Heidi crying on her bed. A quick scan revealed no blood around her, which Karina took as a good sign, but her friend's sobs signaled that something was wrong.

'Heidi, what on Earth is going on?' asked Karina in disbelief.

'I don't know. The right side of my body hurts me so badly, and I can't stop crying,' Heidi responded quietly.

'Shh, Shh. Ticla went to get help for you. You are not alone. You have us. You're going to be fine. You'll see.' Karina's words were meant to calm Heidi down and bring some relief. She was trying to help her friend in a situation that was completely beyond her control. What else could she do but try to give her some hope and solace? That, and a hug. Heidi looked like she was going to pass out at any moment. Karina felt the raised temperature on her friend's body. Maybe she was coming down with a fever or a bad flu. Maybe it was contagious, and she was at risk too. It did not matter anymore; the entire world was coming down with a much severe malady, one that could kill everybody on the planet: the World War. Karina felt like crying too, out of another kind of pain. What was the point in holding back all this tension and being brave? She had a million reasons to cry out loud, yet the tears did not come. Her whole being felt dry as a stone. Her pain was not physical; it was like a blanket covering her, like a cocoon, but it hurt nevertheless.

After a few minutes that seemed like an eternity to Heidi, the nurse entered their room with Ticla following. Ticla was speaking animatedly about Heidi's condition, as if she was afraid that if she stopped talking the nurse will turn and leave them. There was a plea in her words, a plea for help, a plea to make everything alright, a plea for their own sanity. When she saw Karina's look, she instantly knew that Heidi's condition was deteriorating with every minute. Little did she know that Karina had her own demons to fight, and Heidi's illness had catalyzed all the reasons Karina had for being afraid.

'Good evening, I'm Anna, the nurse. What seems to be the problem?' asked the lady who had just come in.

'Good evening and thank you for coming. I can barely feel the right-hand side of my abdomen, and the entire right leg. I feel nauseous because of the pain too,' Heidi answered as best she could.

'Alright, just lie on your back and let me examine you. You have fever. It's not too high, but enough to make you weak.' The nurse started to palpate Heidi's abdomen, putting some pressure on the right-hand side. Heidi's response was a series of wails. The nurse took her time examining the patient inch by inch, and when she was finished she said, 'This is definitely an internal problem, perhaps an infection of the appendix. The fact that you have high temperature is not a good sign. How long have you felt this pain now, and how often?'

'The pain started about a month ago, and burdened me almost every day, but never with such intensity as in this last week,' Heidi said.

'You were in pain for a month and did not say a word to us?' Ticla asked with visible indignation.

'I thought that it was a cold from the humidity in the basement. I was waiting for it to go away. Instead it only became worse,' Heidi explained.

'I see.' the nurse said. 'Right now you need medical attention that I cannot provide. I will phone the hospital to send an ambulance to take you there. I'll report your case to the colonel as well. Just lie here and calm down. Help is on the way.' With that she left the room to take care of all the arrangements.

The three girls were shocked by what they had just found out: Heidi was so sick she was about to be taken to the hospital by ambulance. Fear and pain made Heidi cry louder, and the two friends panicked even more. It was a nightmare for all of them. Ticla thought that she and Karina should try to encourage Heidi and give her strength, but she felt so helpless and drained of energy. She felt like crying herself, and all she could do was throw her arms around Heidi and let the stream of tears fall down her cheeks. Each of them had pushed themselves too hard, and now all that they could feel was desperation for one reason or another. After all, each of them was so young, so far from their families, exposed to dangers, and ultimately so scared of this dreadful war.

It did not take long before the siren of the ambulance was heard. Heidi started to panic, looking around, not wanting to go anywhere.

Karina stood up and grabbed some essential things for Heidi to take with her to the hospital. This gave her a purpose and helped her to focus on something useful for her friend, instead of becoming over-whelmed by her own anguish. Soon after that the two Red Cross helpers knocked at the door, holding a stretcher. The nurse was with them. Heidi was still fully dressed in uniform and made an effort to get up from the bed. The pain did not ease at all. She did not want to get on the stretcher, but the effort to walk was harder than she thought. The two paramedics helped her from each side and finally she was able to make one step at a time, moving with the speed of a turtle. Karina gave a small bag with Heidi's necessities to the nurse to take to the hospital. She and Ticla walked Heidi all the way to the ambulance on the street. Some other girls came out on the hallway or to the front door to see what was going on. Heidi was as white as the hallway wall. Her suffering was written all over her face. Before she got into the car she turned to meet her friends' eyes and waved good bye. With that, the ambulance doors closed and it sped away.

At the hospital she was taken to the admissions room, where she met a doctor. He was the doctor who had seen Teresa more than three months ago. Heidi recognized him, but the doctor did not remember her. The pain was sharp and she could hardly maintain her composure. However, she had a faint hope that she would get better once the doctor had diagnosed and treated her. For whatever reason, maybe her intuition, she trusted him. He had done the best he could for her sister and right now that was enough for Heidi to feel safe under his care. After a quick examination, the doctor left Heidi lying on the wooden bed and looked for the nurse. Heidi had time to look around and take in the hospital emergency area. The building was solid, and looked at least a hundred years old, with nice architectural elements and white marble floors. Some other patients were hosted in the same large room. Some of them looked asleep, while some were awake, the suffering written on their faces.

The new environment caught Heidi's interest for a few moments, but her body did not allow her to explore as much as she would have liked to. Her own pain kept her attention on about her own survival. While she was waiting for the doctor to return, she tried to distract herself from the imminent fear by thinking about something pleasant, maybe something from her past, a nice memory from her childhood, something to give her some relief.

This is how she found herself thinking about Confirmation day and her relationship with God. At the age of ten, she was due to receive communion in the Catholic Church in Traisen. The event was supposed to be the most important day of her life up until that time, the day she became an active member of God's church. One of her mother's friends was supposed to guide her through the ceremony, along with a group of other young girls from her school. The custom was that all the girls were to wear white dresses and white flower wreaths on their heads. Confirmation was to take place in late spring, on the last Sunday of May. The preparations began about a month before. The most important piece was the little white dress. In 1935, the great recession was being felt right across Europe, and goods and money were limited. Josephina, her mom, struggled to get, make, or borrow a dress for Heidi. Her mother's friend, Heidi's companion to the ceremony made it clear that she would take on that task only if the girl was to be properly dressed in white. Heidi's mother had made an arrangement to borrow the dress from a neighboring farmer, promising that, in return, she would work a week in the summer helping with the dry grass. The farmer had a daughter five years older than Heidi, and the dress was available. In fact, that dress became a source of money or free labor for the farmer every year when somebody needed the outfit for the Holy Ceremony. With the dress problem solved, Josephina Souisa was happy, and looked forward to her daughter's confirmation. There was only one little problem: even at the age of ten Heidi knew what she wanted, and it was not a white dress. She thought that white did not flatter her skin, and blue was what she really liked. Now, in the agony of pain and fear, Heidi remembered how she had stood in front of everybody in church wearing her favorite blue dress that her parents had given her for Easter a year before. She went through all the trouble to leave the house in the white dress under her parents appreciative looks, and change into the blue dress in the little barn owned by one of her friend's parents, only to be rejected at church by her companion who was angry about the color of the dress and refused to walk her to the altar to attend the ceremony. Yes, she remembered the scene as if it had happened yesterday, and the outcome was that she skipped confirmation and returned home dressed in blue. Of course, her mother was very disappointed and scared that something bad would come their way because the Evil's work had multiple facets. However, Heidi stood her ground, convinced that if she was a child of God, He would love her no matter the color of the dress she was wearing. Now, what had happened in the past made her wonder if such a supposition was indeed true, or was she destined to pay for her blue dress and the lost communion with God from eight years ago, and die right here and now in the hospital room. With that thought, she lost consciousness.

The doctor found her in that state when he returned. He had just made arrangements for surgery in the operating room. There was no time to waste. Her appendix was already infected and had to be removed, otherwise she could have died. The nurses wheeled the bed as fast as they could and the doctor got ready. It was late at night, but no other emergencies came in and he could focus on Heidi's condition.

The surgery took about an hour, but Heidi did not open her eyes for another hour and a half. When she did, she saw that a nurse was sitting beside her bed, dozing off. It was still dark outside, and Heidi wondered if it was still the same night as when she had been admitted to the hospital. She had no idea what happened to her or how long she has been unconscious. What was strange was that she felt no pain. Trying to investigate her condition, she realized that she had no feeling in her right leg and hip. She almost started to panic when the nurse opened her eyes and saw her awake.

'Oh, you woke up! I'm sorry, I fell asleep. I'm Nora, your nurse.'

'What happened to me? Am I paralyzed? I can't feel anything on the right-hand side of my body from the waist down!' Heidi told the nurse, and started to cry.

'Paralyzed? Oh God, no! You had your appendix removed, and must still be under anesthesia. Actually, you were very lucky. If you had waited another day you could have died. The infection was spreading quickly,' the nurse told Heidi.

'Is that right? I'll be fine, then?' She could not believe how many things had happened since she fainted. And a new day had begun. The window was letting the sun light come in already. God had saved her this time. Perhaps, He liked her blue dress after all. Heidi smiled at the thought, but only briefly, because the anesthesia was beginning to wear off and she was starting to feel the area where the cut had been made. The doctor came through the door and smiled at her.

'How is my patient doing? You must still be under the sedative, but in a couple of days you should be able to walk again. The recovery will take few weeks, but after that you'll feel like new again. Please do me a favor and do not push yourself, give it time to heal. I'll see you again tomorrow.'

'Thank you, doctor. I'll take your advice,' Heidi responded with gratitude.

The next couple of day passed slowly, since the hospital was boring and the days seemed longer. Ticla and Karina found time to visit Heidi and check on her condition. After the scare they had been through that night, Heidi's friends were relieved that everything had turned out fine in the end. On the third day the doctor advised Heidi that she would be released from hospital the following day, and that she was eligible for a week of medical vacation which she could spend at home. Heidi could not believe that she was about to go home. She was so happy. She asked Ticla to send a telegram to her parents and let them know that she had had surgery, and was coming home for a week. By the time Heidi left the hospital, her father had sent a message back which was somewhat bizarre when Heidi read it.

"Bring home one bottle of Pilsen beer. The doctor will help then. Your father."

Back in her room Heidi tried to understand what the message meant. Being a pragmatic person, one thing was clear to her: she had to go home with at least one bottle of the well known beer. But how? The alcohol was sold only to men in stores. She could not just walk in, grab a bottle and pay for it. She needed somebody to help her. But who? She was slowly walking to the dining room to check the dinner menu, when she passed by the main entrance and was greeted by the on duty soldier. He was a friendly man who got along with all the girls and sometimes closed his eyes and let them in late at night after their curfew. His name was Martin.

'Hi Martin. How are you?'

'Hi. You are the girl that went to hospital a few nights ago, right? How are you feeling? I heard you had surgery. Are you all right?' Martin asked, happy that he had someone to talk to. His duty as the concierge was boring most of the time.

'I'm fine now, thank you. I'll go home tomorrow for a week to recuperate,' Heidi answered and headed toward the dining room. But all of a sudden she had an idea, and she turned back to Martin.

'Listen, when do you finish your shift? May I ask you a favor?' said Heidi, full of hope.

'I'll be off duty by seven this evening and back on tomorrow at seven. Why?'

73

'If you don't have plans for tonight, maybe you could help me?' Heidi asked cautiously.

'My only plan for tonight is to go and have a drink with my buddies and after that go to bed. I've been working long hours this whole week. Ask me anything you want.' Martin started to wonder what she had in her mind. Some girls were quite wild and open to adventure, but this one was always reserved and grounded. She and her two friends were good girls. He had felt sorry when the other night they took her by ambulance and he had almost said a prayer for her then. If she needed help, he presumed it must be something important to her, and he would be delighted to offer his services.

Heidi was trying to decide whether or not to ask him about the beer. Finally, she realized that he was her only hope of making her father's wish come true, and spoke up. 'The thing is that I'm going home tomorrow morning and I just received a telegram from my father. He asked me to bring him a bottle of Pilsen beer, and I don't know how I'm going to purchase it. I have money, but nobody would sell it to a girl like me, you know…' When she finished, she was red with embarrassment.

Martin found her and her request sweet, and answered with a soft smile 'You would like me to buy the beer for your father, is that it?'

Heidi nodded, her blue eyes still looking down. She was not used to talking to men, let alone to ask favors from them. The only man she felt comfortable with was Thomas, Elisabeth's cousin in Vienna. He was like a big brother to her, and she never blushed in front of him. The Vienna episode seemed so long ago. Here she was now standing in front of a soldier asking him for help in a matter that she could not do herself.

'That is not a problem at all. I'd be glad to help you and make your father happy. I will go and buy the beer right after I get off duty here. How many bottles do you want?' Martin asked with a happy grin.

'Really? That is so nice of you. You have no idea how grateful I am. I'll bring you some homemade cookies when I come back. I think three bottles will suffice. I'll give you money right now. Thank you, so much.'

'I'll bring it to your room as soon as I come back tonight. You take care of yourself on this trip home, and get well soon.'

With that, Heidi gave him the money and thanked him one more time before she went to dinner.

Later that evening, while Heidi was busy packing things in her small suitcase, she heard a knock on the door. Ticla jumped from her chair to go and open it.

'I think it is for me, Ticla. I'm expecting someone,' Heidi said mysteriously.

Ticla stopped in her tracks and looked suspiciously at Karina. Heidi walked slowly to the door. She felt the glares of her friends on her and began to smile, making them even more curious about what was going on. She opened the door and saw Martin standing there with a paper bag on his hands. She made sure that the girls inside were not able to see the visitor, but that only made them more curious and they tripped over themselves to get a peek at the person in the hallway.

Heidi took the package and thanked Martin again. He wished her a safe trip and sent greetings to her father. Then, Heidi shut the door and turned toward the center of the room, only to see her two friends staring at her with an offended look.

'Could you explain to us what that was all about? Who was at the door? What is it with this secret visitor?' Ticla went off like a machine gun.

Heidi started to laugh so hard that her belly hurt, and instinctively she pressed her hand over the surgery scar, trying in vain to stop the convulsion. Her laugh only intrigued Karina and Ticla even more.

'What's so funny, Heidi? Tell us, so we can share your amusement,' Karina continued Ticla's inquiry.

'You girls, you look like a couple of old gossipers at the community dance! What are you thinking? That I have a secret admirer who paid me a good-night visit? I can't believe it. This is so funny!'

Karina looked at Ticla, then back to Heidi.

'I think that the appendix you had removed has made you sarcastic, huh?

Ticla finally found her words and advised Heidi that an explanation was needed and that she did not find anything funny in the whole matter.

Heidi loved her friends, and to see them mad at her was the last thing she wanted. Finally she started to tell them the entire beer story, beginning with the puzzling telegram she received from her father that morning. After that, she took the three bottles out of the brown bag and packed them carefully in her luggage.

'The funniest thing is that my father does not even like beer.'

'Maybe it's for your mother, or Teresa,' Ticla said.

All of them looked at each other, processing what they had heard, and then all of a sudden they burst into laughter. It was a good evening. They forgot about the war and about work for a few minutes and let themselves be eighteen year old girls, sharing a secret and a story.

The following day Heidi said her good-byes and took off for the train station. Before she left, Ticla told her that when she returned they wanted to know who had drunk the beer. Her remark brought another wave of smiles to each of their faces.

Chapter 7

Heidi's trip home was uneventful. After two train connections, one in Vienna and the other one in St. Polten, she arrived in Traisen by sunset. It was almost a full day journey, but Heidi enjoyed every minute of it. The scenery on the sunny day all along the way made her feel free and happy. It was a big change from the environment she had lived in for seven months in Pilsen. All this was further heightened by the anticipation of meeting with her family again! In the end, the suffering and the surgery were well worth it, since, as a result, she was able to enjoy this gorgeous day and go home, even if only for a week. She thought about how life sometimes brings you challenges and at other times rewards you with happy moments. Everything went well that day. She received help with her suitcase at every station, she sat in the window seats on both trains, and there were no delays with the trains' schedules. When she finally arrived, the sun was sending orange rays through the valley, painting the sky with a lovely light. On the station's platform three people were waiting for her: her mother, her sister Teresa, and her brother Johan. When she got off the train all three of them started to run toward her, hands in the air, ready to hug her!

'Heidi, welcome home! Look at you; I'm so happy you are here!' Josephina Souisa said, tears of happiness filling her eyes.

'Good to have you home, sis.' Teresa hugged Heidi and kissed her on both cheeks.

'Heidi, I'm so glad you came back. Here, give me your suitcase. Let's go home. Dad cannot wait to see you,' said Johan, and his face was radiating with joy.

Heidi was overwhelmed, and became emotional while she hugged each of them with love. Finally, when she could speak again, she rushed everyone out of the station and headed home to see her father and her younger sister Louisa.

She would have run to the house, but her strength was limited. The operation had not healed completely, so she had to walk slowly and carefully. When they arrived home, Frantz Souisa was waiting at the top of the outside stairs, smiling.

'Heidi, my girl, welcome home! Thank God that I see you home again!' The father embraced the daughter with love.

'Father, I'm so very happy to be here with you. I tend to think that my appendix has done me a huge favor. The suffering was worth it, since, as a result, I get to be home with you for a week. Better than nothing, huh?' Heidi spoke from her heart, and it was full of joy.

'Let's go inside and let me look at you. How are you feeling?' Frantz continued.

'The surgery still bothers me every now and then, and will do so until it's completely healed, but that is ok. I don't mind it. I'm home!' Heidi said.

'Hey sis, this suitcase is quite heavy. How did you manage to carry it? What did you put inside?' Johan asked as he deposited the luggage on the living room floor.

Teresa wanted to ask Heidi so many questions about what had happened in the center after her departure, and about the ordeal that her sister had to endure, but their parents stole Heidi's entire attention. She heard her father ask Heidi, 'Now, let me ask you, did you receive my telegram?'

'Yes Father, I did and nothing could have intrigued me more than what you wrote in it.'

'Why is that?'

'Why?' Heidi started to smile. 'What was all that about the beer? Out of everything in the world you asked me to bring you beer. You don't even like beer. That is why!'

'So, were you able to bring some, then?' Frantz asked anxiously.

'That was not a joke, this strange demand, was it, Dad?'

'A joke? No! It was actually very important that you brought it. Did you?'

Josephina looked at her husband as if he had just lost his mind or something. Teresa did not have a clue what the two of them were talking about. It was the strangest conversation she had heard in years. It was like father and daughter were talking in a secret code. The funny thing was that even Heidi did not know what was going on.

'That is so funny Dad. You really expect that I brought you the beer. Why is it so important to you? Yes, I brought three bottles of Pilsen beer. Johan is right. The suitcase is heavy because of it. Now be so kind and illuminate us as to what you need the beer for?' Heidi concluded.

They saw Frantz rubbing his palms, pleasure written all over his face.

'Three bottles? Excellent! Good girl!' he said and with this he sat down on the sofa.

'Well?' Heidi asked, her curiosity pushed to the limit.

'Yeah Frantz, go on and tell us what's with this beer, after all?' Josephina said to her husband still wondering if he was alright.

Finally, Frantz Souiza understood how this dialogue was driving everybody in the room to suspicion, and began to laugh with all his heart. When he could speak again he said 'I admit this is funny, and it could seem foolish on my part, but Heidi, my dear, you just got yourself an extra week vacation with that beer. Everybody, Heidi will be with us for two weeks. Isn't this nice?'

'Father, I do not know what got into you, but my papers show that I'm due to be back on August 6th, one week from now.' Was her father loosing track of time?

'Ha ha, this is what you think, but tomorrow morning, after we pay a visit to doctor Miller here at the clinic in town, you'll get an extra week to stay home. How does that sound?'

'Sounds like I have no idea what you're talking about. Why should I go and see the doctor here in Traisen? I'm fine,' Heidi went on. She was going nowhere tomorrow, why should she?

'Ok, enough with this cat and mouse game. I spoke to doctor Miller as soon I received your message that you had had the surgery. I was concerned about your condition and how serious this illness may be. He assured me that you'll recover to your full strengths once the cut heals. He also told me that if you could bring him a bottle of the Pilsen beer that he is so fond of, he would make all the arrangements for you to get another week off to recover. I trust him, and he has the authority to extend your stay on the basis of an examination of your condition at this time. We give him the beer and he gives you one more week of vacation that you deserve anyway. Does it make more sense to you now?'

Heidi was totally bemused by what she has just heard. Teresa, her mom, and even Johan were totally startled.

'Is that right, Dad? Is it possible for me to spend more time home with all of you? That is wonderful news!' She was happy and surprised and gave her father a hug full of appreciation. Afterwards, everybody in the room burst into cheers and had a good time.

The next day, the visit to the doctor confirmed the plan that Frantz Souisa had revealed the night before. Doctor Miller was very grateful for the beer and pleased with Heidi's healing process. He directly sent a message to Pilsen, stating that Heidi Souisa needed more rest than was initially recommended extending her medical vacation by a week. With that, Heidi was free to enjoy her stay without worries.

August was a beautiful month in Traisen. The mountains had a majestic green colour, the sky was blue, and being home was refreshing emotionally and physically. Josephina Souisa cooked fresh tasty meals, Teresa helped her out of her fondness for food, Johan, who had now turned sixteen, had become a real help for the family, and Heidi was spoiled by everybody, or so she felt. Louisa, the youngest of the family, behaved like a true twelve year old and was jealous of Heidi, who, since coming home, was receiving most of their parents' attention.

Every day Heidi and her father followed the news about the war, and on occasion discussed it together. Luckily, there were no developments around Vienna for the two weeks that Heidi spent at home. She had a chance to relax. She caught up with Teresa on what was new around Traisen and briefed her sister about how things had changed in Pilsen after she left the army. Heidi was happy that Johan was becoming a fine young man with good manners and much courage. The only one who annoyed her was Louisa and her lack of responsibility. Heidi noticed that thanks to her mother's garden, food was not such a big problem during summer time, but overall, in Traisen, there was a shortage of goods and money. She thought that if the war lasted a few more years her family would become poor, along with everybody else around there.

One day after another passed, and at the end of the two weeks Heidi returned to her duties in Pilsen. She started to dread all the good-byes, but she had learnt by now that all good things, just like the bad, eventually come to an end. Nothing lasts forever.

When she arrived at the Communication Center back in Pilsen, after a long day of traveling, she was tired and already home-sick.

In the hallway, she met Ticla coming out of the dining room.

'Heidi, is that you? You did come back!' Ticla said as soon as she saw Heidi.

'Hello to you, too!' Heidi said without any enthusiasm, and headed toward their room. Ticla followed her up the stairs and together they entered the room where Karina was reading a pamphlet about work.

'Here you are Heidi, you did come back after all!' said Karina, visibly surprised.

'Yes, unfortunately I had to return. How are you?' Heidi responded.

Ticla sat down at the table and began her inquiry. 'You are late one week, you know? We thought that you had done something foolish and deserted the army. We were so afraid that you'd end up in Martial Court. What happened to you?'

Heidi now understood why her friends' welcome was so cold. They had been scared that she would not return at all. Of course they did not know that her stay was extended and she was allowed to be one week late. With that, she started to unpack and fill the table with all the goodies her mother and Teresa had made to bring along with her: cookies, cheese, apples and a loaf of freshly baked bread. Ticla and Karina watched the food with interest. It was a reminder of their own families, and the food their mothers used to make.

'Here, you two come and take a bite of everything I brought. My mother and Teresa packed all these for the three of us, not only for me,' Heidi invited her friends.

'Cookies, and cheese, and homemade bread? Heidi, these must be delicious!' Ticla and Karina started to taste the food and praised the cook.

The three of them enjoyed dinner, talking all throughout its duration.

'So Heidi, how come you stayed home longer than expected?' asked Ticla.

'Because of the beer!' Heidi said.

'What? Did you drink the beer all by yourself and got drunk not sober up for a week?' Karina laughed.

'You think that I'm joking, but I'm serious. The beer got me an extra week vacation', Heidi replied.

'How?'

'Well, it turned out that my father talked with the doctor in Traisen before I went home and told him I had had surgery. The doctor asked for a bottle of the Pilsen beer that he likes so much but has not been able to buy since the war started. Apparently, I was his only hope for getting it, and in return he extended my vacation by a week for medical reasons. He took care of reporting to Col. Schloss, so no Martial Court for me this time,' Heidi assured her friends.

'That is great! Good for you! I'm glad you came back. Thank you for this regal meal you've laid out for us,' Ticla said, looking happy.

'Yeah, thanks for the tasty food Heidi. I'm happy you enjoyed your stay home. I wish I could go home for a week, too,' Karina added.

'Now, if you could excuse me for a minute, I have to go and give Martin this small parcel in appreciation for helping me,' Heidi announced and disappeared through the door. When she returned, they continued to talk about life in Traisen and Austria in general, before they called it a night and turned off the lights.

The rest of August passed quickly. Heidi was busy with work. Every day something happened in one place or another all across Europe. It looked like the Allies' focus was on liberating Italy and Sicily, along with attempts at destroying the German facilities that had started to build the new V-2 rocket. The Eastern front was dominated by the Battle of Kursk, where the Soviets gained victory over the Axis powers. The Germans retaliated and secured their positions in their occupied territories. Martial Law was instituted in Denmark, replacing the Danish government.

In September, the Allies forced Italy out of the war with the signing of the Italian Armistice. Mussolini had to flee and sought refuge up in the mountains. Hitler became aware of the danger that awaited him after losing the support of the Italians and advised the evacuation of civilians from Berlin. In an attempt to turn things around in Italy, Hitler rescued Mussolini and sent German troops through Greece to regain control over southern Italy. The operation was successful in mid-September. Throughout this month, increasingly violent battles took place from east to west and from south to north. The Soviet Union declared war on Bulgaria, British submarines attacked a German battleship in the North Sea, and local governments across Europe started to help Jewish people to flee across the ocean or to Sweden.

In October, Corsica was liberated by the Free French Forces and Italy declared war on Germany.

Heidi turned nineteen on October 11th, and again her birthday went by largely unnoticed. Ticla and Karina offered to take her out after dinner to the Corner Café for tea and a biscuit, but something came up in the center, their shifts were switched around and they could not find the time to do it. She did receive a telegram from her family, but that was all.

The war continued with its turmoil throughout November, with more raids and bombs, and more casualties.

Chapter 8

At the end of 1943 the war had intensified all over Europe. The communication center in Pilsen was busy following event after event, each one more frightening than the last. Col. Schloss made sure that the work in the center was running smoothly and efficiently. The girls put in long hours and a lot of energy.

However, in the week before Christmas, Heidi and her friends found time to unwind and even go into the city to buy a few things and to get in the Christmas spirit. At St. Bartholomew's Cathedral, groups of singers sang carols, in the central square the trees were decorated with sparkling garlands and stores' doors were decorated with green pine wreaths. The Corner Café had a festive atmosphere, with candles on the tables and a nicely decorated Christmas tree in the middle of the large room. If they could have forgotten about work and all the news they received every day about attacks and battles all across Europe, Heidi, Ticla and Karina might have been able to enjoy the winter holidays, even being far away from their families.

Karina was especially upset about all the bombings that had occurred in Germany in the last couple of months. Teresa sent Heidi a letter about life in Traisen, telling her how the family was doing, wishing her and her friends a safe and merry Christmas. Ticla received a Christmas card from her parents too.

On Christmas Eve an announcement was made and posted on the black board: whoever was not on duty that afternoon or that night was to visit the hospital and meet with wounded and sick soldiers who had no relatives or family to keep them company over the holidays. Karina was due to work that evening, but Heidi and Ticla were free. The curfew of 10:30 pm was lifted, and a group of girls were ready to head to the hospital for a good cause: to help someone who was suffering and spread the Christmas spirit. The gesture was a very thoughtful one for the usually rigid German army.

Again, Heidi and Ticla were inseparable. As they entered the hospital, a nurse greeted them with gratitude.

'Good evening, young ladies. I'm Nora and I suppose you are here to share your Christmas Eve with the less fortunate sick soldiers who are lonely, to show them that they are not forgotten, and make them feel better at this time of the year.'

Heidi recognized the nurse from the previous summer when she had undergone surgery. She was glad that, in return for the nurse's kindness during her recovery, she could now help her by looking after one of her patients, if only for few hours.

'Merry Christmas, Nora!' Heidi responded with enthusiasm, followed by Ticla. Then her friend pulled her aside and whispered in her ear.

'Heidi, I'm not sure I am up to this task. It makes me nervous to talk to strangers. What should I tell them?'

'I know how you feel. I'm nervous too,' Heidi replied, and then she turned toward the nurse and spoke louder.

'Nora, we are willing to help, but we don't feel too comfortable about keeping company with men we don't know, sick or not.'

'Oh, no need to worry. They will be happy just to see you there. You do not have to do much, just hold their hands and tell them few things about why you came here tonight,' Nora advised the girls.

'Maybe we can meet the ones who are suffering the most, who will not be able to listen or talk to us too much. We can hold hands all right, but talking is another story,' Ticla pleaded.

'All right then, I can find two people who are not very alert and will not talk much, if at all. How does that sound?' the nurse asked.

'It sounds good. We appreciate it,' Heidi agreed. Ticla also showed a sign of relief. The nurse led the way to the second floor and into a large room where patients were lying on narrow beds. They passed a few girls who were already attending to patients and reached the opposite end of the room where Nora showed them two men who seemed to be asleep. They did not look wounded, since no bandages could be seen, but their illness must have been serious as they looked lost to the world.

'Here you are. These are two soldiers who came from the North African front with malaria. The disease is not contagious anymore, but they are still very weak, and sleep all the time. You can each pick one, and relax.'

'Thank you, Nora,' Heidi said, and then the nurse left them to return to her duty, but not before adding, 'No, I thank you for coming here and doing this. You will be just fine. Your support is much appreciated.' Heidi looked around and pulled a chair close to one of the beds where a young man was lying. He seemed to be asleep or maybe sedated in order to alleviate his pain. She could not imagine how much he was suffering or what his life had been like in the past. He was a man who had fought in the war and, if he recovered, would maybe have to fight again. What were his dreams? What did he believe in? What could she possibly tell him to make him feel better?

Ticla sat down beside the other bed, looking at the other patient and perhaps wondering the same thing as Heidi did. The moment was awkward, and they did not know where to start or what to do for these strangers.

The one attended to by Heidi moved his head and made a little noise. Heidi was startled and instinctively took his hand and held it. Feeling the soft touch, he moved again and gently squeezed her hand. Heidi could feel his warmth, probably due to the fever. She started to talk.

'Shh, Shh, Shh, you are not alone. I'm here to help you.' She did not know what else to tell him.

Hearing her soft voice he tried to open the eyes, but the eye-lids seemed too heavy. Then he squeezed her hand again, trying to get energy from the connection.

'You'll be all right. The worst has passed. The nurse said that you'll recover,' Heidi found herself babbling just to prove to herself that her presence was useful.

The man shifted his head and finally opened his eyes, while Heidi stared at him.

'Did I die and go to Heaven? You must be an angel...' Heidi heard him say. He was awake, and he was talking to her. She could see that he had to put a lot of effort just to do this. She felt a wave of compassion for him.

'Hi, I'm Heidi Souisa, and you certainly are alive. As a matter of fact, you'll make a full recovery if you have patience. Tonight is Christmas Eve and I'm here to spend it with you. Would you like me to stay and keep you company?'

He hung on every word she said, trying to make sense of what he heard. A pretty girl was holding his hand and talking to him, and it was Christmas Eve! It must have been the night of miracles! It made him very happy despite the illness that kept him in that hospital bed. He couldn't help noticing how pretty she was and how intelligent her beautiful eyes looked! Were they blue? She asked him whether he wanted her to stay. Of course he wanted her to stay! She was a breath of fresh air to him, a heaven-sent fairy.

'Please stay if you can. You make me feel better already. Forgive my weakness. My name is Francis Ubertal…'

'Nice to meet you, Francis. Now take it easy, and save your strength. I'll stay with you for few hours. Where are you from?' Heidi started to speak all of a sudden, forgetting her shyness.

'I'm Austrian, from Vienna. I was deployed in North Africa, in Morocco for the last year, before I became sick. I've been in the war for the last two years. How about you?'

Heidi could not have been more surprised when she learned that he was also Austrian. That discovery made her want to communicate more, and melted all the reservations that she had at the beginning of the evening. She instantly felt at ease, and grew fond of him.

'This is so strange! I'm from Austria too, a little town close to St. Polten called Traisen. Have you heard of it? It's about 60km away from Vienna.'

'Really? I'm glad to hear that we come from the same area. What are you doing here in Pilsen? I see that you are in the army, by the look of the uniform,' Francis said feeling all of a sudden much better. This girl, Heidi, seemed to him an angel on a holy night. His spirit improved instantly, and the physical weakness faded away, lost in the excitement of the moment.

'Oh, I am part of the telecommunication company at the main Communication Center here in Pilsen. We follow the aviation deployments and the air raids all over Europe. I've been here for a year now. My friend over there is Ticla, I mean Mathilda. She's also from Austria, somewhere near Salzburg.' Heidi gestured with her hand towards Ticla who was sitting by the other bed and talking quietly with the other patient.

Francis turned his head to see Heidi's friend, another young Austrian lady who looked absorbed in a discussion with Robert, his colleague of both combat and suffering. They had both come a long way. They had to fight on the front, and then fight malaria. Sometimes it seemed like they had lost both battles, sometimes they had hope that they would make it, but they could never foresee that some strangers would care about how they felt on a lonely Christmas Eve. And yet here they were, enjoying the company of two fine and brave young ladies whose purpose was to improve their spirit, if only for few hours. Now, that was more than they could have wished for Christmas. It was wonderful!

Francis turned back toward Heidi, still holding her warm and delicate hand. He felt power coming through that point of contact, and an exchange of positive energy. He closed his eyes for few seconds and took a few deep breaths, letting himself be flooded by the peaceful feeling transmitted through human touch, and the peaceful thought of being and belonging. Heidi thought that he had fallen back to sleep and deep inside felt herself disappointed that the conversation was cut off short. She would have liked to ask him more questions about himself, and share with him some of her own thoughts. But then Francis spoke again, opening his eyes and looking into Heidi's.

'I've been in this hospital for one month, and this illness has drained not only my physical strength but also my desire to live. I come from a family with military ties. My father is a retired colonel and my older brother is an officer in the Bavarian Regiment. I was one of the leader officers in Morocco. If I recover, I'll probably be promoted to a higher rank officer and sent back on war duty.'

Heidi listened carefully to his story. He wanted to tell her as much as he could about himself, but it was tiring and he had to pause every so often. She filled these gaps with her own story. She told him about her enrolment at the age of seventeen, and about her sister who became sick and had to leave the army, about the bombardment in the spring that had terrified her, and about her good friends Ticla and Karina who kept her going each and every day.

Francis told her about Vienna and the neighborhood in the outskirts of the city where his family lived in a nice big house that her mother kept in excellent shape even during the last few years of war.

In return Heidi spoke about her family in Traisen and her father's shoe business that had suffered during the war, and how that it did not matter much as long as they were in good health, and safe.

By dawn Francis and Heidi felt like best friends and could not be-lieve that they had talked the whole night and the time had passed so quickly. Back home, Christmas morning was the time for opening presents. Francis thought about the warmth of his family in Vienna, and the many Christmases when presents and a decorated pine tree reigned in the living room while the vanilla smell of cookies came from the large kitchen. His mother served eggnog and cognac during this time, while the gifts were opened creating a festive atmosphere. Now here he was, with no presents, cookies or drinks, but feeling happier than ever, simply by looking at this girl who chose to spend her spare time with him, giving him solace when he needed it most. That, and hope, and joy. Heidi's presence was the most beautiful gift he could have received. His only regret was that he could not give her anything in return, and he feared that he would not have another chance to see her again. While all these thoughts crossed his mind he found himself talking.

'You coming here and meeting me was the most beautiful Christmas present I've ever received. I cannot express how much it means to me. My only regret is that I have nothing to offer you this Christmas morning. I don't even know if you'd like to see me again and I fear that if you wouldn't, I'll be very disappointed. But Christmas time is for hope and joy, and I think there may be a chance that we remain friends and that I'll have the opportunity to treat you the way you deserve to be treated. What do you think?'

'I think about how scared I felt last night before I met you, and how good I feel now after we talked all night long,' Heidi said. Francis hung on each word, waiting for an assurance that he'd see her again. When she stopped, he became sad instantly.

Heidi was looking for the right words, self-absorbed in her own insecurities. A glance at the big clock on the wall told her that she and Ticla were due back to the Center. Pressured by time, she spoke quickly. 'I'll visit you again as soon as I can. You have to promise me that you'll take care of yourself and get better soon. If you need anything, let me know via courier. I'll come back tomorrow afternoon if my shift does not change. Please have faith in me, you are not alone anymore. You've got yourself a friend. I have to leave now, but I'll be back. Merry Christmas, Francis!' and with that Heidi leaned forward and gave him a hug. He was as happy as a small child who had just been given a long awaited present. He almost choked back tears of happiness. When he could talk again, he said 'Merry Christmas Heidi! God bless you! I'm not going anywhere; I'll be here waiting for you. Go now. See you soon!'

Heidi told her friend that they had to leave. Ticla looked disappointed, like she had just been awoken from a nice dream. The time had flown by so quickly; it must have been because it was spent in good company. Ticla said something to Robert and then quickly joined Heidi. They walked together across the long room and down the stairs, rushing toward the hospital's exit. It was already late and they were due back in a few minutes. The cold air outside felt refreshing and the walk invigorated them. But most of all it was the memory of the night, when they met two wonderful men, that put a spring in their steps.

'Let's not spoil this great day by being late and getting punished by the colonel. I want to go back to the hospital and visit Francis as soon as I can,' Heidi told Ticla, catching her breath. They were almost running.

'Me too! I mean, to see Robert. He is so wonderful. I hope he'll get well soon. He said he would be honored if I would visit him again. Can you believe it?' Ticla added, trying to keep up with Heidi. The street was almost empty at that early hour. When they reached their building they were 20 minutes late. They knew that the rule was to register at the front door and log their time of return. The colonel checked the register daily, and being on time was something that he was strict about.

When the girls entered the large hallway knowing that they should have left the hospital sooner, they were ready to face the consequences. Instead, they were greeted by a cheerful concierge, Martin.

'Merry Christmas, ladies!'

Heidi could not believe their good luck. She knew instantly that Martin was on their side, and the log in the register would not show the delay.

'Merry Christmas, Martin! We are so sorry for being late.'

'Late? What are you talking about? Don't worry about that. You ladies are right on time! Now run and get ready for breakfast,' Martin said with a wink.

Ticla and Heidi were already climbing the stairs to the second floor toward their room, happy that they escaped the colonel's punishment. Once behind their bedroom door, they hugged each other and giggled with relief, while Karina opened her eyes waking up from her sleep.

'Oh, you are back. I was so tired. You two look happy. What happened?' said Karina, stretching her body.

Ticla went on without a second invitation. 'Merry Christmas, Karina! What a nice Christmas Eve we had! We met two young officers who are true gentlemen. They are still sick and weak physically, but they are smart and caring and they want us to visit them again. One is from Vienna and the other is from around where you live, Leipzig in eastern Germany.'

Heidi continued, full of enthusiasm, 'I sat with Francis. He is twenty four years old. He is from Vienna. Robert is German. They are friends, and were together in the same battalion in North Africa where they caught malaria.'

'Well, I'm glad you had a good time. Remember how terrified you were last night before leaving? There was no news here, which is good news. Christmas time should be for celebration, not fighting. Let's go and see if we have a decent breakfast on this holy day,' Karina concluded.

'Good idea,' Ticla said. 'I also want to check when I have time off, so I can go back to the hospital. Hopefully on New Year's day we can spend some more time with our new friends.'

Karina noticed that her friends were totally wrapped in their thoughts about the two officers they had just met. Were they falling in love with them? She kept the thought to herself.

The dining room was decorated with garlands and small branches of pine tree. Breakfast was larger than usual, and tea came with a piece of fruit cake. Some girls ate it, and some saved it for later. Heidi and Ticla put it aside, wrapped in a napkin.

The day passed quietly. They worked for a few hours, then rested for a bit, and enjoyed lunch and dinner which consisted of tasty food and more cake. The next day, in the afternoon, Heidi and Ticla found time to return to the hospital for a short visit. They both had butterflies in their stomach and an accelerated heart-beat. Francis was the first to spot them coming. He gave the signal to Robert and the two of them welcomed the young ladies with happy smiles.

'You made it! You did come back! You have no idea how glad I am seeing you again!' Francis said and made room for Heidi to sit on the edge of his bed.

'How are you feeling? I told you I'll come if I could, didn't I? Here, I brought you something: a piece of fruitcake. You like it, don't you?' Heidi asked as she revealed the slice from the napkin.

'You are so sweet, you know that?' he said looking into her beautiful eyes, trying to understand how he had been lucky enough to meet her. She was beautiful, caring, smart, and right there offering him fruit cake.

Heidi, seeing that he did not take the cake, feared that he could not eat, or did not like sweets. She looked toward Ticla and saw that Robert was eating the piece that her friend had brought him.

Francis sensed her distress and added quickly, 'This piece of cake must be very good.'

'It is, and it's yours.'

'Thank you so much for thinking of me. I'd like to share it with you, so please break it in two and let's have it together.'

'No, it is for you, you need energy. I'm fine.'

'Please do me this favor and have half of it.'

Heidi smiled, tore it into two equal pieces and handed one to him, saying, 'All right, I'll eat it so you can be sure I don't poison you!'

'Heidi, darling, that is not what I meant. Even if it was poison, I would have eaten it if it was from you,' he said with a smile, and took the cake with a weak hand.

They both enjoyed the tasty fruit flavored cake while holding hands. The moment was sweet, literally and figuratively.

Ticla and Robert seemed deeply engaged in a whispered conversation. Heidi and Francis talked about themselves and their life before the war. The common ground was Vienna and all its beauty. They deliberately avoided the subject of war and disasters. All they wanted was to feel happy for the time they spent together. Happiness was so invigorating that Heidi lived in the moment, enjoying every bit of it. Francis was getting better every minute when he was in Heidi's company. When she wasn't there the hope that she'd come back kept him going. Also, when they were alone, the two men had begun to talk more and more about how lucky they were to have met these two fine ladies and how much they meant to them.

The four of them spent New Year's Eve together. By then, the men were able to lean on the pillows in a sitting position, and they felt better and had a good time.

Heidi, Ticla, Francis and Robert welcomed 1944 in a celebratory mood, despite the dangerous war that was still raging all over the world.

Chapter 9

Following the aggressive intervention of the Allied forces in Europe, the Nazi Army suffered heavy losses on the battle fields. This coincided with an increase in hostility from the civilian population of the occupied territories. The beginning of 1944 brought more air strikes over Berlin. The Red Ukrainian Army forced its way to Poland, the British army continued to put pressure in Italy, while the Americans were defeated in their attempt to seize control of Southern Europe. The war intensified, however, the German Army started to lose grounds. The number of prisoners of war in labor camps in the Soviet Union was increasing. The Nazis had no choice but to begin enrolling teenage boys in order to fill the gaps created by the fallen soldiers. This triggered significant hatred toward the German Army from the families of the newly recruited young men. The German uniform became a target of that hate. In Pilsen, several street attacks occurred against the German military forces in an effort to weaken the occupying power.

Immediately after the New Year Col. Schloss advised his staff to be careful when outside the Center. A few days later he ordered that any woman going out into town was not to wear her military uniform for safety reasons. The population of Pilsen and the underground Resistance Movement were ready to take their frustration out on the unarmed female population of the German army.

Whereas the year before Heidi, Ticla and Karina had had little interest in leaving their building during their spare time, since they had met Francis and Robert, the former two could not wait to go to the hospital for short visits.

'Heidi, I do not have any winter civilian clothes. Do you?' Ticla asked her friend, feeling frustrated.

'No, neither have I. I asked my father to send me money from my bank account in Austria, and I plan to go shopping,' Heidi replied.

'Do you know what the exchange rate is when you purchase something in the store? I went to buy a pair of shoes yesterday. It is a complete injustice: two marks for one crown. In other words I had to pay double the advertised price,' Karina interjected with disappointment.

'Really? Why is that? Is it legal? At the bank the crown and the mark are at parity,' Ticla said reluctantly.

'The Czech banks will not exchange your money; they'll only deal with their own people. When they see your name, they refuse to perform any transaction. This is how they support their people,' Karina went on.

'As soon as I get the money from back home, I'll have to go and buy clothes anyway.' Heidi decided helplessly.

'You're right. I'll come with you. We need a few garments to be able to go out to the hospital. God knows, our poor friends must think that we have given up on them. We haven't seen them for a week now,' said Ticla.

Karina thought about her friends and their new male friends for a moment. Then she spoke her mind.

'I envy you, you know? Each of you met a man you seem to care about. That gives you a purpose and something to look forward to, not to mention that it improves your personal life. All of a sudden the war falls into second or third place in your life, and this new friendship helps you cope better with the reality. I think you two have found something special. I envy you, but in the same time, I'm happy for you. I hope to have the chance to meet your friends soon.'

Heidi looked at Karina, stricken by what she had just heard. She had never looked at this new relationship that way, but Karina, being more objective, was completely right. Francis had brought feelings into her life that she had not known before: excitement, restlessness, anticipation and desire. Was this what happiness meant? It was true: ever since she had met Francis the war had faded into the background and lost its front-stage place in her life. Was she losing focus? Was it a bad influence? Whatever it was, it felt so right and so good. Francis's well-being was a big part of her daily thoughts, and the visits were the highlights of her week. Yes, she needed to see him as much as he needed to see her. They were in complete harmony during the time they spent together. She could not stay away from him for long, and knew that he needed her visits like the very air he breathed. This was why she would have to go and buy civilian clothes at any price as soon as possible, and be free to do whatever she felt was right for her. All these thoughts made her write a long and heartfelt letter to Teresa at home. Her sister was her best confidant, and she needed to share this new experience with someone.

Within a couple of days Heidi and Ticla were all set for a shopping spree. With money in their pockets and a longing for freedom and security, they headed towards the commercial district in downtown Pilsen.

'Let's try to find a coat first. That will cover whatever we wear underneath. We need a coat and a hat. A hat would give us a chic fashionable look.' Ticla advised Heidi.

The tailor's shop was a delight. Coats hung in a row, in a variety of colors: grey, dark green, dark blue and burgundy.

'Good afternoon ladies!' the salesman greeted them.

'Good afternoon,' Heidi responded, while browsing the coat rack. 'What can I offer you?'

'We are looking for a winter coat, please,' Ticla said with her eyes on the green ones. Heidi was already set on blue.

The salesman rubbed his hand with satisfaction. It was unusual for him to sell coats, and it looked like these two young military ladies were determined to buy, rather than simply look at his merchandise like most of the people who came in. In no time Heidi and Ticla had tried on a few coats and admired themselves in the large mirror. The sizes were perfect, and the colors suited them completely. There was no way they would not buy the coats, but choosing the hats was more difficult. The selection wasn't very diverse, however, they were both able to find a matching hat. Heidi settled for a light blue one with a small border that intensified her blue eyes, and Ticla opted for a burgundy one with a larger border which gave her a chic look. When they were ready to pay, they remembered Karina's prediction: the price would be double for them because they were going to be paying with marks, not crowns. With a bit of persistence, however, they persuaded the salesman to give them a discount, given that they were purchasing expensive garments.

Once back to their room, they paraded the new acquisitions in front of Karina's admiring eyes. It was still late afternoon and they were off duty until 10pm. In an urge of the moment they decided to pay a visit to the hospital and see Francis and Robert. With their new coats and fashionable hats they left the building feeling very pretty. Martin, at the front door, wished them a nice evening and complimented them on their look.

At the hospital, Nora, the nurse, noticed them right away but did not recognize them. They looked as if they had just stepped out of a magazine. Only when Heidi started to talk to her did Nora realize who they were. By now Heidi and Ticla were familiar to the hospital's staff. Nora told them that the two officers they had befriended were doing better and better, and thanked them again for their kindness and their visits.

The two girls then rushed toward the second floor. Their elegant walk did not go unnoticed by the patients they passed by. When they approached Francis's and Robert's beds, the two men were sitting up, eyes glued to the two new apparitions who entered the large room. By the look on their faces, neither of them had recognized Heidi and Ticla yet. What they found unusual was that the two mysterious ladies were coming straight toward them.

'Holy Mother of God, these two movie stars are looking straight at us, Robert!' Francis said.

'You're right. I haven't seen such elegant ladies since I was in military school in Berlin, four years ago,' Robert remembered.

'Wait a second, that's Heidi!' Francis exclaimed.

'Are you sure? Is that Ticla?' Robert could not believe what he was seeing.

The girls got closer, wearing their most seductive smiles, while their admirers looked at them in awe. All kind of thoughts were crossing each man's mind! Had their lady friends left the army? Were they aware of the consequences of quitting their jobs? Was the war over? What was going on outside the hospital in the city of Pilsen?

'Hi, Francis! How are you doing?' Heidi greeted her friend.

'Heidi, darling, what a lovely surprise to see you! You look gorgeous! Why are you wearing civilian clothes?' Francis asked right away.

'I'm glad you like my new coat and hat. They are brand new, and cost me an arm and a leg, but it's all worth it if I can come and see you,' Heidi said with enthusiasm.

'I am a lucky man. I was wondering when I'd see you again.'

'The reason I have not come for the last few days was because Col. Schloss ordered that anyone leaving the building should not wear the German uniform anymore. It is too dangerous to be recognized as a member of the German army. I had to wait for my father to send me money from my Austrian bank account to buy civilian clothes. So far, I only bought these two pieces, and I rushed to see you. Tomorrow I'll go and shop for a couple of blouses and a skirt. See? I still have the uniform underneath the coat right now, but outside nobody knows that. Now tell me everything about the last days I haven't seen you,' Heidi said

'So it's become unsafe for Germans to walk on the streets? This is not a good sign. I'm glad Col. Schloss thought to protect you and forbid the uniforms for his staff. You still have to be careful, though. You only speak German, and anyone can tell where you came from,' Francis said, concerned.

'I know what you mean. The color of the clothes is not going to protect us from the dangers out there. I'll be careful, I promise. By the way, how do you like my new acquisitions?' Heidi asked, all smiles

'You will laugh knowing that when you two walked into the room, Robert and I thought that we have just seen two movie stars.'

'That is funny indeed. Thank you for the compliment.'

'You're welcome! You are so wonderful to me, and so beautiful, do you know that?' Francis was happy, really happy, simply to see Heidi and hold her delicate hand, which he kissed gently.

Ticla and Robert were also happy, and equally involved in a whispered conversation they both enjoyed.

The next day Heidi, Ticla, and Karina had the chance to go shopping again, and the experience was again both bitter and sweet. Bitter, because prices were higher for them than the rest of the Czech population and sweet because new clothes have always appealed to women, no matter the age or times.

After buying a crisp white cotton shirt, a knitted blue blouse and a black bell-shaped skirt, Heidi waited for her friends to finish making their purchases. Ticla settled for a dark blue pencil skirt paired with a grey shirt and a burgundy sweater, and Karina opted for a dark grey "A" line skirt and a purple sweater with pearly small buttons. Once out of the store they were ready to head back to the Center, but on the way they passed a lingerie boutique. The window displayed delicate undergarments. Ticla stopped in front of it, mesmerized. She had never seen such beautiful underwear in her life: lace and silk camisoles, embroidered pants and bras, not to mention the silky stockings with decorative guarder belts.

'My Goodness! Do you see what I see? These must cost a fortune, but they are worth every crown,' Ticla said in awe.

Heidi was also taken by the beauty displayed in the shop's window. Karina, on the other hand, tried to figure out what were they seeing: these light pieces of underwear could surely not keep someone warm in winter time.

'Let's go in and have a closer look,' Heidi decided suddenly.

Ticla did not wait for a second invitation and led the way inside the store. The door bell made a crystalline sound, and right away all three were greeted by an elegant middle age lady who looked like the owner of the shop.

'Good afternoon, young ladies. Welcome to "La Rose"! I am Madame Fleur, and I'll be happy to show you the lingerie collection brought here from Paris.'

'From Paris? Wow!' Ticla could not contain her surprise.

'Yes, please feel free to browse through the entire store, and let me know if I can help you with anything,' Madame Fleur said, smiling.

Heidi, Ticla and Karina looked around, already imagining how they would feel wearing any of those garments.

Karina, though, had a quick reality check. 'You are not going to buy any of these, are you?'

Ticla answered:

'Maybe I will. Heidi, what do you think?'

'I think it would be a waste of money, but I wouldn't blame you for that. I may pick one or two items myself.'

Hearing that, Karina started to believe even more firmly that the men in the hospital had something to do with her two friends' sudden change of character. She thought that Heidi and Ticla were already in love, but they did not know it just yet.

'You know what? You two should go ahead and buy some nice lingerie. After all, it came from Paris,' Karina said.

Half an hour later they left the store, each, including Karina, holding a little package wrapped in expensive looking paper from Paris.

Once back in their room they displayed all the items they had bought on their beds, and one could easily have seen that their spirits were high and their heart-beat stronger. Looking at their new purchases they felt happy, they felt feminine, they felt beautiful.

Outside, the world was consumed by the war, and the girls were fully aware of the fact that they were part of it, but for an afternoon they could forget about it and let themselves be nineteen year old ladies with hopes and dreams of love, peace, and a normal life. The rest of the week was calm for Heidi and Ticla, allowing for a few visits to the hospital and happy moments in the company of Francis and Robert. Karina was amused to observe her friends getting all dressed up before leaving. They looked beautiful and happy every time they went to meet the men.

Day by day Francis and Robert became stronger and their illness started to heal. By the end of January they were able to get out of bed and take short walks inside the hospital. Heidi and Ticla were thrilled by the progress their friends were making. By then they had become closer and let themselves enjoy the time spent together. Nora told Heidi that the speedy recovery of Francis and Robert was partly due to the good influence that she and Ticla had had on the patients. The nurse assured them that the men would be able to leave the hospital much sooner than was initially thought. This good news brought joy to all four, and consolidated the strong feelings that they had developed for one another.

Chapter 10

Heidi filled her days with work and visits to Francis. Sometimes she went alone, sometimes with Ticla, depending on their schedule. The war was in full force on all fronts, but somehow, when she was not on duty, she felt free and her spirits were high. She looked forward to meeting Francis any time she could. Teresa replied to the letter she had sent her regarding this new friend, and Heidi felt that her sister was supportive of her new feelings. As Karina noticed too, Teresa was convinced that Heidi and this young officer would eventually fall in love with each other. Heidi was young and the new experience thrilled her. She grew very fond of Francis, and his well-being was one of her main concern.

The recovery was going well every day, and while Francis gained strength he became more caring and protective of Heidi. At only twenty four years of age he had already lived through the war and survived a bad disease. He had a good upbringing and education, and he was a fine, honest gentleman for whom Heidi was one of the most important people in his life.

Francis knew that, once he would have fully recovered, chances were he would be sent back to the front. The joy of being able to spend time outside the hospital with Heidi was overshadowed by the possibility of leaving Pilsen altogether at the call of duty.

It was a Sunday afternoon in late February, when winter lost its power and the first snowdrop flowers were sold on the street corners, that Francis told Heidi how he felt about her. They were out together for the first time, at the Corner Café, enjoying hot coffee and a few freshly made biscuits. He still lived in the hospital, but his condition was much improved and allowed him to go outside the building every now and then.

The fresh flowers placed on the table in front of them created a romantic atmosphere. Francis's hand on top of Heidi's gave her a pleasurable feeling of warmth. Happiness exuded from their words. One could see the sparkle in their eyes, as they were a refreshing picture of love.

'You look wonderful, and you are wonderful to me. Every time I'm alone, all it takes is to close my eyes and your image comes to me so clearly that I feel like you are there with me. All I can think about is you, you know that? I never thought that I would meet someone like you, Heidi,' Francis said full of passion.

'You are a master of words, but it is exactly how I feel about you too. I pray for you, I long for you, I live for you,' Heidi admitted, not without blushing.

'Sweet darling Heidi, did I tell you how happy you make me all the time, and especially now, with your words?' While saying this, Francis leaned over and brushed his lips over hers. Then he waited for her reaction before kissing her with passion right there in the Café, ignoring the other customers. For Heidi, the world stopped spinning and time stood still. She felt suspended in the air between the sky and the earth, light as a feather. The first kiss! The first man in her life! The first love! She hung on to the sweetness of his lips, the delicious pressure against hers, and to her total abandon to Francis's touch. When they finally parted, their eyes looked deep into each others, speaking without words. The magic was there, the love in the air! Francis gathered his composure first and said softly, 'I am the happiest man alive right now, sweet Heidi! My heart is beating only for you.'

'I think I can say the same thing, Francis,' Heidi admitted, still on cloud nine. So this was what love meant. She was mesmerized by her new feelings. The whole world had a new horizon. They forgot about the war: it was as if love truly could conquer all.

When they left the Corner Café, they walked hand in hand towards Heidi's building and Francis bought her a small and delicate bouquet of flowers from a vendor. Before she headed inside they hugged and kissed again, whispering farewell in each other's ears.

Heidi passed Martin at the front door and greeted him with a happy smile before she went to her room where Karina and Ticla were having a joyful conversation.

'Heidi, I'm so glad you came home, I have the most wonderful news to share with you!' Ticla said, hardly able to contain her enthusiasm.

Heidi was already overwhelmed by her own experience, but Ticla seemed not to notice. While taking her nice coat off she heard her friend saying, 'Robert proposed to me. He asked me to marry him. Can you believe it?'

'Really? That is great! What did you say?' Heidi asked, trying to be calm.

'What? You react like you knew it already. Aren't you surprised?'

'I'm just happy…. for you I mean. I'm very happy. Did you say yes?'

'Of course I said yes!'

'Then, congratulations are in order. Let me give you a hug my friend! I wish you two lots of happiness!'

Karina was looking at Heidi and realized that her friend was caught up in her own romance. She saw her putting the flowers in a glass and looking pensively at them. Karina thought that Heidi must have had news of her own but was not ready to share it just yet. She chose to say nothing about it. The rest of the evening was filled with Ticla's excitement and plans for her future. The men would be released soon from the hospital and housed in the military quarter at the German army base, not far from the Communication Center right there in Pilsen. There was a strong possibility that once they were considered capable to fight, they would be sent back to the battlefield.

The following week the engagement was made public throughout the center, and Ticla received congratulations from almost everybody. Col. Schloos told her that she would be entitled to one week vacation following the wedding.

Heidi and Francis were happy for their friends and the four of them got together whenever time permitted. On the other hand, the two of them were happy about their own romance, which flourished and gave them much joy. Francis, being more mature and accustomed to military strategy, was looking into ways to keep Heidi safe and teaching her how to survive the dangers of the war. Heidi meant the world to him, and he had her best interests at heart. Even from the hospital he had known that the war was not going well for Germany, in particular on the Eastern front where the Soviets were gaining territory.

'Dear Heidi, I care for you more than I care for my life. I would like to protect you always and make sure that you are safe and happy. This war is becoming too dangerous in Eastern Europe, and in a few months the Red Army will probably be advancing toward us at a rapid pace.'

'I don't want to talk about war right now, not when I'm with you. I know what's going on outside of these walls.' Heidi said, sounding annoyed, but she knew that Francis was right.

'Listen to me, my love. It is not that I want to talk about war. Quite the opposite! When I'm with you I feel like nothing can harm us, and our love is enough to keep this world going, but the dangers are out there whether we like it or not. I want you to be prepared for the worst and be safe all the time. So, listen to me: we do not know what the future will bring our way, but we do know that we love each other and we want to stay alive and survive this terrible time, don't we?'

'My father said the same to me, to keep safe and not take unnecessary risks.'

'Your father is a wise man, and he loves you very much too. That is why you should always try to stay away from danger. Look, when I leave the hospital, which I think will happen soon, I'll have to go to the German military base here in the city. For a while they will give me some clerical or training tasks, but if the war doesn't end soon, I may have to go back to the front. When I'm gone I need to know that you'll be in a better place than Czechoslovakia. The Russians may come here, and they are rough people. Their army has no discipline and they are a lot more dangerous than Americans.'

'Do you really think the Russians will arrive here?'

'Unfortunately, they will. It is only a matter of time. That is why I advise you to take any opportunity to move anywhere to the west, and never towards the east. If you see transfers to other centers in Germany or Austria, take them without a second thought.'

'But that means to leave you here, and I'll be alone. I do not want that, to be apart, I mean.' Heidi could not bear the thought that she and Francis would eventually be separated by the war. She became sad.

Francis saw the sudden change of her mood, and hugged her with love. He did not want to upset her; he only knew that if something happened to her he could not live anymore. What he felt for Heidi was hard to put into words. It was as if he lived for her and through her. He had to make sure that she would always be safe.

'I know your advice is right and I trust you like I trust myself. I promise you that I'll look for ways to move west, but it would be unbearable to leave you behind here in Pilsen,' Heidi managed to say, looking into his eyes.

'I know, my love, but there will come a time when I'll be gone to the front too, and you shouldn't stay here, in the path of the Red Army,' said Francis.

'I see what you mean. I'll look into opportunities to secure a better position. Now let's forget about the army and have a good time, shall we?' she asked him with a sweet smile.

Melting in her lovely hug, Francis thanked the universe that he had found her. He wanted to hold her for the rest of their lives, and he was certain that Heidi was the woman he wanted to marry. He did not tell her that, but deep inside he was sure and hoped that she felt the same way. After he was going to be released from the hospital he would let his family know about his plans. His brother had been in touch with him and knew about Heidi, but his parents hadn't been informed yet.

Robert and Ticla set their wedding date for the end of May. Robert was supposed to go and meet her parents in Austria and get married there. Afterward, Ticla would go with him to Germany during the week vacation they were entitled to.

In the next few days Heidi looked into the ads on the center's board and found a training session for the new communication equipment that was supposed to be held in Vienna for a month. She shared the news with Ticla and Karina and told them the reasons they should consider enrolling in it. Karina was all for going, but Ticla was reluctant, not wanting to be apart from Robert. Heidi talked about this opportunity with Francis, who was happy to hear about it. Actually, he was so pleased with Heidi's determination to follow his advice that he encouraged Robert to persuade Ticla to go too. Francis knew that the girls shared a special bond and Heidi would have been happier if they went together. Vienna was a safer place than Pilsen, and from there they could get a much better placement.

It was the beginning of March when the three girls left Pilsen for Vienna via Prague. The men had just been released from the hospital and started to work at the German military base in Pilsen. Francis had landed a teaching and training position within the department, and Robert a clerical job at the enrollment quarter. Their departure was tearful, but it was for the best, for they were at least temporarily sheltered from the horror of the war. The men promised to keep in touch and, one way or another, to be reunited with them soon.

Right after they arrived in Prague Heidi and Ticla felt the impact of being apart from the men they loved, and started to wonder if the training enrollment wasn't a mistake after all. But the beauty of the city impressed them so much and with Karina's help they coped with reality easier. Prague had something majestic and charming that even the war had not destroyed: the nineteenth century architecture of the elegant buildings, the pigeons flying over the large plazas, the tall cathedral towers measuring time with powerful bells and the beautiful gardens, which at that time of year started to bloom under the spring sun. The three friends spent their spare time exploring the beauty of the capital city. Heidi and Ticla managed to talk to Francis and Robert over the phone a few times, and that was enough to keep their spirits high and allowed them to enjoy their stay.

When the week was over, they were transferred to Austria for the remaining training period. It was Karina's turn to be in awe when they reached Vienna. Heidi felt like a local in the capital of the waltz, and with pride and excitement guided her friends through the centuries-old streets. In a way, the entire training period felt like a vacation, despite the fact that news from the front was quite disturbing at times.

All Ticla could think about was her upcoming wedding and Robert. Heidi understood her feelings, since she herself was thinking of Francis. Karina, on the other hand, felt free as a bird and grateful for the opportunity to travel and see new places.

'I cannot wait to go back to Pilsen. I miss Robert so much,' Ticla said, longing for her lover.

'Don't complain again, my friend. In three weeks we will be back, and you'll have enough time to plan your wedding. Maybe you should look for a nice dress while we are still in Vienna. What do you think?' said Heidi, trying to lift her friend's spirit.

The three of them were enjoying a calm evening in the backyard. Occasionally the trainees gathered there at the end of the day to unwind and relax under the warm breeze of late March.

'I can do that, I suppose. Oh, I hope Robert misses me as much as I miss him. What do you think?' Ticla asked in a melancholic tone.

Heidi was thinking the same thing about Francis, but she did not want to show it. Instead, she assured Ticla that her fiancé must have felt miserable too because of her being away. Karina did not have anybody waiting for her, and all she needed was right there where she was. Furthermore, she really liked Vienna, and the thought of going shopping for Ticla's wedding dress was quite appealing.

'Well, I believe we should go out tomorrow after class and look for a dress. In fact, it's a brilliant idea to pick the dress from Austria, your country!'

Ticla's face became radiant and her melancholic mood disappeared instantly, replaced by excitement.

'That is exactly what I'll have to do tomorrow! How come it didn't crossed my mind sooner. My wedding dress purchased from Vienna…that is perfect. I don't think I'll be able to sleep tonight! I'll be dreaming of the dress. Heidi, do you know any stores around here that might have something appropriate?'

'I'm sure we can find some boutiques to choose a nice dress from,' Heidi responded, feeling happy for her friend.

The next day didn't go as expected. Training took longer than usual and by the time the students were dismissed it was almost evening, and they had no time to go shopping. Ticla felt like a child who has been robbed of her favorite toy. Her friends had to find a way to consol her by discussing plans for her upcoming wedding day. Later that week, Ticla bought her dress from a small but elegant store in Vienna. It was made of soft white chiffon with a simple bodice, boat shape cut around the shoulders, and a full voluminous skirt at calf length. The sales lady advised her also to buy a silk white rose broche for her hair. With that, Ticla was all set for her big day. Heidi and Karina admired her sincerely, imagining the wedding Ticla was so excited about. Her happiness was contagious and all three of them were caught up in Ticla's wedding dream. Unfortunately, they would not be able to attend the event, since it was taking place in Ticla's home town, but being part of the preparation was enough to feel the wedding spirit.

The next day started like a beautiful spring day, and for once it matched Ticla's good mood following the dress purchase. It was already the beginning of April, but nature looked as if it were way ahead of the season. The morning courses were interesting and Heidi had a good understanding of the lectures, enjoying some of the challenging parts.

When she had a few minutes for herself she allowed her thoughts to fly back to Pilsen, where Francis was.

She missed him dearly. She had taken his advice to come to Vienna for the training, but she would rather never have left Pilsen only to be with him. In a way, she had wanted to put their relationship to a test and see how it felt being apart, and maybe he needed to do the same. Now she knew for certain that she had strong feelings for him and could not wait to see him again. It almost hurt being alone. Her heart was heavy, and as much as she tried to keep her feelings to herself, she knew that Karina noticed her heartache. Finally, she now understood her sister's sadness upon coming home from Grof Hoiu's castle two summers ago while being in love with Hans. At the time she had been too young, and did not know how to react or help Teresa. Love was magnificent when the lovers were together, and torture when they were apart. Also, her love for Francis put everything in perspective: the war was still the monster in waiting, but somehow she felt stronger and less afraid of it. The sense of togetherness gave her hope and purpose in life. Heidi was always fond of her family and roots. Her father had instilled a sense of belonging in her at an early age, but now, for the first time, she had found her true self and place in the world. She would fight for herself and her loved ones until her last breath. The war would eventually end, but what she learned along the way would help her to carry on no matter what. And what a journey her life would be!

On the evening of April 3rd, all hell broke loose. The alarm systems went off across Vienna, announcing an unexpected air strike. The students complied with the emergency procedure and rushed to the shelter.

'My Goodness, I can never get used to these alarms, even though we initiated so many during our service in Pilsen. Do you think they would drop bombs on Vienna?' Ticla asked Heidi once they reached the safe room in the building's basement.

Heidi squeezed her friend's hand and looked around to locate Karina. The German girl was just coming through the door trying to find them.

'I was among the last girls to leave the training room, and before I was out the door the teacher was talking on the phone to the Major State. I overheard that the Allies' targets are further east of Vienna. They will only fly over the city. I hope that is right.' Karina said.

'It's still daylight outside. It doesn't seem like Vienna could be their destination at this time,' Heidi reasoned.

'Do you think Pilsen is safe?' Ticla added, worrying about Robert.

Seeing how much she cared about her fiancé, Karina's heart went out to her friend.

'I'm sure the officer said east, not north, Ticla.'

'I hope you're right, my friend. I hope we will all be safe and survive this raid together. What would I do without you two?' Tears of gratitude filled Ticla's beautiful eyes.

The roars of planes were heard outside. The people in the shelter stopped talking, and then the silence of the room was replaced with the planes' passing noise, and fear. After a while, the room went quiet again, and then the end of alarm went off and everybody let out sighs of relief. The enemy had passed by without striking. This time, the target was elsewhere.

That night they found out that Budapest and Bucharest were severely hit by bombs in the most devastating Allied attack on Eastern Europe thus far. The German bases in Romania suffered a second attack two days later, on April 5th, when the US forces bombed the oil fields and refinery plant in Ploiesti, about 70 km north of Bucharest. These events marked a big success against the Nazis and shook the confidence in the German leadership in Hungary and Romania. It may have been a turning point for the war.

Ten days later, Heidi, Ticla and Karina left Vienna. They could not wait to return to Pilsen and be reassured that life could bring them warm moments of love and solace, stolen from uncertain dangerous times.

Chapter 11

Heidi entered her room feeling exhausted. She was due for her shift in an hour. She had just met Francis at the Corner Café for the first time since returning from Vienna two days ago. They were both happy to see each other. There was no doubt that Francis missed her as much as she missed him, and their reunion was a blessing after weeks of being apart. But the question as to whether they were together or apart in war time was not one over which they had any control. Any day they could be called to their duties, and God only knew when or if they would be able to meet again. This was especially the case lately, with the war having intensified all over Europe and it seemed like the Allies were determined to push the German armies' limits. Francis told her about the air raids over Eastern Europe and the progress that the Red Army had made coming west. All these signs, in Francis's opinion, led to only one conclusion: the Germans were bound to lose the war. It was only a matter of time before that happened. It was not that any of them were pro-war. They were dragged into it without having any say in the matter, but being on the losing side of the barricade was going to be tough and risky. If only Hitler would have mercy on his people and stop the insanity before it was too late! Francis told Heidi that it was unlikely that something like that would happen. He had been appointed to train the new generation of the Nazi Army: sixteen and seventeen year old boys recently enrolled. His job gave him shivers, thinking that those teenagers were supposed to fight the American and Soviet armies.

Heidi was still thinking of all that Francis had told her, and felt hopeless about her future for the first time in a long while. Karina saw her sadness and could not understand what was wrong with her friend.

'Heidi, you are back. How was your date with Francis? Are you upset about something? What is going on?'

'Oh, Karina, I'm sorry I did not see you here. I thought I was alone. Oh, my friend, Francis is adorable and I'm so blessed to be loved by such a gentle, caring, and smart man. And he was so happy to see me, but the news about the war anguished me,' Heidi said, turning on the light.

Karina saw tears in her friend's eyes. She did not know what to do: whether to ask more questions or just leave Heidi alone to deal with whatever was troubling her. She decided to keep quiet and be there if Heidi needed her. But Heidi did not look like she wanted to talk, and decided to just lie on her bed, pretending to relax or sleep. In fact, she needed to sort out her emotions and thoughts, and deal with reality one step at a time.

When Ticla arrived home that evening, Heidi had already gone to work, and Karina was asleep. The fact that there was nobody there to talk to annoyed Ticla, who was eager to share her happiness with the entire world. Robert had been very affectionate, and their upcoming wedding plans had figured prominently throughout their entire meeting.

The month of April flew by quickly with the abundance of events that shook Europe from the Atlantic to Ukraine. More bombings in Romania and a massive air strike in Paris put the German occupied territory in jeopardy. The rebel resistance movements in most of the European countries disrupted Hitler's domination.

Francis urged Heidi to seek a placement in Western Europe, but no openings were posted at that time. For the time being Heidi did not mind staying in Pilsen, since he was there too. Ticla and Robert were getting ready for the big day, and spent most of their spare time together.

Sometimes Ticla came home very late, after Heidi and Karina were already sleeping, and the three of them hardly spent any time together anymore. When she was not out visiting Francis, Heidi and Karina would enjoy a nice talk and share gossips about what had been happening in the centre. Some other girls were already involved with officers of the German Major State in an unorthodox way. Martin, who still worked as a concierge, knew a lot about these affairs between certain employees and high ranking officers eager to pass the time away from their family and wives in much younger company. This was often facilitated by way of the exchange of money or favors. In times of terror and oppression, the young women could easily fall prey to more powerful and influential men. Heidi realized that the choices that one makes in life are crucial for success or failure. She felt sorry for the poor judgment of her co-workers, and knew that their behavior would only bring them regret later on in life. Karina had the same opinion about the infatuated girls who were stupid enough to pretend that they had found true love, and believed they would soon be replacing the officers' wives. In fact, they would end up being discarded like used napkins at the end of the meal.

'Heidi, I found out that the "ladies", as we call the mistresses in our centre, are planning to attend a party with their officers tonight.'

'This does not surprise me, Karina. Haven't they been doing the same thing every night for weeks now?'

'Yes, but tonight Col. Schloss advised Martin that, due to higher alert, nobody is to leave the premises, and everybody is to be on standby. It was written on the blackboard, remember?'

'Oh, you're right! I saw the note, but since I was not planning to go out tonight anyway, I didn't pay much attention. Do you think our "ladies" would go to town despite the restriction?'

'Oh yes. You just wait and see. They'll find a way around it. It would be too boring for them to stay in, don't you think?'

'Where is Ticla? Still working?' Heidi wondered.

'I left her by the telex machine. I think she's found a way to communicate with Robert by telegram. When he is on duty at telex they can do that. She is so in love... and so are you, isn't it?' Karina touched on the subject with diplomacy.

'Yes I believe I am. Francis is a wonderful man. I'm so lucky he fell in love with me. After all, I'm an ordinary girl from Traisen, whereas he is from a wealthy family from Vienna.'

'Heidi, do not underestimate your qualities. I have never told you before, but you are a wonderful young woman. Your value lies in your caring heart and your wisdom, in your ability to touch other people's lives and bring them joy. I'm so blessed to have gotten to know you and have you around, my friend,' said Karina.

'Karina, I did not know you thought so highly of me!' Heidi looked both surprised and pleased.

'Now you know... Back to Francis, I think you two will end up getting married also.'

'I don't know, my friend. The future is so uncertain, I cannot see that far. We take it one day at a time, and try to make the most of it. I feel like my life is somehow on hold until the war is over, if it actually ever ends...'

'I know what you mean. I feel the same... sacrificing my youth for a later time. Dreadful destiny, huh?'

'In times like these, we should count our blessings and keep going, don't you think?

'See, now you understand what I said before about your wisdom. This is why I'm happy to have you around. You always find a way to encourage me.'

'Now you've made me all emotional. Come here and give me a hug.'

The two friends smiled and hugged each other with warmth. They spent the rest of the evening doing small chores, and by the time they were ready to go to bed, Ticla stormed into the room, bringing news.

'Heidi, Karina, you would not believe what is happening in the other wing of the building!'

'Ticla, you finally decided to come to the bedroom? I thought you would fall asleep on the telex machine,' Heidi said sarcastically, while Karina started to laugh.

Ticla paused for a moment, and then she laughed too. She and Robert had been chatting for hours before she realized how late it was. It was good to stay in touch any way they could. On her way back to her room she noticed something happening on the other side of the hallway and decided to investigate for a bit. What she discovered was hilarious and risky at the same time.

'All right, I know it's late and you wanted to sleep, but what I'm going to tell you now will keep you awake for a while longer. In Room 22, four girls, the ones that befriended the German officers from the Major State and go to parties almost every night, were leaving the building by descending on a rope made of bed-sheets knotted together out of the window to the backyard, and then to the street. Can you believe it?'

Karina gave Heidi a knowing look. It confirmed what she had heard that afternoon. The "ladies" found a way to meet their married lovers. How foolish they were to take all that risk.

'So, this is how they got out. I'm wondering how they'll get back in before dawn.'

'Well, I'm not going to stay awake and wait for them to come back. It is funny enough that they practically jumped out the window for a drink and a roll in the hay,' Heidi said.

'You're right. Let's call it a night and have some rest. Good night!' Karina said, and Ticla rushed to her bed too.

'Good night.'

The light was turned off, and the room went quiet. The three friends were fast asleep in no time.

Loud voices were heard throughout the hallway in the silence of the night. They came from both outside and inside the building. Heidi woke up feeling tired and scared. So did Karina, and when they started talking, Ticla turned, saw the night light on, and propped herself on one elbow, looking around with sleepy eyes.

'What is going on? Is it an alarm?'

Heidi urged her to keep quiet, trying to make sense of the voices from outside their room.

'No, no alarm, but let's listen carefully.'

The noises from the hallway seemed like a woman's cry for help and they could hear rushing steps passing by their door.

'There is an injured girl who fell out of the window at the back of the building. Please open the front door and see how badly she hurt herself,' a female voice pleaded, sounding desperate.

'What are you saying? Who fell out the window? Where?', one of the on duty soldiers said.

That was enough for the three friends to jump out of bed and to rush toward the door, with bare feet and in pajamas. When they stepped into the brightly lit hallway they saw two of the "ladies" talking with the guard, while Col. Schloss was coming down the stairs to see what all the noise was about. Heidi, Ticla and Karina stopped in their tracks.

The officer's voice thundered throughout the building. 'What is this disorder in the middle of the night?'

The soldier took up a straight pose and saluted his superior before reporting the incident and asking permission to investigate what he was told. Then, everybody followed quickly to the back wing of the building and entered a room. The window was wide open and from one of the bed's legs a rope made of blue bed sheets went over the window sill and hung outside along the exterior wall. Col. Schloss went straight to the window and looked down outside. When he turned toward what now seemed quite an audience which filled the room, he was livid with anger.

More girls in pajamas, and two more guards came to the scene, wondering what was going on.

'Corporal, take the names of these two employees who climbed the window, and the two down there in the yard. Send two guards outside and assess the condition of the injured woman, and bring everybody inside the building. Ask the nurse to take care of the medical matter if necessary,' the colonel said.

'Yes sir!'

Immediately the soldier saluted and left the crowded room. Col. Schloss looked around, and continued:

'Everybody go back to your rooms now, and get some rest. Tomorrow morning at 8:00, assembly meeting in the dining room! Attendance is mandatory. Good night.'

With that, he headed to the door, while the girls cleared the way for him to exit. They were still reluctant to leave, being curious about the details of the incident. One of the girls who had gone out and was able to return safely on the improvised rope started to cry quietly. The other one was angry that their escape had gone terribly wrong at the end. Still, they did not know how badly the girl who fell from about five meters had been injured. Instantly Heidi and Karina went to the open window and looked down.

'Oh my God, looks like she is still on the ground' Heidi said.

'Yes, she must be in pain by the look of it. At least she is conscious. Oh, now the guards are helping her to get up.'

'She can stay on her feet. Thank God. She is limping but otherwise she can walk with a bit of help. Hopefully nothing is broken.'

Ticla came from behind, and advised them to go back to their room. Nobody wanted to upset the colonel more than he already was. The three of them returned to their beds but none of them could sleep anymore. They talked about the stupidity of the "ladies", and how it would affect everybody in the center. Punishment would surely follow in the morning. The thought of the meeting was frightening. Nevertheless, the whole story, as sadly as it ended, was quite funny and served the "ladies" right. Before they could fall asleep again, Heidi, Ticla and Karina had a good, heartfelt laugh.

The next morning everybody was in the dining room, most of them looking tired. The "ladies", all four of them, were seated at one table. One of them had some band aids on her arm, and a swollen ankle. When the colonel came, all of them rose and greeted him.

'Heil Hitler! I asked you here this morning to remind you that orders are made to be followed and that military discipline is mandatory. Whoever disobeys the rules will get punished, and military punishment can be tough. What happened last night is outrageous, and the persons who ignored my orders will face the consequences. Now, it is time to go back to work, except for the four of you that are culpable. You'll have to come into my office right now. Meeting dismissed. Heil Hitler!'

Heidi and her friends got up, heading to the basement into the communication room. Another day of war-filled news began.

For the remainder of the week everybody was restricted from going out into the city. Furthermore, Heidi heard that the four girls who had been caught the other night were grounded for two weeks and punished with two hours overtime each day for two weeks.

Since the month of May had begun, spring was in full bloom and so was Heidi's mood. She was happy and in love, and the hours spent with Francis were the highlights of her days. Often they met at the Corner Café, before going to admire the beautiful public garden in the city. A few times they paired up with Ticla and Robert and went to restaurants that featured live music and dancing. Francis was a good dancer and all the outings with Thomas two years ago in Vienna paid off for Heidi. She knew a thing or two about waltz and tango, allowing Francis to lead her on the music's rhythm easily. Sometimes the soirees ended with long conversations about the war's tactics and what was to be expected in the near future. They liked to be prepared for the worst and hope for the better. Francis always had news from the front, which he shared with Heidi, giving her good advice. What was frightening was that Germans continued to enroll young men in the army. All Heidi could think of, was her brother Johan. Teresa sent her letters every month and she knew what was going on at home.

A week before the end of May, Ticla went home with Robert to get married. The day they left was full of joy and good wishes which they received from everybody who knew them. She packed the wedding dress carefully and could not wait to get home. It had been almost eighteen months since she last saw her parents, and now she was bringing them a son-in-law. Heidi, Francis and Karina walked them all the way to the train station and waved to them until the train disappeared from their sight. After that, the three of them went to the Corner Café and had some celebratory drinks and cookies. Karina liked Francis and was happy for both her friends. After a while she excused herself and went back to work, leaving Heidi and her beau to enjoy their evening.

'You know, I'm happy for the soon to be married couple. They take big chances by tying the knot,' Francis said pensively.

Heidi looked at him a little puzzled. 'What do you mean by that? What chances?'

'Heidi, Robert will go back to the front one day, and God knows what could happen to him. I wish him all the best, but war is war, there are no guarantees he will return home safely, or at all.'

'Oh God, Ticla would be devastated if something happened to him.'

'Yes, she would be. How would she go ahead with her life afterwards?'

'She would somehow, but not without a lot of pain.'

'Let's say he becomes an invalid or is taken prisoner and is not able to come home for a long, long time. She would not even know whether he was dead or alive anymore...'

'Oh.'

'Heidi, I love you with all my heart. I cannot even put into words the intensity of my feelings for you. I know you love me too. It is only natural that I want you, and only you, to be my wife. I dream of a good and long life together, but I don't think is right to marry you before the war is over. I love you too much to be so selfish and marry you not knowing that for the years to come I'd be there for you. By the time I'm sent back to battle, the Germans will be losing the war. This is not a good position to be in. I do not want to put you in a situation of being a widow before we even start life together as a couple.'

Heidi listened to him carefully and did not know if his words were meant to make her happy or terribly sad. They did both, actually.

'What are you trying to tell me Francis?'

'My sweetheart, what I'm saying is that I want you to marry me...yes, to marry me....but only after the war is over. Will you marry me then, Heidi?' he asked, and went down on a knee.

Heidi felt a wave of warmth flowing through her body and instantly blushed looking down at him. She was speechless. They were in the city's large plaza by the dry fountain, decorated with Cupid statues. Francis was waiting for her response, while a few pedestrians passed by smiling at them. Finally, Heidi recovered her composure and said the word with great determination and happiness:

'Yes!'

Francis got up and lifted her off the ground, swinging her through a full rotation before he kissed her with passion. He was a very happy man.

'My sweet darling Heidi, thank you for saying yes to me, I'll be a loving husband and will always cherish you. We are engaged now, aren't we?'

Heidi caught her breath and said "yes" again. Her heart was jumping out of her chest. She was happy like she had never been before. Francis looked deep into her eyes, kissed both her hands, and said, 'I should put a ring on your finger now, but I could not find one single gold jewelry store in Pilsen. All of them were owned by Jewish people and they have all fled the city. I will give you my necklace. I have it from my mother and I know it's real gold. Here…' He took the delicate piece of jewelry off and held it in his hand showing it to her. It was the most exquisite necklace with a delicate gold cross. Heidi had never owned something like that. It was beautiful. Then he offered to put it around her neck while she lifted her hair, revealing her white skin. The moment was magic. He looked at her. She was beautiful. She took his breath away when they kissed again. Up in the sky the moon was round and bright, and the May night was star-studded.

When Heidi returned to the dorm, she was alone. Karina was on duty. She sat down on her bed and replayed in her mind the events of the evening, smiling to herself and feeling on top of the world. A few blocks away Francis was also day-dreaming in his dark room, too excited to sleep. He had told his parents about his intentions concerning Heidi and had their blessing. He did not know much about Heidi's family, but all he needed to know or have, was Heidi. She was wonderful, and he could not wait for the war to be over, to be able to start living his life with his fiancée.

Heidi's engagement surprised and pleased Karina the next day when she found out. She respected Heidi's wish not to make it public, like Ticla had done, since there was no date set for the wedding, yet.

The week Ticla was away turned out to be full of personal and public events for Heidi. Her love for Francis fuelled an optimistic attitude and sweet dreams, but on the other hand the war's developments and the pressure that the Allies were putting on Germans all over Europe, doubled by the stubbornness Hitler displayed for winning the battles at all costs, worried her.

When her friend came back as Mrs. Mathilda Grunne, Heidi had mixed feelings, but did not know why. It was mostly because of the war, but also because she had found a new sense of life that she now knew Ticla had had for a while. Ticla, being a married woman, was now in a different league. Heidi had started to understand that since she had said "yes" to Francis. The three friends stayed up a whole night to talk about the wedding and the honeymoon spent in Robert's town. Ticla was happy and more mature than before. She had a good time with her family and Robert was embraced with love by her parents. Robert's family was good to her, and made up for the lack of comfort and rough surroundings of their home, in a remote village in Eastern Germany. Since they had come back to Pilsen Robert had returned to the German Major State and was really busy with his job, hardly having any free times to see Ticla. It was frustrating for both of them, but they were a family now, and that made them stronger, united.

Chapter 12

The first week of June 1944 had the Nazi Army pondering a possible attack by the Allies in north-west Europe. Regiments of infantry were placed along the French and Belgian shore. There were already walls built to protect against a sea invasion, which would have been possible only at low tide. Mines were placed strategically on the beaches, and the Germans thought they had everything under control. Furthermore, the weather which was nice in May, deteriorated at the beginning of June. If the Allies' troops intended to land in Normandy they needed clear skies and an uncovered bright full moon. The month of May was full of action and the German superior generals were long overdue for a relaxing weekend. This is why most of them took leave on the first weekend in June to spend with their families. The weather was lousy, but that was a good sign for the Germans. They thought that they had everything under control and not much was going to happen that weekend.

Heidi was planning to spend her day off with Francis, and was looking forward to it. Since Ticla had returned, she had been feeling a bit under the weather. Maybe she had come down with a cold or something on the week after the wedding. She and her now husband did not look forward to company other than themselves, which left Heidi and Francis on their own as well.

Around 9am, before she was out the door to head into town for her date, Heidi was stopped by an internal order that everybody was due in the Communication Room immediately. Disappointed about the sudden change in her plans, she descended into the basement, followed by a very moody Ticla and a sleepy Karina. Once at the telex machine Heidi read the messages: "Massive landing of the enemy in Normandy.

Disembarkation by sea and by air! Code Red!" She took the piece of paper and gave it to Col. Schloss, who almost tore it apart while grabbing it from Heidi's hand.

'Everybody at the work stations! State of emergency! Nobody leaves the Center. Hurry, hurry!' he thundered throughout the old building. The girls were coming quickly out of their rooms, many trying to tie a shoelace or to button up the uniform while rushing to their stations. Some thought that it was an air strike coming over Pilsen, some were confused not knowing what triggered the chain reaction running throughout the building. The telex machines and the telephones started to type and ring. The noise level in the room increased quickly. The Nazis were hit hard by the Operation D-day that began that morning when united divisions of British, American and Canadian forces spilled onto the north Normandy beaches and began the invasion into German occupied territory in France. The French Resistance helped the Allies to escape the German attacks, and hit the Nazis where they least expected. Hitler was fuming with anger. A week later he launched a V-2 flying bomb attack on Britain as a response to D-day invasion. He was convinced that the V-2 bomb was his secret weapon that would allow him to win the war. For the rest of the month more and more V-2s were launched toward the Western Europe.

At the beginning of July, Ticla was felling downright miserable. What she thought was stomach flu had not gone away, and every morning she was sick, unable to eat or get out of bed before noon. She tried to move her shifts around for the afternoons and evenings in order to be able to keep up with her duties, but that meant that she could not see her husband as much as she wanted to, since he was mostly off duty in the evenings. Karina and Heidi were surprised that Ticla was feeling so lousy, while the two of them felt perfectly well. It seemed that the flu was not spreading as one would have expected.

One evening, when Heidi was coming home after spending a lovely afternoon with Francis, she found Ticla alone in their room, crying.

'What's wrong, my friend? What happened?" Heidi asked right away when she saw her.

'Heidi, I do not know what to do! I think I'm going to die soon,' she said, while a flicker of relief shone in her eyes seeing Heidi back.

'What are you talking about? Why would you die? Nonsense! I know the war is intensifying, and times are uncertain, but why do you think you're going to die?'

Ticla blew her nose and continued:

'Ever since I came back from my honeymoon vacation I've been sick, and I'm not getting any better. How long has it been now? One month? The nausea, the tiredness, I even feel dizzy sometimes...'

'Ticla, listen to me, you are going to be all right. The flu bug will surrender soon, and you'll get better.'

'Wait a minute, this is not all. I even missed my period this month, and sometimes I have really bad cramps, but that is all there is to it,' Ticla went on with sadness.

What she has just heard made Heidi think for a second, and then she turned and looked Ticla in the face:

'Did you just say that you missed your period?'

'Yes. I'm so messed up, I'm dying,' Ticla concluded.

'Oh my God!' Heidi exclaimed, while Ticla started to cry again, afraid of her future, or rather the lack of it.

'Ticla, stop crying, you silly! Do you know what all these mean?'

'Heidi, I'm so scared. Why is this happening to me? I'm so young and newly married; I do not want my life to be over just like that...'

'Ok, Ticla, listen to me. You have no idea, do you? Look, let's sit down and analyze your condition. You are nauseous every morning, you feel tired, and you missed your period: you may very well be pregnant, my friend. You'll have a baby, my dear!' Heidi started to laugh and put both her hands to her mouth, wondering if Ticla would be happy, or terrified by the news.

Ticla opened her eyes wide in disbelief. What had Heidi just said? She may be expecting a child? Oh God! She could be! All of a sudden she felt calm, and happy. The tears dried on her cheeks, and her eyes begun to sparkle. She was really happy. She hugged Heidi and thanked her for being there for her. Karina came in soon thereafter. She had gotten used to Ticla's mood swings, but this time she looked relaxed and happy.

'Karina, my friend, Heidi thinks that I may be pregnant. Can you believe it?'

'Heidi is a smart girl, I believe she is right. That is so wonderful, Ticla. Good for you!' Karina said with relief.

Heidi realized that Ticla's condition had to be confirmed by a medical professional in order to be sure and decide on the course of action.

'Ticla, you should go and talk to the nurse before you break the news to Robert, do you understand? You have to be sure before you start dreaming.'

Ticla agreed that Heidi was once again right. She was so excited that she just turned around and left the room to speak to the nurse. After she left, Karina and Heidi pondered the situation and talked about their future.

As expected, the next day Ticla's pregnancy was confirmed, and immediately the paper work began for her release from the army. When Ticla broke the news to Robert he was beside himself with joy. It would have been a continuous celebration, but Robert had not been feeling well lately either. Not like Ticla's, his condition was more serious, and a consultation at the Military Medical Office revealed that he might have had a relapse of his previous illness. He was bound to be released from the army based on his diagnostic. Nevertheless, before Ticla was set to go home for good, Heidi, Francis and Karina organized a get together, partly baby shower and partly farewell party, where they shared good wishes, heartfelt laughs, and as well as some tears. They promised to stay in touch and, given the fact that they had become like one big family for the last nineteen months, Ticla's departure was hard on her friends. On the other hand, it was seen as a sign of the normality of life, and hope for the future.

One evening in mid-July Heidi and Karina sat in their room talking about life and all that had happened.

'Heidi, do you realize that we started here as a group of four and now look at us: we lost Teresa first, now Ticla. It seems that the two of us are doomed to fight this war until the end. Do you think this is fair?' asked Karina pensively.

Heidi thought about it herself. It has been a dangerous journey and it was far from over. If anything, they grew weaker by being the only remaining two. The power of numbers had dissipated everywhere in the Nazi Army. To make up for the loss, the new contingent of soldiers was made of youngsters not much older than children. Francis was telling her about the regiment that he was training, which had the age average of 17.

'Karina, let's not become too depressed over Ticla's and Teresa's departure. To each his or her destiny! At least we have our good health, and we have each other. Actually, I have good news, and bad news to share with you right now.'

'Oh God, no more bad news, please. Tell me what it is?'

'The bad news is that next week on Wednesday, Francis will leave Pilsen to join the detachment that he instructed at an undisclosed location...'

'Oh Heidi, that must be awful for the two of you. I'm so sorry!' Karina understood how her friend must be feeling.

'The good news is that Francis's superiors will organize a farewell party for his and some other young officers' departure. And guess what? We, me and you, are invited and will attend the banquet. Actually, Francis told me that Col. Schloss has already been informed and he will participate as well.'

'What? Are you saying that we will go to a party organized by the German Major State? Good Lord, what am I going to wear? When is the event?'

'This weekend! We have two more days to get ready and we definitely should go out and shop for gowns, since it is going to be a formal dress code.'

'What? I cannot believe it!'

'You better believe it, my friend. Col. Schloss gave us the whole of Saturday off, and tomorrow afternoon we can go shopping. How does it sound?'

Karina was happy, and not afraid to show it. After all, who would not enjoy a party after so many months of work, work and work. Heidi had never seen her so exuberant. All of a sudden, Karina changed her happy face, struck by the realization that Heidi may not share her joy, since the party was associated with Francis' departure.

'Heidi, pardon my foolish enthusiasm. I did not mean to hurt your feelings. You must be upset about Francis's leaving.'

'Don't be silly. I'm glad you're happy and looking forward to this party. I'll enjoy every moment that I can spend with Francis, and I'll not let the fear overcome me. We will go and have fun. We all deserve it.'

The two of them started to dream about the banquet, and felt like Cinderella.

On Friday afternoon they headed into town to buy their dresses, and they did buy beautiful gowns, along with pretty pumps. The whole shopping experience was pleasant and made them forget about all the worries in the world, if only for a few hours. The next day Heidi spent with Francis. They went to the park, which was covered in wild flowers and high grass. They had a picnic under an old oak, watched the birds and listened to their songs, but most of all they looked into each other's eyes and imagined their future together in a better world. Then they went to watch a movie, one of the few that were still playing on a limited schedule, and in the afternoon each of them went to their places to get dressed and ready for the party. Francis was supposed to come and pick Heidi and Karina up at around 6:30 in the evening.

The girls spent a long time getting ready, and since there was no full-length mirror, they admired each other with great enthusiasm. Indeed, they looked elegant and beautiful. Their youth, paired with nice dresses and shoes, worked wonders.

Heidi's dress was the color of the midnight sky, with a figure-flattering cut and of floor length. Her copper hair was combed nicely, parted on one side and decorated with a matching blue hair band studded with small black beads. The contrast between the dark dress and the fair complexion of the skin looked somehow angelic. When she stepped into the black pumps and grabbed her black clutch, Heidi felt and looked beautiful. She was full of anticipation of meeting with her beau. The golden necklace with the exquisite heart that Heidi wore all the time, mostly underneath her button-up blouses, was now revealed on her décolleté, giving her an elegant rich touch.

Karina sincerely admired Heidi, but she herself looked stunning, as well. Her dress matched her green eyes, and hugged her body in all the right places. As accessories she had a decorative comb on her curly blond hair, black high heel shoes and a small purse with strings. The evening was important to her, since she had never attended such an event in her entire life.

Francis picked both of them up by taxi cab. When he got off the car to greet them, he was looking sharp in his German uniform with shiny buttons and polished shoes. When he saw Heidi, she took his breath away with her elegance and beauty. He took a bow and kissed her hand before helping her get into the cab. Then he also helped Karina, and when they were all seated, the car pulled into traffic, off to the German Major State Quarter, where the Banquet Hall was. When they arrived, and entered the big room, they saw that it was nicely decorated with wild flowers on each table. The crystal chandeliers hanging from above and the rich red marble floor were reminders of another era, full of glamour and better days. A live band was playing café concert music while the guests were taking their places at the tables. The hall filled up quickly with officers of all ages accompanied by elegant ladies. Karina spotted Col. Schloss sitting at a table with a group of officers and their guests. At Francis's table they were joined by two of his colleagues and another young lady who was working at the head office as an administrative assistant. She was very outgoing and engaged Heidi and Karina in animated conversation. The waiter came to bring them some light drinks and entrees. The atmosphere was delightful and they were having a good time. Francis was happy to be with Heidi in such an elegant setting. There were no doubts that she'd fit perfectly into his high society world when the war would end. She was gracious, smart, well-mannered, and breathtakingly beautiful.

Karina was taking all the glamour in. She had never seen such an aristocratic crowd, except in the movies. It all seemed surreal to her, but she enjoyed it very much. One of the men at their table started to pay attention to her, and soon she was having a good time, forgetting any insecurity she may have had.

At one point a colonel took the stage and the music stopped. He delivered a speech about the "glorious" German Army and its leaders, and at the end he wished everybody who was due to leave the head quarter in Pilsen farewell and a good time at the party. After that the main course was served. Delicious food, good conversation and music in the background passed the time for another hour. When the dessert was served, the band started playing upbeat songs, and the dance floor was filled with skilled pairs floating on the sound of the music. Again Heidi and Francis shared the intimacy of passionate tangos and fluid waltz, dancing in each other's arms, looking into each other's eyes. There were magic moments that evening that none of them would ever forget. They were able to get a glimpse of a good and normal life, if only for few hours. They felt the love, the excitement, the abundance of food, the confidence that nice clothes can give, and the fun and laughter that friends share. It was the perfect evening, the perfect moment stolen from heaven while living in the middle of hell. Tomorrow all would become a cherished memory, but the night was not over yet, and Heidi lived in the moment, feeling happy and in love. So did Francis, who knew that the party was the highlight of his life so far. The happiness he read in Heidi's eyes was so inspiring for him, and so overwhelming in the most positive way. They danced and then talked, and they kissed, and listened to the music.

Long after midnight people were still having a good time and nobody wanted to leave. The party ended at dawn, when private, military and taxi cars took the crowd back home through the silent streets of Pilsen. It was Sunday morning, and a beautiful day was beginning with birds' song and orange sun light. Heidi and Karina were dropped off at their old building. Francis held back the cab for another five minutes, not wanting to let Heidi go inside just yet. Karina was accompanied by the young officer she had met at their table. They were in a good mood and laughing frequently.

Once back in their room, the girls were still dreaming of the magic moments they had just lived. They helped each other to get out of their nice gowns, and then they tried to get a couple of hours of sleep before breakfast. However, they mostly lied in bed recalling the details of the party and how happy and beautiful they felt. By 9am, in the dining room, Heidi looked radiant and, due to her youth, nobody could tell that she hadn't slept at all. She lived on the love and happiness that she had the night before. Some other co-workers tried to find out how the party had gone and asked her lots of questions. Heidi let Karina answer, since her friend could hardly contain her excitement about the most important event of her life. Heidi preferred to keep her thoughts to herself and nurture her inner strength with them. Furthermore, her fiancé was due to leave in a couple of days and she needed time to herself to adjust to this quite saddening situation.

Before Wednesday Heidi and Francis met as much as they could and made plans for the time when they would be apart. Since Francis always encouraged Heidi to seek ways to move out of Pilsen toward Western Europe, they knew that keeping in touch would be hard. That was why they decided to have a base point where somebody always knew their whereabouts. That point was agreed to be Heidi's family in Traisen. Francis knew how close Heidi was to her family and it seemed logical to communicate with her via Traisen. That was the safest way to keep in touch with each other. Francis's parents knew about Heidi and their son's intentions toward her, but Heidi did not feel comfortable about contacting them directly before she actually met them. The main goal for both of them was to stay alive and survive the war. Until they would meet again their hopes and their love would help them take one day at a time.

Heidi received permission from Col. Schloss to go to the railway station when Francis departed. They had a tearful goodbye on the station's platform, along with other young couples that were going through the same agony.

Francis pulled her close to him and whispered in her ear. 'I love you more than anything in my life. I'll pray for your safety and for our chance for a life together. You have to be strong and take care of yourself, and always, always trust that I'll be there for you, my love.'

'I love you too. Please stay alive, and come back to me,' was all that Heidi could respond between tears.

Then he boarded the train and by the time he found a window to wave to her, the car set in motion. She stayed on the busy platform until her blurry tearful eyes could not see him anymore, and then another minute or so looking at the shiny empty rails that lay behind the train that took him away from her. When she returned home, she succumbed into Karina's arms, crying her eyes out and letting out all the pain Francis's departure has caused. It felt like everybody was leaving her behind for one reason or another: Teresa, Ticla and Robert, Francis...

Chapter 13

'Karina, I'd like to talk to you about the posting on the board. Did you notice it?' Heidi asked, full of hope.

It has been almost a month since Francis had left Pilsen, and she was trying hard to follow his advice and transfer somewhere to the west. The frustration about fewer and fewer openings was doubled by the anguish of not knowing anything about her fiancé. All in all, Heidi was feeling miserable and stressed. That was why, when she saw the opportunity to get out of Czechoslovakia, she was eager to take the chance. Of course, she would rather persuade Karina to go with her, since having a good friend to be with is always better than being alone.

'I saw the ad for two positions in Amsterdam at the airport station. I was thinking the same thing, but there is an age condition that we do not meet: 20 years or older.' said Karina with disappointment.

That was true, Heidi thought, but when one has determination there must be a way to succeed.

'Let's apply anyway and see what happens. We've been here for so long, and we have the training required for the job, maybe we can slip in without problems. What do you think?' Heidi insisted.

'Do you remember when we first met and I was being difficult to you girls? It was because I came here alone, while all my training class-mates were sent to Amsterdam. I was so upset about not being allowed to go there. It was again the age that made the difference, and I was too young. You understand that going there now would be a dream come true, so to speak, but would we be able to actually make it?' Karina said, sounding doubtful.

'Listen to me, my friend. You wanted to go there almost two years ago, and I want to go there now, so we will apply and see what happens. Maybe we'll get lucky. Let's go and sign in. We don't have anything to lose, do we?'

Before the day was over the two of them put their names on the applications and started to hope for an approval. Moving toward Western Europe became a necessity if they wanted to have a better chance of survival. The enemy pressured the Axis powers from every direction, and the Russian troops coming from the east gained a lot of territories that summer. It was the beginning of August 1944. The warm weather helped the Allied infantry troops to advance against the German Army. While each front was fought by a different country's army, Germany had to spread its troops all over Europe at the same time, since most of its war partners had surrendered to the Allies. Hitler started to bring in new battalions of 17 and 18 year old soldiers having had a short period of training, practically unprepared for the horrors of the war. Not surprisingly, the failed assassination plot on Hitler on July 20th, 1944 prompted the fanatic leader not only to retaliate against the plotters and their families, but also instigated his thirst for power and revenge at all costs.

Caught in the middle between the Western invasion of the British, American and Canadian forces and the Eastern pressure of the Red Army, Heidi knew that Francis's advice was the right one to follow. That is why, when the applications came back approved, she and Karina were happy to start packing and prepare for the journey to Amsterdam. In order not to carry too much luggage, the girls decided to send home some of their civilian winter clothes. In Western Europe army personnel was supposed to wear military uniform.

The day Heidi and Karina left Pilsen was a hot summer day, bright and shiny. The train trip took twelve hours, but it did not seem that long to them. The scenery captivated Heidi's attention and filled her with excitement. When they stopped in several big city stations across Germany, the people speaking German and the Prussian buildings seemed more familiar than in Czechoslovakia. Even the money they possessed had the correct value. All these details made them feel better and more optimistic. Passing by, they saw some buildings destroyed by bombings, the gory reminder of the long-lasting war, but even that could not alter the good mood Heidi and Karina were in. When they arrived at the Grand Station in Amsterdam, the cooler air of the evening embraced them pleasantly, and in no time they boarded the military bus that took them outside the city to the airport, their new base. After a brief checking of their papers, they were given a small room for accommodation. It being a Friday evening and the weekend already on its way, they were told to report for duty on Monday morning. Until then, they had two days of vacation ahead of them.

'We had a terrific trip, and now we have time off to visit Amsterdam. This is a real treat, don't you think?' said Heidi, sinking into her bed with relief.

Karina stretched her feet after kicking off her shoes. She was tired, but happy. Tomorrow her dream would come true. She would wander through the city she'd longed to see since she came out of training in 1942.

'Heidi, I cannot tell you how grateful I am that you brought me here. It means so much to me. Your guidance and determination really inspires me. I'm so lucky I had the chance to know you. We will definitely go and visit the city tomorrow.'

The tiredness took over them quickly and shortly after, they called it a night and went to bed dreaming of the next day.

Saturday morning began with the sun filling their small room and waking them up gently. After breakfast, they inspected their quarters and the surroundings of the airport building and tower, to become familiar with their new home. Following protocol, they wore the army's uniform, which in the crisp early morning air was comfortable and cozy.

When the first city bus came, they hopped on and headed into the metropolis.

'Heidi, look at these buildings! Aren't they beautiful? They look similar to the ones in Vienna,' Karina said with admiration.

'You're right! Amsterdam is a beautiful city. I believe we are already in the city centre. We better get off the bus at the next stop,' said Heidi.

When they got off the bus, a big plaza opened in front of their eyes. Pigeons were flying in circles before stopping on the centuries-old stone pavement of the square. The tower of the City Hall was standing tall, pointing to the sky with its sharp red roof. It shone under the morning sun, showing off its silhouette. They walked around, sat on an old bench, watching the city coming to life on the gorgeous sunny morning. A few children came out accompanied by their nannies, reminding Heidi about Elisabeth's daughter, the little girl she took care of in Vienna three years ago. The young children ran to catch pigeons, giving rise to a burst of flying birds above their heads, symbolizing freedom and joy. Karina and Heidi felt a sense of peace and normality to life. It was good, like liberation of all the demons and fears that they had harbored inside for so long in the East. Western life seemed better, even during the war. At noon they decided to explore more of the city's beauty, and ended up on a street full of boutiques which lured them with their temptingly decorated windows. The merchandise was nicely displayed and the quality and abundance could make someone forget that the looming war was lingering above. It felt almost as if they had landed on a different planet.

'This is so unreal! I thought that Prague and Vienna were the richest cities by the look of the goods and the elegance of the stores, but now I believe that the further west you go, the richer they become,' said Karina, admiring a window full of shoes for as long as she could stare without raising any suspicion.

'I lived in Vienna for almost one year and I thought that it was very wealthy, but I could still see the marks that the war had scratched on the overall well-being of Austrian society. Here, I'm amazed that everything looks so undisturbed by the war's plague. We should enjoy the day without over-analyzing and without making comparisons. Let's head that way: I can see a public garden down there.'

'You're right Heidi; we've been blessed with this opportunity to visit Amsterdam without the least worries. The sun is becoming very hot; we should hide in the shade of a tree in the park.'

They headed toward what looked like an oasis of green and colorful flowers, eager to give their feet a rest and their soul a recharging dose of relaxation. Before they reached the park gates, their noses detected an appetizing aroma coming from a little bakery, a few steps on the left on a narrow street. The temptation was hard to ignore and, since they had had nothing to eat since breakfast (mostly because they were too carried away by the city's scenery to remember about other needs), Heidi and Karina disappeared inside the bakery in an instant. The display of pies and cookies made them salivate, while the scent of vanilla and caramel filled their senses. There were a few other customers inside waiting in line to place an order. The waiting time was spent in choosing the right cake or pie from a variety of many kinds. When Heidi and Karina got their turn, their minds were set on a slice of apple strudel, a cinnamon bun, and a cheese pie each. They had only German currency to pay with, and that triggered a bit of a discussion with the sales person who was not sure that their money should be accepted by the store. The fear that they might walk out empty handed was excruciating, especially after all their senses had reached a no turning back point, and their appetite was enormous. The owner of the bakery came out from the kitchen to arbitrate the situation. Seeing the two young ladies in German uniform looking so disappointed about the small incident, he decided to allow the transaction to go through. The two starving looking customers left the store in a state of triumphant joy and could hardly contain their excitement, anticipating the taste of their purchase. With the warm paper bags held close to their belly, Heidi and Karina entered the nearby park searching for a bench in the shade. There were lots of wooden benches with peeling paint waiting for them, but none had the benefit of a cool shady spot. Since military protocol did not allow them to just sit down on the grass beneath a tree, they settled on leaning on a stone half-wall built around a man-made pond and look at the ducks that swam in it. The benefit was the shade of a large tree hanging above the water. Nevertheless, the air was hot and the clothes too heavy on their backs.

Heidi and Karina opened the bakery bags and reached inside for the first piece that they were about to savor: the creamy cheese pie. It was delicious. Neither of them had tasted such a culinary marvel since they had left home before the enrolment. Half-way through eating it, though, the heat of the August afternoon made them feel hot and on their foreheads beads of sweat appeared. To ease the discomfort Heidi took off her military bonnet and placed it on the wall beside the brown bag. She ran the back of her hand over her forehead to wipe off the sweat and felt the air brushing her skin and her hair. It felt better. Karina did the same and both of them continued to eat the apple strudel and started to relax and talk about food and sweet memories. To rest their feet, they sat on the stone wall, dangling their legs with relief. It had been a long time since they felt so careless and happy. The park, with its natural environment which reminded them of the beautiful places back home, the comforting food, and the bird's song made the afternoon perfect.

'What are you doing over there? What a shameless and forbidden behaviors for members of the Third Reich Army! You two, get over here right now!' a male voice thundered over the harmony.

Heidi and Karina froze in their position, not knowing what to do. The scare was almost painful. They looked toward where the voice came from and saw an angry German officer staring at them with hatred. The bite they were chewing on almost made them choke. Heidi jumped off the wall, stood up straight and saluted with her hand to her temple. When she could not feel the edge of the bonnet with her straight fingers she knew she was in trouble. The salute is the first and utmost important rule learned in the army. Breaking it can be catastrophic for one's military career. While Heidi looked around to find the bonnet and put it on, the officer was already heading their way walking on the tall grass, his face red with indignation. Karina stumbled around to do what Heidi was doing, her heart sinking in her chest. When the three of them were face to face, the officer, whose rank was a colonel, started to shout at them, full of rage.

'Which battalion are you from and what are you doing here behaving like peasants? I will report you to the Martial Court and have you thrown into a labor camp! I do not want to hear any excuses. You come with me right now to the check point at the Military Major State Headquarters.'

With that he turned and they had to follow him. Quickly the girls put the half eaten strudel in the bags along with the cinnamon bun they wanted to save for later that day, straightened their composure and reluctantly and quietly followed him out of the park. What they felt inside was a combination of fear, helplessness and anger. The colonel was marching under the afternoon sun eager to get to the office and punish the rebels. All of a sudden, for Heidi, the streets of Amsterdam lost the brightness and fun they had had before. Clutching the brown bag with the remaining cakes was the only reminder of the lovely day they had spent in the city. Karina looked even more troubled about the whole incident and in a reflex gesture Heidi grabbed her friend's arm and squeezed it with affection. They were in this trouble together, and would face it together.

The Major State Headquarter was in an equally majestic building in downtown Amsterdam. The walk took them more than half an hour. Given the circumstances and the summer heat, they arrived there exhausted. The colonel took them through some large rooms before finally arriving in an office guarded by a soldier. Inside, the room was elegant, with a big mahogany desk and a Louis XV armchair, along with a sitting area furnished in the same royal style. Most of the buildings that the Germans converted into their quarters belonged to rich old families that were dispossessed of their assets once the Germans occupied the areas. The colonel moved around his desk and sat down, feeling tired. Heidi and Karina stood inside the room by the door, looking like they would rather escape than take another step toward the middle of the office. Their legs were shaking, partly because of fatigue and partly because of nervousness.

'Present me your papers and identification!' the colonel asked firmly.

Heidi joggled the bag she was holding and reached into her chest pocket for the papers. Her fingers were stiff and it took her more time than the colonel had patience for to unbutton the pocket and hand him what he requested.

'Hurry up, I do not have the whole day to wait for you here. Obviously discipline is not your forte. Tell me your names!'

Heidi stated her name and Karina did the same. The colonel wrote them down and then pressed a button on the desk. A guard from outside entered, and waited for instruction. The colonel gave him the paper with the two names and asked him to verify them in the books. He complied and left the room promptly. Then the colonel looked over Karina's and Heidi's papers, discovering where they came from and what subdivision they were employed in Amsterdam. After an hour or so, they were transferred to another floor in the same building where there was only a long table and four chairs. It looked like an interrogation room. Bad sign.

Once they were left alone in the room Karina almost started to cry.

'My God, Heidi, what is it going to happen to us now? We should have never come here in the first place. This city is a curse for me. Two years ago I could not get placed here, and now that I'm here I'm going to end up in a concentration camp.'

'Shut up, Karina. Do not even say that word. If worst comes to worst we will end up in a labor camp, not a concentration camp. What are you talking about? It is not the same thing.'

'Heidi, do you think we did a war crime by not wearing the bonnets on a hot summer afternoon, or is the colonel overreacting?'

'I don't know, my friend, but I've learnt the hard way that the Germans in the West are more infatuated with discipline and pay more attention to details than where we have come from. Colonel Schloss was a lamb compared to this colonel. He's a wolf. Now we can appreciate more the freedom we had in Pilsen.'

'You're right. What are we going to do now?'

'Nothing, just wait and see.'

They stayed there for more than an hour and the room was cool, cooler than expected. They almost felt cold, or was it the fear which made them uncomfortable? Eventually they became hungry again and remembered about the brown bags they carried. There was no point in being more miserable than they already were, so they both started to eat the leftovers of the strudel and then the cinnamon bun.

All of the sudden they heard steps coming down the hall, and could not swallow the bite they had in the mouth fast enough before the door flung wide open. The colonel and another female officer came in, looking furious. Heidi and Karina stood up at once.

'Heidi Souisa and Karina Schwartz, have you both come from Pilsen?'

'Yes, we have sir,' Heidi answered for both. It began to seem like the interrogation she and Teresa had undergone back in Traisen when she was seventeen. She tried to shield Karina like she had done back then for Teresa.

'Did you arrive here yesterday and did you report to the Airport division?'

They must have checked everything by now. She answered again for both.

'How old are you exactly?'

At that point none of them responded. The colonel grew angry again.

'I asked both of you a simple question. I expect an answer!'

'I'm going to be twenty years old in October, sir,' Heidi managed to say.

'You are going to be? I asked you how old are you today?'

'Nineteen, sir.'

'Nineteen, huh? And you?' he shouted toward Karina.

'I'm nineteen… sir,' she mumbled.

'You too are nineteen, then. Very well! Our protocol requires that auxiliary personnel be twenty years of age or older in the Western regions. How come you two were sent here in the first place, not to mention the lack of discipline you displayed in public spaces? Where were you trained?'

'I was trained in Vienna, sir,' Heidi said.

'Answer the entire question. How come you were sent here, being only nineteen? That I want to know,' the colonel went on like a machine gun.

'It must have been a mistake about the date of birth. I do not see any other explanation sir,' Heidi said slowly after taking a deep breath.

That was it. Their little white lie was out in the open. They had put in incorrect dates of birth in the application that they had submitted. It was the only way they could leave Pilsen and come to Amsterdam. Now God only knew what was waiting for them. Karina started to sob, too afraid to face the consequences of their desperate act.

The colonel stared at them in disbelief. Were they insane? Who in their right mind would lie in an official paper? These two could not stop amazing him, in a very bad way of course, but amaze him nevertheless. Without another word, he turned and left the room followed by the woman he had come with. Heidi and Karina were left alone again wondering what would come next. They didn't dare to talk anymore about the wrong they had done, afraid that the walls might have had ears and someone could have listened to their conversation. They just sat down and finished eating, like the food was everything that they had left of their lives. The bun had lost its taste, but at least it gave them something to do while awaiting the colonel's verdict. Two hours later, in the evening, the door opened again and a soldier asked them to go with him. They were walked again into the sumptuous office where the colonel was seated at his large desk. When they entered he looked at them with anger, and said:

'Heidi Souisa and Karina Schwartz, you are culpable of clerical fraud and of not following German army policy. These are important matters that are prosecuted by the army's rules. I spoke to your superior at the airport outside the city, and he will decide what to do with you two, since he was the one who approved your transfer applications. Now you'll be taken back to the airport by one of the army's vehicles. I am very disappointed in you as members of the glorious German Army. Shame on you! Now go, I do not want to see you for a minute longer. Understood?

'Yes sir!'

'Heil Hitler!'

'Heil Hitler!' the girls responded at the same time, relieved that they were about to leave the building.

The trip back outside the city to the airport was so different from the one they had taken in the morning by bus in the opposite direction. The mood was now somber and the joy was gone. Nothing could have prepared them for this awful ending to a gorgeous summer day. At the airport station they were taken to the on duty lieutenant's office and interrogated again about the incident in the city and the doubtful circumstances that surrounded their transfer to that communication station. When they were dismissed, it was almost midnight and the verdict was to be sent back to Pilsen where they had come from. All in all, it was quite a light punishment for a rather serious crime in the army's books.

Exhausted and upset, Heidi and Karina went to bed and fell asleep in no time. After all, tomorrow would be another day. There was no need to suffer more for a situation that they could not change. At least the war had taught them that much: to live one day at a time.

On Sunday morning the sky was grey and dark clouds were hanging over the control tower. Heidi and Karina packed their suitcases and reported to the lieutenant's office to pick up their travelling papers and train tickets. They did not talk much and when everything was settled, the bus took them to the Grand Station in the city. By the time they boarded the train the thunderstorm had begun, followed by heavy rain. For a while they watched the sharp lights that crossed the dark sky and just listened to the thunder and the rain drops. The weather shared their angry mood and disappointment. At least the thunder storm protected them from a possible air raid or bombardment: trains had lately become targets of the Allies' war planes.

After twelve hours, on Sunday evening they arrived back in Pilsen. Col. Schloss, who was informed about their behavior and the incident in Amsterdam, gave them a cold shoulder and sent them back to their old room. The girls appreciated the fact that he did not punish them further. Tired and ashamed by the whole situation, they went to bed for a good night sleep.

On Monday morning Heidi went in the Communication Center and when she sat at the telex machine and started to work, the Amsterdam episode seemed like a dream: half nice, and half nightmare. She was back at square one, but she had learnt a valuable lesson. One should not try to live a lie. It always comes back to hunt or bite you. Those kinds of chances were not worth taking. Heidi knew that Karina felt the same way about what had just happened. With that thought, she put the story behind her and looked forward to new opportunities to achieve her goal and fulfill the promise she had made to Francis: to move somewhere in the Western region, out of the path of the Russian invasion.

That week, on the first afternoon they had off duty, Heidi asked Karina to go out to the Corner Café to lighten their mood and forget about the mess the war had dragged them into. The coffee shop, where Heidi had many sweet memories of Francis, looked different. It had lost its charm and the bohemian atmosphere. They found a table in a corner, and were looking over the menu when a man showed up at their table and introduced himself as Leon Kratsky from the police department. Heidi knew that she had seen him before but could not remember in which circumstances. Karina became scared hearing that he was a policeman, wondering why he had approached them. He was dressed in civilian clothes and was smiling.

'What can we do for you, officer?' Heidi asked with caution.

'Oh, I'm sorry. I must have given you the impression that I'm speaking to you in connection with work. No, no, I was just wondering if I could spend a few minutes with you, if you allow me. I'm off duty, and I'm not pursuing an investigation right now,' he answered.

Heidi looked at Karina, and then made a gesture toward one of the empty chairs at their table. Leon sat down and smiled with gratitude.

'By the way, it's my treat; please allow me to take care of the tab. Now, you may ask yourselves how come I know you.'

'Yes. It's not that I haven't seen you before. You are one of the usual customers here at the Café, but we've never talked,' Heidi went on with confidence.

Karina, still scared about the incident in Amsterdam, did not want to have anything to do with an authority figure, no matter how friendly he seemed to be. She just minded her own business and let Heidi do all the talking with the stranger.

Leon told them that he had noticed them for a long time, and had seen the handsome German officer with Heidi before, referring to Francis, and he thought that everybody could use a new friend, especially in uncertain times like those they were living in. His German was perfect, and his eyes gentle.

'My mother is Austrian, from Upper Austria, and my father is Slovak from around here. I was lucky enough to go to the Police School, and graduate just before the invasion to be able to avoid enrolment.'

'Officer...' Heidi started, but was interrupted right away.

'Call me Leon, please.'

'Well, Leon, we appreciate your friendliness and we sure could use a new friend who is sincere, like you. My name is Heidi and this is my friend and roommate, Karina. I'm from Austria and she is from Eastern Germany. The young officer you've seen me with before is my fiancé. He left Pilsen to go to the front a while ago.'

'Nice to finally meet you ladies and I'm grateful that you allowed me to,' Leon said cheerfully.

Then for a short while nobody said anything. The waiter brought a tray with delicious looking pastries and a pot of fresh lemonade. Leon had ordered it for all of them, and it took the girls by surprise. The afternoon passed by quickly, and his company was becoming quite enjoyable.

That evening Heidi told Karina that she should have been friendlier toward Leon and could have had more fun. For the next two weeks the three of them met regularly at the Corner Café, and always had a good time together. Eventually Heidi told Leon about their escapade to Amsterdam and the big scare he gave them the first time they met following that dreadful incident out west. Her confession explained the reservations that Karina had towards him at the beginning. Leon showed a lot of respect for Heidi, treating her like one of his dear friend, but it was Karina who intrigued him the most. The German girl was still shy, and it was a challenge to get her to open up to him. Both of them were looking forward to these meetings. The bond they shared after such a short time was typical of the fast-paced life people lived during the war.

The news from the Eastern front made headlines when, on August 23rd, 1944 Romania, a strategic ally of the Nazi Army, surrendered to the Red Army and decided to take the side of the Soviet Union in the war against Hitler. This act tipped the balance over the edge and shifted the powers of the Eastern European battles. All of the sudden the Soviets had a clear path toward Central Europe and help from the Romanian army, which was very familiar with the German Army's strategy and positions.

Heidi's biggest fear about fast advancing troops toward Pilsen was confirmed, and it was the time to leave as quickly as possible, as Francis always advised her to do. Having had a failed attempt under her belt only weeks ago, the chances of another transfer were diminished, but she was determined to keep trying. Karina, on the other hand, was too frightened by their previous experience, and more inclined to stay put than try to leave again. Her decision was influenced by the new turn the friendship with Leon had taken as if by itself: he was falling for her, and she was so amazed about her new feelings that she wasn't even sure what she wanted anymore.

'Karina, a new opportunity to move to a communication station in Brno was listed on the board today. It is still in Czechoslovakia, but further west. What do you think?' Heidi asked her friend, full of expectations.

'Oh, no, not again, Heidi! I'm scared of taking any more chances,' Karina answered honestly.

'What? You should be scared of not taking chances. This is what surviving is all about, don't you see? We cannot set roots here and just wait for our lives to end, when we have an opportunity to do something about the circumstances we find ourselves in.'

'Yes, you've always been optimistic, but I'm not, and the Amsterdam episode proved to me that we cannot change our destiny. It will always haunt us and bring us down no matter how hard we try.'

'Karina, listen to me: what happened in Amsterdam was a case of bad luck, and sometimes we have to lose in order to become stronger and win the next time. You cannot give up just like that. You have to get up and try again and believe that next time the outcome will be as expected.'

'I expect nothing good anymore. I'm sorry. I do not want to hold you back. By all means go ahead and apply and take the chance you want to. I wish you luck and I admire you for everything you are and have done for me, but I'm not coming with you.' Tears were flickering in Karina's eyes when she said that.

Heidi looked at her friend and gave her a hug, almost crying herself too. She understood that Karina was shaken by the war, and was trying to deal with a bigger than anticipated dilemma, one involving Leon. Her friend was developing feelings for the police officer, who begun to show a lot more interest in her friend. Love was the best thing that could happen to anyone, and from her own experience Heidi knew how intense these feelings were, and how they can take precedence over any other reasoning in one's life.

'Karina, you and Leon have something special going on, am I right?' Heidi asked gently.

Karina looked into her friend's blue eyes and let out a deep sight.

'I like him more than I thought. He is gentle and caring and really fond of me. Is this what love is all about, Heidi? Tell me my friend, because you must know better. If I get butterflies in my stomach every time he walks in in the Café, does it mean I'm in love with him?'

Heidi smiled, and talked softly.

'You cannot wait to see him and be with him, right?'

'Right!'

'You also feel like nothing else matters more than spending an hour with him around, right?'

'Right!'

'You think of him when you cannot go and meet with him, and wonder what he's doing and if he feels the same about you, right?'

'Right!'

'Then, my friend, you are in love with him, and that is wonderful. It gives you a purpose in life, gives you joy and gives you strength.'

'Do you think so?'

'I know it. I'm happy for you, and I believe that Leon will take care of you even if you stay here, and even if the Red Army arrives in Pilsen. He looks like a strong, wise man. Do not be afraid to share your feelings with him and to be happy. Life is too short not to take and enjoy all the blessings that come your way. I shall not say any more words about you coming with me to Brno. You found love and the meaning of your life here with Leon. I wish you both the best of luck. Me, on the other hand, I have to do what my heart tells me to, and I'll apply for the transfer tomorrow morning. I'm glad that, if we have to go our different ways, at least I know you'll be fine with Leon, and not alone. God bless us all!'

Karina stared in awe, processing what Heidi has just said. A wave of happiness and contentment came over her and her life seemed all of a sudden more bearable and full of new hopes, which was unusual given the circumstances. Heidi was such a smart and empowering girl, and she felt so blessed that their paths crossed and that they had made the most out of the time they lived together. It was now time for a change, one that both of them were ready for, and were at peace with.

Chapter 14

In the next few days, just before September 1st, Heidi's application for Brno was approved, and once again she started to pack her belongings and get ready for her departure. This time she was confident that she would leave Pilsen for good, and sent a telegram back home to her father about the transfer and the division she would soon join.

Karina and Leon took Heidi out for supper the day before she left, and the three of them had a good time. After all, each of them got what they wanted. They appreciated the fate that brought them together and hoped that the future would spare them from any further bad luck. The new pair was in love and Heidi was happy for them. Saying good-bye had a new meaning, because this time it was about going to a better place, or so she thought.

When she arrived in Brno and reported to the Third Reich Head Office, Heidi learnt that the accommodation building where the Radio Relay was, still needed work to be finished. It was a remote area 20 km outside the city, apparently still under construction. The personnel recruited to work there had arrived too early and it was decided to keep everybody for a week or ten days at the headquarters in Brno, to help with telecommunication work while waiting for the final destination place to be completed. This gave Heidi the opportunity to get to know the new environment, and the new city. She was always eager to explore new places. She was proud that she had visited Vienna, Pilsen, Prague, Amsterdam and now Brno. She was not in a position to look back and analyze, but the war, despite the hardship and the risks, had helped her to see places that would otherwise have been impossible for her to see, especially at that age.

From the army's point of view, Brno was similar with a German city. Most of the locals spoke German, and the German uniform was respected on the streets. She could see that the city was more civilized, and discipline was instilled in the army's forces. In a way, Heidi felt safer here than in Pilsen. Maybe that was what Francis meant when he persuaded her to go west.

The Communication Center in Brno was much bigger than the one in Pilsen. They employed also civilian personnel for the retransmission of the information received through the military channels. However, the original content was always coded when it was received by the non-army workers. The large room was divided by a thick glass wall on which the coded information was written for the civilian team to relay it further. The messages on the glass were written with colored chalk. They had to be written backward, like in the mirror, in order to be read from the other side of the wall. That was not an easy task, and only a few of the army's employees were able to accomplish it. Heidi volunteered to try, since she was able to write with both hands: right and left. Soon she discovered that she was doing a good job and was given this task for the duration of her stay in the city. She found this type of work enjoyable n and she embraced it with enthusiasm.

On her third day, she received a telegram from home. Before she had read it, Heidi prepared herself for the worst not knowing what had happened. She was almost afraid to find out. Her father told her that Johan, her younger brother, would be in Brno for a couple of days that week, before he was dispatched to an infantry regiment somewhere in Eastern Germany. He gave Heidi the address where she could find her brother on Thursday, and maybe even on Friday, that week. Heidi re-read the message a few times to make sure that she understood it correctly. Johan had enrolled in the army, and she knew nothing about it. Of course, she was too busy with her own life to even think that anything would change at home. Her brother has just turned seventeen in May and now he was enrolled in the army. Heidi imagined the anguish her parents must have been through when they found out, and how hard it must have been to see their only son taken to the army. She felt like crying for all the families that had to send their children to fight a war that wasn't even theirs.

Thursday, the day her father talked about, was going to be the next day. Heidi had to make some arrangements and ask her superiors for the afternoon off, in order to go and look for her brother. She could not sleep most of that night, thinking of her family, and of Francis. It was one of the toughest nights because she felt lonely and sad. Luckily she did not have those thoughts too often, but that night Heidi felt hopeless.

Thursday morning she woke up more tired than when she went to bed the night before. She worked half the day, and by noon she was restless and eager to go and find her brother. She did not feel like eating much at lunch and by two in the afternoon she received the pass to go out.

It still felt like summer. The weather was dry and sunny that year. Brno was a much bigger city than Pilsen, and, like in Amsterdam, the German uniform was mandatory everywhere if you were enlisted in the army. In a way Heidi missed the laid-back life in Pilsen and the freedom of wearing civilian clothes in the city. Walking toward the address that her father had sent her to, she was thinking back over all the years that she had been forced to live far away from home, and everything that had happened since she last saw Johan more than a year ago. Heidi thought that he must have changed and wondered how he would look wearing the German uniform. She didn't realize that, self-absorbed in her thoughts as she was, she had begun to walk faster and faster, and was already closer to her destination. She had just started to pay attention to her surroundings, looking for the building number, when she found herself walking toward her brother. At first she thought it was an apparition she was looking at, but when Johan smiled at her in surprise she begun to run toward him and call out his name.

'Johan! Johan!"

The young man opened his arms and embraced Heidi with a warm hug. He was happy to see her, and Heidi was beside herself with joy. She threw her arms around his neck, laughing and emitting sounds of happiness. Johan kissed her on both cheeks joyfully.

'What are you two doing? This is unacceptable behavior! Yes, I am talking to you!'

The words hit Heidi hard. She looked around, and behind her was a German officer standing tall and looking offended. Johan was in a better position to see the angry man, two steps behind his sister. As if in slow motion, he let go of Heidi and stood still, preparing for the military greeting, while Heidi regained her composure, and turned toward the officer with the same intention.

'Where do you think you are, at a farmers' market? You should show some respect to the uniform you're wearing, by not behaving like peasants.'

'With all due respect sir, he is my brother and we haven't seen each other in more than a year. We met on the street and we were taken over by excitement. We apologize, sir!' Heidi said, begging for some understanding.

The incident that took place in Amsterdam was too fresh in her memory, and she was scared that she and Johan would end up in an interrogation room as had happened with her and Karina. She could not believe how unlucky she was, to be in trouble again. No matter how hard she tried, she could not escape the watchful eye of the German discipline. Johan was still holding her hand, and no matter how old he was now, he looked to her like her little brother, and Heidi could not help but protect him. She looked at the colonel and felt his anger and disgust. Suddenly, something flashed in her eyes. When she turned her head in the direction of the flash, she saw a few bystanders, and a photographer taking pictures. Some faces smiled to her in a supportive manner. They were civilians from Brno, complete strangers from a foreign country who showed solidarity for a human gesture of brotherly love. Silent looks that spoke volumes for the siblings who displayed spontaneous affection, caught in a happy moment of finding each other far away from home, in such uncertain times. Encouraged by all these, Heidi spoke her mind with confidence:

'Sir, we understand that we were carried away by the joy of seeing each other in the street, and we are sorry if in any way we offended you. My brother was enlisted a week ago and he is in transit to a military base to serve in the German army. He is seventeen and I'm nineteen. I've been working for the Third Reich since I was his age. We are from Austria. I ask your forgiveness for any wrongdoing we may have done here today.'

'I knew that you must be outsiders. German people have discipline in their blood, but you, look at you, you are the ones that give a bad name to our glorious German Army. Shame on you!' He stopped and looked around to the crowd that by now had formed a circle around the three of them. After a pause he continued:

'Never, dare to be so disrespectful again! Do I make myself clear?'

'Yes, sir,' Heidi and Johan answered at once.

'Heil Hitler!' the Colonel said and then turned on his heels and left.

The people on the sidewalk started to cheer and clap their hands, pleased that the superior officer had left, and the siblings were left alone. Heidi and Johan tilted their heads to thank the crowd and went to find a place where they could talk privately, and spend a couple of hours sharing news from home and from the army.

'Sis, that officer scared you, didn't he? What a character! Are all of them so rigid?' Johan started to ask as soon as they were seated at a table in a small but cozy bistro.

'In Pilsen I never had a problem with my superiors, but everywhere else they seem to be so arrogant and strict. Let's forget about it and you better start telling me about the parents and Teresa.'

'Mom and dad were broken-hearted when I left. They are so concerned about me and you. They gave me loads of advice and told me to pass it all on to you. You must know by now how to stay out of trouble, so I'll spare you all the details.'

'Our parents are wise people, Johan, you should listen to them. What about our sisters?'

'Teresa is working at the wool factory. She is happy with the job. It gives her a distraction from the war, and all the bad news that we hear every day from the front. She must be in love with that man, Hans Ellis I believe that is his name, because she always asks the mailman about letters. She received a couple this year, informing her he was in the East, somewhere in Ukraine. Teresa was so happy to learn that he was all right. Ever since then she has continued to worry, and, as I said, work fills her days with other thoughts for a while.' Johan paused to sip the beer that was just brought to their table, along with a cold herbal tea that Heidi ordered for herself.

'Louisa, on the other hand, is as wild as a gazelle. All day long she spends at her friends' houses and does nothing at home. Mom and dad would like her to help out, but she just disappears and comes home when she is hungry. Last week, dad got really upset with her behavior and taught her a lesson. When she came home in the evening and sat at the dinner table he sent her back to where she had been all day to ask those people for food. Louisa went to bed that night hungry and angry. But, guess what? After that she started to come around and help mom in the house. It was so funny, but it worked.'

'I hope they will be fine. You were a lot of help for the family. Too bad you could not stay home. Do you know where you'll be serving, which front?'

'There are only two options: east or west. They did not tell me anything. Probably will be a short training period before I get dispatched anywhere. What about you, sis? I heard Teresa telling mom that you got engaged to an Austrian officer. Is that right?'

Heidi blushed, and looked surprised. 'Yes, it's true. His name is Francis. He is from Vienna. He was very sick last winter when I met him in the hospital. Now he is in good health and is working with young soldiers like you at an undisclosed location. We haven't been in contact since July.'

'Well, I think congratulations are in order then. I want you to be happy, Heidi. You deserve it.'

Heidi's heart intensified its beat, thinking of Francis, and afraid that she would become emotional, she changed the subject quickly.

'What luck that we were in Brno at the same time. Next week I'll go to my destination, the Radio Relay station in a farmers' field about 20 km outside the city. We have to make sure we move as far west as we can in order to survive. Do not forget that, Johan. If you ever have a chance to choose, always choose the west over the east!'

Johan agreed with a nod and looked at his watch, which was his father's. He had been given it before he left. Heidi noticed it as well, and almost felt her eyes becoming wet. She missed her family so much. Johan finished his glass of beer and the cheese pie they had, and said with a sad look, 'It is time for me to go back. I'm due in half an hour. It was nice seeing you Heidi, and may God help us to meet again all together.'

'I'll walk you back to your building. I'm free the entire afternoon. Let's go. I don't want you to be late. Discipline is important, isn't it?'

The late afternoon brought more people on the streets and they had to be careful to greet all the superiors properly, in order to stay out of trouble.

In front of the large door of the German Army's building, Heidi and Johan said their good-byes, making the moment as short as possible to avoid getting emotional over it.

On her way back across the city, Heidi thought about what Johan had told her about their family, and wondered about their future. Back in her small room she cried, letting all the tension and frustration out along with her tears, before sleep finally overcame her.

The next morning was a bright day. Heidi's mood was restored to a certain extent and she was having breakfast in the dining room with some other women, when she heard her name called out by a girl who was reading a newspaper.

'Heidi, this young woman here on the front page, looks like you! Or… wait a minute, is that you?'

All heads turned toward Heidi, and then they all got up to get closer to see the newspaper's page. Heidi was confused. Finally, when she heard all the giggles of her colleagues over what they were seeing, she got up from her table and came closer to see. The others moved away to let her grab the newspaper and read the front page. The headline read "Heartfelt vs. Heartless" in bold big letters. Below it was a picture of her and Johan holding hands, but looking in fear at the angry officer they had met the day before. The article followed below the picture. Heidi started to read it. The whole story was about the incident on the street the day before. The writer was sympathizing with her and Johan and criticized the reaction of the German officer. The reunion with her sibling was called heartfelt, and the officer was the one who was called heartless. Heidi smiled with appreciation for the way this had turned out in the paper. She only hopped that the officer himself would see it and read it, and of course Johan, but she had no way of knowing whether this would happen. Her co-workers pushed her aside to get a glimpse at the article and the picture. Heidi handed the paper back, and went back to finish her breakfast. After all, she became a very important person on the front page. She felt vindicated for all the sadness the German officers had caused her in Amsterdam and yesterday in Brno. There was still God's justice!

For the remaining days in the city, Heidi focused on her work in order not to let herself think of more personal and delicate matters. In a way she was anxious to leave that place and go to the fields where her station was. She wanted some peace and quiet and a place she could call a temporary home, with people who shared the same interests and work as her. That was why she was relieved when three days later she took the bus and headed to the Relay Station in the middle of nowhere.

The place was peaceful. The radio relay tower overlooked the hilly region like a lonely soldier guarding a deserted battlefield. The long and low building housing the dormitories blended into the scenery like a big dune between the curvy plains. It had small windows with wooden boards to close over in emergencies. The station at the bottom of the tower was a solid two-storey structure meant to weather the winds and the high snow in the winter. There was a navigation equipment room, an office for the supervisor of the operations, and a meeting room that served various functions from training to guest room, depending on the situation.

The personnel was limited to two guards on duty and two on standby, six female workers for the telecom operation, among which Heidi was included, and a lieutenant who supervised all the activities. When she reported for duty, Heidi was welcomed by Lieutenant Van Grover, a Dutch engineer who showed her the equipment and told her the basic rules of the site. She was supposed to share the bedroom with another five girls, and for the main meal of the day they all were fed by the neighboring farmers who were each assigned two people. The farmers' houses were spread between the hills and could only be reached on foot. The road that linked Brno to the Radio Station was a narrow dusty stripe in the dry weather and a muddy one when it rained. Very seldom did a military car drive there. Carriages and wagons pulled by horses were the mode of transportation of choice.

Heidi found the spare bed in the bedroom and put all her belongings on top of it. The other young women looked at her and then started to introduce themselves. Their names were mostly German and Heidi could not focus on any conversation that the others wanted to strike up. She was tired and a bit annoyed with the living conditions she had just discovered. Her thoughts were somewhere back in time at her parents' home, and even at the Communication Center in Pilsen where she had friends and a lover, and somehow all these seemed so far away and lost forever to her. She was not going to cry feeling lonely, but deep inside she was sad. Ever since she had seen her brother Johan in military uniform, she had been beside herself with worry for his safety. It looked to her as if the worst of the war was yet to come, and the depressing setting of this new location reinforced her unhappy thoughts. When she unpacked her suitcase she made a mental note to send home her remaining civilian clothes, since there was no use for them in the farmland. That first night she dreamt of Francis, and in the morning her mood had visibly improved.

At supper time she and another girl named Cora, the short form of Corrine, went to the farm down the hill where they had a decent meal. The farmer's wife was from a Czech village near the Austrian border, and her cooking was similar to Heidi's mother. The food was a blessing in war time, and Heidi appreciated the hospitality of the farmer and his family.

By the time Heidi had become used to the new lifestyle and the new job, the leaves of the trees had changed color and fall took summer's place. Soon after, Heidi turned twenty years of age. On October 11th, 1944 she realized that for the first time nobody around her knew that it was her birthday. She decided to let it slip by unnoticed, and did not give it another thought, trying to put aside all the sadness and sorrow of her loneliness. Two decades of her life were gone. She counted her blessings: good parents, loving siblings, dear friends lost along the way, and a love worth hoping and living for. Would the new decade be as good as the past ones? The answer was unknown.

Chapter 15

Surprisingly for November, it was a bright nice day. The plains and hills were almost grey where the grass had changed color after the dry summer. The leaves were long gone from the trees, and the only green patches in the scenery were the pine trees which climbed up to the heights. The mountains in the background stood tall as the train approached the peaceful little town of Traisen.

The man was feeling anxious to arrive. It has been a few months that he had been dreaming of this moment. The war had got in his way, and he could not do it sooner. Ironically it was the war that had facilitated this trip for him, and despite the anguish of what would follow in about two weeks time, right now he was happy for what he would do with the remaining time before going back to the frontline. He had just spent a week with his parents. They looked so much older than they were, and since he has seen them last time they had acquired some silent illnesses which made their lives harder than they already were. It was only the house itself that seemed unchanged and the homey feeling that exuded from it. When he left, he almost broke his parents' heart. The dreadful moment hunted him along this train trip, but he tried to think of better moments that might lie ahead.

The train pulled into Traisen station shortly after noon, and he got off on the platform. He took a deep breath of the mountain air, looked at the yellow building of the station that was bright in the sun, shook his army boots, straightened his military coat, brushed his fingers over the casket's brim, and started to walk toward the street. His sense of direction helped him spot the way to the main street, to the Town Hall. He walked slowly, taking in the appearance of the town. He was pleased to see that even during the war people in Traisen were taking care of their surroundings. Some pedestrians he crossed paths with were looking admiringly at him, and greeted him. People were friendly too, he thought. He crossed a bridge over Traisen River and arrived at the city's square, guarded by a few leafless old trees, before he turned right on the main street toward Town Hall.

When he entered the building, he looked for someone to ask a question. Some people were waiting in the hallway for their turn to receive their monthly food stamps. All of them turned toward the newcomer and looked him up from head to toe, not knowing who the stranger was. Most of the waiting area was filled with women. They were all ready to start a conversation with him. This made him smile, and he greeted them courteously.

'Good Afternoon! I'm just wondering if anyone can help me with a piece of information. I take it that you are locals, and in this close-knit community anybody knows everybody,' he said in an appreciative tone.

'Good afternoon, officer! You don't look like you are from around here, are you?' A middle-aged woman answered his greeting.

'You are right, indeed! I'm only visiting Traisen, and I would like to meet with the Souisa family. Do you, good people, know by any chance where I can find them?' the stranger asked politely.

'Souisa, did you say? Could you tell me more about them? Maybe I can figure out who you are looking for,' the woman said.

The other ones started to whisper among themselves, trying to guess who this officer was looking for. The man looked at them hopefully.

'Mister Souisa is a shoe master. Maybe you know him: Franz Souisa.'

'Oh, you should have told us that from the beginning. Of course we know him. He has two grown-up daughters that were in the army. Wait a second, I think one is still in the German Forces, and now his only son was enlisted not too long ago.'

'There is truth in what you've just said. I'm looking for this same family. Could you show me the direction to their home, please?' The man was happy to learn that he was on the right track in his mission.

The woman paused and then she spoke slowly.

'What is that you want with the Souisas? Good Lord, you do not bear some bad news about their kids, do you?' She asked with a terrified look.

The stranger quickly made a negative gesture with his hand.

'Oh no, God no! I sure hope everybody in the family is well at this time. I'm here to visit them for a totally different reason. I'm sorry I scared you by coming here in Traisen. I should have known better, and told you up front that I do not bear bad news for anyone in this community.'

A sigh of relief crossed the old tall hallway. People looked at him with less anxiety now, and the same woman started to give him all the information he needed to reach his destination. He thanked them with profound appreciation and then he left the building. Outside, the sun warmed the November day and it was pleasant to walk to the address he was given. He felt happy and content. He did not notice that, right after him, his informer rushed out of Town Hall and headed in the opposite direction in a big hurry. The woman was almost running toward the wool factory, hardly catching her breath when she entered the plant.

The way to the Souisa residence was pretty much like going back to the station. He crossed the bridge again, and stopped for a minute to look at the playful fish that swam in the rapid water. He gathered his thoughts, preparing himself for the meeting. Then he looked up toward the mountains and the sky, like a ritual for getting strength. After a while he started to walk again at a slow pace, taking in all the surroundings. The air smelled like freedom, the day was getting brighter for him. Finally he would do what he had been waiting to do for a long time now. When he arrived in front of the three storey house, he looked up at the third floor for a few seconds before reaching for the iron gate's handle to get to the narrow stairs on the side of the house. After he had climbed them half-way through, he heard the gate opening again behind him with a squeak. He turned around and saw a young lady staring at him while catching her breath, a sign that she had run. He almost had a vision of another young lady that never left his mind, but the person he was seeing was somebody else. She started to smile at him, visible relieved. He smiled back to her.

'Francis? Is that you?' the young woman asked him.

'Err, yes. You must be Teresa, Heidi's sister, aren't you?' he replied.

'Oh God, it is you after all... and you're right, I'm Heidi's sister. What a surprise to see you here. But forgive my manners, please go on, let's walk upstairs and inside the house.'

They shook hands and together went up to the third floor and inside the house.

Josephina Souisa was cooking in the kitchen when she heard voices in the hallway. She looked at the big clock on the wall and saw that it was only a quarter after one in the afternoon. Teresa would still have been at work at that time, and Louisa was helping the farmer up the hill to sort the potatoes they harvested that fall. It was one of the few days when Louisa did something useful after school. Who could have just come in and be talking so animatedly? She pulled the cooking pot from the stove, dried her hands with a kitchen towel, and headed toward the entrance. What she saw frightened her: a young German officer was talking to her older daughter, Teresa. "Good Lord, spare us the bad news. Let my children be safe and alive", it was her first thought, and instinctively she made the sign of the cross over her chest.

'Mom, we have a visitor!' she heard Teresa tell her. Josephina could not be more surprised by what she saw and heard. It was very unusual for an officer to visit people in Traisen unless they had some news to deliver in person about the young soldiers who were in the army. Her heart beat intensified and her legs grew weak. She had to pull a chair up and sit down. Teresa saw that her mother was pale and realized that she was scared by Francis's arrival. She herself did not know what brought Heidi's fiancé here to their home, but from Francis's eyes she knew it was something good, and nothing to worry about.

'Mom, come here, I want you to meet Francis, Heidi's fiancé. He came to visit us. There is nothing wrong. You can relax and invite this gentleman to have a seat. I'll go and tell dad. Are you all right, mom?'

Josephina's color came back to her cheeks. She now felt embarrassed by her behavior and her lack of hospitality. She got up from the chair and went to greet Francis and give him a heartfelt hug. The man was moved by the warm welcome and took a seat as Heidi's mother indicated. He looked around and saw that the house was clean and tidy, very small compared with his parents' mansion, but cozy and warm nevertheless. He felt like he belonged to this family, and being part of Heidi's nest seemed so right to him. Then, a door opened on the left side of the living room and Teresa came in followed by a man. He was walking with a cane, but held himself tall and his eyes were sharp and witty. Francis rose from the chair and stepped toward him to introduce himself properly.

'Mr. Souisa, please allow me to introduce myself: Francis Urbertal. Sir, I'm very pleased to finally meet you, and yours.'

'Mr. Ubertal, I'm happy to meet you in person. I have heard a lot about you, and all have been good things. I hope you come with good news, and my house is open to you anytime,' Frantz Souisa said and offered the visitor a warm handshake.

'There may be some suspicion about my coming here, but I assure you that it is an honor for me to meet you all. I have a short vacation and I visited my parents for a week, and now I have some important things to talk to you about, sir, before I go back to the battle.'

'First of all, it is lunch time, and the food is ready, so you will dine with us. Please make yourself comfortable and let's sit down at the table. My wife will serve the meal in no time, right Josephina?'

'Right, right! Teresa, please help me set the table, and let the men talk alone.'

Teresa followed her mother in the kitchen. Once they were there, sounds of admiration and surprise could be heard as the women started to analyze what had just happened.

The men stood a bit in silence as they gathered their thoughts. Then, Francis started to talk.

'Mr. Souisa, you must know that I have strong feelings for your daughter Heidi, and I believe she is the most wonderful woman I've ever met. I can see now where all her compassion and love came from. It is this beautiful family she grew up in, that made her the way she is. I command you for being such a good father. Heidi thinks the world of you, sir.'

'Heidi is a good girl. One can always count on her. She is smart too,' Frantz said with pride.

'I completely agree with you sir, and I want to assure you that I respect her, and love her with all my heart. This is why not long ago I asked her to marry me and she said "yes", making me the happiest and luckiest man in the world. My intentions toward her are most respectable and serious. I came here today to ask her hand in marriage from you, her father. I hope that you find me trustworthy enough to accept my request and I promise you that I'll never disappoint her or you, sir. In these days and times our lives are always in jeopardy, but if we all come out of this war alive, I'll marry Heidi in front of you, your family, my family, and God.'

'Son, you and Heidi have my blessing! I only hope that the future will be kind with us and ours. You must know that my only son was taken to the army not long ago and so far we know very little about him.

Thank God that Heidi could move a bit toward theWwestern region, and now she is in Brno at the Radio Relay station outside the city. Johan met his sister for a few hours back in September before he headed to the training camp. No matter how old they are, I'll always worry about my children. I'm a veteran of the First World War, and I know how dangerous the war can be. But why am I telling you all these? You yourself know the war better than I do now. I wish you to be safe and come home at the end of it.'

'Sir, thank you very much for listening to me and for allowing me the chance to have Heidi's hand in marriage. I know how the war destroys many families, and I do not want Heidi to be a victim of these awful circumstances. I won't marry her before the war is over. We decided to wait and focus on our survival. Once the war is over, we will tie the knot. It is not my intention to leave a widow and possibly an orphan behind. That is why we will remain engaged for now, and marry later.'

'I think this is a wise plan and I command you for having my daughter's well-being at heart. You are a man of honor and I'm honored to have you in my house. Now, let's go and have something to eat, and perhaps we can celebrate a little with a glass of wine. I still have a couple of bottles from before the war in the pantry,' Frantz said with a wink. They got up and went into the kitchen to join Teresa and her mother.

The atmosphere became relaxed and the four of them started to talk about Heidi. Then the topic changed to Francis's family in Vienna, and at the end it turned to what had happened that very day since he had gotten off the train in Traisen. There were some laughs about the way in which Teresa was informed by the woman at the Town Hall about Francis's arrival, and how the rumors that a handsome officer had come to see the Souisa family had spread quickly around town. Everybody was talking about it when Teresa left the workplace to investigate what was going on. People suggested that the stranger was looking for Teresa. Even Teresa's heart skipped a beat thinking that it might have been Hans Ellis, her fiancé with whom she had lost contact lately.

Frantz Souisa was glad that Heidi's future husband was a good man in every way. His daughter deserved to be happy. After they finished the meal Francis said that he must get going and catch the train to Prague, and then to Brno. His intention was to spend his remaining vacation time with Heidi, and since now he knew where to find her, he was eager to meet with her. After all, it had been a few months since he last saw her, and he was missing her so much. He thanked the ladies for the meal and Frantz for listening to him and being so supportive.

Josephina quickly put together a small package of some leftovers and fresh fruit and gave it to him to take along and share it with Heidi. When Francis said his good-byes, the women had misty eyes, and Frantz shook his hand with pride and love.

On his way back to the train station he felt happy and content about doing the right thing and asking for Heidi's hand from her father. The thought that he would meet her soon put a spring in his steps. Bystanders on the street admired the young officer, wondering what brought him to their small town.

It was already mid-afternoon. If he took the first train to St. Polten he could catch the connection to Prague, and from there it would be easier to get to Brno. With some good luck he could be there before midnight.

Back at the Souisa household, the official engagement of Heidi and Francis was the topic of many joyful conversations. Heidi's beau made a terrific first impression, and everybody had only appreciative words about the visitor they have just had. Teresa made a note to write Heidi a long letter about the encounter Francis had with the villagers and their parents. It sure was something to talk about, not to mention all the gossips that would follow.

*

It was raining all day in the outskirts of Brno, as November was notoriously gray in that region. But the rain did not bother Heidi, who was working in the communication tower. Her mood mirrored the weather, which could have been a burden for her, but in the last few weeks she had managed to live with her sadness and became immune to almost every emotion. Sometimes she wondered what happened to the optimistic girl that she used to be back in Vienna and even in Pilsen, but she usually brushed that thought away and tried to focus on the work she had to do, without over-analyzing her life in that secluded area outside Brno. If her sour mood was the price for moving west and being safer, she was willing to pay it. She did not interact much with any of her colleagues, only with the farmer's family where she had supper daily.

It was late at night, and Heidi was finishing the last paperwork that she had for that day. After that she would go and get some dreamless sleep before another rainy day started again. The war was getting closer and closer to German occupied territories. Each day Heidi's heart sunk with fear for the fate of the two men she loved dearly: her brother and her fiancé. She knew nothing about either one, and that was the main reason she lost her smiles and optimism. On the way to her small bedroom she tried not to think about all her fears for her loved ones which would definitely destroy any chance at a good night's sleep. It happened before on so many nights… She was about to start to undress and go to bed when the telecom went off and called her name. She jumped with surprise and buttoned up her uniform. Hesitantly, and encouraged by her roommates, she left the room and headed to the main office where she was due to report, based on the call. She tried to keep her heart-beat in check, but it was too hard to calm down all her fears of bad news.

When she knocked at the office door, she noticed that her hand was shaking. She took a deep breath, telling herself that she was a soldier and soldiers should be brave. When she opened the door her superior got up from his desk and came toward her at the door. He smiled to her and slowly he slipped past her and out of the office. Heidi could not understand why the lieutenant had left the room and left her there inside alone. Only then she noticed, in the dim light of the office, that she was not alone. From the chair in front of the desk a silhouette was beginning to rise. She only saw its back, but when he turned, and she saw who he was, Heidi let out a cry of joy and ran to Francis' wide open arms. Encircled in his hug, she laughed and cried at the same time, while he swept her off her feet and swirled her around in the middle of the small room.

'Oh, my God! Francis, you found me! You are here. I'm so happy, I cannot even speak.'

'Yes, my love, I'm here and right now you don't need to speak.' Then he kissed her, and all the words were swallowed in that unique moment of rediscovered love and passion. When they finally parted their lips Francis spoke with a grave voice:

'Go grab some clothes and let's go. I have a car waiting for us to go to the city. You've just got six days of vacation to spend with me. Do you want to be with me Heidi, my sweet Heidi?'

'What? We can spend a week together in Brno? Oh! That is wonderful. Come with me to pack a few things and off we go!'

They headed hand in hand to Heidi's bedroom, and Francis sat on an old chair while his fiancée threw a few civilian clothes in a bag. She looked so happy and beautiful even after a long day of work. When she was ready he took her bag and both of them went outside in the rain rushing toward the car that was waiting. The joy they felt was indescribable. All the way to the city they were extremely happy, not noticing any bumps on the muddy road, which were hard to avoid on such dark night.

Chapter 16

The next morning Heidi and Francis woke up late, since it was the early hours when they arrived at the hotel and fell asleep right away. The first look out the window told them that the sky had more rain to shower on the old city, but for once the bad weather had no impact on the young pair and the two of them could not have been happier, just because of being together. The hotel was a solid four-storey building with tall ceiling rooms. It had a cage elevator in the middle of the lobby, but as many other technological things, it was not working. This gave Heidi the opportunity to admire the elegant stairwell to the third floor where Francis booked the room for a week. Even late at night and under the dim lights, she noticed how much architectural character the hotel had. It lived up to its name: The Majestic.

Now, after a few well-deserved hours of sleep, the room looked fresh and cozy. The old style furniture was well maintained and sumptuous. It was the perfect setting for a dream vacation spent in the company of a loved one. Heidi was happy, truly happy, and so was Francis. They unpacked the few civilian clothes they brought with them, put aside their German uniforms, dressed like normal people and headed out to get something to eat. The parcel that Heidi's mother had given Francis the day before had been devoured right after they checked in.

Feeling comfortable and madly in love, they reached the street and walked toward a bakery where they could have a tasty breakfast and freshly brewed coffee. Seated at a small table in the aromatic shop, they indulged their senses while devouring the cheese pies they bought.

'I know it sounds odd but, to me, right now, this is heaven!' Francis said looking into his fiancée's eyes.

'I completely agree. My heart and my soul are full of joy and happiness. Your arrival was so unexpected. I had felt so depressed for so long, and now I'm overjoyed,' Heidi confessed.

'I'm happy that I met your parents and we received their blessings. It was something I've wanted to do ever since we got engaged. My parents are looking forward to meeting you as well. All we have to do now is to stay alive and wait for this war to end.'

'This is not an easy task, is it?' Heidi asked rhetorically.

'No, my love, it is not, but let's be optimistic at least now that we are together, shall we?' Then he leaned forward and kissed her softly.

When they finished their breakfast, they decided to go and see a movie at one of the few remaining theatres. It was a sad love story, but at least they were able to escape the November rain. They would have enjoyed a comedy more, but society was not in a laughing mood and most of the movies were sad ones. They also played documentaries with footage from the front, labor camps, and of course Hitler's appearances at special events. Heidi and Francis were not interested in those. They lived through similar events, and a movie about the sad reality would not have impressed them. The fictional story that they watched that early afternoon was a love story cut short between a rich American woman and her French lover who had to go to the front in the First World War, and did not come back. Heidi cried a bit at the end, being touched by some similarity with her own life. Francis comforted her and tried to cheer her up, which, of course, he succeeded once they were out in the rain again.

They returned to their hotel room for a little while. Francis had a radio transistor that he had brought from his parents' house and tried for a short while to tune to some news programs. He intercepted a Czech radio station and understood nothing. Then he gave up, knowing that news is always bad news, and not wanting to upset Heidi again. The rain drops' rhythm on the window sill made them sleepy, and, since the room was warm and cozy, they decided to lie down on the bed and rest in each other's arms.

'Oh, I know that outside is raining and the war is out there too, but here, now, being with you, it is heaven, my dear Heidi! Did you ever notice that your name starts with "H" as in "Heaven"? There must be a good connection between those "H"s!' Francis was holding his fiancée close to his heart, and started to caress her with love.

Heidi abandoned herself in the sweet pleasure of her lover's touch, before she herself felt the urge to stroke his hair and the nape of his neck while taking in the masculine scent of his shaving soap mixed with the rain. The heat of their bodies created a warm blanket around them, and their breath became heavier. It was an undiscovered and new pleasure when he kissed her. Heidi trembled in his arms and responded to all the sensations he gave her. His hand moved along her lean body lightly as a feather, letting her ask for more and making her move closer to him, while his lips never left hers. It all seemed like a slow dance on the horizontal plane of the bed, more like floating on a cloud. Heidi encircled her arms around Francis's torso, pulling him towards her. He gasped for air for a few seconds and then he looked deep into Heidi's eyes. He saw love and desire and lost himself in that blue sea of warmth and sweetness.

His hand continued to caress, but her clothes were in the way. His fingers found the buttons of her blouse and the skirt she was wearing, and gently, with her help, freed her from the first layer of clothes. More comfortable and excited by the exposure, Heidi lay there in the French underwear made of silk and lace, the very same she had bought almost a year ago in Pilsen, from Madame Fleur. Francis's eyes browsed her body, admiring its firmness, freshness and its perfect curves covered by the elegant undergarments which had a pleasuring touch. He was speechless, but his eyes spoke volumes about how much he loved her and how happy he felt at that moment. Heidi had thought about this moment many times before, but nothing came close to the emotions and the pleasure she felt just lying there under her fiancé's gaze. She was happy that she was wearing the nice French camisole set that wowed Francis instantly. The power of seduction was amplified, and it felt good.

In an instant he took off his first layer of clothes, while his eyes were glued to Heidi's sweet, flushed face, looking up at him. There was no embarrassment or fear, only love and desire in anticipation. The next kiss brought them close to each other and the touch of revealed skin sent grooves of warmth through their young bodies. There was air, earth, and fire around them for almost an hour. Two lovers as one body, one breath and one heart-beat, discovering each other, letting themselves float on the wings of love. When they could not wait any longer Francis held her tight and cried her name, almost in despair, before collapsing beside her on his belly, one arm spread across her waist, and the other underneath his body. He groaned a few times while his body trembled on the thick mattress. Heidi was too self-absorbed in her own overwhelming sensations brought upon her by this new experience to notice Francis's last relief lying beside her. When all was over, he kissed her again and then he spoke:

'You are wonderful! Your beauty, inside and out, is every man's dream. I'm so happy and so lucky that I found you, and you are in love with me. I will always cherish you, protect you, and love you. You can trust me completely, as I trust you. I cannot wait for the day when you'll be my wife and my love for you will have no barrier. But right now, Heidi, you rest assured that I love you and I have your well-being in my mind, and I will make sure you won't get pregnant, my darling. We do not want to complicate things during the war, do we? Relax and let me hold you a while longer before we go out for dinner.' Heidi smiled at him and he smiled back and, soon after, they fell asleep in each other's arms.

The next few days went by quickly. The rain never stopped, which kept them mostly indoors. That wasn't necessarily a bad thing, since their room became a nest of love and passion. When they went out they ate at some local restaurants with a homey ambiance and good food. Francis, being an officer, earned good money and he loved to spoil Heidi with the finest of fine things. One day they spent a lovely evening at Astoria, an elegant restaurant for Brno's elite, one of those places that not even the war could change or destroy. The patrons were mostly men in German uniform accompanied by well dressed women, but Francis and Heidi, both wearing civil clothes, fit in without a problem, passing for locals. After dinner, they enjoyed a glass of wine and some live music. A few couples went out on the dance floor. Francis asked Heidi to dance, and in no time they were swirling around performing a perfect waltz. They had a good time and were making life-long memories together.

The last full day they spent together was bitter-sweet. The anguish of Francis's departure troubled Heidi most of the time. She was a strong and well-grounded young woman who knew that all good things eventually come to an end, but this time the end was frightening her. The future frightened her as well. The present was all she had, and what she wanted to last forever: her and Francis together.

Francis, on the other hand, felt strong and brave. He wanted to make sure that his fiancée stayed safe until they met again, and spent most of the day teaching Heidi survival skills and giving her advice. That day he told her that should something happen to him in combat he would not end up in a war prisoner's camp. He would not come back to her unless he was in one piece and able to fulfill a normal life with her. He did not want to put Heidi through any sacrifice, knowing that she would be better off if he died, rather than come back as an invalid. He wanted nothing less than a perfect life together. When he told her that he would always keep one last bullet in his pistol for himself should there be a need for it, Heidi cried and clung to him with all her strength, but his will was more powerful. She had to accept it out of respect for his beliefs. She knew that he would come back to her if he could, but only if he was as strong and as manly as he was now. He was the man she loved and he loved her back. The war was something that they could not control, but he was determined not to let the war control him. The last bullet in his pistol would give him the choice and power over the war. That was Francis's rule for the war's game.

As far as Heidi was concerned, she had to stay alive no matter what. Francis wanted it that way. He taught her as much as he knew about tactics and common sense for the war's trials.

The morning they had to part ways, ironically, the sun came out and the rain stopped. It was a small solace for their painful good-byes.

When he dropped her off at the Relay Station outside the city, the last hug was the longest and most desperate. The last kiss was the sweetest and most affectionate. When Francis's car pulled away on the muddy road, Heidi waved her handkerchief for as long as she could see the car before it disappeared at the horizon. She then wiped the tears from her face and returned to her small room. Majestic Hotel became a memory... left back in the past. It felt like her life was over. It felt so very sad being alone again.

Chapter 17

Heidi had been working in the radio relay tower like a robot ever since she returned from her vacation with Francis. There was nothing to interest her outside work, and she was glad that she could throw herself into a routine job that did not required much interaction with her fellow colleagues. She did not feel like socializing, but rather wanted to seclude herself in her dear memories of her fiancé. She missed him so much.

Francis had sent her a brief letter about ten day after he left, which she now carried with her everywhere she went. Sometimes when she was alone she would take the paper out of her tunic's pocket and re-read it. Every time she did so she discovered new meanings in his written words. It was like the letter had a soul of its own and communicated with her. It was Francis's love for her that transpired from it. It gave her hope and strength, but also an objective view of the war, and all its implications. It was real and true as Francis himself was. He was more concerned for her safety than he was for his own, and told her that the Eastern front was hell on earth and she should find a way to move further west. Brno was still considered to be in the Red Army's path toward Berlin. He told her that his deployment would most likely be to Eastern Europe and that he already had a company of newly trained teenage boys to lead into combat. Not a very good situation to be in, thought Heidi, with winter and the Soviet army fast approaching. When she was not thinking about Francis, she worried about Johan, her brother. From the brief messages she received from her father she understood that Johan was still in training in Eastern Germany.

When December arrived with its cold weather, the lumber dormitory building felt more like a cave than a house. The wooden logs with which the stove burnt were always short in supply. With the danger of Czech partisans hidden in the nearby forests the administrative staff of four soldiers, was afraid to go too far and get more logs for the stoves. The farmers' houses were warm and cozy, but they could not spend much time there. They went once a day for their meal and then quickly returned to their base. The hours of daylight became shorter and the dark harbored many dangers.

The isolation of the remote site was very depressing. Heidi was on the verge of breaking down. She had come a long way from her first training in Vienna two years ago, and so many things had happened since then. She wondered how Gloria from Lilienfeld was doing, and where Ticla and Karina were? All the good friends she had made along the way were long gone. It was time for her to do something and move out of that unfriendly place. But where to? No postings for new jobs or training were to be found.

Around Christmas, she was surprised by a nice parcel she received from home. The last letters she sent to Teresa must have made her sister aware of her somber mood, and she must have told their parents. Her mother, Josephina, had put together some cookies, some dry cheese, a few apples and a small bottle of homemade cherry liqueur, and sent it to Heidi as a Christmas present. It was a touching gesture that brought warmth to Heidi's soul, and tears of joy to her eyes. Since Christmas was a time for sharing and good deeds, she decided to invite all her colleagues and the guards to join her in celebrating by enjoying some of the treats she had received.

On Christmas Eve, after everybody had come off duty and was gathered inside the dorm around the hot stove, Heidi displayed the parcel's contents on the old table and had everyone's attention in no time.

'Everybody, please come over here! We have some Christmas treats courtesy of my parents. There is enough for everyone,' Heidi announced.

The other four girls and the three guards approached the table and looked at the feast that laid there. One girl ran back to her room to bring some fresh bread that she had received from the farmer's wife earlier. Seeing that, another disappeared only to come back with a two big slices of apple pie, a gift she received from her host in the village. They put everything together and gathered around the table. In no time the cheese was cut in small pieces, and so was the pie. Even the apples were cut in quarters. When Heidi unveiled the bottle of liqueur from under a napkin, everybody let out a sigh of pleasure. That was the treat of the evening, and so welcomed on a cold December night.

'I know that we did not have much time to spend together, but on a night like this we should be merry and enjoy a few moments of relaxation and indulgence, don't you think?' Heidi said.

They were all young people who had been serving in the army for years. Heidi was wondering who had the most years of experience, but she pushed those thoughts away and urged the others to help themselves and start eating. They used their metal cups as glasses and poured an equal amount of the red cherry-scented liquid in each of them. They then cheered and made a toast to "Good health and safety!" The liqueur was smooth and sweet, the alcohol warming.

'Heidi, give your mother my compliments for this elixir when you see her. It is divine!' one of the soldiers said.

'My mother and my sister are gifted cooks. My sister worked for rich people for years, and she learned to be a chef. I'm not surprised this cherry liqueur is so perfect. It is made according to a famous recipe.'

'How old is your sister? I may want to marry her, since she is such a good cook!' the other soldier said with a wide grin.

Heidi and the other girls laughed out loud.

'Then you'll be my brother-in-law!' Heidi said between giggles.

They ate and drank and got along well. Heidi felt again the closeness with her comrades as she had felt in Pilsen. It was a good feeling, and it was as if she was reunited with her own old self again. She liked being with people. The atmosphere was relaxed and pleasant. They told jokes and had good laughs between the bites of good food.

All of the sudden the sound of a dog barking caught their attention, and they at once went quiet to better hear. It was not an illusion. Somewhere outside in the dark night a guard dog gave the signal that danger was approaching. Instinctively the soldiers grabbed their pistols they had put aside while the little party had been going on. The girls looked around in fear.

'Let's turn off the lights and have a peek outside through the windows,' Heidi said. The girl beside her ran and turned off the light switch.

The darkness enveloped them. Each of them stayed still for a few seconds to adjust to the dark room. Then, once they could find their way around without tripping on each other and the furniture that surrounded them, they moved with caution toward the blank windows, lowering themselves below the window sill. The moon was covered by a thick blanket of clouds, making the night even darker. So much for the Christmas' bright star spreading the ray of light on which the angels would descend! No such luck!

The barking was all that could be heard, and nothing could be seen.

'Do you think the partisans would make a move tonight?' a girl asked quietly to no-one in particular.

'It very well could be,' a soldier answered while squeezing his weapon to make sure it was handy.

The Czech partisans were a permanent threat. They had congregated in the nearby woods and kept an eye on the relay station ever since Heidi joined the site in September. On every trip she took to the farmer's house she kept looking out for movements at the edge of the forest, but never saw anything suspicious. It was like a continuous danger laid in wait, hunting her, a psychological battle with an unseen enemy. Until now, that is. Heidi moved quickly over to the window facing the forest, and cautiously tried to browse the horizon. There was not much to see. Even the dog stopped barking, and in the silence she only heard the breath of her peers inside the building.

'I believe that whatever it was that scared the dog is gone. We should relax and continue eating the good food Heidi's sister and mother sent her.' It was one of the soldiers speaking, but Heidi and the others were not so eager to relax after the scare they had had.

'I think it would be wiser to keep the lights off for the rest of the evening. Better safe, than sorry!' Heidi said in a low voice. She received the agreement of the rest of the crew. They moved away from the windows and around the table again. Their eyes were used to the dark by then, and they easily found the food and cups. For the remainder of the night the building sat in total darkness, blending into the hills' scenic profile, while inside a small party went on celebrating the Christmas of 1944.

*

The New Year of 1945 came without glamour. All of Europe was reeling from the plague of war. Hitler grew more and more anxious to recapture the areas he had lost control of following the Allies' pressure. The smart V-2 long range guided bomb, of which the Germans were so proud of, was launched frequently at targets such as British and Scandinavian cities. The territories lost in France and Belgium during the big onslaught the previous summer were difficult to get back. Attacked from west and east, Germany begun a year that could have marked the end of the war, finding itself in the position of the loser. The high-ranking officers must have known that already, since the main focus had shifted from an aggressive offensive to a cautious defensive in an attempt to limit damage.

Where Heidi was, at the relay station, the somber reality was not known. The lower ranking personnel of the German army were kept in the dark. Most of the operations remained secret. She was desperately seeking a way to move somewhere closer to her home. It was also an especially heavy winter, which added to her anxiety. There was no news from Francis or Johan. That fact alone could have put her in a bad mood for weeks. It looked like nothing good would ever happen again. When she was at the lowest of the low in terms of hope, a message came through the wires that caught her attention instantly. She read it twice before handing it over to her superior. It could be her escape. The message concerned training being held in Austria near Linz. It was for the air force personnel and required skiing skills since the base was up in the mountains. The message was broadcast to several relay stations, and asked for ten positions to be filled by young women of at least twenty years old.

That night Heidi tossed and turned, thinking about the opportunity that she saw in the message. She was not supposed to ask any questions until the ad had been posted. Also, she could not share the news with any of her teammates. She had to live with the news without being able to do anything about it. She was so desperate to apply and get out of there. Linz was like home to her after all the years spent in Czechoslovakia. She prayed to God to help her get the ticket to go back to her country, if only for a few months of training.

She was beside herself with joy when the following morning she saw the ad posted on the board. The good Lord must have answered her prayers. All that was left to do was to apply and then pray for an approval from her superiors. Three days later her name was on the list, and she was due to leave in a week. After she signed the papers in the lieutenant's office Heidi made a plan about what she had to do before leaving. First she thanked God for helping her, and then she wrote a letter home to advise her family about her transfer. She was told by her supervisor that she would receive a new uniform from the head office in Brno: the gray air force attire. Pragmatic as she was, Heidi put together a parcel of her remaining civilian clothes to send home. In the Alps, where the new Air Station was, she would not need clothes other than the uniform. The last time she had worn civilian clothes was with Francis. Each garment brought her a flood of dear memories. She folded everything with care, taking her time to remember each day she had spent with her fiancé: a movie, a dinner, a hug, the passionate nights, and all the rainy days that they spent together. Last but not least she packed the silky French lingerie that always made her feel feminine and sparked Francis's desires. She smiled when she closed the cardboard box, sealed its lid with pink band aid and tied it up with a rope. The best moments of her life were related to the box's content. She thought that her entire life might as well fit in a box.

Not wanting to spoil her good mood, she busied herself with packing the things that she was to take with her to Linz, of which her gas mask was the most important. In a few days she was due to leave, taking a huge step in the right direction, or so she thought. Indeed, when she boarded the microbus that came to take her to the Third Reich Major State in Brno, she could sense her freedom on the horizon. Her intuition told her that she was starting her journey home. Austria was her destination. Austrian soil was safe enough for her. She was determined to do whatever it took to make it home safely, and wait for the end of the war, and for Francis to come back to her. She couldn't even look back at the relay station she had left behind. She was only looking forward. She had in her heart all she needed to take with her, and the rest was not important anymore. There were no close friends to say good bye to, nor a picturesque sight to please her eyes. The relay tower was left behind standing tall and solitary on the top of the muddy hill, while the car shook from pothole to pothole on toward the city.

Chapter 18

When the train pulled into Linz station, it was still dark outside. It was a bit after 7am on a cold January morning. Heidi had been traveling all night long, coming from Brno to Prague where she switched onto the train to Linz. The previous day she had spent in Brno, at headquarters where she prepared for her transfer.

First, she made a trip to the Central Post Office where she sent the parcel with her civilian belongings home. After that, she received her new air force uniform along with the papers for the new Air Force Station, with its code name Sabina. She had to attend a four hour preliminary training session for her new job. She was amazed by how interesting the topic was and excited that, for once, she would get to do something that was challenging and enjoyable at the same time.

The change of uniform also did her good. She liked the well-fitted gray tunic and the comfortable pair of trousers. The new light grey shirts were crisp and almost elegant. It being winter time, she received an equally nice calf length coat with shiny double breast buttons. A winter hat and a spare summer bonnet completed her wardrobe. The boots she had been wearing before were exchanged for a brand new pair, and she was told to go into the city to buy some underwear and a sweater using an allowance for that purpose. She was given a train pass and instructions on how to get to Linz and where to report once she arrived there.

Heidi spent the afternoon shopping for a few things for her, and some food for the trip. In the evening she went to the rail station feeling tired but happier than she had been in a long time. Carrying her little suitcase in one hand and the box with her gas mask in the other, she boarded the evening train and looked for an empty seat. There were plenty of them. People had given up traveling long ago, and the only passengers were part of the armed forces. Used to not trusting anybody, Heidi was afraid to fall asleep, preferring to stay alert and awake. In Prague she changed trains with only ten minutes to spare. That was a good thing, since she would not want to wait around at that late hour in the rail station's waiting room. God only knew who she could find there. It was not safe for a young woman to travel alone at night time, but Heidi was brave and determined to make it to Linz in one piece, safe and sound.

The second train was even more deserted, and she could easily have stretched her legs and lain down on an empty bench, but instead she chose to sit up straight and stay awake. The lights on the train were dimmed for camouflage purposes.

Most of the time she thought of Francis and wondered where he was. Her mind was occupied with happy memories and the good times they had shared together. She did not dare to think about the future: it was something that she did not want to anticipate, feeling sheltered from disappointments that way. The war did not allow people to dream. Times of war were meant to be lived every moment as if they were the last. War times were dark times, like the night she was seeing outside through the dirty window, harboring danger and death. War times were to be lived in the present, and did not leave room for anything other than survival instincts. So she survived that night, and made it to Linz one winter morning when the first rays of daylight stabbed the darkness of the early hours.

Heidi hopped off the train and gathered her luggage. She took a deep breath of fresh cold air, and headed toward the back of the station where some cars were waiting. She stood there pondering her options for getting to the city's core, when someone approached and talked to her.

'Good morning! I'm waiting for a young lady. I'm to pick her up and take her to the Air Control Station. Would it be you?' the stranger asked. He was in German uniform too, and Heidi saw that the rank was the same as hers. She was a corporal. Heidi was surprised to meet him out of the blue, and grew a bit suspicious.

'Good Morning! If that is indeed your mission, you must know the station's code name and my name as well. Am I right?' Heidi asked cautiously.

'Oh, I'm sorry. I should have started with that: Sabina and Souisa Heidi.'

'You seem to be right on both counts. What is your name?' she was relieved that someone was there to take her to the Air Station, and that she would not get lost in Linz.

The soldier gave her a smile along with the information she requested.

'My name is Peter Kosh. Are you Austrian? I see that you speak like the locals here.'

'Hi Peter. I'm from Traisen, near St. Polten. What about you?'

'I'm from Austria too, somewhere near Graz. Ready to go? The car is parked right there. If we rush a bit, we may have time for breakfast before we head up into the mountains. Let me help you with the suitcase, and follow me, please.'

Heidi looked at him while he grabbed her luggage and turned toward an army car parked nearby. She had been on Austrian soil for less than five minutes and already things had started to look better. She did not have to struggle to get to the Air Station because Peter was there to take care of that, and he seemed friendly enough to have breakfast with. She needed a large coffee and some sugar, since she had been awake for more than twenty four hours already. With a smile, she followed him and got into the back seat of the car. Peter climbed onto the driver's seat and started the engine. It choked a few times before he put the car into gear and drove away. The engine noise was so loud that they could not even attempt to talk. They would have had to shout in order to hear each other, so they preferred to drive in silence through the city. As promised, Peter stopped in front of a house just outside Linz. It looked like a farmer's house and Heidi was surprised when Peter got out of the car and went around opening her door. She did not know whether it was good manner, or a simple order to leave the car. Her astonished look made Peter laugh.

'Heidi Souisa, please follow me inside this house. They serve a delicious breakfast here. Don't look so afraid: nobody's going to bite you. These are good people.'

Heidi had to comply and entered the house, which turned out to have a cozy dining room inside. They sat at a table covered with a plaid table cloth and in no time a girl who looked no older than ten, showed up carrying a tray much larger than herself, with two big cups of coffee, a pot of milk and two pieces of fresh, warm bread. She blushed when she set it on the table, and Peter complemented her on her waitressing skills.

'Thank you Helga. Say hi to your mom from us. She has a big help in you, you know that?'

'Thank you. Bon Appetite.' With that Helga disappeared behind the kitchen door.

Heidi smiled and tried the black coffee that she so desperately needed. It was good and warm. She started to relax and enjoy breakfast. Peter ate as well, and throughout the meal they talked about the air station and its surroundings. Heidi found out that Sabina Station had a "sister" named Hermina a few kilometers away. Sabina was served by female personnel and Hermina by men. The last mile to the tower was inaccessible by car, and could be reached only by foot, and in winter, by skiing. The aviation stations were always on the heights, where the radar got a good signal. In ten minutes, Peter had taught Heidi the logistics of the area and the duties they covered. Much invigorated by the food, coffee, and the conversation, Heidi went back to the car and Peter drove her toward the mountains to her destination. Again she was left alone with her thoughts.

When they entered a village situated high up on the mountain, Peter stopped the car and looked back to Heidi.

'That's it. We're here. Final destination, Miss Heidi!'

'Well, thank you for bringing me here, Mr. Peter,' Heidi replied with mischief. She liked his personality.

'From here on, there is a path that takes us to the Air Station. It is a thirty minutes walk all the way up. Coming down is much faster if you are skiing, which, at this time of the year, is preferable. They have skis up at the station, but right now we'll have to walk. I'll help you with the suitcase.'

'Peter, that's very nice of you but I can carry it myself,' Heidi protested.

'You must be a brave girl, but trust me; it is not an easy job to get up there. Here, I'll take the suitcase and you can carry your gas mask. Agree?'

Heidi nodded and handed him the little suitcase. She prepared herself for the stiff walk. They passed through the village, meeting a few locals who greeted them warmly. The people spoke her own language and it made a big difference for her. Heidi was happy to be in her home country and among her co-nationals.

There were patches of snow on the uphill path. They walked through a leafless forest. The morning light was filtered by the tall trees.

Half-way through they stopped to catch their breath and look around. There was no movement made by animals or birds. All of nature was still, and the only noise was that made by their own progress. By the time Heidi had started to breathe heavily, the forest ended and an almost flat plateau opened in front of them. The snow there was thick and the wind was blowing.

'Here we are, Heidi Souisa! Welcome to Sabina Air Force Station!' Peter said with a smile.

'Oh, this looks like an airport tower! And all these antennas...' Heidi wondered, seeing the site.

'Wait until you see inside, Miss Heidi. But first of all I have to take you to the Lieutenant's office and then show you your room. Five star hotel, if you didn't know it.' He laughed, and she laughed too, following him to the main building that looked like a mountain chalet. Inside it was warm, or so Heidi thought after being outside for almost an hour. She reported to the commandant and he welcomed her there. A large room upstairs was the women's dormitory and she was advised to take one of the empty beds, make herself at home, and in an hour to meet the commandant again for an orientation tour in the tower.

Heidi was surprised to find her suitcase waiting for her by the dormitory door, but Peter was nowhere in sight. She opened the door, grabbed her luggage and took in the large room full of beds. There must have been about ten beds, some of them on two levels, one above another. Nobody was there and she spotted one stand-alone bed that looked unoccupied. She checked the bed sheets, and they were fresh and unused. She sat down on the blanket and, opening the suitcase, took out some necessities and then closed it, pushing it under the bed. Since there was not much to do with her hour of free time she had on her hands, she decided to go and see the rest of the building.

Beside the large dorm there was another room that looked like a dining room with three old tables. It connected with a small kitchen. From the hallway she found another room where a big stove was cracking with logs on fire. Inside it was furnished with old furniture, giving the impression of a meeting, training, or living room.

When she ventured to open a door in the back of the building beside the main office room, she was surprised and embarrassed to see Peter lying on one of the three beds inside. She stepped back, trying to close the door as quietly as she could. Peter was not sleeping, just stealing a few minutes of rest after the trip to Linz he had to make to pick up

Heidi. As a matter of fact, he was just thinking of her with his eyes closed. He heard the door opening, and under normal circumstances would have been jumping out of bed in no time, but somehow he knew that whoever was coming into the room was not an intruder. Without opening his eyes, he saw her through the curtain of his lashes. He did not want to talk to her since she was already scared, and shyly backed out of the room.

After that, Heidi quit wandering the building and sat patiently on a chair in the dining room waiting for the lieutenant to meet her for the grand tour and work instructions.

The first week on the job Heidi learned a lot and with the help of the other co-workers and roommates she became more accustomed to what she had to do. There was a lot of responsibility involved. They controlled the air traffic of the German war planes from the moment they appeared on the radar until they were far enough away to leave Sabina's coverage and be handed over to another station, most likely Hermina. Each girl was assigned a plane and followed it on the screen and through radio communication within the Station's area. A small mistake could cause a disaster and loss of lives, which was why they had a strict schedule and were supposed to be well rested and alert on the job. They worked six hours daily, went down to the village once a day for a decent meal, and then studied the new codes that were changed frequently due to security and espionage concerns. In the morning they had breakfast, made by rotation among the personnel of the Station. Everybody took turns in serving at the small kitchen. Heidi loved being on duty there every six days. It was a pleasant change of pace and made her feel like she was at home, with the only difference being that her family was now her colleagues, the three male soldiers, and the Lieutenant.

While the girls always rushed to their jobs in the tower, Peter always lingered a bit longer in the dining room, making small talk with Heidi while she waited the tables after breakfast. She appreciated his company and occasional help, and they soon became friends. She was on good terms with the girls too, since they all slept in the same room, but she did not grow especially fond of any of them in particular. However, her social life was far better than the one she had had in Brno. Soon, she was at ease with her new life on the mountain and no longer felt depressed. The trips to the village, made mostly on skis, were enjoyable, and the people she met with down there were her people. She still did not trust anybody, but she felt welcomed wherever she went. For the first time in two years she was content with her life, under the circumstances. Somehow she accepted what she could not change and focused on her job, which she liked. She still had her worries about the fate of her brother and her fiancé, but her mission was to survive the war and stay sane.

Daily, war planes flew over them and Heidi followed them on the radar one by one. She used a coded conversation with the pilots. It was a highly important operation and Heidi gave her very best to accomplish it. She liked her job and, most importantly, she was very good at it. The Lieutenant noticed how fast a learner she was, and knew that he had one of the best employees he had ever had at Sabina Station. It was as if Heidi realized for the first time how important her actions and quick thinking were in protecting another human being's life, the pilot's. She took it very seriously and with full responsibility. Deep down she knew, thanks to Francis's insight, that the Germans would lose the war, but until it was all over, she had a duty to protect the lives of her people. The paradox of the situation hit her so many times, but she was enrolled in an army that forced her to live by its rules, regardless of her beliefs or feelings.

Up in the Alps the war was more a shadow than a reality. It was like she was watching a horror movie. There was nothing she could change about it, and it could not physically threaten her. The threat was at a mental level; however, she was already self-trained to withstand the burden.

Her work-mates were very much like her, strong young women who took one day at a time and made the most out of it. It was a more mature environment than the ones she had been in before. This suited her well, since she had come a long way through the war. All the life experience she had since leaving her small town at the age of seventeen had taught her much, and made her a brave young woman. And what a journey it had been so far!

**

The days went by quickly. March had already arrived.

That morning, after she served breakfast in the dining room, Peter, her new friend, came to help her with the dishes.

'Heidi, in appreciation for the excellent breakfast, let me give you a hand with cleaning up. You woke up so early today to have everything ready for us. You must already be tired.'

Heidi smiled at him and said ironically, 'Speak for yourself, Peter! You are the one who takes naps every opportunity you have. I'm fine, not tired at all. I like serving and preparing breakfast. It's something that reminds me of the normal life I had before this war started.'

'What do you mean about me taking naps? Oh…' He suddenly remembered. 'I wasn't sleeping when you walked in on me on your first day here.' He said it with a wink.

Heidi blushed instantly remembering her wandering around just minutes after she had set foot in Sabina air station, and how she opened the door to the soldiers' room not knowing what room it was.

'Did you see me back then?'

'Of course I did. I tried hard to pretend that I was asleep and not laugh out loud seeing the expression on your face.'

'The expression on my face! What was so funny about that, huh?'

'You looked like a deer caught in the headlights!'

'I did not expect to see you there, and I was embarrassed about intruding. I did not know that was your bedroom.'

'Don't worry. You were so cute that I pretended to be sleeping in order not to scare you even more. Now you mock me that I'm a lazy person. How nice of you!' He was teasing her.

'Peter, I'm sorry if you felt that way, and I'm sorry about that incident back then. Here, you can dry the dishes and let's forget about it.'

'Now that is a huge honor, Miss Heidi! You actually think I can be useful at something. Pass me the dish towel, please.' He was happy to be around her, and took every opportunity he could to make that happen.

In fact, Peter was very fond of Heidi. It must have been because he was the first person from the station who met her and something about her wits and friendly attitude had appealed to him. He was two years older than her. He had been serving in the army for five years already and was badly injured once when he was fighting in Northern Italy two years ago. He had been shot, but the bullet luckily missed his heart and got stuck in his lung. His commandant would not let him die on the battle field, and carried him on his back to the nearest camp hospital where he had surgery in order to have the bullet removed. Afterwards he was sent to Berlin to recover, and after five months of convalescence he was re-deployed to Sabina Station as auxiliary personnel. He had looked death in the eye and cheated it. He was lucky to be alive, and that was why his personality was so outgoing. He knew that life was precious and took his time to cherish it. He also knew that his good luck was probably wearing thin, since he had used a big chunk of it when he survived the shooting, and wondered if he still had enough luck left to be able to win Heidi's heart. He liked her so much, and that was why he was out around her every chance he had.

'I was just thinking that we can go skiing to the village later and have lunch together. Soon the snow will begin to melt, and then there would be no more skiing. The other day I saw some spring flowers in the sunny part of the forest. What do you think?'

Heidi was not on duty that day. She loved skiing. Spring was coming and the snow was disappearing fast. The days were getting longer too. Peter's invitation seemed tempting. Through the window the day looked warm and bright.

'Peter, I was planning to spend the day looking over tomorrow's navigation codes, but I suppose I can do that later in the evening. I think we can pay the village a visit and have a decent meal while we are there.'

'Great! Let's finish the job here and get ready to go!'

Peter looked happy like a little boy on his birthday. He wanted to get to know her better. There was an attraction toward her that he could hardly hide. Heidi was smart, pretty, and fun to talk to. The other girls were too shallow for him. He was determined to take this friendship to another level. After all, he had nothing to lose, but everything to gain.

When everything in the small kitchen was in place and cleaned up, Heidi went to her room to dress properly for a ski trip to the village. Peter was waiting for her outside with the skis ready.

The day was bright and the morning light was filtering through the trees like a sheer curtain. The snow glittered under the sun. A perfect early spring day with mild temperature!

'Are you ready to go?' Peter asked Heidi with a big smile. His blue eyes were brighter from the reflection of light around them, and from the fire that burned inside him.

'I'm ready. This is a gorgeous day. Let's not waste a minute more!'

The slide downhill was a pleasure. Heidi always found skiing relaxing and fun. She was good at it. She smiled all the way down to the village, while she found her way around the tall trees on the serpentine slope. Peter, being protective and caring, went behind her. From time to time Heidi let out small cries of joy that were music to his ears. She was like the goddess of the mountains, floating on the snow.

When they arrived to the village, they took off the skis and stored them in a shed that belonged to the army forces, and then they headed to the main building on the street, a dining hall owned by a farmer. His wife and daughters worked there while the farmer and his young sons were in charge of the farm itself. He had cows, pigs, and chickens, and supplied all the goods to the small restaurant his wife ran. It not yet being noon, lunch was being prepared and a delicious smell came from the kitchen. There were only a few patrons inside at that morning hour, but still more than there would be on a summer day when the villagers had more work to do than in spring. Of course the war had taken most of the young men and women away. Those left behind came in mostly to hear the latest news and gossips from the community.

Heidi and Peter sat at a table by the window. They both needed to catch their breath after the effort they had put into skiing. Heidi's cheeks were red and her eyes were as blue as the sky. She looked beautiful and happy. She also felt good. Her anxiety and depression, that had lingered around her for months in Brno, was now completely gone. She was back to her true self.

Peter, looking at her, could hardly contain his excitement. He wanted so badly to share his feelings with her. His courage had built itself up over weeks, and that day he was ready to express himself and reveal his affection. He got up and went to the kitchen desk to order some hot tea and biscuits. He was nervous and needed something to do before he talked to Heidi about himself.

Back at the table Heidi was thinking how wonderful it was to have a true friend like Peter and smiled towards him. Her smile gave him butterflies in the stomach and wings to his soul.

When he returned with the tea cups and the plate of biscuits he was ready to speak up his mind and heart.

'Here you go: peppermint tea and fresh biscuits for an amazing girl!'

Heidi laughed and returned his compliment.

'You're pretty amazing too, you know? I'm so lucky that you picked me up at the rail station in Linz two months ago. I was so lost when I arrived here, literally and figuratively... and depressed too. But look at me now: I like my job, I have a good friend, I'm in great shape because of all the skiing I'm doing, and I'm among my people. If only the war would come to an end sooner... and...' She stopped in mid sentence, not knowing if she should continue or not. She took a long sip of the tea and decided to drop the subject.

Peter was all ears and did not want her to stop talking. After all, she had started to reveal something about herself and he was very interested in finding out more.

'And?' he asked hopefully.

'I left home and enrolled in the army at seventeen. I learned a lot along the way and I've been in danger a few times. The war is so complicated, and complicates people's lives in so many ways. I would lie to you if I told you that all these years were lost to me. In a way they have given me new opportunities to grow up fast, and taste and appreciate life.'

She stopped again. It sounded like a monologue. She was talking to herself, analyzing her recent past. Peter was more interested than ever in listening to her. She needed a listener, someone she could speak to in order to sort out her feelings and her fears. She needed a faithful friend, and she thought she had found one.

'Heidi, you're seeing the good things that happened to you even in this nightmare. You're incredibly optimistic, and I'm lucky I met you. You have made this whole ordeal bearable for me. Ever since you joined Sabina Station, I've been happier than I have been in years. You have a gift in making people happy, you know that?' he said with caution. He did not want her to stop her confession. That was better than what he thought, and would make his own confession easier.

Heidi felt encouraged to speak and let her trail of thoughts flow. 'There were good things happening to me along the way. For the first time, I fell in love with a wonderful man, who I met in the most unusual circumstance. He was very ill but recovered completely. He taught me all I needed to know to survive, and gave me hopes for the future. I pray to God that he will remain safe and come back to me one day. He is my fiancé. I also made good friends with my roommates in Pilsen and we took care of one another. They taught me that friendship is a reliable relationship based on trust and compassion. Coming here I found the same values in the people I met, you included, and I've got a challenging and important job that I love doing.'

Heidi continued to talk about her war experience, but Peter wasn't hearing her anymore. In fact, he went deaf when he heard the word "fiancé". It was like someone had hit him very hard on his head and the world went spinning around him: Heidi was engaged. The girl he was so fond of was not available. Her heart belonged to another man. Oh

God! In that very moment he wished he had died two years ago when he was shot. He felt like his life was over anyway. He had such high hopes for a chance to win Heidi's love, but all was shattered when she told him about her life. He almost felt nauseous and, in an effort not to throw up, he drank the tea all at once. The warm liquid gave him some physical relief, but nothing could relieve the burden in his heart. He looked at her, taking in her pretty face, and her gentle speech, aching for another outcome of that meeting that he wanted so badly to be a date, and was not, and would never be...

Peter was a man of honor and realized that Heidi was not responsible for his misery. She knew nothing about his affection for her and had never encouraged him in pursuing her as a lover. She was a devoted friend, and a very lovely one. What he had just found out about her hurt him, but he could never betray her trust in him. She considered him her friend and opened her soul to him, and he could not disappoint her in any way. He had to be strong and act like a man. It was better to have her in his life as a friend than not to have her at all. No, he would not burn all his bridges by hurting her. She was too dear to him. She would never know how much he liked her and how much he would have loved her if only she was available, which she obviously was not.

Heidi felt good. Recounting her life in the army was like a needed confession. She felt lighter and at ease after she finished. How lucky she was to have someone like Peter listening so patiently. He was a good man, Heidi thought, and gave him an adorable smile. Little did she know how much she had hurt him in the last few minutes and how strong Peter had to be not to show his pain. Life was never fair, was it?

Peter found the strength to look Heidi in her eyes and offer her his friendship and support without lying. She meant a lot to him, and he wanted to have her in his life as much as he could without scaring her away.

'You are a remarkable young woman and you've been through a lot during your service in the army. I'm glad you ended up on this mountain, and let's hope that we will live long enough to talk about this time as a long gone memory. Now, let's take a stroll in the village and visit the market place. We can grab some fruit and cheese to take up to the station. Besides, the day looks so wonderful: sunny and breezy.'

'That would be lovely. Let's go, my friend.' She got up and helped him clean the table. When they stepped outside, the sun enveloped them in a warm light.

At the market they bargained for some nice apples and even a jar of plum jam that they promised to share at the station. They had different tastes in cheese, but managed to agree on a piece of dry old cheese that would last a while. Peter put the produce in his backpack. Back on the main street they met a group of villagers talking about the latest news. When they approached them, they found out that the Eastern front had been pushed toward Hungary, getting closer to Austria. The source of the news was not very reliable, but the people were propagating it anyway. Heidi thought about Francis and her brother. They were out there on the battlefield. Her heart ached for them. Peter saw the sudden change in her mood and understood her concern. It showed him how committed she was to her fiancé and how much she cared about his well-being.

'We do not know for certain what the situation is, and for now we should focus on our duties. Don't be sad, Miss Heidi.' It was a nickname that only he used. Heidi always smiled hearing that. She smiled again and nodded. They had better return to the station. Going uphill took much longer than coming down, and a lot more effort.

Back at Sabina Station they went about their afternoon chores. Peter felt sad, but Heidi did not notice since he made every effort to keep his appearance unchanged. Heidi was invigorated by the physical exercise, the fresh air, and all the talking she had done. Inside and out it was a good sensation, like rejuvenating her body and soul. Peter was a great man — she thought—a true friend.

Chapter 19

Life at Sabina Air Station carried on as usual. The month of March was busy with war planes flying by on missions, or on surveillance. There was something going on every day. The Germans consistently bombed England and Belgium with V-2 rockets. It was an attempt to move the balance of the offensive to their side. Hitler was desperately seeking a way to hit the enemies hard, but did not have much luck. The Red Army was coming from the east with determination, and on its way governments surrendered and turned against Germany, making friends with the Russians. It was like a domino game: once the first brick fell, all of them came down. First it was Romania, then Hungary and, in mid-March, Poland. The circle of German influence was getting smaller and smaller.

The people in the village listened to forbidden radio stations and knew quite a lot about the Eastern and Western fronts. When Heidi and her colleagues went down to eat or to buy food supplies, the villagers always had news for them. Heidi knew that spies were sometimes infiltrated among the locals and that they would spread odd news in order to catch the less than loyal German Army's personnel, and potential deserters. She knew how to stay away from the rumors and not to react to the possible instigation. After all, she was wearing the German uniform and had to be careful about what to believe and what not to.

Peter was also a smart soldier, and advised Heidi not to listen to all the news from the village. Up at the air station it was business as usual, without much updates from the war. The only thing that seemed odd was the fact that, by the end of March, most of the operations were moved to Hermina Station.

One afternoon, when Heidi had just come back from the village with two other roommates she stopped to chat with Peter in the living room. He was cleaning his pistol and could use some company while doing such a boring task.

'Oh Peter, I'm glad you're here. You won't believe what the rumors are in the village!' Heidi said, still excited about the trip she had taken with her mates.

'Hi, Miss Heidi! What do you mean? What rumors?' Peter asked with interest. He was still moved every time he was around her. His heart could not let go of the feelings he had for her, but now his head was on his shoulders and kept his heart in check. He had no remorse whatsoever about his broken romance. She was still one of the dearest human beings in the world to him.

Heidi threw herself on the old armchair, feeling tired.

'Well, the rumor is about the Red Army cornering the Germans and getting closer to the Austrian and Czechoslovakian borders. Everybody was talking about it and asked us details, expecting that we knew all about it.'

'Oh, that… I hope you girls did not engage into such conversation with the villagers, did you?' Peter was afraid that Heidi and her colleagues could fall into a trap set up by the informers.

'You know me better than that, don't you? My lips were sealed, and once they started on the subject I urged the girls to leave the place. But still, what if all those rumors are true, Peter?'

'We don't know for sure, but it could be possible.'

'Then, what happens to us here? Would we be taken prisoners, and sent into labor camps? The Russian are tough people, especially with women. '

'I don't know. I believe you should be careful and, at the right time, when nothing matters anymore, you should hide and become a civilian, in order to stay safe. But don't talk about this with anyone, Heidi. Just do it when the time is right. That would be the only way you could avoid prison camps and all the misery that happens there.'

Heidi listened carefully. That was good advice, coming from a good friend.

Peter looked at her with misty eyes. God, he still loved her. He would not accept something bad happening to her. If she could only let him take care of her, she would be forever protected, but she was unaware of his feelings and would never run away with him.

'Peter, you talk like you know something that I don't know. What is that?'

'I wish I knew how this war would end and when, but all I know is that Hitler is going to lose, and the end will come.'

'Peter, please tell me what you know. I have a feeling that you try to shelter me from some bad news.'

Peter was torn between duty and friendship. He knew something about the plans that the lieutenant had for the girls. He did not know when the order would come to have the girls sent away. Where, he did not know.

'Heidi, I heard something about this air station being closed in the future and all the operations being moved to Hermina Station. It is not for sure yet, but there is a strong possibility that they would do that. It is not only the Red Army coming from east, but the Americans are pushing at the western border, too. Austria is on their path to Germany.'

Heidi's heart ached for Francis and Johan. It seemed to her that they were in much greater danger than she was. Her face became worried and sad. Peter felt sorry to scare her, but it was the truth that he told her.

'Then, it looks like there is no easy way out of this mess, is there? Thank you for being such an honest person and a good friend. I will think about what you have just told me and come up with a contingency plan. Now please excuse me, but I think I'll go to my room and rest a bit. I'm on duty in two hours.' She got up and tried to smile, but tears filled her eyes instead. Was she scared, or only emotional? She was not sure anymore. She was only human.

Peter opened his arms and was surprised when she actually let him hug her in a fraternal way. After that, she left the room feeling a tiny bit better. He stayed there watching her walk away, wishing he was more to her than a good friend.

A week later, on March 29, the Allies took Frankfurt and the Red Army entered Austria. The next day all the young women received letters of dismissal from Sabina, and papers for reporting to various Major States of the German Army. The lieutenant asked them to come for a meeting in the living room and broke the news to them. They were due to leave in another week. Heidi looked at her letter and saw that she had been sent back to Brno. That was a huge disappointment for her. How could she leave Austria again, especially when the Red Army was getting closer? But orders were orders and she had no choice but to comply.

195

Peter found out about the decision of the Major State and the departure of the girls and offered Heidi support and advice. His task was not easy, since Heidi was on the verge of breaking down.

'I believe that the Russians will arrive in Vienna any day now. Their bombers circled the Austrian air space, with some bombs dropping on the outskirts of the capital.'

'Peter, my home town is not far away from Vienna, I'm worried sick about my family.'

'Right now you should be worried about yourself, Heidi. You are an active member of the German army and you are also a woman. You should definitely hide from the Bolsheviks. They are barbaric in comparison with the Americans.'

'I know, my fiancé told me about them. What am I supposed to do, Peter?'

'You'll be leaving Sabina Station in a few days. Be alert and play it by ear. Take any opportunity that may arise, and take care of yourself. Remember, there will be no heroes on this side of the barricade. Once it's all over and we emerge as the loser, the rest of the world will hate us …we'll even hate ourselves. So, no heroic acts are required at this time. Do whatever is best for you and do not look back, if you know what I mean.'

Heidi looked at him in wonder. He really wished the best for her. He was a great friend. She got up and hugged him with affectionate friendship and gratitude.

The last days on the mountains passed quickly. When everything was ready for their departure and the luggage was packed, Peter drove Heidi and two other girls to Linz rail station. They did not talk much during the ride, each of them thinking about the future and all the dangers lying ahead. At the rail station the other two girls said their good-byes and rushed to their train to Berlin. Heidi had a couple of hours to spare until her train to St. Polten was due to depart. Peter kept her company until she boarded the second to last car of the train, which he advised her as being safer than the front of the train. When they had to say their good-byes, the moment was equally awkward and emotional. Heidi felt like she was losing a good friend, while Peter could not let go of the woman of his dreams. He still loved her hopelessly, and wished her good luck and a good life. He had become a better man because of her and was strong enough to let her go. With a grave voice he wished her well and kissed her on the cheeks, before lifting her onto the car's steps and giving her the little suitcase and the gas mask. She had tears in her eyes, and tried hard not to cry openly. There was so much sadness in her soul. Too many departures to places she did not want to go to, too many dear people left behind, too many fears to face, too much to deal with only to stay alive.

When the train set in motion, Heidi waved to Peter for as long as she could, watching him become smaller and smaller on the platform. She was feeling lonely and scared. The future was looking darker and darker to her. She had a bad feeling about it, but nothing could prepare her for what was about to happen on that trip.

It was a bright April day with blue sky and warm sun. She was still wearing her winter coat over the gray tunic and pants. She put the suitcase by her feet along with the gas mask box. The people around her were mostly civilians. They were debating the latest news, and Heidi listened to them without participating in their conversation. What she was hearing was that the Soviets were taking over Vienna and heavy bombing had happened on the previous days around the nation's capital. She was thinking that even though she was working with the air force she knew nothing about those events. The Germans must have held back that news in an effort to keep up appearances in front of their troops. But why? Heidi could not understand how Hitler could be so blind as not to see that they would be defeated by the Allies. Why was he so cold-blooded, pushing the German Army practically to suicide? What was she supposed to do in Brno if the Red Army was about to take over Eastern Europe? While all these thoughts were crossing her mind, the train was heading east toward St. Polten. They had been travelling for less than an hour when the alarm went off throughout the train. People panicked and started to scream. The train personnel was running from car to car making sure that everyone knew what to do and where to hide. The alarm was informing them of air raid threat. The few soldiers travelling on the train got up and advised people to seek shelter under the benches.

Heidi pushed her suitcase aside and made herself as small as she could to fit under her seat. The others around her followed suit. Some children began to cry and all kind of panicked noise filled the car. One soldier shouted for everybody to keep quiet and listen for the planes' engines. He mentioned that it was important to know which direction the attack was coming from to know on which side of the train car to hide.

Heidi was all ears, but what she heard the loudest was her heart beat. The train was going slowly but did not stop. People were scared and could hardly contain their composure. Then the plane's noise began, at first like a hum of thousand of bees and increasing by seconds until it was a gory roar. Heidi could locate it as coming from the opposite side from where she was hiding, and knowing that she was in the right place she braced herself to become smaller and covered her ears in an instinctual gesture.

Outside, the planes came in a formation of three and lowered their altitude to better aim their guns at the train. When the target was in plain sight and within the gun's radar, it started shooting for a few seconds, and then flew over. People in the train screamed and by the sound of it some might have been injured. The old train was still moving like a wounded animal. Heidi felt her face wet and checked it with her hand to see if there was blood. The liquid was not red and then she realized that it was her tears that washed her. Was she crying? She did not know what was happening. The noise from the planes faded away. She tried to get up and look around. People were scared and some were injured. They cried for help. A soldier came out of nowhere and his voice was heard over the screams like a bolt of thunder.

'Attention! Listen up, everybody! The attack is not over! The planes will come back. This time they will hit us from the other side and we have to be prepared. Move under the left-hand benches right now. They will be back in no time.'

Heidi knew that the soldier was right. They had to come back and would strike again from the opposite direction. She moved quickly to a narrow spot under one of the seats across the aisle. Few people followed the instructions, while the injured were agonizing where they were. A mother with a young child handed him over to a man beside Heidi. She made room for the little one who was crying in despair. Heidi saw that the child's mother was bleeding from her shoulder. She wanted to help the mother but all of the sudden the noise of the returning planes stopped her, and instead she made herself as small as she could under the bench, and made sure that the child beside her was protected as well.

The raffle of the bullets stabbed the train roof and a few of them fell like rain drops on the car's floor. The smoke and the noise were unbearable. Finally, the train came to a complete stop, while the planes were flying away. The attack lasted only thirty seconds, but it felt like an eternity. Time was losing its dimension. When the soldiers announced that the air ride was over, people started to come out of their hiding places, terror written all over their faces. Next, word spread that the locomotive was damaged and they were trying to fix it. In the meantime the travelers looked after the wounded and searched for family members who might have gotten lost in the ambuscade. Heidi had only herself to look after and gladly helped her immediate co-travelers to get on their feet and calm down. The little child was exhausted by the terrible scare and crying. His mother was becoming paler and paler due to the blood she was losing. Heidi helped her to uncover the wound. It was only a deep scratch, not a bullet hole, but the bleeding was bad. She found her suitcase thrown under another bench and took out her winter scarf. With that she made a good, tight bandage for the woman's shoulder to stop the bleeding. After that, she handed the child to the mother and looked around to see if there was anything else she could do for the others. She was blessed to be alive and ready to help. Unfortunately, she saw the soldiers carrying some bodies from car to car toward the front of the train. There were casualties.

The next hour passed quickly while people recovered from the shock and the pain. By 10am the train set in motion again and pulled like a tired horse through the hills of Upper Austria. When almost everybody was beginning to feel more relaxed, the siren started to ring announcing another air strike. The horrifying signal sent everybody back into panic. Heidi was sure that the second time the attack would be worse. She got down on the car's floor by the mother and the child she had helped earlier. The woman was doing better. She had some water and the wound was not bleeding anymore. The child slept for a while but when the signal started, he woke up scared. The train picked up speed as if trying to run away or hide from the danger. Ten minutes later the planes were seen in the sky coming from the north. Heidi hid herself under the bench. She was scared. All the years in the army could not prepare her for the day she was having. Her instinct told her that the train would be hit harder this time. The planes flew over a few times, back and forth, without shooting. Their approach was terror inducing for the people on the train. The fear was general and most of them thought that the end was close and they would not make it.

Then the sky went quiet for about five minutes that seemed like an eternity. Flickers of hope that perhaps the attack was over appeared in travelers' eyes. Some began to stretch and get out of their hiding places. Heidi began to move her body under the bench when her fine hearing detected the sound of an engine. She saw that people were up and about and shouted at them to hide down on the carriage floor. Just as they looked at her in dismay, the bomb dropped and the train shook like a dry leaf in the autumn wind. Some of the people were thrown to the floor, some just went flying through the broken windows of the car. Screams were heard throughout and then smoke smell filled the air.

Heidi opened her eyes, afraid of what she might see. She was at the end of the train, and her car was still standing. The smoke was coming from another place, not from within. She could not see any flames. Some people were crying, some were cursing, and some were just moaning in pain. She was not injured. The bench had kept her sheltered from the debris and the explosion. She got up and looked outside. Broken glass was everywhere. The mother and the child were badly shaken by the bomb's tremor, but otherwise all right. That was good. She was being protective of them. Other travelers weren't as lucky, though. A few were badly injured by the fall they had taken. Outside there were some bodies lying on the dry grass. They must have been thrown out from the train. The on-duty soldier in charge of the train's safety announced that everybody who could move was to get off the train and go into the nearby field. The bomb had dropped on the locomotive and there would be a fair amount of time before the train would be set in motion again.

Heidi gathered her gas mask and the little suitcase and headed to the door. On the way she looked back at her neighbor with the young child and urged her to get up, helping her with the toddler. The air was becoming hard to breath. Coughing and stumbling over the debris they managed to disembark and headed toward higher lands along the railway. They were in the hills of Upper Austria, nowhere near a village or town.

The waiting time was spent attending to the injured people and encouraging each other to calm down from the shock. That was hard to do when the old locomotive was still fuming, while it was removed from the garniture and pushed away through a nearby rail switch that had to be fixed prior to that task. The rail personnel managed to ask for help from a depot, a few kilometers away. They stayed there for almost three hours, assessing the situation and trying to solve all the problems. The new locomotive that was brought to the site was much smaller but it was all that could be found in an old depot in Amstatten. By early afternoon everybody was asked to get back on the train and slowly they set in motion once again. Heidi was wondering if she would ever make it back to Brno, her final destination. She thought that the planes that bombed her train were American or British, but the soldiers that came with the new engine were talking about the Soviets getting closer. When it started back on its journey, the train had broken windows and the crisp April wind was blowing in Heidi's ears. She looked around and everybody was cold and uncomfortable. The good thing was that it was a sunny day. Rain would have been much worse.

By the time they arrived to Lower Austria, toward Melk, the noise of planes could be heard again. People were at the end of their strength. Panic engulfed everyone, and space under the benches became so crowded that people started to push each other aside to get a better spot. Survival skills had kicked in, Heidi thought, and so she helped the mother with the child to fit in beside her. That was the worst day of her life so far. The war showed its brutal side, and was indeed frightening. The planes approached with a horrific sound and within seconds dropped a bomb in front of the train. The car shook again, and dust and smoke was raised to the sky. The horrifying quake lasted a couple of minutes but the aftermath was sinister. They were under attack for the third time that day. When the planes flew away and they let sign of relief, Heidi got out and headed to the exit along with some other people. Once on the side of the track she saw that the bomb had exploded about fifty meters in front of the locomotive. The rail was damaged and torn apart. Some trees and bushes were burning in the vicinity of the track. It looked impossible to get past that section of the railway. The next half hour was spent again assessing the situation. The verdict was that all that could be done was to walk beyond the disaster site and another train would come and take the passengers to St. Polten. Some people were unable to walk. Some were carried by relatives or acquaintances and some by total strangers. Slowly they moved along the track like a sad pilgrimage looking away from the burning debris. After another hour, a train with only two cars pulled up in front of them and a few soldiers got off to give people instructions. In the first car were to be put the wounded and their caregivers, while the second car was for people able to stand and take care of themselves.

Some passengers started to ask the new crew and soldiers what was going on in St. Polten and if the bombers were flying over the city as well.

Heidi and the others found out that St. Polten was already occupied by the Russians and that there were no air raids over the city, but that the Red Army was taking it with assault. So far they had left the civilians alone, but whoever was in German uniform was considered a target.

Hearing this, Heidi was scared and confused. Not knowing what to do, she approached one of the soldiers who had a higher rank and asked:

'Pardon me sir, may I ask for a piece of advice?'

The man looked at her in surprise. Where did she come from? She was wearing German Air Force uniform. She must be on a mission.

'Good day, young lady. Go ahead and ask your question, but first tell me what in the name of God are you doing here?'

'I have an order to go to Communication Headquarters in Brno, Czechoslovakia. I have to report there by noon tomorrow.'

'Good Lord, lady, you have no idea what is going on only few kilometers away from here. Austria has been invaded by the Red Army on the east and by the Americans in the west. They are advancing and closing the circle around us. In Czechoslovakia the situation is even more unstable since the partisans are attacking the Germans from within. There is no way you'll make it to Brno alive. Where are you from? Eastern Germany?'

'No, I'm Austrian, from Traisen a town about thirty kilometers south of St. Polten,' Heidi said.

'I have heard of Traisen. It is in the mountains, right?'

'Yes, not very far from here if you go over the hills and into the mountains.'

The man was thinking what to say and then spoke his mind.

'Listen to me young lady: it is too dangerous for you to even try to go to St. Polten. The Russians are rough people, and they chase after women like flies after honey. Being in uniform, you are also their enemy. They will catch you and I don't even want to think what could happen to you. Since you are a local and your home is not that far away, you are better off not getting on this train. Go home. Forget about your duty in Brno. The war will soon be over and we will have lost it. I do not want to say more, but that is the best you can do to save your life.'

Heidi could not believe what she had just heard. The sergeant must have known the real situation. It wasn't as if she was talking with a villager whom she could not trust. She was torn between taking his advice and running home, and boarding the newly arrived train and continuing her trip to Brno. She had to ask one more question. The sergeant was already busy urging the civilians onto the train.

'Pardon me for bothering you again, but do you think I should at least get to St. Polten and then decide what to do?'

The sergeant looked at her thinking. She was young and while he could not tell her age he knew that she must have been in the army for a while now since her insignia were visible on her shoulder. She also must have been well trained in radar and telecommunications, since her uniform was of the air force. She was sent to a foreign country that was swept by battles on the ground and in the air, and she was an Austrian whose home was not that far away from where they were. He made up his mind and decided to help her make the decision that would be best for her. There was no time for any more bravery in this war. It was almost over and a lost cause. Nobody wanted to see any more casualties, even though Hitler was determined not to give up. Hitler was a fanatical fool. He liked being a sadist, and played with people's lives, but then and there he, Sergeant Miller, could make a difference for this fellow comrade, a young woman of his nation. He spoke in a tone that gave Heidi no room for uncertainty.

'What is your name?'

'Heidi Souisa.'

'Heidi Souisa, St. Polten is under Russian attack. In a day the entire region will be occupied by the Red Army. There is nobody who can keep the Soviet troops from gaining control over Lower Austria. They are taking over our land as we speak. You'd be taken prisoner the moment you get off this train and try to go anywhere. You must leave now and never look back. Take off the military signs from your coat and roll in some dirt so that your clothes do not look like a uniform. Whatever military identification and written orders you have, you must destroy at once so that nobody can trace you as an active member of the Third Reich. Take your gas mask with you and put a change of clothes into your pockets. Get rid of your suitcase, since you'll need your strengths and energy to walk across the mountain. If you have any food with you, take that along too. Here, I can give you my compass. You'll make better use of it than I will. Go south-east and be aware of your surroundings. You might find some farms along the way and people can guide you to the right path to Traisen. Don't tell anyone where you come from and your military background if you want to live. Now, do not waste any more time. Go! You have a few good hours before the night sets in. Good luck!''

Heidi took the compass from his hand and, still surprised by his words, nodded. He turned to attend to his task of boarding people on the train and get going. When he was about ten feet away he heard Heidi yelling after him.

'Thank you, Sir. God bless you!'

He turned to wave to her. She waved back and smiled with gratitude. Then she turned on her heels and started to take the insignia off her epaulets and rummage though her suitcase. Quickly, she grabbed some underwear and a pack of dry biscuits and stuffed her pockets with it. Next, she took the papers from her breast pocket and tore them to pieces. Last, she threw away her suitcase with the remaining belongings, took the gas mask case in her right hand and started to walk rapidly away from the railway. She did not look back, but heard the noise of the train set off in motion. She took a deep breath and headed toward the mountains and began her journey home.

Chapter 20

Heidi had been walking for about three hours before she dared to stop to catch her breath. She sat on the gas mask box by a leafless bush in the forest. She had used the compass to head in the right direction, but she found a path through the forest that she figured would take her somewhere. As long as it headed southeast she was on the right track. Or so she thought. Now that she had stopped walking, she looked around and up to the sky. The trees were bare and the sky was still blue above her. Her boots were covered in mud and her trousers and the coat's lower edge were stained and slightly wet. At least she had some biscuits to eat and some sugar cubes for building up her energy. She knew that she would find fresh water in the mountains and was not worried about thirst. What worried her was the approaching night. She was not sure how and where she would spend the night, but tried to be positive and not panic thinking about it. She still had about another two good hours of day light and then she would look for a shelter for an overnight stay. She had grown up in similar region and knew that most of the wild animals were not hibernating at that time of year, and some small predators could have come out of hiding by April. So, she considered night time to be a threat for her, and had already decided to spend it in a safe place. With that thought, she stood up and resumed her walking with faster steps. She was surprised that being alone in the wilderness did not scare her a bit. She assumed that nothing could be worse than the attacks that she survived on the train earlier that day. Also, the fact that she had left the army and was going home to her family put a spring in her steps. She then started to think about her parents and her sisters who were at home. How were they coping with the Russian invasion? Heidi decided that if God would allow her to arrive home to her family, she would not let anyone harm her loved ones. When that thought went away, she found herself thinking of Francis. He must have been sent to the Eastern front and had to face the Red Army. She knew that Francis's task was the most dangerous one. She prayed for him to be safe and protected. There was nothing she could do other than pray. She also thought about Johan, her brother. Only God knew where he was. Only God could help them all. While all these thoughts were going through her head, she realized she had walked to the edge of the forest. In the valley was a village. She stopped and assessed her options. After all, she was a trained soldier and she could make use of her strategy training.

Heidi decided to walk around the edge of the woods and hide behind the bushes and other patches of greenery for camouflage. She got as close to the village as she could while remaining out of sight. She read the name of the village on an old faded sign from a fair distance, and was relieved when she realized that she was on the right path. She was still not close enough to her home town. She decided not to go through the village and avoid talking to anybody. She was afraid that some German soldiers might be there and might recognize her dirty uniform. It was safer not to be seen by anybody. Right then, she knew that she had enemies on both sides of the barricade. Watching out for any human movement from the village, she managed to go around it and kept walking southeast. She heard noises coming from the yards where a rooster or a hungry pig screamed for food. It was a familiar sound of peaceful life that filled Heidi's heart with warmth. The sun was setting behind her. Daylight was fading away, letting the dusk set in. Heidi passed the village and was rushing up the hill looking for the path she had deviated from when the forest ended. By the time evening came, Heidi was rushing on the other side of the hill and could see the path taking her toward another mountain. She also saw a farmhouse in a remote area. She decided to spend the night there. Crossing the field and avoiding a muddy, soggy patch of land, she approached the farm. She stopped about fifty meters away from the house to ponder her next move. The windows were covered by wooden blinds, but she could still see the lining of the light inside. Outside there was no movement. Still suspicious about who might have been living there, she decided not to knock at their door. Instead, she went toward the barn to look for a place to stay overnight. She did not want to take any unnecessary risks. She looked around the barn and saw a hole in the wooden wall. She approached it and squeezed herself inside. It was dark, but the smell of domestic animals and the warmth of their breathing were reassuring. She could find a bale of hay and made an improvised bed for the night. Heidi settled herself on an alcove and closed her eyes. She was fast asleep in no time. She was very tired. Sometime during the night she woke up not knowing where she was. She heard some movement in the darkness but soon realized that it was a horse. Then she relaxed and went back to sleep. In the morning, the rooster announced that morning had arrived. Heidi was up on her feet and with great caution found her way out of the barn and ran over the field toward the woods. She did not want to be seen by anybody at the farm. That way she was safe, and would not involve strangers in her actions. When she was sheltered by the trees she stopped and ate the remaining biscuits and a sugar cube. She realized that if she decided to knock on the farmer's door she might have received some decent food, but it was not worth the risk. She wanted to get home more than anything. She was close enough to make it to Traisen by late afternoon if she was lucky. Once the day began, the morning fog settled in the mountain. At that point Heidi had to rely only on the compass reading. In her mind she thanked the sergeant who gave it to her. He was a good man. She then spent a good part of her trip thinking of all the good people that had helped her along the way since she left home to enroll in the army. The list was not very long, but those men and women had made a difference in her life. She would never forget them.

First it was Thomas and Elisabeth, during her first year in Vienna. Then it was Gloria from Lilienfeld who, with her needy personality, gave Heidi a purpose to protect and guide her, and therefore a good feeling about being helpful. Then came Ticla, with whom she bonded instantly, and Karina, who taught her that under a tough appearance sometimes you can discover a true friend if you take the trouble to persevere. Even Martin the doorman in Pilsen had helped her and cared for her. Next, it was Francis, who loved her with all his heart. Peter form Sabina Station was a true gentleman and friend. He gave her good advice and looked after her well-being while she was up in the mountains. He boosted her spirit and made her live a life without depression. Last but not least were the soldiers from the train which she escaped from, and the sergeant who sent her home at the right moment before it was too late.

By noon the sun dissipated the fog, and Heidi found herself up on the heights overlooking Traisen. She deviated from the path by following the compass and arrived sooner than expected. Of course, the downhill walk was a challenge at least, since there was a stiff slope she had to descend, but nothing could stop her at that point. She could almost see her house from where she was. She made a sigh of relief and pondered her immediate move to go to where she wanted to. When she started her descent to the valley, she realized that it would be harder than she initially thought. The soft and muddy soil was slippery and a few times Heidi landed on her derriere on the slushy soil. When she was about half-way to the bottom of the hill, she noticed that the town looked deserted. Not a soul in sight. Some army trucks were parked on a few spots on the town's main streets but that was all she saw. She was coming from the north side of the town. When she finally reached the outskirts of the Traisen, it was easy for her to rush through the back streets and cross the river over an improvised pedestrian bridge made up of a wide tree trunk, and take the shortcut toward the railway station and then run toward the building she had grown up in: her home. Her heart was pounding in her chest with anticipation and emotions. She took two steps at a time on the side of the building to the third floor apartment. She was about to yell to her family that she was home, but, when she turned the corner to the backyard where the entrance was, she saw the door wide open. At that time of the year they still needed heating in the house, and nobody in their right mind would have left the door open for the cold to get in.

Heidi stepped inside and closed the door behind her ready to surprise whoever was at home at that time of day. Instead, when she entered the living room she stopped in horror. What she saw was her home having been turned upside down, like a robbery had just taken place. The furniture was damaged and things from the drawers were spread on the floor. She ran from the living room to the kitchen and then to the bedrooms and her father's shoe repair shop. She could not find anyone. She was all alone. Her home had been vandalized and her family was gone. Fear that they could be dead sent a shiver along her spine. Getting her bearings after the first shock, she looked around at the devastation. She saw her family's belongings trashed and shredded and all the damage that had been done. By whom? She did not know what to do next. The house was cold and she was all of a sudden very hungry. She checked her pockets and found a sugar cube and sucked on it, while she started to plan what to do next. The main goal was to look for her family, but she felt weak and tired. She let herself slip onto the floor and grabbed her knees with both arms, resting her head on top of them. She tried to work out what might have happened, but her head did not help her much. Her eyes rested on the floor and saw a picture torn into pieces. The image became blurry when tears filled her eyes. It was the only picture she had from Francis. He was wearing the German officer's uniform and was featuring a handsome smile. He had given it to her when she went away on training to Vienna exactly a year ago. After she returned from training, and Francis asked her to marry him, she sent the picture home to Teresa, so that she could see her fiancé. Now the picture was lying there on the floor shredded to pieces. Who could have done all this damage? Heidi blamed herself for not being more interested in the news and not knowing what was happening in her town. She remembered that she had not seen a soul on the streets, and then she got up and headed out the door. She ran downstairs to the neighbors' apartment and knocked at the door. Nobody came to open it. Cautiously she tried the door handle. It cracked open and she peeked inside. It looked similar to her home: vandalized and deserted. She did not step any further. Instead she turned and went back upstairs. She found nothing more than a deep hatred in her soul for the ones who had done all the harm to Traisen people. She did not know who they were but she hated them so much. She could cry a river to let all the sadness out of her chest, but there was no time for crying then. She was cold and hungry and once again she focused on her survival. She went to the kitchen, which now looked more like a dump, and checked the stove. She saw that she could use it. She picked up the parts of a broken stool and shoved the wood inside. She looked for matches in the cupboards, and after a few minutes she found some in a small box. With some old paper she managed to start the fire in the stove. Then she looked for anything that she could eat. By sheer luck she discovered three old potatoes no bigger than an egg, with wrinkled skin and spiky growths. She cleaned them of the poison growth and put them on the stove's black top. Then she waited. Soon she realized that it would take an eternity for her meal to be ready, and she put the tiny potatoes directly inside the stove on the side where the ashes were incandescent. She made sure to watch them and turn them on each side. The baked potato smell filled the kitchen and Heidi took it in with all her senses. The warmth coming from the fire felt good. She was becoming relaxed, as if in by an induced trance. When she took the first potato out of the stove she held it in her hand feeling the heat in her palm before taking the first bite that tasted like heaven. The pleasure of a warm meal sent her into a sweet reverie. She felt happy to be alive and to be home. She had to regain her strength and then look for her family, but right there and then she was content eating a delicious potato in her kitchen. She devoured the first one and then she started the second one while taking care of the last one which was still inside the stove. She must have dozed off for a bit, since she did not hear the steps coming from outside. She jumped out of her skin with fear when she heard a loud voice.

'Achtung! Put your hands up!'

Instantly she raised her arms still holding the half eaten baked potato. Her eyes were big with surprise and fear looking at the gun pointing at her. The German soldier was looking at her, making sure that she was not dangerous, and then he lowered the gun.

'What are you doing here? Are out of your mind? What is it with the fire in the stove? Move away!' He was angry. He pushed Heidi aside from the stove and started to put down the fire with a shovel that he picked up from the floor. The third potato flew out of the stove covered in ashes and rolled on the floor. Heidi caught it right away, burning her hand.

'Ouch!' She cried and dropped it in her lap. Then she carefully grabbed it using a handkerchief and hid it in her pocket. The German soldier, who was corporal, extinguished the fire and turned to face Heidi.

'The smoke was coming out of the chimney, do you know that?'

Heidi, not wanting to be intimidated by the intruder said with irony:

'That is what usually happens when there is a fire. The smoke comes out, like in the old saying "No smoke without fire"!'

'Pardon me? Which planet are you from? Are you insane? What on Earth made you start a fire?'

'I was cold and hungry. I baked three old potatoes and tried to warm up a bit. I have just come home and I found all this mess. I don't even know if my family is alive, or their whereabouts. What is happening here in Traisen?'

He looked at her perplexed.

'Where did you come from? Don't you know that the Russians are shooting from the eastern hills? They are ready to take over the town. We managed to stop them for a short while but we do not have the resources to keep them away. It is a matter of days before they will defeat us. The looting and the damage you see around were done by them

210

during the night. The barbarians sneak into town and steal food and goods, protected by the dark. Most of the local civilians fled their homes and are hiding in a bunker by the old school west of town. They were too afraid to face the Russian invasion during the night time. Furthermore, they look at women like bulls in heat. If I were you I wouldn't stay here overnight, and the fire is out of the question, too.'

Heidi listened to all the horrific news. The Russians were there. Her family had run away and God only knew if they were alive. She would have to go and look for them at the bunker. She was on her feet, ready to leave. The corporal stopped her by grabbing her arm.

'Where do you think you are going?'

'To the bunker, to look for my parents.'

'You must have really have fallen from the moon or something. Haven't I just told you about the Russians? Do you want to be an easy prey for them or what?' He was very serious, but Heidi almost smiled.

'What do you suggest then? I came all the way across the mountain walking alone for two days to get home. Before, I was on a train that was bombed three times in five hours. I need to find my parents and my sisters, and nothing will stop me from doing that.' She pulled her arm from his grasp with a sudden jerk. She also gave him a look that spoke much more than she had already told him. She was determined to leave.

He saw her anguish and despair and spoke gently that time.

'In half an hour it will be a good time to walk to the bunker. Both armies will take a break to eat and recharge their ammunition magazines. I will make sure you get there safe and sound.'

'I see,' Heidi said, not very convinced. She had a lot to think about. On one hand she was still concerned that someone may recognize her uniform even though it was dirty, and on the other hand she could not wait to find out about her family's fate. She knew only too well that as a civilian she had to comply with a German soldier's orders. So she just sat on the broken sofa and waited for the time to pass.

When they were ready to go, Heidi made sure that the door was shut behind her and the windows closed too. After all, it was her home, and she hoped that one day she would come back. The corporal urged her to stay behind him and they walked quickly along the buildings, watching out at every corner. The biggest challenge was when they had to cross the river. They were exposed on the bridge, and they had to run as fast as they could from one end of the old structure to another. Once they reached the old Town Hall they were in the German controlled area and it was easier to walk. By then Heidi could not wait to arrive at the hiding place of her people. She started to run, leaving the corporal behind. He did not bother to follow her anymore. He understood her rush and left her alone. It was safer on that side of town. He still could not figure out how she had appeared out of nowhere, since it had been more than a week that the entire remaining civilian population had sheltered in the bunker or at a nearby farm. Finally, he just decided not to give it another thought. Women were always a mystery to him.

Heidi gathered all her energy to be able to rush to the shelter. She was anxious to see whether her parents were there or not. What she had discovered at home was heart-breaking. She could not forget the shredded picture of Francis on the floor. How much hate one must have to take it out on a simple photograph, and how they had looted the house! Heidi thought the Russians may come out the winners of the war, but that would not make them even half as civilized as the Germans were. At that time, the Russians were her enemies. When she passed the old School House she saw the large barn she used to play in when she was a child. Back then the kids discovered the basement of the building which was locked and which scared them very much. There were a lot of stories told about it, but the truth was that the bunker was built during the First World War by the locals as a place to hide from the combat. It served well then, and obviously it did so now too. Heidi found her way inside the barn and into the basement. She had never been inside the bunker before and was surprised to see that it consisted of one big, dark room crowded with people. Her vision adjusted to the dim light inside, and looked at the faces that started to stare back at her. She browsed all the strangers she passed by, while searching for her parents. There were lots of people, some even sleeping on used clothes or blankets; maybe some were ill or perhaps just exhausted. She was having a hard time seeing all the faces and realized that it would take forever to check everybody in the room. Then she had an idea to shout out her family name.

'Is there anybody by the name of Souisa? Please listen to me, is the Souisa family here? Does anybody know them?'

The room went quiet while everybody paid attention to her. People started to look around to see if there was someone who could respond to her question. Heidi saw all eyes on her and heard nothing in response. She almost felt like bursting into tears from the fear that her loved ones were not there. She wiped her forehead with the back of her hand in exasperation. Then a female voice was heard from the crowd.

'I'm Souisa. We are over here! Who is asking?'

Heidi turned to the direction where the reply came from. Her heart was about to jump out of her chest. The voice resembled to Teresa's. Her sister! Good Lord! She had found her sister! From the mass of people Teresa came to Heidi, unsure of what to expect. When she finally saw her, she put her hand over her heart and rushed to her. When they embraced each other, there were tears of joy in their eyes.

They did not speak, not being able to, for about a minute. When they both realized that it was not a dream but reality, and Heidi was indeed back, Teresa took her hand and led her through the bystanders toward the side of the bunker where she had come from. Heidi was both happy and worried. It was obvious that Teresa was not alone there, and that she would show her who else was hiding there with her.

When her sister stopped, Heidi looked down on the cot and saw her mother trying, but unable, to get up. Beside her, their father was lying on his side and seemed to be asleep. Heidi threw herself to Josephina's weak body and hugged her with all her heart. Then she looked toward her father, who stirred, awoken by the movements around him.

'Frantz, Frantz, look who's here! Heidi came back home!' Josephina said, with unexpected joy.

'Dad, it's me. Are you sick?' Heidi knelt beside him and took his hand. Tears of joy washed her face. She had found them after all. They were alive. From then on she would make sure that they would be all safe. She would look after her family and help them survive. The end of the war was near, and from then on she would battle anyone who was a threat to her and her loved ones. While she made that pact with herself she felt a hand patting her shoulder. When she turned she saw Louisa, her younger sister. Louisa looked changed from the last time they met. She was almost fourteen and had grown a lot in the last year. She was Heidi's height, and had a womanly body. Heidi hugged her, relieved that the entire family was there relatively safe for the moment.

Over the next couple of hours they shared all the good and bad news. The good news was that their prayers had been answered, and they were finally reunited; the bad news was that they were hungry and exhausted. Some of the people in the room were also sick and they feared a pandemic. Their parents were weak, and the sisters were scared of the Russians invasion and all the dangers that they might have to face. Heidi found out that food was almost finished, and they were surviving on water and dry bread from the army's supply. Basically, they were dipping the bread in water to soften it enough to be able to eat it. There was no nutritious food around, and everybody was constantly hungry. Whatever they were able to bring with them from home when they fled in a hurry, was gone after one week. Heidi realized that her father's condition was deteriorating due to the lack of food. He had not been a healthy person to begin with. Apart from his left leg that was injured by a bullet in the First World War, he was also suffering from an internal illness to his gut. He was suffering in silence because of the conditions they were all forced to live in. Heidi was hungry as well. That day she had only three biscuits on the road and one and a half baked potatoes at home. She felt the left over potatoes in her pocket. She took it out and divided the food into four portions for her parents and her sisters, while she settled for some dry bread. While eating, they talked about what had happened to their home and how the enemies were attacking Traisen every day from the side of the mountain. The fear had pushed the town's population to hide in the bunker. The German regiment based in Traisen was trying to keep the Red Army at bay, but it looked like soon they would lose control on the Eastern side of the Traisen River. Shots were fired from one side of the valley to the other, and German soldiers were at the end of their rope in terms of ammunition and strength. Heidi found out that there was an agreement between both armies to cease fire for one hour between five and six in the morning every day. This was deemed the "sleeping hour". Usually, at that time, people came out of the basement to get some fresh air and bring fresh water from the old school's fountain.

Heidi took Teresa aside and had a word with her.

'Sis, I have an idea. Our parents and us, we need some real nourishment if we want to survive this war. Father is suffering quietly and mom is losing her strength. They need some decent food, and so do we.'

'Easier said, than done!' Teresa said with skepticism.

'Listen to me! I have an idea. You said that the farmer up on the hill is still living in his house. That means that he has food. He must have milk and eggs and other things, don't you think?' Heidi looked like she already had a plan.

'The farmer regrets that he cannot deliver produce to the people in town. He must have much more than he and his family need.'

'Really? Hmm… Teresa, I have an idea. I would like to go to the farmer's house tomorrow morning during the "sleeping hour". Actually, I'll definitely go.'

Teresa looked at her sister, questioning her idea.

'Heidi, you've just arrived here, God only knows how you made it, and now you think of risking your life again for a piece of food? You could not be serious.'

Heidi realized that Teresa was terrified by what had been going on in her town for more than a week and also by her sudden arrival, but she would explain the long story to her later. At that moment she was tired and needed some sleep before waking up very early to make the trip over the valley and up to the mountain to the farmer's place. Nothing could change her mind. Her family was too important to her to at least try.

'Let's get some rest now and we'll see what we can do in the morning. Do we have a clock or a watch around here?'

'Dad has his old watch on his wrist. I had to sell mine a while ago for some fabric for a jacket that now must have been stolen from the house anyway. Oh, Heidi, it is so good to have you back. I love you sis, I missed you all these years.'

Heidi hugged her sister and then curled up on the floor beside her parents to steal a few hours of good sleep. After all, home was where one's heart was, and she could very well call the bunker home since she was there with her family.

When she woke up, Heidi thought that she had slept in and looked for her father's hand to see the time. It was dark, but the florescent dial of the watch showed a quarter to five. Good. She still had time to get up and go. She figured that one way trip to the farm would take her about twenty minutes, if not less. She knew the route. She got up. Teresa sensed her, and also woke up.

'Heidi what are you doing?' she whispered.

Heidi turned and put her index finger to her lips, advising her sister to keep quiet.

'I'm going to try to get some real food. Go back to sleep before you wake up everybody in here.'

'No, Heidi, don't go, please… It is too dangerous,' Teresa pleaded.

'Teresa, trust me, I know what I'm doing. I'm trained to survive, I'll be fine. See you in an hour or so.'

'No, wait! I'll come with you!'

'Now you listen to me sis: you stay here and take care of mom, dad and Louisa. They need you here. We cannot leave them alone. I'll go and ask for some food and come back. You have to trust me with this. If

I do not come back in an hour, chances are I've decided to stay over at the farm and come back tomorrow morning during the "sleeping hour". Do not panic, and keep everybody calm here. Do you understand me? Now wish me good luck and go back to sleep.'

Teresa looked at Heidi in dismay. Since when had her sister become so self-assured and bossy? Heidi was younger than her, and should have listened to the older sibling. Soon she realized that she could not stop her. Finally, she whispered "good luck" and let her leave.

Heidi's trip to the farm turned out to be uneventful. In the darkness and the cool morning weather she did not encounter anybody. When she arrived at the farm she went straight to the big barn. She knew that farmers wake up early and attend to the animals first thing in the morning. Sure enough, the farmer was filling the stales with hay and his wife was milking a cow.

'Good morning, hard working people!' she said to them, making sure that they heard her.

Both of them looked toward her startled, and could not believe the shoe master's daughter was standing in front of them. Where in the world had she come from at that hour?

'Good Lord, Heidi Souisa, what are you doing here?' the woman asked, not sure if she was seeing things or if it was Heidi in the flesh standing in front of her.

'I came from town. I'm in a bit of a hurry. I have to go back before the cease fire is over. I was wondering if you have some spare food to give me for my family. In the bunker there are about fifty people who are suffering from famine and are becoming sicker by the hour. I took advantage of this quiet hour and came to see if I can bring them some food.'

'Good girl! I was wondering why they never sent anybody here to get food. I guess nobody had your courage. When did you come back home? Josephina told me that you were still in the army last time I spoke to her.' The farmer's wife was up on her feet and putting an arm over Heidi's shoulder, she led her out of the barn toward the house.

'Yesterday,' Heidi said.

'Let's give you something to eat while I put together a parcel with food to take with you. You must be in a hurry!'

'Yes. Thank you.'

Heidi ate a regal breakfast by the war's standards, consisting of bread, boiled eggs, cheese and raw milk. The farmer's wife filled up a basket with cheese, bread, four boiled eggs and two big bottles of milk. In another fabric bag she stuffed some potatoes, carrots and a few onions, along with more cheese and bread. When all was done, Heidi got up and asked what time it was. It was twenty to six. She knew she had to rush back to make it on time. She put the bag across her body like a back pack and took the basket in one hand, gave a hug to the farmer's wife and thanked her profoundly. When she passed the barn she yelled her thanks and farewell to the farmer, and set off at a fast pace toward Traisen. The weight of the food slowed her down and she was afraid that she would not make it and run out of time. The lucky thing was that she was going downhill and she used gravity in her favor. It was still dark, right before dawn. Her heavy breathing pounding in her ears, balancing herself between the bag on her back and the basket in her arm, making sure she did not spill the milk, she started to run once she reached the town's streets. There was not a soul in sight. Few minutes after six, she passed the old school house and crossed the yard to the barn just as the first shots were fired from the Russian camp on the hill.

Theresa got up and headed to the bunker's door, terrified that someone had fired a bullet at her sister. She should have been back by then but was not. On her way out, in the dark stairwell to the ground level of the barn, she collided with Heidi.

'Good Heavens, girl, watch out!' Heidi yelled, annoyed that someone had almost knocked her down and smashed into the precious wicker basket.

'Heidi! Thank God you're back right on time. I heard shots out there!' Teresa was beside herself with relief.

'Oh sis, here, take this basket. Handle it with care otherwise you'll spill the milk. It almost broke my arm all the way here.'

Teresa grabbed the basket and turned back to the bunker followed by her sister.

Inside most of the people were awake due to the noises from outside, mainly the shooting. They looked at the two young women who were caring a big basket and an equally big shoulder bag. It did not take long for them to realize that it was food that they brought in. Some of them started to ask questions and beg for a piece of food. Teresa stopped to think what to do. Heidi pushed her forward toward the place where their parents were. Then she took off her shoulder bag and started to take out all the food. Teresa followed her, checking out the content of the basket. Frantz, Josephina and Louisa were looking at the abundance of food, thinking that they were still dreaming. Heidi improvised a table cloth from one of the napkins that the bread and cheese were wrapped in, and urged her family to eat. Louisa did not wait for another invitation and grabbed bread and cheese. She stuffed her mouth and moaned with delight. Then Frantz looked at Heidi and asked her quietly where it had all come from. Heidi handed him an egg and bread and told him to eat first, and then she would tell him the whole story. The people around came closer to look at the Souisa family, and their breakfast. Heidi got up and spoke loudly to everyone.

'What you see here is the food that I brought from the farmer on the hill. I took the chance to go there this morning during the "sleeping hour" when the shooting ceased, and asked the farmer for food. My parents are very weak and I feared that they would become ill without proper nourishment. I risked my life out there but I succeeded. I brought good food and milk. It is more than my family needs, and whatever is left over we will give to all of you, but first I need to make sure that my parents and my sisters are not hungry anymore. The farmer on the hill has produce and food that they can spare, but I could not carry more by myself. I'm welcome to go back any day I want, but that is all that I can bring. I made it back just in time before the shooting started, and I took a huge risk by doing that. I will go back when we need more, but I cannot bring food for everyone here. When I go next time, if anyone here volunteers to come with me, I would appreciate it. However, we cannot go there in large groups. That would anger the enemy and they can be very ruthless. After my family eats, the rest of the food will be distributed to all of you. Next time I go to the farmer, I'll take one person with me in order to be able to bring more food. The following time, I can take the same or another person with me for the same reason, but never more than two people. That way we do not catch their attention. Now just be patient, and everybody will have something good to eat today. Tomorrow morning we may have more than today.'

Teresa looked at Heidi in awe, and so did her parents. She was all of a sudden in charge of their well-being and of that of all the others as well. Everybody listened to her and did what she told them to. She gave them hope and food and some of them saw her as their rescuer and hero. Life in the bunker took a turn for the better because of the young woman who came out of nowhere to take care of them. Frantz thought the same thing, and felt very proud of Heidi. She was indeed the child who inherited his courage and determination. And she was wise too. He thanked God for bringing her home. He knew that Heidi was able to look after all of them. He was tired and weak, but his daughter would handle whatever would come their way. He could finally relax and let her be in charge.

For the next ten days Heidi made the trip to the farm, accompanied by another young woman from the refugee group, and fed everybody with the food they brought. One day the farmer's wife did not have the bread baked, but they were given the dough half baked and raw and had to finish baking it at the bunker, cooking it over a primitive fire. The people were happy to have good food every day, even though it was not much when it was shared among everybody, but it was much more than they had had before. While the bunker's population found a new quality of life, the fight over Traisen intensified and the Germans lost some key positions in town. The bridge over the river was controlled by the Russian, and they were free to advance toward the middle of town.

The German troops in Traisen weakened and the surrender of the town was seen as imminent. One day, a small commission of one officer and three soldiers descended into the bunker to announce that the following day everybody was to be moved by trucks toward west through the mountains. The German forces would follow the evacuation of Traisen, since the battle of the town was lost. They negotiated a ceasefire for two hours the next day for the civilians to be moved out. The order was that everybody got ready for departure.

Frantz Souisa would have rather gone home than anywhere else, but he had to listen to the soldiers. Heidi organized an evacuation plan for her family, arranging who took care of whom and making sure that everybody stayed together and boarded the same truck. Later that evening another commission came to do a head count and decide on how many trucks they needed. After that task was completed, they advised the civilians that one truck would suffice and they needed to get ready. During the raid through the bunker, one of the sub-officers recognized Heidi.

'Wait a minute! I know you! You were one of my students five years ago.'

Heidi froze when she recognized her teacher from grade eight. He was always mean to her. Out of all the people in the world, it was he who crossed her path again. She sensed trouble.

'Right, Heidi Souisa, the shoe master's daughter. I thought you were in the army. How come you are here?' the teacher continued.

Teresa's warning system went off, understanding right away what the sub-officer was implying. He could declare Heidi a deserter. Heidi had told her the circumstances in which she had come home, and her clothes could confirm her actions. She would have given Heidi civilian clothes but they did not have any. They all left home with only what they were wearing at the time. She was filled with fear for Heidi's fate.

Heidi felt all the eyes in the room on her and knew she would have to say something. That stupid pig could do her lots of harm. She stood tall and spoke with as much confidence she could find within herself.

'I'm flattered that you remembered me, Herr Professor. Unfortunately my memories of you are not so fond, and I do not want to talk about the old times now.'

He was startled that she dared to confront him in public like that. The little bitch, he thought. She would not let her get away with that so easily.

'Frauline Souisa, may I have a word with you outside? As far as I'm concerned, you are still an active soldier and your obedience is required.'

Teresa froze when she heard that. Heidi gave her a long look and then spoke to the sub-officer.

'With all due respect, sir, I have to tell you that I was discharged from the army a few months ago, and I do not consider you my superior, nor shall I take orders from you any more than anybody here in this shelter. I have no reason to follow you outside.' She said the lie with confidence, without even blushing. Her survival skills had kicked in once again.

The teacher wanted to say something to put her in the corner, but the people made a protective circle around Heidi. Idiots, he thought. Then he turned and left the room followed by the soldiers who witnesses the scene without interest.

The next day, on April 20th, 1945, the evacuation took place. At one o'clock in the afternoon a truck pulled into the old school house yard and the order came for everybody to get out, embark, and leave. Heidi organized the departure with Teresa and helped their parents to get out. The day-light almost blinded them, and slowed them down. The guards urged everyone to hurry and climb in the back of the big truck. The refugees were mostly women, old people, and kids. It was hard for them to board the truck and the process was delayed by several failed attempts.

Finally, the guards started to give them some help instead of only orders. When the Souisa family's turn came to board the truck it was a slow process to lift Frantz and Josephina onto the truck's platform. Louisa jumped on without problems and Teresa followed her. When Heidi's turn came, a hand pulled her aside by her shoulder. It was the teacher, telling her that even though she was released from the army, as she had said the previous day, the effort that the army made for her should be repaid through volunteer work she should perform for the army. Because of this, she was not allowed to leave with her family, but rather she was to follow with the regiment later that day. The bastard had gotten back at her with a below the belt shot. Teresa yelled Heidi's name at the top of her lungs, terrified that she would lose her sister along the way. Her mother started to sob and her father made the sign of the cross, praying for God's help. The people waiting in line behind Heidi were urged to pass by and climb into the truck, while Heidi looked at her family, afraid that she may never see them again. Before the embarkation was over, the teacher went away and one of the guards winked at Heidi. She was standing by the truck trying to find a solution to the problem she was having thanks to her hateful teacher. Nothing came to her mind and she almost panicked thinking that she was going to be left behind, but then she noticed the guard's look. Instantly her mind went into overdrive. The soldier whispered to her to stay close and be ready to jump into the truck when he gave her the signal. Heidi's heart skipped a beat. There was a faint hope that she could still sneak in and leave with the others.

When all were ready to go and the soldiers pulled the cover over the back of the truck, Heidi got the signal to jump on it. She did it seconds before the prelate covered the back of the truck and the engine started. She was pulled inside by the other people and found her way to her family while the truck started to move. Heidi thought that the helpful guard had just joined the gallery of good people she had met along her journey throughout the war. God bless him and his Heidi thought, and let herself be embraced by Teresa, who was happier than she could express to have Heidi back.

The road took them away from home, but at least they were together, and that was a good sign, right then and there. It was not a place or a house that mattered to them anymore, it was the life of their loved ones and staying together, which made all the difference.

Chapter 21

The trip took about two hours. The truck shook along the potholes on the dirt road. When it was going uphill the people had to hold onto each other to steady themselves to keep from falling out. When it was going downhill, they did the same in order not to squash each other against the front board. Some of the travelers got motion sickness, some just sat there helping as much as they could. They were not told where they were going to, and some feared that it might be to a labor camp. They could trust neither the Russians they had to flee from, nor the Germans who were panicking and losing their grip on the war. At that point the civilians were caught in the middle and suffering the consequences of the actions of both armies. When the truck came to a painful stop, and the brakes squeaked hard, the prelate was lifted by a couple of soldiers, and Heidi saw that they had stopped in a village. The streets were empty. The order to disembark was given in an intimidating tone. As a result, people rushed to get off the truck. This was not an easy task especially for the older people. When they were all standing on the road, they were directed toward Town Hall where they would be assigned a placement with a host. In a small room, the mayor of Steinakirchen am Forst was trying to sort things out and direct the newcomers to a place to live. Mostly, there were single rooms in the school or abandoned apartments. When he had to deal with bigger families, he would place them with farmer families in the hills, who could host them. The village was in the mountains, about thirty kilometers west of Traisen.

When the Souisa family's turn came, the Mayor counted them and decided that for five people it was the best to send them to a farm outside the village. There they could find food easier and could also help the farmer with some chores. When the paper was signed and directions given, Heidi and Teresa guided their parents and Louisa to the nearby hill to their host. It was late afternoon already and they were afraid that night would come before they could reach their destination. By sheer luck, while walking on the dirt road, a carriage came from behind and gave them a lift close to the farmer's house. The last two hundred meters were inaccessible by vehicles, and they had to walk. They passed the large barn and headed to the house. The farmer came out to talk to them and looked at the mayor's papers. Then he gave them a long look and stepped aside to let them in. The sun was slipping behind the mountain. Once inside, they met the whole family, which consisted of a wife and three daughters, two teenagers and one about Heidi's age. They appear to be friendly and eager to meet Heidi, Teresa, and Louisa. The farmer's wife took out some food from the pantry and laid it on the table for the guests to eat. They were hungry indeed. They started a conversation over dinner and got to know each other better. The topics revolved around the war and the Russian's invasion. Also, Heidi found out that Steinakirchen am Forst had no German troops to control the village. If the Red Army reached near there, there would most likely be no fights. Once again, that day Heidi thanked God that she had not been sent away from her family. Whatever came their way, they would at least be together.

For the first four days life at the farm was quiet. Everybody helped and they got along well together. Furthermore, no shots were being heard like in Traisen, and the Souisa family had some time to relax. But then, one evening at the end of April, things changed all of a sudden.

One night when the two families were getting ready to go to bed, a loud knock at the door scared them all. At first they wanted to turn off the gas light and pretend to be asleep, but a second knock, more powerful than he first was heard, and the door showed signs of giving in. The farmer went to open it. He made a gesture toward the others to hide in the back room. When he opened the door, the third knock was about to begin. In the door Heidi saw two soldiers. When they started to speak she realized that they were Russians. Her heart sunk in fear. Teresa pulled her back into the hiding spot. They could hear the conversation. One of the Russians spoke perfect German.

'Good evening. I am the commander of the Third Division Pravda and I wanted to stop by and say hello to you and yours.' With those words the second soldier pushed the farmer aside to clear the path for his superior into the house.

'Now that we have met, we are wondering if you have any leftovers from your dinner to spare,' the officer spoke again.

The farmer shifted his weight from one leg to another and, with a mad voice, said 'What the hell do you think you are doing, showing up at my door asking for food? We do not have any food here. We are poor and starving ourselves.'

The soldier, hearing the loud tone, held the rifle up. The commander put a hand over it and lowered it, and told the solder:

'The master of the house would be nice enough to take care of his guests without you threatening him.' Then he turned to the farmer: 'Am I right?'

'No, you are not welcome here, and I have to ask you two to leave now,' the farmer went on. The officer did not look pleased by what he was told, and the soldier grew more alert. The situation was escalating by the second. The officer started to move, checking the room. The soldier went to the front door and slammed it shut.

What happened next was completely unexpected. Heidi jumped out of her hiding place before Teresa could stop her. She went to the middle of the room and looked at the farmer, then spoke. 'You'll have to give these men what they asked for. I'll set the table for their dinner now.' The farmer grabbed her by her arm and stopped her.

'You just go back in the back room and wait there. We have no food to share with the enemy. Do you hear me?'

Heidi escaped his grip and looked him in his eyes.

'We do have food, and will share it if you don't want to see all of us dead.'

The Russian officer listened to the conversation with interest. The soldier did not pay attention, probably because he did not understand the language.

Then, from the back of the room an older man came out, looking tired but determined to say something. It was Frantz Souisa. He looked at the farmer and then at Heidi before speaking.

'Hans, we are grateful that you let us live here with you and yours, and we understand your reasons to be upset, but I believe you should listen to my daughter, and welcome these two men into your house. We do not have much of a choice here, do we?'

The farmer was unsure of what to do. He gave it a second thought and then he gave up, threw his hands in the air and told the newcomers to sit at the table. His family and Heidi's came out of hiding.

The farmer's wife rushed to bring some food, helped by her daughters. The officer sat down and asked Heidi to join him at the table. He was intrigued by her courage and authority.

'So tell me young lady, where are you from? I take it that you are a guest here too, and this wise man must be your father. You two look alike.'

Teresa came to Heidi's side, ready to protect her. But Heidi did not need protection. Heidi was protecting all of them.

'I'm from Traisen, a town about thirty kilometers east of here,' Heidi answered.

'Traisen? We passed through your town a few days ago. It looked like a ghost town, not a soul in sight. How did you get here?'

'We are refugees and were shipped here a week ago.'

'I see. You must be afraid of us, aren't you? But we came to liberate this nation and we are not your enemy. We left families back home too, and we do not attack civilians. Mmm… This bread is as good as my grandmother used to make… and the butter is delicious. Thank you.'

The soldier was shoveling everything into his mouth like he was famished. The officer had good manners. They both ate, and drank herbal tea. When they finished the meal, they got up to leave. The officer thanked the farmer for the welcome and from the door he turned to tell them one more thing.

'My troops will pass Steinakirchen am Forst tomorrow. While I'm in the area I can guarantee that no harm will come to any of you. The farm will be left in peace. But after I'm gone, anything can happen. You make sure to take care of yourselves. I know that some of my co-nationals have a bad reputation, and I'm not saying that is not true. I can only control so many, but not the whole Red Army. I think that this young lady here has a good understanding about what is going on and you should listen to her in the future.' With those words he gave Heidi a long look and a smile. Then he said something in Russian to the soldier and left.

After that visit, nobody felt like going to bed anymore. They sat together and talked about what had just happened and what they should be aware of in the future. The bottom line was that the Germans were gone and the Russians were advancing to the west day by day. As the officer had mentioned, some soldiers were hard to manage and they could be a threat to the Austrian people, mainly the female population. That had to do with the rough habits and bad reputation that the Russian

Army had. In a house full of young women, the farmer and Frantz Souisa had many reasons to be worried. The next day was calm and they began to relax, but the following day, in the evening, another knock on the door brought a Russian soldier who asked for water. He drank a big cup of it and asked for a bucket full of water to take to his mates. That was all he needed and he left. For another two evenings one soldier showed up under one or another pretext.

On the fourth day Heidi and two of the farmer's daughters took a trip to the neighboring farm two hills away from their place. They wanted to relay a message from their father regarding the beginning of spring plowing for the potato plantation. That was a task that Heidi volunteered to take on, accompanying the girls aged seventeen and eighteen. During the day it was supposed to be safe to walk around. When they arrived at the neighbor's house, they were stunned by what they discovered. The house was locked. They yelled to the host to answer the door. After a little while a curtain moved at one of the windows. Heidi waved her hand and gave a friendly smile to whoever was looking out. Two minutes later the door opened and the three of them stepped inside. The darkness was thick due to the covered windows. Heidi saw three silhouettes seated in a corner, and their mother was trying to comfort them.

'Good Lord people, what is happening here?' Heidi asked frankly.

'Who are you and what are you doing here with my neighbor's daughters?' the older woman asked.

'My name is Heidi Souisa. I'm from Traisen. My family and I are living with your neighbor for the time being. Are these your daughters? What happened to them?'

The three poor creatures looked like they were badly beaten and scared. One spoke to Heidi, fighting back tears.

'Two nights ago we were attacked by Russian soldiers. They broke into our house and took us from our beds and had their way with us. They threatened to kill my father if he intervened. They locked our parents in one room and took us into the other room and raped us; all of them by turn.' The girl started to cry openly. The other one took over and continued the story.

'They beat us and slammed us when we protested. Pigs! After they finished, they took food from the pantry and sat at our table and ate while watching us cry, lying on the floor. Sadists! They then pulled their trousers up and took something from their pockets which they threw at us, saying, "Here, you have these, because you were good girls" and laughed. When they left it was almost morning.'

Heidi understood what had happened. She was not entirely surprised. Everybody had warned them about these kind of behaviors. She knew that it was only a matter of time before the soldiers knocked at their door. She needed all the facts to be able to come up with a strategy very quickly.

'Holy Mother of God! You said that they were three?'

'Yes. Three pigs.'

'Did you see them before that night?'

'Yes, they came by, in turns, each one every evening prior to that.'

Heidi thought for a moment.

'They came before to ask small favors, right?' she asked.

'How do you know that? That is exactly right! Are you a mind reader?'

'I wish I was, but I'm not. We have received visits every evening for the last four nights now. We are six girls in the house. I suppose they will keep coming for another two nights and then they'll attack in a pack at the end. Exactly like they did here… Oh my God! We do not have much time to get ready for a counterattack.'

Her farmer's girls came closer to Heidi, as if already seeking shelter. Heidi remembered why they had gone there in the first place, and urged them to deliver the message their father had told them to. While they started to talk to the mother, Heidi had few more questions for the neighbor's daughters. They were obviously still in distress, but she figured that it was better to talk about what had happened than to keep it all bottled up inside.

'We are afraid that they will come again one of these nights. What can we do to protect ourselves?' one of the girls asked Heidi.

'You should hide, and your parents can tell them that you went away to some relatives in the village when you're actually hidden under the bed or somewhere. Just don't give up. Quit being a victim. Fight for your lives.'

'Easier said than done,' the mother of the girls intervened. 'These soldiers have guns, and no hearts.'

'Yes, and besides, they think that they did nothing wrong, since they paid us with some fancy pieces of lingerie,' the older girl mentioned to Heidi.

Fancy lingerie, Heidi thought. Where on Earth had these barbaric sadists found women's lingerie to give away, just like that?

'What lingerie? Do you still have it? Could you show it to me, please?'

'Oh, sure we can. Come with me to the other room. There are silk camisoles and beautiful bras, and some embroidered pants, all with French labels, not Katyusha flannel underwear.'

When the girl opened a drawer, inside were a few pieces of Madame Fleur's boutique's items that Heidi knew all too well. She could not understand how, by a twisted game of fate, her very own lingerie, shipped home when she left Brno, had fallen into the hands of the Russian soldiers. She felt like crying, but kept her composure in order not to look like an idiot in front of the girls who had gone through hell the other night. The only explanation was that the Russians looted her house and paid for their orgies with the goods they had stolen. Idiots! How she hated them for all they did, and were about to do.

'What you have here are goods that were stolen from my house in Traisen. I know it sounds strange, but I bought these items in Pilsen, Czechoslovakia more than a year ago, and in January this year I sent them home from Brno,' Heidi said.

'Really? You know what? We do not want them. As nice as they are, they remind us of the most horrific nightmare we have ever had. Take them back, if they are yours.'

'No, not after they touched them, I do not want them back. Do what you want with them, burn them for all I care, it does not matter anymore. What bothers me so much is that they have profaned everything they have touched. My fiancé's picture was torn to pieces in the middle of our living room. What they wanted to prove by doing that I really don't know, but they are capable of doing us a lot of harm. Thank you for talking to me about your dreadful experience. I hope God will help you recover from your ordeal. I think my host's daughters and I better get going now. You take care of yourselves.'

Heidi took her companions and returned back to the farm. She told her and the farmer's families about what had happened at the neighbor's farm, and tried to put together a contingency plan for their defense. They had already received four night visits, but since there were six young women in the house, Heidi figured that there would be another two nights before the soldiers came after them. That meant two full days were left. She talked to Teresa and their host's oldest daughter.

'Too bad that we do not have a young man here at the farm! My father and your father are not in any shape to fight with one soldier, let alone six of them,' Teresa said, at a loss for ideas.

The farmer's daughter then said something very odd, and quickly retracted the words that had slipped her lips. She mentioned that her brother would not count as a man in the house. Heidi's sharp thinking noticed that, and asked more questions.

'What do you mean, your brother? Where is he? I did not know you had a brother.'

'Oh, I don't have one… I suppose. He is as useless as a rotten tree in the middle of a lake. Forget I even mentioned him.'

'No, no, please tell us about him. Where is he now?'

'I told you, he is useless.'

'Listen to me: I do not care how useless he may be, I need to know where this brother of yours lives,' Heidi pushed the girl to keep talking.

'In the basement,' she replied.

'Excuse me? Say that again,' Heidi could not believe what she had heard.

'Look, my brother is a very sick person; sick in the head. He is kept in isolation because he is a very unsocial being. He was in a hospice for years, but this winter they sent him home because of the shortage of food. My parents were forced to go and pick him up and bring him home. We had to lock him in the basement so he wouldn't harm himself or others. Are you satisfied now? Any more questions?' The girl was irritated and nervous at having to reveal the family secret to complete strangers.

'I'm sorry to hear the tragic story, but thank you for sharing it with us. I think we can ask your brother for help.'

'His help? Ha! He is not good for anything. He is a madman.'

'Even madmen are good for something if one knows how to work with them. For the problem we are having, he may be the only help we can get, unless you want to procrastinate and be hurt like the girls we visited today. Take me to the basement where he is locked, please. I'll talk to him and ask him to help us.'

'I do not think you know what you are about to get into. He is more like an animal than a human being. My parents locked him up for a good reason.'

'I want to see him anyway. I'm not scared. Take me to him,' Heidi insisted.

The girl looked at Heidi and, throwing her arms in the air and rolling her eyes, turned and headed to a door that was always locked. She took a key from her apron pocket and then opened it. Heidi followed her down a stairway. The girls stopped in front of another closed door and from a small table she took a gas lamp. With a match she lit the lamp to provide some light in the dark stairwell. Then she unlocked the door and called her brother's name, Hans. Heidi came closer at the threshold.

'Hans, you have a visitor. Her name is Heidi, and she wants to see you and speak with you. Do you want to talk to her?' his sister asked cautiously.

Heidi stepped inside the basement, holding the lamp to better see her surroundings. A silhouette was standing in the dark like a shadow. She began to question her judgment about facing this man, but it was too late to go back. She was not a coward. Besides, Teresa knew what was going on, and if she was in danger she would yell to her sister for help. She stepped inside the small room, and was hit by a heavy smell. Then, she held the lamp higher and the light revealed a face that looked more like a gorilla than a human. Heidi held on to all her strength not to scream out loud. She was terrified and sorry at the same time. She stared at the man in utter shock. He covered his eyes from the light, and took a step back as if he was afraid of something. Heidi started to talk to him with a shaky voice that grew more controlled with every word.

'Hello Hans, my name is Heidi and I came here to visit you and invite you upstairs in the house. Would you like to come with me and your sister?'

His sister frowned, not sure if allowing him out of his room would be such a good idea after all. Heidi knew what she was doing. She needed him out in the open. He was a human being and she was determined to treat him as such.

'Hans, would you like to come out of this basement and be with the rest of us, your sisters, your parents and my family?'

'I don't know. Are there any dogs upstairs? I'm afraid of dogs. Dogs bite Hans.'

'Oh, there are no dogs in the house, or at the farm for that matter, but if we see dogs that would want to bite you, you can bite them back. You have more power than dogs have.' Heidi was trying to train Hans for the possible encounter with the Russian soldiers. She figured that playing a bit with his mind would be to their advantage. She was pleased that Hans was not an aggressive madman, as his sister described him. He was ugly and smelled awful, but with some patience Heidi thought that he could serve her purpose: to keep the enemy away from the girls.

Encouraged by Heidi and his sister, Hans came out of his room into the daylight. When Teresa saw him she was shocked too. Heidi called Louisa and his other two sisters and told each of them what to do. One was supposed to bring water to wash him, one was sent to bring a pair of scissors, one to get her father's shaving knife, and some soap, and one to get some fresh clothes from the farmer's closet. They took advantage of the fact that the parents were busy with the work outside, and did not have to justify what they were doing.

Heidi and Teresa started to cut Hans's long and dirty hair, while his sisters put a bucket of water in front of him and with some wet cloths washed his eyes and forehead. They helped him get out of the dirty clothes and washed his bony body. Hans was happy that six girls were taking care of him. When they cut the long beard, and he needed a clean shave, Heidi went outside to look for her father. She did not know how to give him a proper shave. When she asked her father to help her, Frantz Souisa was surprised by Heidi's plan, but he followed her back into the house and tried not to let his repulsion toward the poor creature released from his basement cell, show. Trusting his daughter's judgment, he shaved Hans's face, careful not to cut or harm him. After that, he actually looked human again. Next, his sisters wanted to cut his fingernails, which had grown long and curvy, like claws. Heidi stopped them.

'Hans, we will let you keep your long fingernails. You can use them to fight dogs if they ever come here. Do you understand me?'

'He, he, I can fight dogs with my fingernails. Good. I like that,' Hans grinned.

Teresa exchanged a quick look of approval with Heidi for her brilliant idea.

Heidi's idea did not seem that brilliant to Hans's parents when they came home late afternoon and saw their son out in the open, all cleaned up and smiling. They were against having him free in the house, considering it a threat to others. Heidi had explained the reasons for bringing him out of the basement, and once again Frantz had to reassure them of his daughter's better judgment to his host.

'Let her deal with the situation we are in the best she can. She knows what she is doing, and you have to trust her. Heidi is smart, and if someone is going to save us from the orgies that the Russians are taking part in, then she is to be in charge, because she really can save us. I give you my word that Heidi will keep everything under control and Hans will not pose any danger to any of us here.'

That evening all of them had a good dinner, and Hans actually behaved well, and enjoyed the company. Later, another soldier knocked at the door asking for a glass of milk, looking around the room and leaving. He was the fifth one. Heidi made sure that Hans and the soldier did not see each other. Hans was their secret weapon, in the fight that would most likely take place the following night.

The next morning Heidi summoned all the girls for a meeting. Together they went over a well organized plan for "welcoming" the soldiers who would come that night to harm them. She would not give up the fight like the neighbor's girls. The six of them walked around the house and into the barn, looking for places to hide. They went up a ladder to the barn's attic, which was half full of hay. They explored the place and made six hiding places using piles of hay. Then they decided on an emergency escape route from the attic to the ground floor through a hole in the upper floor, making sure that the landing would have enough cushioning to prevent any injuries. After that, they went about the day's chores. In the evening they had an early dinner, after which the girls and Hans sneaked out of the house to the barn. All of them used the ladder to get up in the attic, and got to each hiding place. Hans was told to sit on the hay and keep quiet. Heidi and Teresa grabbed the end of the ladder and moved it from the middle to one side of the barn, close to the pigs' sewer box. After that they got into their positions and waited. They were prepared to spend the entire night in the barn if necessary. It was already dark outside, and even darker inside. The moon was sending a foggy light from behind a thin cloud. Around nine, they heard some voices speaking Russian outside. Then they heard the steps walking around the barn and powerful knocks on the house door. By the noises, Heidi knew that there were quite a few soldiers. When they grew impatient, they yelled to the farmer to open the door or else they would shoot. The threat made the girls feel goose bumps, but nobody said a word. Finally, the farmer opened the door and the soldiers walked in, eager to find the girls. There were six of them. They ignored the people in the house and pushed them aside, calling for the girls. When they couldn't find them, they became confused for a minute and started to talk among themselves, probably unsure whether they had the right farm. After a while they became angry and, in broken German, asked the parents where the girls were. The farmer started to say that they had been sent to the village with a message for the mayor and hadn't come back yet. The way he said it, without much certainty, showed that it was a lie. The soldiers became even angrier, and for a moment Frantz and Josephina Souisa thought that it would be the end for them. While one soldier pointed a gun at the farmer, another one said something that made them change their minds and, instead of shooting, they decided to search the house for girls. After all, they had gone there to have some fun, not to kill. Each room, pantry, and even the basement were searched. When they found nobody, their rage built up. They started to quarrel in their own language, storming out of the house like madmen. Frantz and his wife ran to the window to see what they were up to. The noise outside grew louder when they kicked buckets and other objects in the farmer's yard out of frustration. Then they stormed inside the barn. The adults in the house began to pray for the safety of their children. They could not do anything to help them. It was all up to Heidi's plan to work out from then on.

The soldiers stopped inside the barn to listen and to get used to the darkness. A cow moved in the stable and they turned toward where the noise came from. They whispered something and all six of them spread out to explore the wooden building. Up in the attic the girls held their breath in fear, feeling like running, but knowing that everybody had to wait for Heidi's command first. Hans was quiet too, which really impressed Heidi. Maybe he was not that mentally challenged after all. One of the soldiers stumbled over the ladder positioned in its strategic place by Heidi and Teresa. He called for his mates.

'Hey, over here! I found a ladder going to the attic. Should I explore what is up there?' the soldier yelled to the others.

They all rushed toward him. Heidi heard them making jokes and laughing while they started to climb up. The moment was close. She had to wait for the last one to climb the ladder before giving the two signals she had planned. The soldiers enjoyed the mission, and by then they were almost sure that their victims were hiding in the attic. The situation was becoming interesting. The cat and mouse game has started. It pumped their adrenaline and some of them felt more excited in anticipation. The place was perfect for what they had in mind to do. Almost like in the movies. With the tips of their rifles they stabbed the hay piles, still talking and laughing. Then they heard a scream from the other side of the attic.

'Run, run to the hole! Hans the dogs are right in front of you. Get up and fight them. You can fight them with your claws. Go and get them boy!' Heidi gave the orders in a firm voice and waited to see what the others were doing. The farmer's girls and Louisa jumped out of their hiding places, making the hay that covered them burst in the dark like little explosions. They ran to the well-known escape hole, away from where the soldiers were standing still unsure of what had just happened. In the moment of confusion, Hans popped from about two meters in front of them, and with a sharp, animalistic scream jumped at them, scratching their faces. He kept jumping up and down, aiming for the soldiers' heads. The Russians were caught unprepared, and could not even understand what creature was attacking them all of the sudden with such a forceful reaction cutting their faces, and eyes. Some moaned in pain and fell on their knees, some were looking for a place to hide, two were turning to look for the ladder to run downstairs. It was an ambush that Heidi and Teresa watched with terror and satisfaction at the same time. The bastards were getting a lesson they would not forget easily. Once Hans started the fight, seeing that he could overpower the enemy, he had a blast. He did not give his victims a moment of break. He kept attacking over and over again, chanting, "Hans is not afraid of dogs. Hans fights bad dogs!" When he had knocked all the soldiers down in the hay, he had an idea of his own. He started to push them down from the attic. Not seeing what was happening because of their wounds and being completely disabled, each soldier was pushed over the edge of the attic by Hans. They landed in the pigs' sewage box and were covered in dirt and pig waste. That was the victory moment that made Hans an instant hero. Heidi and Teresa approached the edge of the attic and looked down. The soldiers were trying to get up from the slippery dirt. After several failed attempts, they'd gotten out of the large box, and they were limping towards the barn's gate, taking off like a herd of wounded animals covered in pig waste, holding their palms over their badly scratched faces. All six of them were running away thinking that they had just seen Satan in the flesh and blood.

Heidi and Teresa, still up in the attic, approached Hans, who for once in his life looked happy and accomplished. The girls praised his courage and strength and guided him toward the rescue hole helping him descend. They reunited with the other four girls on the barn's main floor.

When the two groups were together, Heidi told them that it was safe to go back to the house. At the gate of the barn they were met by their worried parents, who were rushing to see what had happened inside. When they saw that their children were safe, they hugged each of them individually, and went back together into the house. It was quite an eventful night, but everything worked out for the best in the end. Hans' hands and clothes were stained with his victims' blood and everybody helped him clean up while thanking him for being their savior. The parents were given a rundown of the events that took place inside the barn, and in the end everybody was able to have a good laugh at the Russian soldiers' expense. Heidi's plan worked. They were safe, and have taught the Russians a lesson that night. Eventually the enemy would retaliate and strike again, but until then the Souisa family had time to plan their defence. That was what it was all about, Heidi thought: being one step ahead of your enemy. It was a basic survival rule that Francis, her dear fiancé, had taught her and she would never forget it.

Chapter 22

The next day in the morning, everybody at the farm were still sleeping due to the events that happened the night before. It was a gorgeous day. May rolled in with good weather and Mother Nature was blessing the hills and mountains with a new fresh green coat of awakened vegetation.

'Teresa, wake up. The sun is high in the sky!' Heidi shook her sister gently, afraid that half of the day had passed already.

'What? I had such a good sleep. No dreams, no nightmares. Is everybody still sleeping in the house, or are we the laziest ones?'

'We are the first ones awake. We should have been up by now and prepare for the Russian's counterattack. I have a strong feeling that tonight they will come again, and this time they'll be really angry. We have to find another way to defeat them.'

'Oh, Heidi, how long do we have to live like this? Always in fear, always on the defense, always on the edge…'

Teresa braced herself, not sure that they would survive after all. Heidi was already up, making sure that the others got up and began their daily chores. There was no time to waste. The enemy was watching them. She knew that. An hour later, in the large kitchen around the table, the young people of the house were brainstorming another defense plan. After a few possible scenarios, they decided that the hiding place had to be the big barn again. With that, they stormed outside and headed towards the barn. The mess left behind by the soldiers was a constant reminder of their presence and threat. The farmer's oldest daughter suggested repeating the same approach as the night before, since it worked so beautifully, but Heidi knew that the soldiers were not stupid enough to fall into the same trap twice. She went up the ladder to the barn's attic to think and explore new possibilities. For lack of a better idea, the others followed her up there. She started to shovel and spread the hay around. She uncovered the attic floor and looked at the old boards. She jumped up and down a few times to test their resistance, and then she came up with a new idea that nobody would have thought of. She ordered Hans to go downstairs and grab a saw and bring it to her. Hans did what he was asked with a great deal of pleasure. He had rediscovered a new life and new opportunities that he had never had before in isolation. He was not a madman, he was only slightly mentally challenged, but his physical abilities were intact. In no time he presented Heidi with the tool she needed, and when Heidi began to try to cut a hole in the attic's wooden floor, he took the saw from her and did the job himself, making everybody notice his good skills. When the first hole was finished, it was large enough for a person to fall through. Heidi thanked Hans for a job well done, and moved around to find another place for a similar one. The girls got the idea that Heidi had in mind, and spread around to look for other places for new holes. The hay was gathered in piles and Hans gladly cut hole after hole according to Heidi's instructions. Some areas were not suitable for such alterations since there connected to main structural boards, and they did not want to destroy the attic. They were only setting a few traps for the uninvited visitors. Heidi authorized about six holes to be cut in well-chosen places. They left the holes uncovered during the day, to make sure they did not fall in the traps themselves. Then Heidi looked for places to hide. Above the attic was a net of beams that sustained the barn's roof. She asked Teresa to help her reach one of those beams. Like a monkey she grabbed one and balanced herself on top of it as if sitting on a horse. She was comfortable doing this, but she wasn't sure how the other girls would feel about climbing the beams. In order to lure the soldiers up to the attic and have them fall through the traps, they would have to be up and above it.

'Right now we will do a rehearsal. Each of you has to pick a beam that you can climb on your own or with a little help. Then you have to hold onto that beam for dear life. Do you understand?' Heidi's words took them by surprise.

The younger girls tried to climb up onto the lower beams. Heidi asked Hans to give them a lift. Louisa and two of the farmer's daughters climbed up like they were getting up on a tree. Once all were in positions Heidi noticed that they were grouped on the same side of the attic like a flock of birds. Heidi explained to them that they should be more spread around, so that when they lured the soldiers to the traps they would be sure to fall down. The strategy was to attract the enemy to each hole they had made. Teresa helped the girls to get off the beams and Heidi indicated to each of them which beam they had to position themselves on that night. Hans was supposed to help them get to their posts, cover the holes with hay, and then hide in the cows' stable. His role was more passive that time. Heidi did not want to expose him to any danger. He was a good young man. He was very respectful and obedient to everything Heidi asked him to do.

The rest of the day passed quickly. Teresa still did not think that the soldiers would come back that night. She liked to believe that the attack they suffered the previous night would keep them away from the farm for good. She thought that Heidi's plan seemed a little exaggerated, but she did not dare to stop her sister and undermine her authority within their group. After dinner, when the dark surrounded the hills and the fields, the six girls and young Hans slipped unnoticed into the barn. Within minutes they had all climbed up their designated beams and soon thereafter Hans finished covering the holes with hay. He then descended the ladder, climbed into one of cows' stables, and made himself a comfortable nest while grinning with accomplishment. The heat from the cows' breath kept him warm and he was about to fall asleep. After about an hour, the awkward position the girls were in made them extremely uncomfortable and some of the younger ones, including Louisa, started to complain. Heidi quickly advised them not to become complacent, since the dangers that they were hiding from were much more unpleasant than the discomfort of holding onto the barn's beams. Outside it was quiet, with only the night bugs and frogs' songs to be heard. Half an hour later, the barn doors flew open with startling noise. A group of soldiers, whispering something in Russian, walked in. They had guns. The fresh air coming from outside woke Hans and made the cows move. Hans realized that the enemy was close, browsing the barn. Quickly he shifted in his hiding place and covered himself with more hay. The soldiers did not pay any attention to the noise coming from the cow's quarter. They knew that animals were there. Then one of them turned on a flash light and scoured the entire main floor. When they found the ladder, the light beam followed toward the attic. One of the girls became too afraid, seeing the light and the soldiers, and burst into a hysterical scream. Instantly the light from the flashlight found her up on the beam. The soldiers were thrilled to see her. She looked like easy prey. The first one was already half way up the ladder when another girl became scared and started to scream from fear that the soldiers would get her. That started the chase, and the soldiers could not wait for their turn to get up on the ladder and drag down the young women. They knew that they would get what they wanted. There was no doubt of it. The six of them were up in the attic in no time, trying to locate the girls. Due to the rush, and by pushing one another, the flashlight was dropped onto the floor, and when it hit the ground it went off, leaving everybody in pitch darkness. The soldiers swore in frustration while trying to adjust their eyes. Everything had gone well for them so far, but some feared that the damn barn was cursed, always bringing them bad luck. The only relief came when Heidi began to talk out loud. She was giving instruction to all the girls to start to make noises, like playing a cat and mouse game to force the soldiers to separate from each other and come and get them. Once again, the girls' voices, the fact that they may as well have been blindfolded, and the chase itself, put the attacker in a challenging mood to dare and go and get them. They could almost feel the pleasure they were about to get from the little witches who defeated them the night before. Sweet revenge was so close. They began to move, with each of them picking a target, and once they were all ready to jump and drag the victim down from the beam, the unexpected happened again. Somehow, each soldier stepped onto thin air, and with a big thud fell down through the holes, landing on the ground. Pain and frustration spread throughout their bodies, since some of them had hit the floor very hard. One of the rifles they were carrying went off and the noise from the shot sent all the animals into frenetic chaos, filling the barn with cries of agitation. Again, it was as if they had landed in hell, and nothing went according to plan. Some got up and limped, and some could hardly move and had to ask the others for help. A free fall from more than three meters onto a hard surface between tools and boxes was the last thing they expected. Besides, if the animals became loose, scared by the firearm, they would trample them under their feet. It was wiser to run away than to make another attempt to catch and rape the girls. With great effort and much pain the soldiers left the barn like a group of defeated wolves. When they had gotten far enough down the hill, Heidi called Hans to come and help everyone climb down from the beams. He gladly complied and after few minutes they all returned to the house safe and sound. Again the parents were worried sick, especially after they heard the shot earlier. For most of the night, the girls related to their parents the chain of events from that evening. They then all went to bed exhausted.

At dawn the next day Heidi was up and found her father seated on a rock in the yard. She walked over to him.

'Good morning Dad! How are you? You look tired.'

'I slept well, but not long enough. When I woke up I kept thinking of our day to day life here at the farm. You, my dear, were smart enough to trick the Russians two nights in a row, but our luck will wear thin one of these days. Besides, how can you possibly set another trap for them next time? They are becoming angrier by each day, and it won't be long before their rage pushes them to kill us all, simply because you girls do not give up. I'm really scared of what could happen if we stay here another night. I'm seriously thinking of leaving the farm, going to the village, asking the mayor for travelling papers and returning home. What do you think?' Frantz asked his smart daughter.

'Dad, I believe you are right. It is too dangerous to stay here. They will use whatever it takes to destroy us one way or another. I'll start to prepare my sisters and Mom, and we can be in the village before noon. You'll have to tell the farmer that we are leaving and thank him for his hospitality. I love you, Dad. We will make it home someday, don't you worry.' Heidi hugged her father and ran inside to deliver the news to her family.

The farmer and his family were sorry to hear about the sudden decision of the Souisa family to leave them, but nothing could hold them back. Even Hans Jr. was sad to see Heidi leave. She was the nicest person he had ever met. To help them arrive in the village, the farmer gave them a small wagon to transport their few belongings and a bag of food for the journey. Teresa and Heidi packed everything tidily and made room for one person to sit on the wagon. Their elderly parents were in no shape to walk all the way to the village on their own. They could take turns and sit while the girls pushed or pulled the wagon up and down the hills. The day was nice and the path was relatively dry, making their journey easier.

By mid-afternoon they had parked the wagon in front of the Town Hall and all of them went inside to talk about the passes to travel home. It was May 5th, 1945, and Austria was being liberated from the German occupation from both directions: from the east the Red Army was advancing, and from the west the Americans were approaching. The mayor told them to wait at least another week, until a pact was expected to be signed when the two Allied armies would meet. He told them to be patient and return to the farm for the time being. Frantz Souisa told the mayor that the farm was not a safe place for them and told him about the events of the previous two nights. He told the mayor that, with or without papers, they would head back to Traisen. Seeing his determination, the mayor, who did not want to attract the Russians' attention, persuaded Frantz to wait another day and stay over in a small apartment in a nearby building that was empty at the moment. He also promised him that he would ask for traveling papers for them in the next few days. In the end, given that it was almost evening, Frantz agreed to spend the night in Steinakirchen am Forst and took the apartment keys that the mayor offered him. Tired and disappointed the whole family entered the apartment and got ready to eat for the second time that day. The rooms were nicely furnished and showed that whoever lived there before had good taste and a fair amount of money. Without changing anything, the parents and the daughters made themselves comfortable and began to relax. They all hoped for an uneventful night in which they could sleep for a change. Before turning in to bed, while Josephina was busy making the beds in one of the two rooms and the girls were washing themselves in the lavatory, a powerful gunshot blew the kitchen window in, shattering it in a million pieces. Frantz almost had a heart attack and the women screamed in horrific shock. They all hid on the floor and checked on each other to see if anybody had been hurt. From the street they heard voices speaking in Russian. Nobody dared to move or get up, but Heidi managed to turn off the lights everywhere in the apartment, and tried to calm everyone down. She closed the kitchen door, and locked the entrance door securing it with a table. Then she told everybody to grab blankets and the pillows and sleep on the floor. She did not know why they had been shot at, but it seemed like the danger was over. After about half an hour she dared to look out of one of the room's window that overlooked the main street, and saw that the streets were empty. With that she said "Good night" and fell fast asleep. It was the third night in a row that the Russians scared them to death. She needed some good rest. Teresa, on the other hand, was unable to settle down and sleep. Her weak heart would not calm down. She stayed up half of the night watching her family. The next morning they packed and left the apartment as soon as they could. Before the mayor's office opened, they were already there waiting at his door. Frantz was furious and restless. When the mayor came in, he was onto him right away.

'Good morning, Herr Mayor.'

'Good morning! How was your night? Did you find everything all right?'

'All right, you say? How could it have been all right when not long after we arrived at the apartment we were shot at from the street. Do you have any idea why that happened?' Frantz asked frankly.

'Oh...oh ...how unfortunate. I heard the shooting last night but I did not realize it was directed at that window,' the mayor tried to avoid giving an answer.

'Yes, it was at us that they shot. We are lucky no-one was in the kitchen at that time. But why would they shoot at that window?'

The embarrassment was written all over the mayor's face. Finally, he decided to tell the truth.

'The only explanation I can think of is that a month ago, when the first Russians arrived in the village, the woman who lived in that apartment took a gun and shot a soldier from that window. She was mad because she lost a loved one on the Eastern front. She did it out of revenge, not thinking of the consequences for our community. We were able to expel her from the village to be on peaceful terms with the Red Army and avoid civilian casualties.'

'And what on Earth made you send us there after all that had happened? Do you realize you could have had us all killed? What kind of a man are you? Shame on you!' Frantz was losing his temper. Josephina put a hand on his shoulder to calm him down. Heidi was filled with anger too when she heard the story. She felt like giving the mayor a slap in the face.

'I regret profoundly what happened. I just thought that the story had been forgotten by now,' the mayor tried to defend his bad judgment.

'You know what? I do not find you suitable as mayor, and I have lost trust and respect for you. If you give us the papers to go home today, good; if not, again good. We will leave this village either way. It does not matter anymore. If we stay here we'd be killed by your ignorance and stupidity. If we leave we may get killed on the road, but at least we make the decision for our fate ourselves, not by an idiot like you,' said Frantz, and Josephina felt a chill down her back.

'I told you that the papers are not ready yet. One more day and things will start to look better, believe me,' the mayor said, taken back by Frantz's anger.

'Enough! I take it that you cannot give us the papers today. Then I say "good-bye" to you. We have a long way home and do not need to waste any of our time on you anymore. Josephina, girls, we are done here. Let's go.' With that he turned on his heels, and while dragging his injured leg, left the office followed by his family.

Outside, another gorgeous May day greeted them with warmth. The wagon was ready for the trip. In silence the Souisa family left the village heading toward the forests on their journey home. They were not scared. As a family they had been through a lot since the war began, and they braced themselves for this last dangerous endeavor. Crossing the mountain directly, and staying away from the main roads, turned out to be an extremely difficult task. When Heidi left the army and walked home almost a month ago, she was driven by a powerful desire to see her family. Also, she was young and healthy and had only herself to care for. This second trip home was entirely different. Teresa and Louisa were self-sufficient, but their parents needed extra care and slowed down the entire process. At any given time one parent was on the wagon to rest and the other was walking tiredly along the path. The girls were taking turns pulling the wagon, and sometimes more than one was pulling it. The warmer weather made them thirstier than normal, and they had to stock up on water every time they found a spring. Every bit of extra weight on the wagon put a bigger strain on the girls. Furthermore, they had to try to go as fast as they could to reach home sooner, rather than later. The time spent on the run was dangerous, since they did not have traveling papers and, if caught by the Russian authorities, it would have been nothing but trouble, and possibly even a big threat to their lives. By evening, they had covered about a third of the distance. It was time to find a place to spend the night. The path they took was away from the villages, and deep in the mountains farms were hard to find. They arrived at a hunting cabin in the middle of the forest. It was deserted, and had not much furniture inside apart from a single wooden bed, a table and a bench, but it would provide shelter from wild animals and cold weather for the night. Heidi and Teresa made sure that everyone was inside the cabin and, with a few clothes and dry grass they made sure that each of them had a place to sleep. They were extremely tired, physically and psychologically. During the night they heard the howling wolfs. In the morning, they all shared a quick breakfast which consisted of bread and water. Before the sun was up shining through the trees they were well on their way. They looked like a small procession passing on a lonely road seeking the freedom they lost many years ago. Tired and hungry, by mid-afternoon they came to a farm. The cows pastured lazily on the stiff green hill, but no humans were in sight. Heidi looked at the small house between the high trees.

'Teresa, I would like to go to that house and see if the farmer is home. I intend to ask him permission to stay over the night, if possible. You better stay here with mom and dad and keep Louisa from wandering around.'

'Heidi, do you think it is safe to go there alone? What if there are soldiers in the house. There is no movement around the house. What if they are all dead inside? My goodness, sis, it could be a trap.' As always, Teresa imagined the worst.

'Well, either way we have to find out what is going on. We have to call it a day anyway. We are exhausted and famished. These cows have milk. At least we can try. Wait here. I will signal you with my hand. If all is fine, I'll wave to you with one arm. If something is wrong, I'll cross my arms above my head. Do you understand me?'

'Why, Heidi! I'm scared. We could get in trouble here. How am I supposed to help if you cross your arms?'

'Good question. Let's think about a plan.' Heidi just wanted to calm Teresa down. There was really not much to do if the house was a trap. They had no chance of escaping alive.

'You and the others hide here in these bushes. I will take the safe route around the house, listen for clues, and spy through the windows. Don't worry about me. I can run and hide somewhere. Just stay here and do not come out until I wave to you.'

With that, Heidi left while Teresa set up the camp behind the blucberry bushes. The house was quiet. In the yard there was a small shed with some hay where the cows slept at night. Heidi investigated the surroundings but found nothing suspicious. She lowered herself down and came closer to the house. She looked through the dirty window but was not able to see anything. It was all blurry and too dark inside. She decided to try the door. Cold sweat ran down her spine when she put her hand on the door knob and pushed down. It was unlocked. The door gave way with a long squeak. Heidi was shaking when she stepped inside. Her instincts told her that something was wrong, but she could not stop. She felt like running away but her feet were glued to the floor, her eyes trying to adjust to the poor visibility of the room. She left the door open; mostly to be assured that she had a quick way out. She took a few steps inside; it looked to be empty. She crossed the room to the kitchen. She stopped in her tracks. Nothing could have prepared her for what she saw.

She let out a sharp cry while looking at three bodies lying on the floor. They were tied up and had scarves over the mouths. Heidi went straight into a panic attack. She could not move, paralyzed by fear and shock. There were one man and two women spread on the kitchen floor. They looked dead to Heidi. They must have been the people who were living there. No blood was visible from where she was standing. Then someone moved slightly and made a faint sound, and Heidi felt like she was about to jump out of her skin. She thought she had imagined it, but one of the women was really moving, awoken by Heidi's scared cry. Seeing that, Heidi tried to put herself together and approach the woman to check on her. To gain courage she started to talk to herself, and her voice filled the silent room with life.

'Holy Mother of God! What happened here? Let's see if anyone is still alive. Who could have done this to these poor people? What should I do now? This one moved a bit. I have to untie the scarf over her mouth...'

'Mmmm.... help...' the voice called to Heidi.

Heidi started to release the cords and elevate the woman's head. Once she did that, the woman opened her eyes, tears falling down her cheeks. She was about Heidi's age. She could not speak yet, but let out some deep coughs. Seeing that the girl had come back to life, Heidi had hope that the others might do so as well. She rushed to untie the older woman and check for her pulse. It was a faint one, but it was there. She was alive too. Next, she reached for the man, who looked like he had been severely beaten and still unconscious.

'Who are you?' Heidi heard the question coming from the girl. It was a good sign that she was able to speak.

'I'm just a traveler passing by your house. I decided to see who lives here and possibly spend the night if it's not too much trouble. My family is with me, too, but they are hiding in the bushes until I give them the signal to come. We are good people from Traisen trying to go home. My name is Heidi. Can you move? I'll be right with you as soon as I help your parents.'

'Oh, God bless you for stopping by. We were robbed and beaten by the Russian soldiers, I do not even remember when. They left us here, tied up and unconscious to die. I'm so thirsty...' She looked like she would faint again. Heidi got up, grabbed a pot from the cabinet, filled it with water from a bucket she saw nearby and held it to the girl's mouth to drink. She took two big gulps and thanked Heidi with her tired eyes.

The remaining water Heidi threw over the older woman's face and she started to move. She was coming to her senses. Next she did the same for the man. The water had a good effect on them. He moved too. They were all alive. Heidi remembered her family waiting in the bushes and she ran outside. The girl cried after her not to leave, and to help them. Heidi assured her that she would be right back in a minute.

Out of the house she looked around to the hills, but all she saw were the cows eating grass. There was no immediate danger. She faced the bushes where Teresa was hiding and waved frantically with one arm until she saw her sister's head above the bushes. Teresa waved back to Heidi and then she disappeared to organize her family to walk over to the house. Heidi rushed back inside the house, which seemed strange to Teresa. When they arrived and walked inside, Heidi was attending to the farmer's family as best she could. The women were feeling better but worried sick about the father who looked to be in a really bad shape. When the Souisa family was updated on what had happened at the farm, everybody was shocked and helped out as best they could. It was heaven sent that they had passed by the house and decided to spend the night, otherwise the farming family's fate would have been a slow death. It turned out that they had been tied up for two days when Heidi found them. They were dehydrated and unable to move. Their house was so isolated, that no-one would have become suspicious about not seeing them, except for the cows perhaps. Frantz, Josephina and their girls, begun to take care of their hosts and prepare some decent food for everybody. The farmer was still having problems breathing, but the women were recovering well. They were profoundly grateful to their saviors and very pleased to have them as guests overnight. Teresa went outside to take care of the cows and she brought in fresh milk. Over dinner they shared the stories of their lives and the ordeals they had all been through. A special bond was created among them, and for the first time in a very long time they had a good time. Of course Heidi was again seen as a hero, which embarrassed her, but the truth was that she was nothing short of a guardian angel. Teresa felt ashamed that she had insisted so much on Heidi not going to the house, and was glad that her sister stuck to her guts and did it anyway.

Their good deed paid off the next day when they left and had a relatively easy journey home. They arrived in Traisen in the late afternoon. The wagon was filled with food and produce that the farmer gave them as a gesture of gratitude. With it they could have lived for an entire week, not to mention it gave them a good start in adapting to the poor conditions they found at home. The damage could be seen everywhere: broken windows, missing furniture, clothes and so on. Their apartment looked like a war zone, but it was theirs and they were together and able to fix things. When they woke up the next day it was May 9th, and the good news that the war was over greeted them like a white pigeon. The old mayor of Traisen sent a drummer on the streets to spread the news. There were not many people living in the town at that time, since the majority had been sent away as refugees, but the few old people who stayed put and the farmer on the hill received the news with great joy. The Russians and the Americans met somewhere near Linz and liberated Austria from the German occupation. The peace pact was signed and the shooting stopped. Heidi and Teresa went onto the streets and partici-pated in the small meeting that the mayor held to find out more details. The peace terms were still ambiguous, but peace was peace and after so many years of war it was good to celebrate it.

Chapter 23

The summer of 1945 was one of big changes in Traisen, and in Austria in general. During the last weeks of the war, the Allied troops occupied the whole of Austria. The Soviet Union took control of Lower Austria, Vienna, Burgenland and large parts of Styria, the USA took over Upper Austria, the provinces of Salzburg and Tyrol. The French got Vorarlberg, the British parts of Carinthia, Styria and East Tyrol, while the southern part of Carinthia went under Yugoslavia's influence.

On July 4th, 1945 the First Control Agreement for the occupation zones was signed. The Soviet zone encompassed Lower Austria (under the borders of 1937), Burgenland and the Muhlviertel region in Upper Austria; the United States took the southern part of Upper Austria and Salzburg; the British Styria, Carinthia and East Tyrol; the French took North Tyrol and Vorarlberg. In Vienna, the city centre was placed under joint four-power control, while the remaining old districts were divided between the same powers as the rest of the country. In August 1945 the Western powers took control of their respective Viennese zones. On September 11th the Allied Council was constituted, made up of the four commanders-in-chief, acting as high commissioners. They had supreme power of decision and met on a monthly basis in Vienna under rotating chairmanship.

Traisen was part of Lower Austria and fell under the jurisdiction of the Soviets. In the summer of 1945, while people returned to their houses and started the cleanup of the war's mess, the Russian occupation installed itself in the region. Russian troops were placed in Traisen and the neighboring villages. It was hard to look at them as liberators because when they first invaded the country they left a trail of atrocities that the population couldn't forget. They were still viewed as barbarians and troublemakers, making it hard to gain any respect from the Austrians. None of the Allied armies attracted such hate as the Red Army did in Austria. Of course the communist doctrine that they tried to instill made the matter worse. All in all, the Russians were the winners and the commanders that gained the least amount of respect from the people they claimed to have liberated. The war was over, but the price Austria had to pay was way too high. They exchanged the German occupation for another one. The First Control Agreement was to last for ten years.

Heidi's family spent the rest of 1945 fixing their apartment and trying to survive. Shortly before Christmas they were able to replace the boarded windows with real ones made of glass, which was a big achievement. After eight months of hard work and sacrifice their home was cozy again. They deserved to relax and enjoy some good cheer over the Holiday Season. Their prayers were for the safe return of Johan, Francis and Hans Ellis. The three men meant the world to the Souisa family. German and Austrian prisoners started to come back home from the Western prison camps, but very few from the Eastern camps. Some happy families were reunited in the last months of the year. Every day the train brought back one or two young men who looked more like ghosts coming from hell: thin, weak, with hollow eyes, and some with wounds or infirmities that made them hard to recognize, but happy to be alive and back home. Heidi found herself wandering around the train station every time the train pulled into Traisen. She looked from a fair distance at the passengers, searching for the loved ones. Sometimes, she approached the newcomers and asked them where they came from and who they were. She felt like a one-person welcome committee, but she needed pieces of information to solve a puzzle of life and death in the war's aftermath. On Christmas Eve, chores and preparations for the holiday kept everybody busy at home. Heidi did not have time to wait for the afternoon train from St. Polten. Teresa was baking bread in the oven and Louisa was cleaning the house, a task that she wanted to refuse but could not. Frantz was lying on the bed troubled by some pain in his ill leg while Josephina and Heidi were outside shoveling the fresh snow that had fallen that day from the stairs to their apartment. The cold weather got to their bones and they rushed to finish the task before their toes went numb. When mother and daughter were about to turn back to the house, the old entry gate squeaked open. The women looked back down the stairs and what they saw made their hearts jump out of their chests.

'Johan?!' was all Heidi could say. Her mother looked like she was about to faint and Heidi jumped to hold her from falling. The man started to jump two steps at a time and was hugging both of them in no time. Yes, it was the beloved son and brother that they prayed for. God granted them the best Christmas gift ever. The family was reunited. Tears of happiness steamed on Heidi's cheeks as she rushed everybody inside and saw the surprise and joy on her father's face. It was truly a miracle that Johan had come home in one piece, and aside from some signs of exhaustion he was all right. That Christmas was the best that they ever had, filled with happiness, long talks, and good food.

In the last months of the war, Johan was deployed in the battles on the German and Polish border, and right before the end of the war he was taken prisoner and put into a prison camp that was administrated by the British in East Germany. When the Red Army arrived he was already in the camp and did not participate in that confrontation. That was his luck, and the main reason he was still alive. In December 1945 it was agreed, by the Allied Forces, to release all the war prisoners under twenty years of age. Johan was eighteen at that time. Life in the prison camp was tough but bearable, and made Johan stronger and more determined to survive. After all, he was a Souisa too and proudly walked in Heidi's footsteps.

The New Year of 1946 came with more hopes that Heidi's fiancé, Francis, and Teresa's Hans Ellis would also return safely one day. The sisters followed the news closely and spoke to other soldiers that came home to Traisen trying to find out more about their loved ones' fates. Neither of them received any leads in the matter. In the mean time, they had to adjust to the new rules instilled by the Soviet domination. It was not unusual to see Russian soldiers walking on the streets, especially after dark. Goods were rationed and distributed to the population according to a waiting list. When a shipment of furniture or household items came to town, a committee made up of a few locals and Russian authorities took care of it. Unfortunately, the post-war times brought out the worst in some Traisen residents, who figured that being pro-communist would bring them advantages. Furthermore, people who were active members in the German Army found themselves being ridiculed by the Russian acolytes. Heidi, who out of her good nurturing character was always helping others, was a few times a victim of these two-faced people, and denied her rights in getting goods from the community. It was sad to see how torn apart the society became after the war and under foreign regime. Even the reminder of the help she gave people in the shelter, by risking her life in order to bring them food from the farm, was not enough to place her in the good books of some influential people. Once again it was proven that trust was a rare commodity, and enemies were infiltrating within Austrian people like the plague.

At the beginning of 1946 more and more prisoners were released and came home. Some were healthy, while some had illnesses that put them in hospitals before they could travel home. Heidi and Teresa were still waiting for their fiancés. All they could do was: wait. There were no leads to pursue in finding any information about them.

One day in April, Heidi received a letter from a stranger. She was surprised and intrigued by it. The man asked her to meet him, and said the he had something to tell her in person. He was living in Lilienfeld, a town about twenty kilometers away from Traisen. She showed the letter to Teresa. Her sister advised her to meet that man and listen to what he had to tell her. Heidi replied to him and invited him to her home any time he could come. The following week a young man knocked at their door and asked for Heidi. Spring was in full blossom and the backyard was green and inviting under the warm sun.

'Good day! I'm Leon Rihter and I'm looking for Miss Heidi Souisa. I believe she's expecting me,' the stranger said to Teresa when she answered the door.

'Good day! Are you coming from Lilienfeld?'

'Exactly! Is Miss Heidi home? Or should I come back later?'

'Oh. She is home. I'll tell her you are here. Please come in!'

Leon did not know what to do. He would have rather waited outside.

'Please ask her to come outside. I'll wait here by the door.'

Teresa sensed the awkward moment and disappeared inside to look for Heidi, who was cleaning the kitchen.

'Heidi, the man who wrote you is at the door. His name is Leon. Here, take off that apron and clean your hands. He is outside in the backyard.'

'What? Why didn't you ask him to come in?'

'I did, but he declined. Here, put on this sweater and go outside. He's waiting. I'll put together a snack for him just in case he decides to stay for a while longer. Now you go sis. Good luck!'

Heidi rushed outside and almost stumbled over Leon on her way out.

'Hi! I'm sorry, why don't you come in? I'm Heidi!' She was nervous and curious, and acted strangely because of that.

'Hi, Miss Heidi! I'm very pleased to meet you. Please forgive my intrusion, but I needed to talk to you in person.'

Heidi almost smiled when she heard him addressing her as "Miss Heidi." That was what Peter at Sabina Station had called her. Strange how memories come back triggered by a simple word! That time seemed so far away. So much had happened since… so much more to find out about…

'If you don't mind, we can sit here on this bench in the garden,' Leon said and waited for her to sit down. The sun was warm. He sat beside her, looked at the grass for a long moment, and then he began to talk.

'I came home from a war camp in Hungary last month. I was there for eleven months. It was hell on Earth the way the Soviets treated us, but I was fine. At the matter of fact, I wanted to be there more than I wished to be released. When I was sent home as a free man, I was sad and annoyed. I would gladly still be there than here today. I have dreaded this moment for almost a year now.' He stopped and took a deep breath. Heidi listened without understanding.

'My brother came home at Christmas time from a similar camp in East Germany, but he was so happy to be home and so were we. Why aren't you feeling the same way? Do you have family in Lilenfeld? Is your family all right?'

Leon sighed again, lost in his thoughts, realizing that Heidi had no idea why he had come. She was more concerned about him, a stranger, than about herself. How could he prepare her for the truth, how could he tell her the truth? He felt like running away right then, before saying another word.

'Miss Heidi, before I was taken prisoner by the Red Army, I was a corporal in the Fifth Detachment of the Eastern Reich, and my superior was Lieutenant Francis Ubertal.'

His words hit Heidi like a brick on her chest. It cut the air supply in her lungs and she moved backwards, slamming her back against the bench. When she could breathe again she said with a faint voice, 'I'm all ears. Please tell me the whole story… you came here for.'

Leon looked at her, and then again at the green grass, and finally he started to talk.

'We were deployed in Hungary in January last year. It was cold, but we survived. The Lieutenant trained us well in that respect. We made trenches while waiting for the enemy to come closer. After a month or so the air strikes began, but we managed to survive them too. By mid-March we got the message through the wires that the Russian tanks were approaching. We were a detachment of about twenty five soldiers all together, part of a battalion spread along five square kilometers. On the morning of March 25th we received the alarm that Soviet tanks were coming our way. It was a foggy day; one could not see even ten meters ahead. We got to our position, but could not see the enemy ahead. Next thing we knew a projectile exploded right beside us. We could not see for a few minutes, the smoke and the fog was all around us. We started to call for each other and we were pleased when everybody in our group responded. That meant that they were alive. When the smoke dissipated, I saw the Lieutenant not far from me. He was wounded but it was hard to tell how badly. I went to his side and he told me that he could not move his legs. I looked down and saw blood on his uniform. The others came around to him too. He was so good to us always and took good care of us, like we were his own brothers. He gave us the order to retreat toward the west to hide from the enemy. We got ready to carry him, but he stopped us. He said that his wounds wouldn't allow him to recover anyway, and he urged us to run and leave him there. Of course we did not agree to that and tried to lift him anyway, but then he got upset and ordered us to go without him. He gave us the compass and ordered us to run westward, as fast as we could. Our only chance was to run and not look back. Most of the soldiers complied, but I stayed with him trying to convince him that there was hope for recovery and I'd help him come with us. He told me that if I wanted to do something for him, there were two things he wanted my help him with. The first was to come and see you. We had spoken about you before and I knew where to find you. He was happy that I was from this area and I knew about Traisen. The second was unimaginably disturbing. He gave me his pistol and ordered me to shoot him. It was his last wish on this Earth: to die before the enemy got to him. I could not do that. He begged me, but I could not. Then he understood and took the pistol back. He was bleeding badly by then. He yelled at me to run and catch up with the others, reminding me to stay alive and meet you when the war was over. I turned and left him there in the trench, following his wish. I was not even twenty meters away when I heard the shot. He did the job I could not do. He took his life before the enemy found him. He was a great man and our savior. He knew that the war was lost for the Germans, and he tried to limit the damage. He set us free and gave us guidance to safety. He loved you so much. He told me about you and your service in the army. He said that you were the bravest and sweetest woman he'd ever met. I can see he was once again right. I'm so sorry we lost him, Miss Heidi.'

After he finished talking he put an arm around Heidi's back to comfort her. She let him do it as she knew that the hug was passed on by Francis himself. She felt tears falling down her face but she could not remember crying. It was strange how her body reacted to the soul's pain. Her mind went blank and she almost had an out of body experience, like she was looking down at herself seated on the bench with that young man who looked as shaken as she was. Then the sky, so blue above her, surrounded her with its immensity. Somewhere up there was Francis's soul looking down on her with all the dreams and hopes that they once shared, smiling at her like an angel. A communication channel between two worlds was established and was waiting for transmission in a completely new dimension. Heidi felt love along with pain and sorrow. She understood why Francis chose death over a disabled life. He wanted to give her everything that a good husband could offer, anything less than that was not an option for him. His wounds would have prevented him from leading a normal life. He did not want to become a burden to anyone. He was a brave man, with a realistic vision about things and events. He loved Heidi more than his own life. He set her free to have a chance at a good, long life. He set her free against her will; he pushed her to a better life. Heidi understood that and respected it. She was sad, but not angry. Francis's last wish was for her to be happy. As he told her in Brno, she deserved a better future than taking care of an invalid. That was why they did not marry right away. Now all she had to do was to go on with her life and live it for both of them. She needed to move on for his sake and be as happy as she could for him. With those thoughts her ethereal body came back to Earth. Heidi got up and asked Leon to come inside and have a snack with her family while she would tell them the sad news. He agreed to help her do that and followed her into the home.

The grief had several stages and each member of the Souisa family dealt with them as they came. Francis was mourned by everyone, since he touched the hearts of all of them during his brief visit he paid before he was sent to the battlefield.

That spring Heidi started to work at the factory outside of town mostly because she needed to distract herself from her broken dreams. It was a British-owned company that was producing tools for the wool industry. Abandoned during the last years of war, the plant came to life again thanks to some local entrepreneurs who reopened it. Teresa and Heidi applied to work there even though it was a difficult commute on the factory's truck. Most of the workers were locals, and managed to repair and restore the production in less than a couple of months. As soon as the British owners found out that the factory was back in business they saw a good potential for their own people and families and, since they still made all the decisions, the Austrian workers started to be laid off and replaced by young English people brought in by management. It was a big injustice, which angered the local workers who tried to escape the rigid communist regime of other factories run by the Soviets. Heidi did not like what she was doing but it was all right because it served its purpose. Heidi was acting like a robot, not paying much attention to the politics that went on in the factory, and the acts of sabotage that her co-workers were involved in. One day she was caught in the middle of an injustice. The machine that she was working with broke down. After the investigation and troubleshooting, it was found that the outage was caused by human error which Heidi was blamed for. As a result she was fired. The injustice upset her, but having been fired was something of a blessing. Later the person who had actually been culpable was exposed, and Heidi was offered her job back but declined, saying that by then she had found another job. That was only a partial lie, because she was due to take on a babysitting job in Vienna in autumn. Similar to five years ago, she came across an offer to take care of a little boy as a live-in nanny. Leaving Traisen was a constant desire for Heidi which hadn't changed.

Late August, while still at home, a neighbor asked Heidi for help. Her son who had come back from a war camp was badly ill, and instead of coming home he was transferred directly to the Military Hospital in Vienna. The mother was anxious to visit her son, whom she hadn't seen for years, and asked Heidi to accompany her to Vienna. The heart-broken mother had never been to the country's capital, and was afraid to go alone. She insisted on Frantz Souisa letting Heidi make the trip to the hospital with her. Heidi was thrilled to help her neighbor and gladly prepared herself to go. They took an afternoon train since it was the only choice they had, and got a connection from St. Polten. On the second train, they met a couple of middle aged men who were very friendly. They lived in Vienna and were returning home from Salzburg. Heidi planned to spend the night in the waiting area of the Vienna Central Rail Station and go the next day to the Hospital. There was no point in trying to arrive at the hospital late in the evening. The neighbor left all the arrangements to Heidi's judgment. When the men learned about the women's plan to sleep in the train station, they offered to host them overnight in their small apartment located on the Danube quay. Of course Heidi trusted nobody, and first she declined the offer, but once arrived in Vienna, the night was falling over the city and the waiting area was very crowded. The two men insisted several times, and somehow Heidi and the neighbor agreed at last. They hopped into a streetcar and half an hour later they arrived at the apartment. It looked very much like a man's home, with basic furniture and bare windows. They were given a spare room with a double bed. Heidi decided to sleep fully clothed and the neighbor followed suit. It being late, they said good night and went to bed. The men seemed to be pleasant people, willing to help. The conversation they had on the train was about the day to day life and the new social system instated after the war. Heidi did not speak much, following her good instincts to be cautious with the strangers. The neighbor was amazed by the big city and the people that lived in it, including the two overly friendly hosts. She was like a child at a theme park. During the night, Heidi woke up and felt thirsty. She reached for the bag she had brought from home to get her bottle of water. The room was dark. She found the water and was about to drink when she heard people talking in the next room. A sliver of light was coming from under the closed door of her room. She was not imagining things. The two men were talking in a low voice behind her door. Heidi listened carefully to catch the topic of conversation. She felt entitled to eavesdrop out of concern for her safety. After all, she was in the house of two complete strangers. The neighbor was sleeping peacefully by her side. Heidi stirred and got off the bed. She came closer to the door and lowered herself to the floor, grabbing her knees with her arms and resting her chin on top of them. She was able to hear clearly, even though the men were talking quietly.

'Hmm…what do you think? Can we use it?' one man asked the other

'Of course we can use it! What do you mean?'

'Hum… but it is a baby…'

'It is what it is. We can cook it as any other small animal or chicken. The meat is tender and nobody would tell the difference from a young pig. Meet is meat and we and our mama need nourishment.'

'I don't know, aren't you afraid that the soul of the baby would haunt us if we eat him?'

'Nonsense. We haven't travelled all that way to come home empty handed. We went to bring food, remember? Here you have food. Look at it as food and nothing else. Mama will be happy to eat a roast, and so would you. After all these years of dry bread we finally will have a decent meal.'

'You're right. Let's put it in cold water for now and tomorrow we will cook it.'

'There you go. Now we understand each other. Let's get ready for sleep. I'm exhausted. Everything else can wait till tomorrow.'

Heidi heard the two men stand up from their chairs and walk to the other room, but her heart-beat was so powerful that she heard it in her ears. She was in shock. What she had just heard made her nauseous. She started to shake like a leaf in the wind, but other than that she could not move. The men's words were in her head. Good Lord, what kind of people were they? And how stupid of her to come here to their home and spend the night. No, she could not move, paralyzed by the horrifying news that she had just heard: these men were cannibals, and murderers. When she did not hear any more noises on the other side of the door Heidi made an effort, got up, and went to bed. She gently shook her neighbor to wake her up. When the woman opened her eyes Heidi put her index finger to her lips to advise her not to talk aloud. After she made sure that they could not be heard, Heidi told the story she overheard in the other room. The older woman became so scared that she wanted to leave the apartment right away. Heidi stopped her. It was wiser to wait until dawn. They could not wander around on Vienna's streets in the middle of the night. Nevertheless, they could not sleep anymore and waited for time to pass, while in a state of terror. When the first ray of daylight hit the city's sky, the two women gathered their belongings and tip-toed out of their room, through the hallway and out of the apartment. Downstairs on the street they let out a sigh of relief and started to walk toward the streetcar stop. It was too early for the first streetcar, but they did not mind waiting.

'Should we notify the police about what you heard the men talking about?' the neighbor asked Heidi.

'We could, but then what if they deny the whole thing and say that I misunderstood, and then they could come after us, seeking revenge? We may get into trouble. We are here to visit your son, not to catch thieves or murderers. Besides, they were nice to us, and did not harm us. I don't think we have enough proof of their crime. What if I misunderstood the whole conversation? We'll never know for sure what was going on. Let's carry on with our purpose and get to the hospital,' Heidi answered.

One hour later they were back at the Central Rail Station where they took a taxi to the hospital. It was half past eight when they reached the big old building on the eastern side of Vienna, which was the Military Hospital. Heidi's memory about the hospital in Pilsen, where she had met Francis, filled her eyes with tears. She took a deep breath to pull herself together and help her neighbor find her son. The nurse led them down a long corridor before they entered a large room filled with beds. Half of the beds were empty, including the one beside the neighbor's son. The mother and the son shared a touching moment when they first saw each other, and tears were running down their faces. They were happy to hug each other for the first time after more than three years. Heidi witnessed quietly the joyful moment and felt happy too, seeing them. She was glad that she could help these people to meet at last. When the excitement of the first moments was over, the mother took some food out of the bag she had brought from home for her son. Everything was much appreciated on both sides.

Later on, the young soldier's gaze fell on Heidi. He knew her from their school years, and from having lived on the same street in Traisen. He asked her to come closer and thanked her for helping his mother come visit. Heidi was glad that the young man was looking better than some other patients in the same room and asked him about his recovery and his experience in the hospital. He has been there for a few months, and would probably stay a couple of months more. He had seen lots of injured or ill soldiers coming and going and had lots of stories to tell, but seeing Heidi there, one story in particular came to his mind. He had to tell her what he had found out not long ago from the patient who occupied the now empty bed adjacent to his.

'Heidi, come closer please, I cannot speak too loud because I'll lose my strength. I have something to tell you.'

Heidi was surprised to hear that, and she thought that the man wanted to once again thank her for her kindness in accompanying his mother. She sat quietly on the edge of his hospital bed and looked into his tired eyes.

'About a month ago on that bed beside mine, was an officer. He was transferred to a rehab center later on, since he was badly injured in the war and his lungs were compromised. He could hardly breathe on his own and he got tired every time he talked. However, we talked a bit about our origins and shared some memories from the battlefield. He was from a military background. His father was a retired colonel from the First World War, and his brother was an officer too.'

Heidi could not understand why her neighbor was telling her the story, but she was interested in finding out more. She let him continue.

'When it was my turn to tell him where I was from he became interested in finding out more about Traisen. That was at least odd to me, but I carried on and gave him a description of the town and surroundings. Then he asked me if by any chance I knew you.'

Heidi frowned and became intrigued.

'He asked about me? How come?'

'Exactly my thoughts! How on Earth he knew about Heidi Souisa, the shoe master's daughter? But then he added that his brother was engaged to a girl from Traisen and even though he never met his future sister-in-law he knew her from his brother's letters. I asked him where his brother was, and he sadly told me that his brother was missing in action. He had fought on the Eastern front, in Hungary and never came home. I was just wondering then if he was talking about you, but since he knew your name he must have been right. Now… I don't know if missing in action means that he would never come back or if maybe there is hope that he is alive, but the soldier was quite skeptical, saying he should have been missing instead of his brother, since nobody was waiting for him at home. He was very devastated.'

'He must have been my fiancé's brother. I know for sure that Francis is dead. Someone came and told me in spring. But, his brother has all the right to live, he has his parents.'

'Well, that brings me to the even more dreadful part. He told me that his parents are dead too. At the end of the war, when the American planes were returning from a raid in Hungary, they dropped a few bombs in the outskirts of Vienna to empty their load. One of it fell on this fellow's house and flattened it, killing his elderly parents. When he came back there was nothing left of his family. Heidi, I am so sorry for what happened.'

Heidi was once again in shock. The pain of losing Francis was buried in her heart, but now finding out about the rest of the family brought her a great deal of sorrow. Her neighbor saw how distressed she looked and got up to hug her. Tears streamed down her face. It seemed that the bad chain of events did not stop with the end of the war. The consequences kept being felt and crushed Heidi like an avalanche. How much more bad news was she supposed to get? What a dreadful fate Francis's family had!

They spent the rest of the day at the hospital. In the afternoon Heidi and the neighbor left. They arrived at the train station just in time for the next train to St. Polten, and out of Vienna they went. Heidi did not talk much, as she was deep in her own thoughts all the way to Traisen. It was quite providential that she had made that trip to the hospital, and found out everything about her never-to-be relatives. At least she received closure on all counts... but it hurt so much. She was alive while almost all of Francis's family was dead. The pain made her came to an important conclusion: she had to live her live to the fullest. She had to do something with the gift of life which she appreciated more than ever before. All the losses she experienced put everything in a different perspective. She was due to start her job in Vienna in September. She was determined to make the most of that opportunity and anything that came her way. The world became a jungle, in which interpersonal relationships were under pressure of political and economical oppression. People did anything to survive. Some stole things and dead babies to eat, some were victims of unbearable suffering, some became traitors and sold their souls to the dominant power for small favors, and even the church took part in compromising actions and greed. Her own country was in ruin, literally and figuratively. In such a poisoned world Heidi had to live and find her way.

Chapter 24

Heidi started her job in Vienna at the beginning of September 1946, eighteen months after the war ended. The city looked different than it did years ago when she had first seen it. Some buildings were in desperate need of renovation, some weren't even there anymore. The people on the streets were a mix of a number of nationalities following the new political ruling. Heidi's employers, Erika and Gunter Shoner, lived in the centre of the city in a decent apartment. Both of them were working for the Ministry of Internal Affairs. Gunter was a consultant specialist, and Erika was the minister's administrative assistant. They were at work most of the day, while Heidi provided care for their two year old son Benjamin. Benjamin was a cute little boy with big blue eyes and curly blond hair. He could easily have been mistaken for a girl, if not for the blue outfits that his mother always dressed him in. Heidi loved children, and she and Ben clicked right away, so much so that the boy never missed his parents when they weren't around. Heidi's duties revolved around the child: cooking for Ben and herself, cleaning after Ben, playing with him and protecting him. She slept in Ben's small room and attended to the boy on the rare occasion he woke up at night. The child was well behaved and, surprisingly, potty trained when Heidi met him.

Erika was a good lady who befriended Heidi right from the beginning. There was a mutual trust between them which built the roots of a pleasant and solid relationship. Erika had a few lady friends her age that she kept in touch with, and Heidi soon became part of that circle also. By the time Heidi's twenty-second birthday rolled in on October 11th, the Shoner family was as close to her as her own. They organized a pretty party for Heidi and she got to open a couple of presents for almost the first time in her life. She received a nice wool scarf knitted by Erika's mother who lived in Traisen, and a chic little purse that Erika had purchased from an expensive boutique. The new job and the new friends lifted Heidi's spirit, and for the first time since her vacation in Brno two years ago, Heidi felt really happy. She wrote a long letter home telling Teresa about the kindness she was surrounded by, and her recent birthday celebration.

Teresa was working at the factory in Traisen. She had a position in the office and was making good money. She was still waiting to hear from Hans Ellis her long time fiancé, but she did not despair, thinking that no news was good news, especially after Heidi had found out about Francis and his family. Teresa wrote back to Heidi about life in Traisen, her siblings and their parents. Johan was employed at the factory as well, and started dating. He was a big help for the family. Louisa, on the other hand, seemed to be good for nothing with her fast temper and laziness. She was only fifteen, but her interest in young men became alarming to her parents. Every now and then the youth of Traisen organized parties without the Russians' knowing. Alcohol was prohibited outside of restaurants and pubs, but some inventive young men managed to sneak some bottles of beer inside the Community Hall all the time. Teresa was doing alright in Traisen and kept Heidi informed of all the events that were going on in her hometown.

Heidi spent Christmas of 1946 in Vienna. The city was dressed in lights and in the park a big Santa Claus made out of straw and hay was displayed dressed in red fabric trimmed with white wool. Little Ben was thrilled seeing it when he visited the park with Heidi. It was a true challenge to take him home without getting him all upset at having to leave. On Christmas Eve, Gunter dressed up as Santa and walked through the door with a nicely decorated, medium size spruce and a white bag over his shoulder, sending Ben into a frenzy. The moment was so special for the little boy. Seeing Santa coming to his home, he started to clap his small hands until they became red. He watched, with big round eyes, Santa putting the Christmas tree on the dining room floor, and then taking out of his bag some toys and handing them to him. He was eager to recite out loud the poems that Heidi had taught him that December to please Santa and collect more gifts. Ben was a delightful child who stole Heidi's heart. Celebrating and seeing Christmas through a child's eyes was the most rewarding present she could receive. Erika and

Gunter was a well-established couple who could afford a thing or two without feeling the burden of a tight budget. The food they had over the holiday season was abundant and they shared it generously. Heidi felt part of the family when she sat at the dinner table next to Ben. They laughed and enjoyed the moment to the fullest.

Before the New Year, the superintendent of the apartment building that Heidi had befriended in the last few months made her a proposition. She always spent New Year's Eve at the Philharmonic Concert Hall in Vienna. During the war the event was cancelled, but reopened at the end of 1945, although with less glitter than before 1940. The upcoming New Year 1947 celebration, was due to reinstate the glamour from the old days. It was supposed to be quite an event, and the lady wanted to take Heidi along to show her how Viennese society celebrated it.

Heidi would have loved to go, but two things were stopping her. The first and foremost was that her employer was a very private person and insisted that Heidi not get involved with ordinary people and gossip about private matters she overheard in the Shoner's household, especially since both Erika and Gunter were working for the government. Erika was also fearful that Heidi would meet someone, fall in love get married and leave her job. The Shoners were so pleased with Heidi's work that they did not want to lose her for one reason or another. That was why Heidi's life was shielded from the outside world as much as possible. When her employers were at work and she took little Ben for walks she met a few people who lived in the building and made some friends. The superintendent, Lisa, was full of life and her husband was a good man. Heidi liked them and became part of their group, as if she was a younger sister to them. The invitation to the New Year celebration was only natural, given their close friendship. But even if Erika agreed to let her go out with her new friends, Heidi would have still had another problem which was not easy to solve. The celebration was a black tie event, and she did not have a formal gown that she could wear.

Luckily, Lisa had solutions for each issue. They were having tea in Lisa's apartment while Benjamin was happily playing on the host's sofa under Heidi's careful eyes.

'Heidi, it would be such a shame if you don't come with us. You must come! Let me think: you could tell Erika that we are going to watch a movie,' Lisa said and a smile bloomed on her face.

'I don't know… I suppose I could, and she might be fine with that, but I still have nothing appropriate to wear. By the way, show me your dress for the occasion! I'm so curious to see it.'

'Oh, my dress is an old one, from even before the war, but I'm lucky I did not put on any weight and it still fits me well.' Lisa got up and went to the wardrobe. She came back holding a hanger with a long burgundy dress made of organza fabric. It had a simple but elegant cut and, in Heidi's eyes, it looked gorgeous.

'Oh my, you'll look like a queen in that dress. See, I have nothing like that in my suitcase. There is no way I can come with you, Lisa.'

'You don't know what I know. You are in luck here. This dress was made by my sister Martha, who is a seamstress and has quite an exclusive clientele. I have always told her that she should open a fashion house and become rich. She really has a gift. I'm sure that she will lend you a nice dress for this occasion if we ask her. You two are about the same size.'

'You cannot be serious, can you?' Heidi asked in dismay.

'You better believe it! I will phone her right now and ask.' Lisa put her dress back in the wardrobe and picked up the phone, asking the operator for the connection to her sister's home. After less than thirty seconds she started to talk with enthusiasm.

'Martha darling, how are you? You must be busy dressing half of Vienna's aristocracy for the New Year's Ball, aren't you?'… Really? …Good for you! Listen, I'm planning to go to the Philharmonic Concert Hall with Ron and a new girlfriend who lives with and works for a family in this building… Yes, she takes care of a lovely little boy; she came in this autumn from the town of Traisen. Going to this party would be like a fairytale for Heidi, that is my friend's name… yes, but we are having a bit of a problem here. Heidi has nothing appropriate to wear…I told her that you may be able to help, especially since she is your size…Aha…Marvelous!…I know it…That would look great on Heidi. She has blue eyes too…Aha… Well honey, thank you so much, I'll see you tomorrow evening then. You have a productive day, Martha! Thank you again! See you soon!' Lisa hung up the phone and presented Heidi with her broad, content smile.

'My dear, you'll have a beautiful dress to wear and you'll come to the party with us. I won't take "no" for an answer, and who knows, you may end up being the belle of the night!'

266

'Lisa, you are fantastic! I would have never dreamt of going out that night, let alone to such an important party. I hope Erika will buy my little white lie and allow me to leave the house for the "movie".'

'She will! She is a good lady and she likes you so much. She is afraid to lose you, you know that, don't you?'

'I suppose you're right.'

'Of course I'm right! Now, tomorrow evening, please come over to meet my sister Martha, and try on the dress. She said that it is dark blue. It would match your beautiful eyes.'

'Thank you Lisa. Oh, it is getting late and Ben has to have a nap. I'll have to go now. See you tomorrow, then.'

With that, Heidi picked up Benjamin, who graciously encircled his little arms around Heidi's neck and they went home to the second floor. Later that evening, Heidi diplomatically had a talk with her mistress Erika, and received permission to go out to a movie on New Year's Eve. The first and most important problem was solved. Heidi was already feeling the excitement of going to such an exquisite party. She stayed awake for hours after she went to bed.

The following evening Heidi went over to Lisa, met Martha, and tried on the loan dress that fit her like a glove and flattered her slender figure. She was able to borrow a pair of dressing shoes from Lisa and her outfit was complete. Looking in the mirror Heidi felt tears filling her eyes and in the blurry reflection she imagined herself standing by Francis' side, like she once did while attending the reception in Pilsen. It was an eerie dream that was cut short, but the sweet memories touched Heidi's heart softly like a feather. She missed him so much! Lisa noticed Heidi's daydreaming, but said nothing, figuring that some things were best left unspoken. After the war, there was so much silent pain in every family and the wounds needed a long time to heal. The dress passed the test and was Heidi's for a night. She and the two sisters had a good time making the final plans for the big night that was two days away.

On December 31st 1946, Heidi helped Erika cook a large meal for dinner, and took Benjamin to bed early. After she finished her evening tasks she wished her employer a happy new year and left. She went downstairs to Lisa's apartment. There, the preparation was in full swing. Lisa was hovering around with her party dress unzipped, gathering her purse's content and looking for her shoes. Ron was patiently waiting on the sofa, looking polished in a dark grey suit. When Heidi arrived, Lisa took her to the other room to have her change her clothes. It was still early but the excitement was hard to contain.

'Heidi, my dear, let's get you into that lovely dress and then I'll help you do your hair,' Lisa urged Heidi. Heidi followed her into the other room and started to peel off her regular clothes. She put on the indigo dress and her white skin glowed in the mirror's reflection. Lisa was at her side admiring her. She started to comb Heidi's dark blond hair. The naturally loose curls bounced like silky springs around her neck and rested on her shoulders. A hint of red lipstick completed her look. Lisa was content with the result and, handing Heidi the pair of shoes, she went back to getting ready herself. Heidi joined Ron in the living room, waiting for the lady of the house to emerge from the other room and get going.

At nine o'clock sharp they were inside the big concert hall, which was full of elegant people. Indeed, the audience was made up of aristocrats, politicians, public servants and members of the Government as well as middle class gents, and all of them blended in a sea of glamour and nice clothes. They mingled in the sumptuous foyer, parading the beautiful dresses and spreading a cloud of cologne and perfumes that made Heidi feel light-headed and happy. She was part of a wonderful event and she loved every second of it. She felt beautiful herself, and for the night she was getting a glimpse into the lives' of rich Austrian people. That was the society that Francis grew up in, and would have been hers too, if she had ever married him. But for that night Heidi wanted to be happy and she let go of the painful thoughts about her lost love. She smiled and talked to Ron and Lisa and some other acquaintances that they met there, and when the first signal was given, everybody headed to the amphitheatre to take their seats. Lisa guided them to the second floor on the right. When she opened the leather covered door, Heidi found herself in a lodge with eight seats close to the stage. Lisa showed her a chair that was made of sculpted wood and had a red velvet cushion. Heidi sat down, and Lisa and Ron took their places beside her. The light was dimmed in the hall, but still sparkling enough to give the whole ambiance a glittering touch. Below their small balcony was a sea of well-behaved people whispering to each other making the entire room sound like a bee-hive. The sound and the light were alluring and enchanting. The stage was covered by a huge red velvet curtain, in front of which lay a beautiful floral arrangement made of white callas and lilies, looking so fresh against the red velvet. Heidi noticed all the details with the wonder of a little child seeing Santa Claus. The second gong was heard and the audience gasped and stopped whispering. One minute later, along with the final gong, the curtain started to lift, revealing a full orchestra on stage. The shiny instruments were resting on the performers' laps. The men were all dressed in black with white shirts and black bow ties. The few women of the Philharmonic Orchestra were seated in the first row and they played violins and violas. They wore long black dresses with white silk collars.

When the Conductor came on stage and took a bow in front of the public, a round of applause burst out at once. Soon thereafter the room was in complete silence before the music started. And the music was divine! Heidi had the program resting on her lap, but was so mesmerized by the concert that she did not dare to take her eyes off the stage and look at it. She noticed that when the orchestra stopped between parts of the symphony, nobody clapped the hands, but waited until the end of the entire piece. Heidi was a quick learner and that night she observed and learned concert etiquette and protocol. The whole experience was so enlightening! The concert had two intermissions when people stretched their legs and gathered in the decorated foyer for drinks and cookies. Heidi had lemonade and a biscuit that Lisa gave her. They were standing on a side of the hallway looking at people talking, laughing, and having a good time. Lisa saw quite a few young men smiling at Heidi when they passed by, but that was all, since Heidi was too delighted by the ambiance to even notice the attention she was receiving. She was almost sorry when the concert was over. All the magic of the music mixed with the flowers on the stage, the tall chandeliers with their soft light and the elegance of the people seemed like a fairytale dream. In the big foyer was a nicely decorated Christmas tree that fascinated Heidi. The last part of the concert was a chorale with a group of prestigious singers who sang happy songs from a well selected repertoire. The concert house was filled with cheers and applause when the New Year came. Heidi was filled with happiness. Lisa and Ron hugged and kissed her, and the entire audience and the artists on stage were standing and celebrating the beginning of 1947. When the conductor signaled for silence the music resumed and everybody sang along with the chorus "Happy New Year!"

One hour later when the concert was over the crowd mingled around the bar for a glass of champagne with biscuits. People did not feel like leaving right away. Heidi did not want that night ever to end. She was mesmerized by the whole experience. She looked beautiful, she listened

to great music, a new year had begun. She hoped it would be better than
the last ones. She felt lucky and good for the first time in a long, long
while. When they finally returned home it was three in the morning and
they were completely tired. Not wanting to disturb the Shoners, Heidi
decided to spend the rest of the night on Lisa's sofa. In the morning she
had breakfast with her friends and then she went upstairs to her employer's apartment. Erika was feeding Ben in the kitchen and Gunter was
reading the first issue of the year of the main Viennese newspaper.

'Happy New Year!' Heidi said cheerfully.

'Happy New Year to you too, Heidi' responded Erika.

'Appi nw yer,' repeated little Benjamin and lifted his small arms
toward Heidi. The child was happy to see his companion.

'Did you have a good time last night?' asked Erika.

'Oh, yes! We came home late, and I stayed over at Lisa's place. I
did not want to disturb you. How was your New Year's Eve?'

'Oh, it was peaceful. After Benjamin went to bed we just had a
quiet dinner and we went to sleep after midnight. Today we would like to
attend the New Year Concert at the Concert Hall at noon.'

'Good for you! I'm sure you will enjoy it very much. Actually, let
me help Ben finish his breakfast and you go take care of yourself and get
ready,' Heidi encouraged her mistress. She was truly happy that Erika and
Gunter would attend a nice event like she did the night before.

The rest of the winter flew by quickly. Heidi took good care of
Ben and in her spare time she socialized with Lisa and her sister. She was
really fortunate to have a pleasant life in Vienna and to be able to take
advantage of her stay there. The little boy was smart and Heidi enjoyed
spending time with him. Erika and Gunter were good people, always
considerate toward her. Teresa sent her one letter every month with the
latest news from Traisen and about the family. Her sister was still waiting
for Hans Ellis to come back to her, and not knowing anything about him
made her sad and hopeless. Heidi wrote back every time telling about her
life in Vienna and encouraging Teresa to be strong and optimistic.

In autumn, around her twenty third birthday, Heidi received a
week paid vacation to go home as a present. Erika wanted to surprise
Heidi with something that would make her really happy. Indeed, Heidi
was pleasantly surprised and it was a Thursday when she left Vienna to
return to Traisen. She was due to come back the following Thursday. It
happened all of a sudden and she did not have time to write a letter
home about her arrival. On Thursday afternoon when she showed up at

home, her family was delighted to see her and she had a very welcoming evening.

There was a lot of catching up to do after more than a year. Traisen had changed a bit. More former soldiers had returned from the camps or hospitals and the old town got a breath of fresh air with the young population increasing. There were activities organized by young people at the Community Hall, including movie evenings and monthly plays or folkloric concert. Fridays were dancing nights when boys and girls along with young married couples had the chance to socialize and have a good time. Heidi also found out from Teresa that in the neighboring villages live music was played by local bands at the newly re-opened clubs. Luck had it that on that Saturday when Heidi was home, in Lilienfeld a guest band was playing at Community Hall. The local restaurants were catering for the event and young people from a twenty kilometer radius were due to attend. It was called the Harvest Ball and Teresa and Johan bought their tickets way in advance. Heidi joined them, and off they went. Transportation was provided by the Traisen Community Service by bus.

The sisters spent Saturday afternoon getting ready and trying on the old dresses that they had. Heidi had a nicer one from Erika, which, with some small adjustments made by Martha, Lisa's sister, fit Heidi like a glove. It looked fresh and fashionable in comparison with Teresa's outdated style, but both of them were pretty. Johan urged them to get going before they would miss the bus.

At the Ball they sat at a table not far from the stage. Teresa went to the buffet and bought some refreshments for the three of them, and soon the band started to play. It was a new group that neither of them knew, but it sounded good and the audience enjoyed it and encouraged it with loud applauses after each song. Johan left the table to mingle and dance with the pretty girls that were present, leaving Teresa and Heidi alone at the table. Heidi was looking around for people she knew, while Teresa just sat there playing with the food and listening to the music. It looked like she was daydreaming and not interested in interacting with the other people. Some young man asked Heidi to dance and soon she was swirling in the vicinity of the stage along with few other couples. Heidi's partner had good dancing skills which really pleased her. They were focused on the steps and the rhythm and did not talk much during the dance. Floating on the song's wings, Heidi found herself looking at the band players. In doing so, something caught her eye: the drummer.

He looked familiar, but Heidi could not place him in her circle of friends, although she had a strong felling that she'd seen him before. After the dance her partner led her back to her table where Teresa was finishing eating.

'Oh, this dance was great, but I'm afraid I'm out of shape. I'm panting like an old dog. What are you doing? You should go and dance instead of sitting here like an old lady,' Heidi said to Teresa. She looked around the big room for Johan and saw him dancing with a pretty petite blonde girl she did not know. Then her eyes fell again on the band's drummer. Grabbing a bite of the food and still looking at that man on the stage, her mind flipping through all her acquaintances', she almost choked on the fried potatoes when she finally remembered the face. Teresa looked at her sister shaking her head: Vienna had changed Heidi. She was more outgoing and spontaneous than she remembered her.

'I'll be right back!' she heard Heidi saying, and then she was gone, like she had just got an important mission to accomplish. It was another impulsive move that Teresa did not understand, but did not give it another thought.

Heidi walked around the dance floor, avoided a few young men who tried to ask her for a dance, and went backstage, all this time her eyes glued to the drummer. When the song finished the lead singer announced a break and the crowd let out a disappointed sigh. Heidi knew then that she was in luck. The band members walked past her going to the hall where friends and family were waiting for them. One stopped and asked Heidi what was she doing up there. He even tried to start a conversation with her, but she gave him the cold shoulder and told him she was waiting for the drummer. The guy yelled back to his band member, not hiding his annoyance, 'Hey, Hans, this girl is waiting for you!'

The drummer looked Heidi's way, put the sticks beside the drums, secured the big shiny clappers, got up and came toward Heidi. He had never seen the young lady in his life. How could she be waiting for him? Perhaps she was a groupie, but, even so, the lead singer got most of the attention, not him, buried behind the drums at the back of the stage. Strange, he thought.

'Are you waiting for me? Do I know you? Have we met before?' he asked, full of interest.

Heidi looked at him with icy eyes. He was handsome and tall, almost intimidating. His blue eyes were in deep contrast with his darker skin and brown wavy hair. He was a good looking man. She regained her composure stood tall and spoke clearly.

'No, we've never met before, but I know you very well. I would like to have a word with you, Hans Ellis!'

'How do you know my name? Who are you?' He was already nervous. He looked around the big hall and then led Heidi to a more private spot behind the stage curtain. There was a table and a few chairs covered by band members' coats and instrument boxes. Hans cleared up two chairs. He gestured for Heidi to have a seat and he took the other chair. He was intrigued and wanted to get to the bottom of it.

'Now I'm all ears. Tell me who you are and what you want?'

'Slow down, mister. I'm not the bad guy here, but you, Hans Ellis, may be! You also may know and remember my sister Teresa to whom you are engaged,' Heidi said.

Hans's face went white and he looked like he was facing a ghost. It was his past haunting him. He did not know what to say for almost a minute. When he regained his bearings he spoke in a hoarse voice.

'Oh my God! Teresa. You are Teresa's sister! Of course! How did you find me?'

'Look, I did not come looking for you. We came to this party as guests and I had no idea you were still alive, let alone that you play in this band. I was surprised when I recognized you. I can see that you are doing quite well while my sister has been waiting for you ever since you left Rosenburg Castle and went to the army. You are a coward for not coming back to her, and she is an idiot for believing that you indeed loved her.'

Hans was struck by her words. He had no idea that Teresa was still waiting for him. The war's hardship washed his memories and the past seemed so faded. Yes, he loved Teresa once, but life threw him on different path and he had to make different choices. It was so hard to explain everything that happened and not look completely inconsiderate. It was hard, but he had to do it.

'I could not come back to your sister when I returned to Austria from Russia six months ago. I was already married then.'

'Married!?'

'Yes, my wife is a Russian medic that I met in the prison camp.'

'You have a Russian wife? You do not cease to amaze me with all this incredible news. I feel pity for you, but I still think you are a bastard.'

'Hold on, young lady! Do you think I did all this to upset Teresa? I was in a life or death situation in that camp and she helped me a lot. Basically, she saved my life. In return she wanted to flee Russia and the only way out was to marry a foreigner. So I agreed, and after one year we were able to return to Austria. It was not like I fell in love with someone else and I have just forgotten your sister and the promise I made to her.' He looked really shaken when he said that. Heidi mellowed a bit seeing him sad and distraught.

'Even so, why didn't you send Teresa a note to give her closure? She would have waited for you until the end of her days. She is in that ball room right now. Do you have the courage to look her in the eyes and tell her the truth?'

'My wife is in that room as well. She must be waiting for me now that there is a break. I have to go to her. I cannot speak with Teresa now. You should understand that.'

Heidi was downright mad. The coward was backing off like a scared rabbit. She decided that Teresa should be spared the pain of seeing the man she once loved so dearly acting as a puppet. It was pathetic. He was pathetic.

'Hans Ellis, you should be ashamed for the rest of your life for the way you treated my sister. You are not worth one single tear drop that Teresa shed for you all these years. I do not want you to ever try to contact her or come anywhere near her. I will advise her of this conversation we had, and what you did. She will be crushed, but eventually she will survive. But you, you will live in a lie. You deserve what you have.'

'Thank you for talking with Teresa about what happened.'

'You're not welcome! Good bye!'

Heidi got up and held her head high when she turned on her heels and left him still perplexed in his chair. She went back among the guests looking for her sister. Johan saw her and crossed over toward her.

'Hey, sis! You look like you are going to kill someone. Are you upset about something?' Johan asked her with a broad smile.

'You better believe that I was this close to killing someone,' Heidi answered, her eyes still browsing for Teresa.

'Who?' Johan said jokingly.

'The drummer!' His sister answered right away.

'Oh ! You sound like you could be serious. Why?'

'Because he is an Austrian who is a Russian worshiper, and a coward bastard! That is why.'

'Do you know him, sis? You described him with quite a few epithets. Who's the guy?'

'Do you really want to know? He was supposed to be our future brother-in-law.'

Johan was confused, but he knew Heidi. She was the fairest person, and if she was so upset at this man there must have been a good reason for it. After another second he realized what she meant.

'No way! Hans Ellis?'

'You are smart, Johan. You figured it out quite quickly. Now I have to find Teresa. Did you see her?'

'She must be around where the food is. You know her passion, don't you? Are you going to facilitate their meeting?'

'Hell, no! He is married to a Russian medic. I'll tell her what I think about this. Oh, there she is. I have to go.' Heidi was boiling inside. Anger and sorrow were mixed in her soul. How could she deliver the dreadful news to her sister without hurting her too much? When she reached Teresa at the food stand she took her elbow and led her to a table to sit down. The band was still on break and people were drinking and talking loudly around them.

'Did you find someone you knew in this entire hall?' Heidi asked with caution.

'I saw the neighbor's sons and a few girls I knew from the factory. Why?'

'The problem with you is that you are too shy, Teresa. You should go out there and dance and have fun. There are quite a few handsome men here that you could meet.'

'I do not want to meet men, Heidi. I'm not available for a new relationship anyway.'

'Yes, you are!'

'Now you just try to tease me, but I'm serious.'

'And why is that? Why you do not want to meet someone who can be good for you?'

'Look who's talking! You already know that Francis does not come back, that he is gone, and still you are alone grieving for him. Maybe you should start making new friends, not me, who still has hope for Hans's return.' Teresa was getting nervous about this conversation. She did not want to upset Heidi, but did not like that pushy attitude Heidi had. Heidi could not wait any longer. She had to cut that malefic cord that tied Teresa up in her own cocoon at once, no matter how much it hurt.

'Teresa, listen to me, Hans Ellis is not coming back to you. Ever. You must accept it and move on.'

Teresa looked like she was in shock. What on Earth made Heidi be so mean to her? What did she do to deserve that? Anger rose in her chest and her heart was pounding hard.

'Heidi, what got to you to talk to me like that? Are you mad at me? Why?'

'Yes, I'm mad as hell, but not at you: at Hans Ellis!'

'God knows where he is now. Why are you mad at him?'

'You're right. God knows where he is. I know too, and you are about to find out, Teresa. He is right here, in this room, along with his new Russian wife. When he is not with her, he plays the drums in the band. You should open your eyes and look around, instead of daydreaming about him all the time.'

Teresa could not believe what she had just heard. Could it be true? She felt like fainting. Heidi put her arm around her shoulders.

'Teresa, my dear, this is hard for you, but I saw him in the band when I danced earlier and I was quite sure that it was him. During the break I confronted him and he told me that he was in a prison camp in Russia for a couple of years and when he was released he had to marry a Russian medic who helped him survive and wanted to flee her country. The only way was to get married and come here as a couple. He said that he had no choice but to do what the medic wanted.'

Teresa was about to burst into tears. All this news came suddenly like falling rocks over her head. She could not believe it, but Heidi would not lie about such a thing. It had to be true. The music had started. The pairs were heading to the dance floor. Heidi got up and went to Johan, who was talking with a couple of girls.

'Johan, I need to talk to you for a second.'

'Jesus, sis, I'm kind of busy right now.' He was annoyed by the interruption. Heidi grabbed his elbow and pulled him aside.

'We are dealing with a crisis here, and you have to help me. I need you to take Teresa for a dance and lead her toward the stage. She has to see for herself that I do not talk nonsense. She has to see him, even from a distance, to get closure. Do you understand me? Now go, and ask her to dance.'

Johan could not ignore Heidi's authority in that matter. He complied with her request and went straight to Teresa. Heidi saw that her sister was reluctant to accept, but finally she got up and followed her brother. They began the dance and Johan was doing an excellent job in following Heidi's instruction. Heidi relaxed a bit. She was under a lot of pressure also. On one hand, her heart went out to her sister's pain, but on the other she was relieved that the wait was over. Teresa could and had to move on. Hans Ellis was history. After the dance, they packed their things and left the party without looking back. Teresa wept all the way home on Heidi's shoulder while the bus drove on the bumpy road back to Traisen. The next day, Sunday, they went to church and after that had a good supper. Teresa got comfort from her family and friends, the way Heidi had almost two years ago. The rest of her vacation was spent catching up with the friends in Traisen. When she went back to Vienna, it looked like she has been away for a year, not a week. So many things happened in such a short period of time! Life was so unpredictable, but it was worth living.

Chapter 25

Life in Vienna was good for Heidi. The little boy she was taking care of was smart and affectionate. She had an easy and pleasant job. Her friends Lisa and Martha always invited her to come along when they attended shows or went to movies. Erika became more flexible toward Heidi's outings during her leisure time. All in all, Heidi was as happy as she could be living in the big city.

From time to time she received letters from home, especially from Teresa who kept her updated with the Traisen news. Her sister was happy again, after the relationship with Hans Elis came to an end. She met a new man from the neighboring village, one that they went to school with, and they fell in love right away. His name was Walter. Heidi read a lot of joy between the lines of her sister's letters. It pleased her that Teresa was finally happy. Also, Johan seemed to have a steady relationship with a girl Heidi knew. It looked to her like her siblings would soon be on the way to marriage. Heidi, on the other hand, had no suitors, and no interest in getting one. Her plan was to live in Vienna for as long as she could and, later on, to move to Switzerland to escape the Russian domination.

The holiday season of 1947 passed with a few parties and good times, and the beginning of 1948 came with lots of snow and freezing temperatures. For more than two weeks in February the city was paralyzed by bad weather. In the mountain villages, people hardly survived the cold and snow. Following that period, Heidi's mom, Josephina, fell ill. It was a combination of lungs problem and arthritis that made her life miserable. Teresa informed Heidi of the situation at home, but even her letters were delayed by the impaired service, and when Heidi received them the news within was already old.

In mid-March, the snow began to melt and the communities had to face another natural disaster: floods. People were scared that their houses would be taken away by the rivers. In the Wachau Valley along the Danube, many fled their properties to reach higher grounds. Everybody was talking about the water levels and the measures to take to keep safe. In Traisen, the Traisen River was high but luckily stayed within its banks. A month later Heidi received a letter from home, but that time it was not from her sister. It was from her father. Heidi braced herself for bad news. She knew that her father would only reach out to her if something was terribly hard or wrong. She opened the envelope and started to read in fear.

"My dear Heidi,

I hope this letter finds you in good health and spirit. However, I cannot tell you that here at home everything is fine, because it is not. We are dealing with a crisis right now and I'm afraid that we cannot handle it alone.

Heidi, your mother is sick. She has been ailing for a while and there are no signs of improvements. Besides the bad cold she had all winter long, now her legs are swollen and she can hardly move. I am old myself and not able to help her or take care of her. Teresa and Johan are busy with their jobs, which are important for us all, and Louisa is good for nothing. Your mom spends most of the time in bed. Someone has to attend to her needs. You'll have to come home and help us. I know this is bad news for you and rather sudden, but you have no choice but to leave Vienna and be with us.

I'm looking forward to your arrival,

Your Father"

Heidi was in shock. She felt sorry for her mom who was suffering and needed help, but her father's words gave her no room to consider the situation and find a solution other than going home herself. It was unfair to her that her father assumed that her job in Vienna was less important than the jobs that Teresa and Johan had back home. In his mind, he thought that Heidi was on vacation in the capital city, not employed. His words hurt her. Tears streamed down her face, falling on the letter. The ink got washed out in places where the paper got wet. She knew that once she left Vienna there would be no coming back. Why was it always her who had to take care of everyone? She had to go to the army, she had to stay in the army, she had to lose Francis, she had to give up on her job and go back home! She knew that her father relied on her more than on any of his children. She never let her family down, she never would, but still, it was ill-fated to always be the one to make sacrifices.

She spoke to Erika as soon as they met. Her mistress was devastated by the news. Benjamin had just turned three, and while he could go to kindergarten, his mother preferred to have him home in Heidi's care. Heidi could not leave for another couple of weeks. Benjamin's enrolment in the preschool program took time, and the Schons could not release Heidi right away. The day Heidi had to say farewell to her employer and her friends was filled with tears and regrets on both sides. Even the little boy was upset, and would not let go of Heidi until his mother took him away to his room.

On the train taking her out of Vienna, Heidi knew that another chapter of her life had come to an end. Going home did not feel good anymore. She wiped a tear from the corner of her eye and set her gaze out to the window on the hilly scenery. She was twenty three years old but already tired of all the trials she had had in her life. She helped everyone she could, but only God helped her. In God she trusted that she would overcome her sadness and sacrifice.

Frantz Souisa was happy when Heidi arrived home. His problems were immediately transferred from his shoulders onto Heidi's. Josephina would get the help she needed. His daughter would know how to handle her mother's situation better than anyone else. And indeed, Heidi knew what to do to be useful to her mom and the entire household. Overnight she became the house keeper, the nurse, and the mother figure for Louisa. Speaking of Louisa, the girl was nothing but trouble, and had given Frantz a lot of headaches over the last two years since Heidi had left home. Louisa was unemployed, did not go to school and her mind was only on men. She had a girlfriend three years older than her who carried her along to all the clandestine parties and places of ill-repute. Heidi had her hands full with her mother and the household to pay attention to Louisa's escapades, not to mention that her younger sister had a temper hard to control. Teresa and Johan were busy with their jobs, and in their spare time they had plans with their respective sweethearts. Heidi felt like Cinderella without the charming prince, and overwhelmed by all the chores she had to do. But the effort paid off, and her mother began to feel better by the day. When the summer began,

Josephina was able to resume her work in the household and Heidi received a well-deserved break. She was still helping around the house, but she did not have to care for her mother anymore. Of course, Josephina's improved condition pleased everybody in the family and the overall atmosphere was much lighter.

Slowly Heidi began to re-connect with a few girlfriends and on occasions go out for walks along the Traisen River or to a movie at the town's Cinema. It was a big difference from the life she had in Vienna, but it was more than nothing. She was a very sociable human being and isolation would have depressed her. Her friend Cathy, who lived on the same street, introduced her to a few young people, most of whom Heidi already knew. Together, on weekends or evenings, they participated in cultural and sporting activities, all of them supervised by the Russian authorities.

Slogans with communist content were hung on each cultural establishment or around the sport fields. It was a psychological burden to see those placards wherever one turned. Heidi realized that the Russians were more aggressive about converting the population to the communist doctrine in the countryside than in the capital city. The target segment was the youth. There were rumors about young women becoming involved with Russian officers and the whole drama of those affairs. Heidi herself received some signals from a handsome Russian captain who tried to lure her by offering her a nice Chaika watch, just as a gesture of friendship, which she declined graciously. Odd things like that only made Heidi realized that she was not where she wanted to live, and she decided to follow one of her cousin's paths and immigrate to Switzerland. She prepared her application papers carefully and sent them away for consideration to Bern. What she was not aware of, was that the mail was screened by the Russians and censored. Also, she did not know that her cousin's successful emigration was due to the fact that she mailed her documents from Upper Austria which was under American jurisdiction. Heidi had set herself up for a long wait which at the end went nowhere, without her even knowing why. Her hopes were high and that got her through each and every day.

On a beautiful Saturday in August, Cathy, Heidi's friend, came over to invite her to a soccer game that was taking place in a nearby village. Soccer never appealed to Heidi. Cathy insisted that it would be fun. She was anxious to meet her boyfriend Will there.

Heidi met Cathy in front of her house. Her friend was all ready for a bike ride to the soccer field which was about six kilometers away.

'Heidi, you've got to come with me. Will insisted that we go there to watch the game. I cannot go alone. Come on, it will be fun.'

'You know that soccer is not my cup of tea. Beside, you have a bike but I don't. You do not expect me to walk all that distance, do you?'

Cathy tilted her head and soon came up with a solution.

'My cousin has a nice bike the right size for you. She will lend it to you, I'm sure. Let's go and get you the wheels.' Cathy pushed Heidi gently along the road toward her cousin's house. Heidi was reluctant but gave in once she realized that Cathy would go anyway, and she would end up alone on such a gorgeous afternoon. Her siblings were all out and about enjoying the summer day. Heidi decided that riding a bike would be fun, and watching the game wouldn't kill her.

Cathy went in to talk to her cousin and came out holding a nice bike for her friend. Heidi took the bike and tried it out, making a few loops on the street. It was running smoothly and she liked it. The ride would be pleasant, at least. Both of them rode back to Heidi's house, to let the parents know about their plans. After that, they were on their way towards the soccer field in the next town.

When they arrived they were greeted by the loud cheers of the crowd. It was the Traisen team against the local team. The supporters were grouped in the outdoor amphitheatre. The girls secured their bikes by the bike poles and headed toward the cheering crowd. Cathy was browsing all the rows with her green eyes in search of Will, her boyfriend. When she saw him at the high point of the arena, she grabbed Heidi by the hand and led the way toward him. When Heidi saw Will at the top of the bench, she realized that he was looking at them as well. He was talking with another man beside him urging him to look back toward the girls, even though that person was more interested in what was happening on the green soccer field. Will was making large signs with his arms to rush Cathy and Heidi to come to him. Cathy was happy to see her boyfriend so eager to meet her, and started to jump two stairs at a time, dragging Heidi along.

'Hello ladies. What took you so long to arrive?' Will asked, pleased that the company had arrived.

'It is all Heidi's fault!' Cathy complained, amused. 'She wanted a special invitation and a nice bike. I took care of both, and here we are!'

'Good girls! Here, please have a seat beside me. Oh, I should make the introductions: here is my good friend Edwin, who is part of the soccer committee. He lives in Traisen too. Have you met him before? Edwin, this is Cathy and her friend Heidi. Move on a bit, please, to make room for these ladies, will you?'

Edwin got up and shook hands with the two young women, moved aside and invited them to have a seat. Together they watched the game, which turned out to be more interesting than Heidi had initially thought. At the end, they found a farmer at the edge of the field selling boiled corn for a few coins, and they all had a piece while talking and laughing. The afternoon went by quickly. When they decided to leave, each of them found their bikes and rode away in formation: Cathy with Will in front followed by Heidi and Edwin. At some point, Will dropped behind and sent Edwin in front to keep Cathy company. Heidi did not understand the move, but said nothing. Will, on the other hand, took advantage of the moment and engaged Heidi in an intimate conversation she was not prepared for.

'Heidi, I'm so glad that you came back. I befriended Cathy only to be able to know you. I think I have feelings for you that make me happy when you're around. I would like to start seeing you from now on.'

'You what? I think you are talking to the wrong person, Will. Cathy is very fond of you and she set her hopes high regarding the relationship with you. I'm her friend and I would not in a hundred years hurt her intentionally. You should pull yourself together and either be with her or not at all, but you and I are no match. Do you understand me? I like you as a friend, but nothing more than that.' Heidi was shaking. All these words came over her without notice and she was terrified by the awkward situation. She sped up to catch her friend and Edwin. Will was shocked by Heidi's attitude and sad at the same time. He understood that his trick had got him nowhere and that he should probably settle for Cathy if she liked him, before she sensed any betrayal on his part and turned her back on him, too. He only hoped that Heidi would not tell her what they had talked about.

When the four of them reached Traisen as the sun set, they stopped and had lemonade, for the girls, and beer, for the young men to settle their thirst. They talked and laughed and had a good time together. Before each of them headed home, Edwin asked Heidi on a date the next day. Surprisingly, she accepted.

Over the next two months Heidi and Edwin were seen together every weekend and sometimes some evenings on weekdays. Actually, they discovered that they were practically neighbors. Edwin was living with his father and his stepmother in the house next door. They were not locals: they had come to Traisen in the years Heidi was away in Vienna. His family came to find employment at the factory in town and after a while they settled there. Their origins were a mix of German and Romanian. Edwin was born in Campulung, a northern region of Romania. He had two brothers who lived elsewhere. His father left Romania at the beginning of the war to find his German roots in Central Europe. Edwin was only twelve years old when he left Romania, but the memories of his childhood spent there would be dear to his heart all his life. He was a poor child but he had a zest for life and a positive attitude. During the war years he was fond of planes and attended aviation school outside Vienna where he was a good student and well regarded by the instructors. One instructor in particular took him under his protection and, along with the aviation lessons, taught him good life lessons that served him well later in life.

Like Heidi, Edwin had his share of drama in his life. Right before he was due to graduate and receive his diploma, during one of the last bombardments of Vienna, the school was hit by bombs and almost a quarter of the students and personnel were killed in the blink of an eye. Among the victims was Edwin's mentor. He was devastated. That man meant more to him than his own father. To make matters worse, the building where the records and school papers were kept was leveled to the ground and burned to ashes. As a result, all the students who were lucky enough to survive saw their training erased from their life and were not able to ever finish the program and get the diploma that would have entitled them to become pilots. Years of hard work and sacrifices were reduced to zero. After the war, Edwin went back to his father's home near Graz. By sheer fluke they moved to Traisen at the beginning of 1948 and rented an apartment next to Heidi's house. Edwin was full of life and no matter where he lived he got involved in community activities, which earned him friends and gave him satisfaction. When he met Heidi he was the treasurer and agent of the Traisen soccer team and everyone who met him respected him.

One could not say the same about Edwin's father, who was a cranky old man who liked to drink and occasionally start scandals in public places. Based on that, Frantz Souisa wasn't too happy when he found out who Heidi was becoming involved with, but, as always, he trusted his daughter's judgment. Then again, he had to worry more about Louisa's actions, rather than any other children he had. The youngest gave him more headaches than the other three put together.

Louisa was a restless teenager who at the age of seventeen fell in love with a much older man, the goalie of the soccer team. She lost her virginity to him and after a short while she got pregnant. When Frantz found out, he told her plain and simple to get married or else he would not support her anymore. Louisa had to give up all her dreams about a fairy tale wedding and marry the father of her unborn child in a modest ceremony shadowed by shame and prejudice. In a close-knit community like Traisen, such weddings were the subject of gossips long after they took place. The new son-in-law was a gambler and a wastrel, who couldn't care less about his new family, but Louisa did not seem to notice.

Teresa and her new beau were more down to earth, and Johan had a girlfriend that the parents approved of. In those circumstances, Heidi and Edwin had a fifty-fifty chance of overcoming the bad reputation of Edwin's family. Frantz Souisa braced himself, not wanting to see Heidi hurt in the future.

***

The spring of 1951 came after a heavy winter and the danger of floods loomed over the region. It was around that time of the year when Edwin asked Frantz for Heidi's hand. He was ready to settle down and start the new life that he had always wanted. He longed for stability, love, and a sense of belonging that he had been seeking his entire life. Heidi was the perfect woman for him. She was compassionate, loving, smart and committed. Her life experience during the war had shaped her character into a brave yet sweet young woman with a lot to offer to her man.

Once she had said yes to Edwin's proposal, the preparations for the wedding set in motion. Frantz and Josephina were happy that Heidi's big day would end the gossip about Louisa's marriage which was still being talked about around town. And they were right. Heidi's big news was embraced by the community of relatives, friends and neighbors with great joy. The wedding dress was offered to Heidi by one of her best friend. It was a beautiful white dress with an ample skirt and an embroidered bodice, completed with a nice tiara and a waist-length veil. The date was set for Saturday May 12th, 1951. Since Edwin was a Protestant and Heidi was Catholic, he was willing to follow Heidi's faith in order to make everything easier for his fiancée. Furthermore, Heidi's extended family was Catholic. They went to the Catholic priest to register for the wedding, about six weeks prior to the event. When they left the church after the interview with the priest, they were rather upset than relieved and happy: the cost of the ceremony was about to put them into a lot of debt, if they could even find the money to borrow. There was a fee for every step they were supposed to take in order to become man and wife. Those made them wonder if the whole thing was worth the trouble. Then Edwin came up with an idea: to check the Protestant church and get an estimate from its priest. The church he was part of was in the nearby village of St. Aegyd. In mid-April on a sunny Sunday afternoon he took Heidi to his church, and after the mass was finished they had a brief meeting with the priest. They were surprised to find out that their wedding in the Protestant church would cost them nothing at all. The church would not charge a fee, but would accept small donations from the guests. That was a pleasant surprise for Heidi, who for the first time had the revelation of how greedy the Catholics had become. She was a good Christian who believed in God and was grateful for the divinity watching over her and her family every day, and especially during the war. She truly believed that, but the institution of the church was driven more by money than by good deeds in her opinion. Knowing that her family would be at least surprised by her decision, she was determined to convert to Protestantism and get married in her fiancé's faith. Indeed, there was a lot of talk about Heidi's wish, but at the end everybody let her do what she and Edwin wanted. The small problem that Heidi knew she would face before and after the wedding was her in-laws. Edwin's parents were nothing like him. They were rough and tough people who tried to make things difficult for the new couple. Their bad attitude had made Edwin almost cut all the ties between them, and once he was married with Heidi the connection with them would become minimal. One of his brothers never came home after the war, but he sent a letter once from Canada. He was doing well living there. The youngest brother was living somewhere around Vienna and came home very seldom, and only in the winter. He was a seasonal construction worker. Edwin knew he would see his youngest brother at the wedding, but after that he would disappear again for months, if not years. His family was a big burden for him, but that was about to change. Heidi and he had plans to apply for an apartment on the other side of the river and live alone. The shortage of housing was a big problem in those years, but Edwin had good reviews on his job and the factory had a big say in apartment distribution. Under the Russian regime, the communist system ruled almost every social service, housing included. The rewards were given based on work and political achievements. After six years of occupation, the majority of the population had learned how to live by those rules.

Heidi's wedding was delayed by one day due to heavy rain, which made it impossible to travel to St. Aegyd church. The floods covered the roads. The next day they received news that the waters had dropped and the roads were still muddy, but drivable. Most of the people would have seen the delay as a bad omen, but Heidi and Edwin were optimistic and happy that they could become man and wife on that Sunday, May 13th. They trusted each other and began their life together fully committed and completely in love. The service was performed in German, so that everyone would understand it, which was different than the Catholic Church which held the mass in Latin. The guests were impressed by the priest's words of wisdom. At the end the generosity toward the church materialized through many heartfelt donations. Even the most Catholic relatives were glad to attend the wedding ceremony and be part of it. After they left the small and picturesque church, the bride and groom, along with their families and guests, headed back to Traisen, where they celebrated.

Soon after she was married, Heidi moved in with Edwin in an apartment granted to them by Edwin's factory. It was a small place on the ground floor of a three-storey building, situated in the centre of town. By September, one more wedding had taken place in the Souisa family: Johan's. Heidi and Edwin were trying to start a family, but did not have much luck. A visit to the doctor revealed that the work Heidi did in the army at the radio wave communication stations was to blame. The radiation that she was exposed to, must have affected her ability to become pregnant. That fact could have upset and burdened a young couple, but Heidi and Edwin did not let it affect their relationship. Instead, Edwin decided that since they would not have children, the best way to spend their life together was to travel as much as they could for leisure. As a result, he put his name down on the waiting list to buy a motorcycle. A car would have been better, but it was not within their means at that time. The waiting could have taken years, but they did not give up the dream. As luck had it, before their turn for the motorcycle came, out of the blue, Heidi became pregnant in the fourth year of their marriage when none of them expected it anymore. The joy and surprise made Edwin withdraw the motorcycle down payment and buy more useful things instead. First of all, he had to persuade the housing committee to exchange the small apartment for a bigger one in the same building, on the second floor. Then, with the money he saved, they furnished it in a very practical way.

When Edwin Jr. was born on November 3rd 1954, his father was at work and his mother was taken by surprise. He was three weeks early. With the help of a midwife and another pregnant neighbor, Heidi gave birth at home. The joy that she had a boy was overwhelming for both parents. From that moment on, Heidi embraced motherhood with all her heart. Edwin Jr. was the apple of her eye, and along with her husband they both took good care of the precious bundle of joy. Heidi was used to children from her jobs in Vienna. Furthermore, her little boy was a happy child with curly dark blond hair, intelligent eyes, and cute as a button. Edwin was very proud of his family, and a good provider for it. Their life had a new meaning. Heidi was happy too. Edwin Jr. was spoiled and loved by both parents. Teresa, who married a few months before Heidi, had two sons in the first two of years of marriage and two years later her husband died of a lung infection. By the time Heidi fully embraced the motherhood, her sister was a widow with two young children.

Their lives became more complicated when Edwin's long-lost brother sent a letter to the family from Canada. He had emigrated at the end of the war and started a new life on the other side of the Atlantic. For years nobody knew his whereabouts, and then, surprisingly, he resurfaced on the world's map. He wrote letters about his life and his new family in Canada, and even made a proposal for Edwin to immigrate to Canada, and join him in Alberta. His letters were full of optimism. Canada was a country of many opportunities and new beginnings. It was a symbol of freedom and a land of promises in comparison with the old and devastated Europe. While Edwin was eager to go, Heidi was more skeptical about the move.

In the mid fifties, more and more young people from Austria, Germany, and Italy were looking for new beginnings in the New World. While America was a preferred destination, the immigration laws were more flexible in Canada. When the Russians had to leave Austria in 1955, the new-found freedom made the population reconsider their options. Heidi's brother Johan and his family applied first to go to Canada. Louisa and her troubled husband followed Johan's example. Frantz and Josephina Souisa watched how their children's dreams to move far away came true. In a year's time, Johan, Louisa and Heidi were bound to leave Austria, and leave them behind for good. Everybody had mixed feelings about the departure, but the one who regretted it the most was Heidi. When she, Edwin and Edwin Jr. boarded the ship in Marseille in June 1957, her heart was torn between the parents she was leaving behind, and the two Edwins she was going with. After surviving the war and the communist occupation, when her country was at last free, she had to move far, far away to start a new life. She could not grow roots in one place. At the age of thirty two, with a two year old son, a good husband, and belongings that fit into four suitcases, she was bound to cross the ocean and build her future in a new country that she would have to call home.

While the old continent's shore faded away behind the ship, holding tight onto her son's little hand, standing by her loving husband, Heidi could not help but wonder what the future would have in store for them. She was a brave woman who always found her way in any circumstances, but then and there, maybe for the first time, she felt that the adventure that they had already begun would be more challenging than the years that passed. She wanted to be optimistic about the change, but all she felt was skepticism.

Ultimately, she shook her head as if to get rid of the negative thoughts, inhaled the salty air of the sea, picked up her child in her arms and decided that whatever would be would be, and that life is worth living when you have your family to care for. Nothing could be as bad as the war was, and she was a survivor of the world's worst nightmare.

Acknowledgments

I've been an avid reader all my life, but I've never thought I would write a book myself. I'm still in awe of my accomplishment.

It all started in the spring of 2009, when I re-established contact with a long-lost high school friend after our 30 year high school reunion. I was not able to attend the event, but, while sharing news and memories that filled up the thirty year gap, she said something that intrigued me. Mihaela Duma, nee Jurca, encouraged me to "write a book and become famous", as she put it. I do not know about being famous, but certainly the accomplishment of finishing my first book is rewarding in so many ways. Mihaela saw potential in me that I was not aware of and I thank her for that.

The storyline is based on my mother-in-law's experience during the Second World War. She lived through hell and came out stronger. Hedwig Ponepal, nee Zuser, became involved in the war at a young age, without any warnings. Her youth was spent in terror and anguish, but her optimism pulled her through. She is a remarkable person who shared her memories with zest and accuracy. I was so impressed with her life's story that I considered it an honor and a privilege to write it. Once I had settled on the book's subject, the flow of events guided me through its journey. And what a journey it has been! My mother-in-law was my first and most important critic. She read the chapters as I finished them one by one, and at times they brought tears to her eyes, or laughter, all along encouraging me to continue. This book is for her, as it is about her life lived on the edge during the long cold night of our contemporary history. She was dragged into the war on the German Nazi side of the barricade. That did not make her a bad person, though, and her personality shone under the dark sky that lingered over Europe all those years. Her story shows the truth about the life of millions of ordinary people caught up in the crossfire of a cataclysm started by a few very dark minds. I thank her for sharing her memories with me, and making this book possible.

I also thank the rest of my family, my husband Erwin and my daughter Laura, who encouraged me to keep writing and offered me their continuous love and support, whether it was by reading my manuscript, or by freeing my calendar of annoying chores in order to be able to sit down and write.

Last but not least, I thank my editor Michael from FirstEditing.com, who took the time and effort to give my text a polished look, and made it an enjoyable read.

I hope that my readers would find my novel – based on a true story – interesting, moving, and meaningful.

Made in the USA
Middletown, DE
18 August 2019